A MOURNING
in AUTUMN

A MOURNING
in AUTUMN

HARKER
MOORE

NEW YORK   BOSTON

Mysterious Press
Warner Books

Time Warner Book Group
1271 Avenue of the Americas, New York, NY 10020
Visit our Web site at www.twbookmark.com.

The Mysterious Press name and logo
are registered trademarks of Warner Books.

Printed in the United States of America

First Printing: July 2004

10 9 8 7 6 5 4 3 2 1

Library of Congress Cataloging-in-Publication Data

Moore, Harker.
A mourning in autumn / Harker Moore.
p. cm.
ISBN 0-89296-775-7
1. Police—New York (State)—New York—Fiction.
2. Women—Crimes against—Fiction.
3. Japanese Americans—Fiction.
4. New York (N.Y.)—Fiction. I. Title.
PS3613.O559M68 2004
813'.6—dc22   2004003583

From each to each . . .
Dianne and Sandra . . . joined at the brain.

ACKNOWLEDGMENTS

The author would like to thank Karen Ross, Herbert Erwin, Gerrie Singer, Robert Aberdeen, Bill Troy, Jim Churchman, Stirling and Migo Nagura, Paul Perkins, and others for the expertise they so generously provide in sustaining Sakura's world. Any errors or creative interpretations are the author's.

Very special thanks to Mel Berger and Colin Fox.

A MOURNING
in AUTUMN

PROLOGUE

The basement was cold and nearly as silent as the death it contained. In the corner, in the darkness, the big Bosch cooler ran with the ambient sound of perpetually indrawn breath. The woman it had been keeping lay naked on the metal table in the middle of the room. A work lamp cut a circle overhead.

He stood in the light. Breathed, openmouthed. Tasting for fear that lingered, for a whiff of the power that still drifted, mixed with molecules of decay. But the power was gone. The moment of transformation slipped irretrievably backward.

The body wraps its mystery in corruption. The defiance of rot.

Despite refrigeration, putrefaction could only be delayed. He drew the light closer, imagining he could detect a nascent tinge of green creeping like shadow in the slope of the belly. He pressed the skin where the dead flesh had purpled with lividity. *Meat* was the thought in his mind.

Not a left thought. Left-brain would still detect some mechanistic elegance in this ruin. Still he was sinister, if the Romans got it right, giving preference to the hand, not the lobe that controlled it. *Sinister* from the Latin. The ancients unaware of that magic cross circuit in the brain.

But there were other kinds of sorcery.

Left-brain picked up the scalpel and made the wide looping cut from shoulder to shoulder. Then a long deep slit, from the midpoint straight down, a cleft from the breasts, through belly to pubis. The wounded flesh gaped, labial and inviting. Right-brain began with the snap and crunch of the cutters, till the breastbone lay open, and the smell like no other rolled in the air. Time to play in the muck.

He was pleased, when it was finished, with his essential rearrangements. Practice made, if not perfect, at least a more satisfying configuration. Left-brain would tidy, would have more to do with this lump. But the *eater of souls* was ever hungry.

Time for fresh meat.

CHAPTER

1

The dawn streets were blue-black and shadowless. Lieutenant James Sakura drove over city asphalt still silvered with rain, wondering if last night's weather had marked real change. Summer had been the hottest he could remember, the heat of July running relentlessly through September—a succession of days so bright and brittle a hammer could crack the sky. Now, on the first day of the new month, the morning had a definite chill. The cold gave an added sense of déjà vu to the ride.

FBI-trained, commander of a special homicide unit within the NYPD, Sakura had thought himself ready that October morning nearly a year ago, when the call had come giving him jurisdiction in a developing serial case. He'd believed himself prepared for the challenges of stranger-to-stranger murder, where the motive for violence was none of the normal human spurs of lust, or greed, or vengeance, but a psychotic fantasy within the killer's mind. He had felt confident of his ability to withstand the added intensity of departmental politics and the pressures of an unrelenting press. He had been handling all these things when his opponent had outflanked him. And if in the end, the killer had been apprehended, if the department had seized the opportunity to create a public hero . . . well, he knew the measure of his failure.

There had been months of leave when he'd considered not returning to the job. But the emptiness at home had forced him back to the thing he did best, if not well enough. If this new summons brought with it a warrior's exhilaration, for his personal life it could hardly have come at a worse time.

A full collection of departmental vehicles had gathered at the mouth of the alley where this morning's body had been found. Sakura pulled his car behind the medical examiner's van and got out, flashing his shield and signing in with the officer in charge of the log.

A grid search was under way in the lot that widened out from the alley, patrolmen looking for anything that might be tied to the crime. Near the stranded sanitation truck with its spilled load, Lieutenant Morris Martinez was holding court within a knot of officers and brass. Martinez had been one of his mentors in the years he'd worked on vice. Sakura waited for his old friend to spot him, and watched while he walked over.

"What brings you to my patch this time of the morning?"

The question, Sakura knew, was little more than perfunctory. Mo was savvy, had to figure what this impromptu appearance might mean. "McCauley wants me to take a look," he answered. "Says he has a bad feeling about this one."

Martinez grunted a laugh. "Must be real bad. The chief don't like you, Jimmy. Thinks you rose too fast."

"He could be right." Sakura glanced over at the clutch of crime scene techs ringing the body. "So, what do we have?"

"Ain't that just like the chief not to fill you in." Mo wasn't letting it go.

"No particulars," Sakura affirmed. "He just said he thinks we might be looking at a serial."

"Could be." Martinez worked the tie at his throat. "Jane Doe here is the second body like this to turn up in the last six months. First one didn't get caught till she hit the collection center. This time we got lucky, thanks to some bad hydraulics. Piston blows on the garbage truck and tosses the load."

"The driver call it in?"

"Yeah, regular civic-minded."

"Have you found anything?"

"Clean so far. Rain washed away any tire prints. I got my guys canvassing to see if anybody saw anything interesting going down since the last pickup." Martinez looked back to where the sanitation truck backed up to the toppled Dumpster. "Driver's already having a fit," he said. "Nobody's told him yet he's got to go downtown."

"The body still where they found it?"

Martinez nodded. "All wrapped in plastic like a Christmas package, just like the first. The surprise comes when you open it."

"Surprise," Sakura repeated. He had detected some particular note of warning.

"You'll see for yourself." Mo's smile was grim. "I suspect you'll be attending the autopsy."

"I saw the ME's van on my way in," Sakura said.

"They're ready to take her."

"Crime Scene?"

"Pretty much finished." Martinez grinned more warmly now, clapping him on the back. "We all just been waitin' for you, Jimmy."

⚶

Outdoor crime scenes were bad, a dumped body the worst. Disconnected. Anonymous. A location with no immediate link to either killer or victim. Little chance for physical evidence beyond the body itself, and whatever hair or fiber might cling to skin, or clothes, or wrapping.

Sakura moved carefully. Mo was an old friend and a realist. Still, all cops were territorial, and he didn't want to ruffle any feathers. If McCauley, as was likely, shifted the investigation to Major Case, then some of these same patrolmen and precinct detectives would be detailed to help his unit with the legwork. Yet the here and the now were his only opportunity to satisfy himself that nothing important would be missed. He walked the lot in his own private grid search, retracing the steps of the techs.

Finally it was time for his undivided moment with the body. He went to where it lay, squatting down on the wet pavement. Getting as close as was possible.

A spill of garbage like vile jetsam issued from the wounded Dumpster, damp and greasy cardboard mixing with other refuse from the restaurant that fronted the lot, marinara sauce and wilted vegetables stewing in the morning's weak sun. And atop it, like the chrysalis of a huge and unknown insect, the winding sheet of befouled plastic.

The shape inside was unmistakably a woman's, but obscured. The layers of Visqueen fogging the contours. The features blurred and indistinct.

Except for the eyes. Some trick of wrapping, or the closeness of the face, the way it pressed against a particular thinness in the plastic. The eyes seemed to float at the surface. A wide and clouded blue. Windows that opened on nothing.

⁂

The rain had disappeared with the night. The sky mid-morning was dry and unclouded, though powdered with city grime. Sakura drove through the tunnel into Queens, junctioning with the Van Wyck Expressway. He hoped he was not going to be late. The plane from Japan was not scheduled to land for a while, but the traffic was always bad getting in and out of the airport. He hated that he was nervous. His wife's homecoming after so many months should bring him pleasure, not make him feel like an anxious suitor. But perhaps that was just what he was. No use to pretend that Hanae's sudden decision to return home meant that all that was between them had been healed.

He had thought for a time that he would follow her to Kyoto, that perhaps this was the gesture that was wanted. But as his leave stretched on, and Hanae found new reasons why it was not yet time for his visit, he had feared she might never be ready to resume their marriage.

It took longer for him to understand that what kept them apart was her guilt. He had known that she felt shame—a Japanese woman's shame for her own violation. He had not considered how deeply responsible she might feel for bringing a killer into the heart of their lives; his own bad conscience had assumed the burden of that. But his wife had had her own part in the silence that had nearly killed her and had robbed them of their unborn child. It was not only he whom she'd needed the time to forgive, but herself.

But forgiveness was a process with no foreseeable end, as he had learned these last few months—a process he believed they might better accomplish together. Perhaps Hanae too had come to this conclusion, and this was the reason she had finally decided to come home.

To come home on the day that had seen the beginning of a new serial case. Were the gods cruel? Or kind? Throwing him into the river where he had almost drowned. Sink or swim. He needed his work. He needed his wife. He had always tried to protect her from the harshest part of his life. He had wanted an island, and had so spectacularly failed.

The sign above the expressway said Terminal 3. He exited, checking the time. Still forty-five minutes before her flight would land. He had left the office in plenty of time, thanks to Darius's urging. Still hard to believe that his ex-partner was now back on the force, sliding into the retiring Pat Kelly's place in his unit. Amazing how much red tape could be instantly cut when headquarters wanted you happy.

Did McCauley want him happy? Maybe, at least, for now. The chief of detectives was not a man to buck his superiors. He had stopped by McCauley's office earlier, directly after his visit to the crime scene, and the chief had made it official. The two female homicides appeared to have enough common features to warrant a move of jurisdiction. The paperwork was still in progress, but Sakura's Special Homicide Unit was now effectively in charge of what looked to be a budding serial investigation. He had met briefly with his team to fill them in before leaving for the airport. There would be a hurried autopsy this evening to justify the conclusion that the two women had been victims of the same killer. He must find the words to explain to Hanae why he could not stay home with her on her first night back. No, not explain. It was not words he needed, but faith. Sink or swim. He felt a sudden eagerness for the sight of her that pierced his heart.

✲

The stillness of the *genkan* was as welcoming as a womb. Jimmy watched as his wife's hand drifted across the heavy silk of her marriage kimono, suspended on a slender shaft of wood in the entrance. For too many months, the kimono, a tangible symbol of their commitment, had hovered like a pale ghost, a painful reminder of what had been lost, and more agonizing, of what yet might be lost.

Hanae's fingernail caught on one of the fine golden threads. "I am clumsy," she spoke softly, a schoolgirl who had somehow failed to please her teacher.

He reached for her hand. It seemed like a round heart beating in the center of his palm. "I love your hands."

"But my fingers are too long for my palms, Husband," she said, her sightless eyes, dark and smiling, fixed on his face.

She had not forgotten his foolish comment, made, it seemed, a thousand years ago. That was good, he told himself. "I must be more careful of what I say, Wife." He heard himself laughing. And the teasing, that too was good.

"Do you hear that, Taiko?" She reached down and roughed the fur of the shepherd's head. The dog's tail made a muffled tattoo against the tatami rug. She bent and unfastened his harness, kissing him on his muzzle. She raised her head, her blind eyes finding him again. "And how are my other friends?"

"They have missed you. But I believe they knew you were coming home. Flitting about as if their cages had grown too small."

She nodded, rising, moving with familiar steps into the living room, to the cages of her finches. *Tee-tee-tee.* Trumpet chirps mixed with spongy sounds of wings fluttering. She extended her neck, pursing her lips, so that her favorite could kiss her. She giggled, reaching inside the cage, bringing the bird to her cheek. "He is fat, my husband. I am afraid you have spoiled him."

"It was my only recourse. He made me pay for your absence, Wife." He watched as she returned the bird, then strummed the bars of the other cages, offering greetings in Japanese, running a finger under a plump breast, across a glossy wing.

He could smell the whiteness of her, an exotic floral scent that drifted from her like breath. And he remembered sitting by her side that first day, years ago now, in the park in Kyoto. It seemed he could not make anything work that day, his mouth torturing the Japanese, his brain scurrying for sensible conversation. It was as though the sight of her, with her lacquer-shiny hair, drawn back against the powdery white of her moon face, had drugged him.

It came as a shock that she was blind. She had none of the affectations he sometimes associated with sightless people. When she spoke, she faced him squarely, her eyes level with his. It was clear to him that she had created her own world, but with bridges enough for others to cross. The absence of sight seemed of little consequence, her instincts and her heart sure and steady guides. She was as complete a human being as he had ever met, and beyond her beauty and kindness, it had been this quality of serene self-awareness that had most attracted him that day in the park.

He moved to stand behind her now, resting his hands upon her shoulders. "Hanae . . ."

She turned inside his arms. "You do not need to apologize, Jimmy. I know there is much to do when a life has been taken."

"Dr. Linsky is waiting to do the autopsy." His voice sounded strangely disembodied. The old fears rising like a beast inside his chest.

"I shall be here," she spoke in Japanese.

He forced himself to silence because he sensed she was glad that he must leave, but not for any terrible reason. There was no coldness, only a sweet shyness that said she needed time to get used to being his wife again. He bent and kissed her, feeling her tremble against his mouth. Then, gently pulling away, she rested her head against him. There would be many other nights, he told himself. For now, it was a gift that she was home.

⚜

The city's basement morgue was a twilight world, fluorescent-lit night and day. The only indication of the lateness of the hour was the relative peace that had settled in the locker-lined hallways. Sakura, who'd come early to the cutting room, was grateful for the quiet, as if alone with the body in the green-tiled space, he might gain some insight that had eluded him in the immediacy of the crime scene. But there was still nothing much to see. Only the dead eyes, grown cloudier still in their chrysalis of plastic, shutting in whatever final image lay trapped within the circuit of optic nerve to brain.

"Thinking of starting without me?" Dr. Linsky had entered with an attendant through the black-aproned doors. He managed to look immaculate in simple scrubs and apron.

"Not part of my job description." Sakura stepped back.

"I find that comforting."

Sakura was silent. Half the game was enduring Linsky's barbs. The ME's sarcasms carried far more sting with detectives he considered incompetent.

The respect went both ways, and Sakura was pleased that McCauley had agreed to forward his request that Linsky perform this procedure. A Linsky autopsy was pure Zen. Never a motion wasted. Each movement completely in the moment. Even with the inevitable backlog, the ME never rushed, no matter how routine a death might appear. He could be trusted to see beyond the obvious.

"I've reviewed Dr. Bossier's report on Helena Grady, the woman whose body was found at the recycling center," Linsky was saying now. "I take it we're assuming that the same person killed both these women."

"The bodies were wrapped the same," Sakura answered. "Both were dumped with commercial trash. The autopsy may show up something different."

"We'll certainly see," Linsky said. He snapped on latex gloves. "Flunitrazepam was found in Grady's system. You probably know it as Rohypnol."

"The date rape drug."

"Yes."

"Anything else?" Sakura asked.

"MDMA . . . Ecstasy."

"What was cause of death?"

"There was nothing definitive, but given a sexual assault situation, asphyxiation was a high probability. Dr. Bossier concluded that Helena Grady was most likely smothered with a dry cleaning bag."

"That's getting pretty specific, isn't it?"

"There was forensic evidence—or rather a lack of it—to support the supposition," Linsky said.

"Which was?"

"No marks on the victim's neck. The thin plastic of a dry cleaning bag clings to the mouth and nostrils, occluding the airways without the need to secure the bag at the throat. And neither were there petechiae, something one might expect to see with other forms of asphyxiation."

"You mentioned sexual assault," Sakura noted. "I take it there was evidence of rape."

"Helena Grady had abrasions in both the vaginal and anal areas. Some of which were possibly postmortem."

"Semen?"

"None."

"The killer must have worn a condom if there was penile penetration."

"That is the most likely explanation." Linsky had finished preparing his slides, and now he looked at the clock. "Keyes is late."

Sakura was content to wait for the technician. Howard Keyes was the best at lifting fingerprints from skin. But Linsky seemed determined to begin the procedure on time.

"We can at least open this." The ME picked up a scalpel and cut lengthwise through the plastic shroud.

The odor was distinctly unpleasant, but stepping forward Sakura was struck first by the image that clocked in and stuck in his brain. "It looks like . . ."

". . . he's been here before us." The ME, completing his thought, was staring down at the neat Y of metal staples that tracked down the torso. "This was also in Bossier's report." Linsky looked up at him. "I think you can be certain, now, that you're dealing with the same man."

🞂

Hours later the vision still haunted.

Sitting behind the desk in his eleventh-floor office, Sakura was only a short distance from his home, but the apartment on Water Street seemed a world away. He hoped that Hanae was already asleep, exhausted by the twelve-hour flight. He could not go home, not yet, with the stink of tonight's autopsy still clinging to his clothes. Its horrors still clinging in his mind.

He's been here before us. He was remembering Linsky's words and the image of that metal Y of staples like a trackroad in the flesh. The persistent vision like an invitation, a token to ride whatever dark fantasy had inspired such a death—a fantasy that seemed to include some parody of autopsy.

His mind had raced with questions that had had to be delayed till Keyes had come and finished fingerprinting the entire surface of skin. But there had been no prints to find. The killer had been as meticulous in removing physical evidence as he had been in closing the body.

Inside had been a different matter. Dr. Linsky had removed the staples to reveal the carnage within the cavity. Every major organ had been cut out of the body, and then replaced.

It had looked at first glance like a bloody jumble, but Linsky had a different perspective.

"Dr. Bossier noted that Helena Grady's organs had been . . . *scrambled*," the doctor had said. "I don't think it's that random, at least not in this case. It's a fairly crude job of reassembly, but it appears to me that the natural arrangement of the organs has been inverted."

Sakura had looked more closely then, and had seen. The reposition of the heart, with its apex tipped toward the right side of the chest. The stomach, liver, and spleen, all reversed. Held together . . . suspended in a silver web of nearly invisible wire.

The phone buzzed on his desk. "Sakura," he answered it.

"I thought you might be there, Lieutenant."

Linsky's voice surprised him. The autopsy had been finished when he'd left the morgue.

"I came back to have another look at the body," the ME was saying.

"Why was that?"

"A purplish mark on the victim's right arm," Linsky explained. "It appeared to be livor mortis, but its position seemed inconsistent. It turned out to be a birthmark. I'll highlight it for you in the photographs. It should help you to identify your victim."

"I see."

"You sound disappointed, James. This isn't television, where the medical examiner solves the crime."

A joke. The use of his given name. It must be later than he thought. "No . . . Thanks," he said. "I look forward to getting those photos."

"You'll have at least some of them tomorrow, and as many of the lab results as I can push through."

"Thank you," he said again, but the doctor had hung up.

He had been sitting in the dark, having switched off the overhead fluorescents. Now he flipped on the desk lamp, settling back in his chair. Was there another kind of mark from birth, he wondered, that made of one a victim, one a killer? Was that not what his friend, Dr. Willie

French, believed, that a serial killer must be born before he could be made? Might that not be the very expression of karma, the misdeeds of past lifetimes encoded like a heritable characteristic within the DNA?

He remembered the Four Imponderables, those principles which the Buddha warned were not to be examined. To do so was to invite vexation, even madness. The third of the four was the admonition against seeking the result of karma. One should never seek to find a detailed link between a volitional act and its effect. Nor should one set oneself up as a judge between good and evil, for to do so would lead only to the intellectual snare of duality, and the suffering which must follow that delusion.

His job was not to judge, but to restore the balance of the law. Only in finding the killer was human justice possible. There was another warning that he remembered, which he would do well to heed—perceiving danger where there is none, and not perceiving danger where there is.

CHAPTER

2

D r. Wilhelmina French stood in the huge window of her Upper West Side office looking down on the busy street. Hard to believe she was actually here in Manhattan, that she had already started seeing patients.

So much had happened so quickly after her father's death. As if despite her escape from Edmond's house so many years ago, he had after all been holding her life in suspension. So much had seemed at an end when her brother had called with news of her father's final illness. She had taken her leave of Quantico to return to New Orleans. Had already left behind, or so she believed, what she had started here in New York.

Now she was back with a vengeance. Her grant might be in limbo—who knew if the government would ever get off its collective ass when it came to LSD research—but official indifference didn't mean there wasn't anyone interested in her theories. Quite a lot of people, it turned out, wanted to hear what Dr. Wilhelmina French had to say about serial killers and the possibility of early childhood detection and intervention. She'd become a bit of a celebrity since her part in the Death Angel case.

Still, the book contract would not have brought her back to New York. She could have written anywhere. She had worked on the outline in her own private limbo, fighting her childhood demons as she waited for Edmond to die. And then Michael had shown up at her father's funeral.

She had not been sure that she would ever see Michael Darius again. But there he was, with no warning, at the cathedral. He had sat with her in the family pew, had left no doubt that he, at least, considered them a couple. She could still laugh out loud, remembering her brother's face. *She'd been holding out on him.*

It was true. She might not phone Mason often, but her brother did expect to be kept informed. Growing up, she'd been the one he could turn to with the vicissitudes of his secret affairs, and in a kind of reverse fairness she'd felt an obligation to confide in him. She had learned that it was good to have his sympathetic ear, that her brother was more to be trusted than any of her friends.

Mason had liked Michael. And Michael seemed to like him. The four of them had ambled about amiably enough that week in the big house. She and Michael in her bedroom every night making up for the months apart, and what had not been said. Mason making plans with his partner Zack. It was the closest thing to happiness the old place had seen since the years when her mother had been alive.

She'd learned to accept happiness in these last few months. She had not learned to trust that it would last.

She answered the ringing phone.

"Willie?" Jimmy's voice.

She smiled. "I'm glad it's you. I've been wondering if it was okay to call Hanae. I don't want to disturb her if she's still resting from the flight."

"I'm surprised she hasn't called you yet. I know she's anxious to see you."

"How is she, Jimmy?"

"She seems fine. I think she's glad to be home."

"I'm sure that she is."

"Did Michael say anything about yesterday?" He had changed the subject.

"Are we talking about the body in the Dumpster?"

"I wondered," he said, "if you'd be interested in taking a look at some photos?"

She let him hear her laugh. "Thought you'd never ask, Lieutenant Sakura."

Margot Redmond watched from a distance the rolling yellow text from the vertical LED sign flicker in twin images upon the lenses of his dark glasses. *I am awake in the place where women die.* Inside the cavernous space the man appeared taller and thinner than possible. The contrast between his fair skin and dark hair heightened in the interplay of paint box colors and tomblike blackness. When his arm shifted inside the crisp white of his shirt, exposing a bit of pale wrist, it was to withdraw one of the small bones laid out in rows on the long table. He seemed to smile, but she was uncertain.

"Mr. St. Cyr. David St. Cyr . . ." She walked up to him.

"Jenny Holzer likes to link ideological statements with the forms and meanings of architecture." He spoke with a slight accent, neither looking up nor acknowledging his name. "Holzer was trying to make sense out of the chaos of death—spreading these bones out in neat tight lines." He turned then so that only one lens trapped the LED script: *Hair is stuck inside me.*

This time she was sure he did smile. He returned the bone to the table, adjusted its position.

"I don't think I'm late. . . ." She checked her watch, conscious of reflections of moving text pooling at her feet.

"I'm early. I wanted to see the Holzer exhibit. I missed it the last time. *Lustmord.*"

"Excuse me?"

"German . . . for sexual murder." He smiled again, glancing over his shoulder, the arc of his arm indicating eight panels of electric signboards broadcasting script in red, yellow, and green. The words, in upper-case letters, scrolled downward at varying speeds. "The voices of the participants—perpetrator, victim, observer."

She glanced down at the table. Saw that some of the bones had little silver bracelets around them. "Are these . . ."

"Human? Yes. I guess you could call them the forensic evidence. Quite a striking statement, don't you think?"

"I don't know what I think." She looked away.

"Such happy insistent colors." Fresh red letters burned across his lenses.

"The message is anything but happy." She saw the words *I hook her spine* pulse down one of the columns.

"Ms. Holzer does what every good artist should. Forces the viewer to look at what he only pretends to reject."

She could feel his eyes through the barrier of the dark glasses.

"Perhaps the sexual murderer is not a monster, but everyman," he said.

She stole another glance at one of the LED signs. *She smiles at me because she imagines I can help her.*

"Come," he said, "let's talk." He moved out of the room, through the annex, toward the main towers of the Guggenheim Museum. She watched him walk, something close to a swagger, with his dark designer jacket opened, his cashmere topcoat casually thrown over his left arm. She could have easily been misled, assumed that everything about him came without effort. But that would have been a false impression. She suspected that he was keenly conscious of every aspect about himself, and that there was exacting deliberateness in everything he did.

"I like this building," he said, gazing up at the glass rotunda. "Wright's giant spiderweb."

In the light she saw that he was young and quite handsome. An anemic aristocratic kind of handsome. In the manner of English gentry and some homosexuals. She couldn't remember if Patrice had mentioned he was gay.

"Frank Gehry did the Guggenheim in Bilbao, Spain." He was talking again. "But I still haven't decided if I like his design. Part of me sees brilliant undulating energy, a steely Daliesque landscape. Another part is reminded of a titanium beast humping its mate." He laughed.

"You don't do commercial?"

"No, I leave the public monuments to guys like Gehry and Koolhaas."

"My husband loved what you did for Brad and Patrice."

He shook his head. "I'm glad they're happy. There are some things I might have done differently. But then, I'm never satisfied."

"A perfectionist?" she asked.

He removed his glasses, and she saw that one of his eyes was blue, the other green. "Is that bad?"

"No, except . . ."

"Perfection is elusive." His bicolored eyes fixed on her.

Unaccountably, she wondered if he thought she was attractive. "Reese and I are happy you've decided to take us on as clients."

"That sounds ominous. You and your husband aren't going to be difficult?"

"No, of course not. We understand how you work."

"Good. Then we shall get along famously."

᠕ᢈᢈᡟ

Hanae sat upon a cushion on the floor of the bedroom. Eyes closed, she counted the strokes of the brush through her shoulder-length hair. She had almost gotten used to the length of the stroke, shorter now, more staccatoed than when she had had hair she could sit upon. Before *he* had cut it. Inside her head she still carried the memory of sitting naked and cold as he'd clicked the steely scissors in a mad dance around her head, her hair cascading, fluttering in pieces to the floor like small wounded bats.

But the man had done more than cut her hair. He had cut into her heart, had cut into her sense of who she was. Had almost severed her marriage to Jimmy. And most painfully, had caused their unborn child to flood from her belly. A living thing no more, but so much blood and water running between her thighs. She had lost almost everything in that house in the woods. Had almost lost her life.

She had retreated to her parents' home in Kyoto after that time. To heal, to allow herself to feel again, to trust her truer self, to rekindle the light inside her head so that no longer would she fear the instincts of her heart. And most surely she had fled to find Jimmy again.

She had first begun to trust her art again in Kyoto. Sculpting on the small table her father had made for her. In the beginning her fingers would not move, trapped in the clay, dead as dry twigs pruned from a tree. Then slowly they had begun to come to life, finding once again in the clay the contours of what her mind saw. Small objects grew under her fingers. A tiny temple, a likeness of Mama's cat, a bird with a long tail. A whole shelf of miniature sculptures, small steps in the slow journey to reclaim herself.

And then there had been the bust of her father. He had fussed and made much of having his image made. Yet he had sat for her in the small garden at the rear of her childhood home. Sat in his kimono, letting her fingers explore and reexplore the planes of his stern Japanese face. But in the end, it had been his smile rising to crinkles at the corners of his eyes that she had found in the clay.

Then there had come the day when she had heard her mother and father whispering. Forgetting the keenness of her hearing, they could not keep from her the horror that had flooded the whole of Kyoto. A four-year-old boy had been taken as he rode his bike in the park, rode beyond the vision of his mother, who chattered innocently with friends, speaking of shopping and the prices of things. It should have been safe for the boy to ride his new bike down the short path, for his mother to speak idly of the best market at which to buy vegetables. Should have been safe, but for a monster in the park that afternoon.

On the fifth day of his disappearance, she had her own blind image of the boy's face floating beneath the water of a pond. Water lily pads spread like a costume hat round his small head, and fat koi nibbled at his ear. He giggled at their touch, bubbles exploding from his mouth in a stream. The image burned behind her eyes steadily throughout the long day. And though the picture she glimpsed inside her was happy, her heart knew that the truth was closer to tragedy. She could no longer remember if it had been the radio or television that had said the boy's severed head had been found in a nearby reservoir, one ear missing due to animal activity.

She had not slept, but prayed all through the night. Prayed for the lost child, his suffering parents, and that her internal vision might be spared. Though in wishing for the last, she knew that this was not to be.

She put down the brush now, and rested her head against Taiko. "I am glad to be home." The shepherd licked her face. "I know. You too are glad."

That first moment at the airport when Jimmy had touched her, she knew she was at last home. She'd smiled secretly against his shoulder as he'd taken her into his arms, remembering well the hard thinness of his body, the square smoothness of his face. She recalled the familiar length of his fingers as he'd taken her hand, the coolness of his palm. And there was the scent of him, Jimmy's smell—green and citrusy and something else uniquely his.

When she had reached inside his pocket for his handkerchief, he had laughed. "I could not tell Mr. Haspel how to fold my handkerchiefs, Hanae."

"He did not do such a poor job, Husband. But it needs my hand."

"Oh yes, my Hanae, we are all in need of your hand."

They had laughed at his joke, but it would not be easy. For either of them. He had come home late last night, and had left early this morning without waking her. She had felt his burden, not wanting this new beginning to start where their old life had ended—with the pressures of his job. But she must make him understand that she did not resent his being a detective, that she could not be protected from the horrors of his work. She must make him believe that what had happened was as much her fault as his.

She had after all befriended a killer, had invited him into their home. She bore an equal share of the guilt. And most important, no secrets should ever stand between them. She reminded herself once more that Jimmy was indivisible from what he did. And if they were to heal, she must make him come to accept this truth as well.

🌿

The fading sunlight seemed to hover beyond reach, a pale competitor to the artificial light that reigned within his office. Sakura turned from the window and drained his cup of tea, reaching for the small jade disk lying on top of his desk. He rolled the smooth green piece round his fingers, and thought of his stepsister's phone call this morning. His father was seriously ill—an unexpected message that caused him to wrestle with the old emotions, the same feelings that had plagued his small boy's heart so many years ago. He was a man who still waged a child's war.

"Knock, knock . . ."

Sakura looked up. "Willie, what a pleasant surprise. How about some green tea?"

"Still trying to reform my dietary habits, Sakura," she said, slumping into a chair. "And don't act so disingenuous. You know I want to see those photos."

"You missed Michael." He poured himself another cup of tea. "I think we might get a positive ID on the victim. An NYU grad student was reported missing on Friday afternoon. Her photo looks a lot like our Jane Doe. Michael and Delia went to interview the roommate."

"No personal artifacts on the victim?"

He shook his head. "But hopefully the birthmark on the arm will make it definitive." He handed her a file. "The first victim showed up about six months ago. Suffocated, then wrapped in Visqueen and dumped for garbage just like this one."

Willie opened the folder and went quickly through the Polaroids taken at the crime scene. She stopped when she got to the first shot from last night's autopsy.

"What's this? Linsky using staples?"

"That's the killer's handiwork. Keep going."

She flipped through the photos. "God, what's he into?"

"That's what I wanted to ask you."

"The organs are inverted. I guess Linsky caught that."

"Yes. So what's it mean?"

"Hell, Sakura, let me work that out in the next five seconds."

He grinned at her sarcasm. "I think you need some of my tea."

"I need some caffeine." She stood up now, spreading the photographs across his desk. "He's real handy with the scalpel and staples. A surgeon couldn't have done better."

"So we look for a doctor?"

She frowned. "Too simple. The inside job is not so slick, but you couldn't expect it to be."

"The inversion of the organs has got to be important," Sakura said.

"Did he do this to the first victim?"

"Yes."

Sakura watched her handle the pictures like pieces of a puzzle, working her theories aloud. "No doubt he went to a lot of trouble. Cutting the organs out, reversing them, and stitching them back. Mimicking *situs inversus totalis*—a complete reversal of the position of major organs—must be primary to his fantasy." She sat down again. "Sexual assault?"

"Linsky got negatives for semen on all the swabs," Sakura said, "but it appears that she was raped like the first victim, both vaginally and anally. At this point there's no evidence to assume anything other than penile penetration."

"There are no defensive injuries?" she asked.

Sakura shook his head. "No. There's nothing to suggest that either of the women was tied up or restrained, and that fits with the fact that both sets of toxicology screens showed positive for Rohypnol."

She was nodding. "Sedation in minutes, an almost hypnotic state followed by unconsciousness. Victims have been known to black out for hours."

"Plenty enough time to rape and kill."

"The unconsciousness may be significant to his fantasy. Raping and killing an unconscious, or more, a dead woman is a lot different from raping someone who is struggling for her life. Certainly more impersonal."

"Hard for me to think of what happened to these women as impersonal," he said.

"Our guy's a real piece of work."

He had to smile at her proprietary label.

※

It was last night's dream that had driven Michael Darius to the morgue this evening. He reached for and pulled a pair of latex gloves from a box on the counter. He signaled the attendant. The stainless steel shelf slid smoothly out of the wall cavity.

Darius drew the green sheet from the victim's face. The cold fluorescence made the raised planes of flesh appear translucent, while recesses dropped away as dark fissures. His first impression was that the girl looked like a victim of Auschwitz.

He exposed the rest of the body. The impression that she'd been confined to a concentration camp was not relieved. Pale and thin, she seemed to have lost more than life. The long neck faded into shadow, and insanely he believed he could make out the faint rhythm of a pulse.

Linsky's fine stitches puckered down the chest, mimicking the killer's pattern, so that her breasts and torso seemed confined by a kind of bizarre corset. Pelvic bones jutted out between the basin of abdomen. He noticed her small delicate feet. The red toenail polish seemed an obscenity.

But this was not how he'd seen her in his dream. Rather she had come to him in a Gigeresque nightmare, an android of finely wrought metals. Of looping tubes and layered plates. Cones and domes. A mechanized whore. She'd jerked unaccountably while faceless workers checked each detail of her metallic seams, the head of each rivet. The only allusion to her true physiology was at the juncture of her groin, where a plasmalike liquid oozed. Her scream from inside the metal globe of her skull had awakened him.

Willie had been at his side. It was still a shock to find her next to him. Sleeping on her stomach, one leg drawn up. Naked, amid crumbled sheets. Real and raw and beautiful like the wood he used to create his models.

The bad dreams had come less often since she had moved in. After all, it had been Willie who had rescued him from the aftermath of his experience with the Death Angel. And his waking life had improved too.

He looked down now, carefully recovering the body of Leslie Ann Siebrig. Death had not completely erased the person in the photograph Missing Persons had sent over. Tomorrow Siebrig's roommate would make it official.

⁕

It seemed to Willie that the wood was lit from within, warm and smooth and glowing. She stood beside the bed that she shared with Michael, running her hand over the exotic grain of the headboard. *It is his soul you feel inside.* She was remembering Hanae's words that day last year in the library, Hanae's hand moving next to hers on the staircase that Michael had made. She believed the words were true. Michael's spirit did move in his carpentry. In this headboard, in all the pieces he had made for this room in the months she'd been away from New York.

Had he known when he'd started that he would ask her to return, to make love in this room that had once been a shrine to that other life with his wife? Or had it only been in the doing that the real healing had come? Was it only when the exorcism was complete that she had been allowed to enter this room as even an abstraction? She didn't know why it should matter, only that it did, and that it was a question like so many others that she would never ask him.

She had been so shocked that first night when he'd brought her things into this room, and not to the smaller bedroom near his work space. She had hidden her reaction in her remarks on its beauty, as if her surprise was not that it existed in this form, but that it existed at all. For Michael could not know that Hanae had told her of the closed-off room where nothing had been changed from the day his wife had left him. He could not know that it was in this room that the killer had surprised her, a demon figure appearing in the vanity mirror, like a punishment, it had seemed, for her intrusion.

Her eyes, unable to help themselves, went to the place where the vanity had stood. Gone now, its fussy opulence replaced by a sleek armoire. But the image of that man remained to haunt her pleasure. As indeed he haunted them all.

She sat back down on the bed, next to some scribbled notes for the chapter she was working. She had finally spoken to Hanae this afternoon. They had talked of small things, as they had in their letters, never about *him,* as if a line had been crossed when each had fled the city. And now, though returned, neither could cross back.

Strangely, it was Michael, of all of them, who appeared to have recovered best. His brush with death had seemed to force some reassessment of what he really wanted. Besides his return to the police force, she knew that Michael was also seeing his boys, the twins that had been born after his wife had left him. That was a good thing, and she did what she could to encourage it, but she suspected that, despite his efforts, Michael had not yet overcome whatever impulse had once made a shrine of this room. He still loved his ex-wife, or thought he did. Which, in the end, was the same.

She wondered if the woman had ever loved him. It seemed impossible that she could, and still have walked out on him in a way so intended to wound. And never, that she knew of, had Margot called or come to visit when Michael was in the hospital.

Stupid to be angry with someone she'd never met. She settled against the piled-up pillows. Life was good. She loved New York. Loved this apartment in the building Michael owned. And her office. That was thanks to Michael too, since he'd been the one to suggest that she start seeing patients, probably to keep her from analyzing him. She smiled. Michael would always be a cipher. What they could share was his work. They'd spent hours last night speculating on this new investigation. Maybe that was the novelty that made him want her. Murder and mayhem, the basis for a beautiful relationship. She laughed out loud.

"What's so funny?"

"Michael." She hadn't heard him come in.

"I brought Chinese." He stood at the closet, taking off his clothes.

"Maybe later." She picked up her notes. "I'm not hungry now."

"I am." He sat on the bed and took the notes from her hand.

✦

The bedroom was dark as a cave. He depressed the play button on the remote, bringing on the *flick-flicker* before the video started in earnest. He frowned at the amateurish quality of the taping, finding inferior technicals almost unendurable. Yet he refused to permit any cinematic ineptness, even his own, to interfere with his concentration. He leaned back and allowed the scene to play.

The camera closed in tightly, panning from the red-painted toenails, slowly moving up the thin thighs, across the pale-haired pubis, to the slim torso, picking out the bridge of clavicle, up the column of fragile neck to the head. A strand of blond hair had been caught inside the mouth, and the pink tongue twisted unconsciously to dislodge it.

A long shot of the body on the table. It remained a white inert thing, since the senses had been tempered. Yet it jerked to life when the plastic went across the face. The arms rose, stiff-jointed. Fingers splayed, grasping empty air. The feet kicking futilely.

Its face, wild and wide-eyed, filled the screen. Its mute scream trapped forever inside its throat. Nostrils sucked hard for breath, its mouth reminding him of the pet goldfish he'd once taken from its bowl. He'd counted that day, with the aid of a magnifying glass, the number of times the circlet of orange mouth had stretched open and shut closed.

And her arms, so like those tiny gill slits, pumping and pumping and pumping, as if their efforts could somehow get the lungs to work. Then shock and struggle at last surrendering to fate.

He paused the video, then rewound to that precise instant when death had come, replaying the exquisite descent of mortality, the dark draining of light from its eyes. That day he had had a stopwatch to time "how long it took" the goldfish. For the human, he'd have to settle for secondhand data using the tape.

He fast-forwarded to the point where the incision had been drawn from shoulder to shoulder, then in a single scalpel stroke through torso to groin. He watched the blood ooze, oil-like, out from the Y-slit. And then Right-brain dug in. Cracking the chest so that it gaped open like a purple-dark mouth. Hands plunged in. Steely scissors snipped tissue. *Wet-click. Wet-click.* Then the unplugging and rearranging. Reordering, till he was satisfied, and the task of resuspension began. Whipstitching the slippery puzzle pieces in place. Left-brain closed, stapling the flesh in tight neat puckers from beginning to end.

Then the body was cleansed. Its skin scrubbed shiny. Though Right-brain loved the sheer humanness of the gore, there was always too much blood for Left-brain. Bodily fluids were so unpleasant. Even his own semen trapped in the prophylactic was wholly distasteful. Though his pubic hairs were less a problem since he'd shaven himself raw.

Later followed the wrapping. Left-brain made certain the edges of Visqueen were neatly folded, the duct tape delivered in economical, straight lines. Though Right-brain believed such fastidiousness was foolish.

He stopped the machine. Listened to the whir of the tape rewinding. He would replay the video. But this time he would focus more fully on the moment of its death. Next time he would play it purely for pleasure, pull on latex gloves, and masturbate.

CHAPTER

3

Michael Darius hated these formal identifications. The secondhand apprehension impossible not to feel in the drab cramped space of the viewing room. The anticipatory grief breathed in like fog, standing with a stranger who was preparing to have to say "yes," it was her daughter, or her husband, or in this case her roommate whose number had just come up in victim lotto.

Maggie Hoffman radiated anxiety like a dark sun. It had taken a lot of convincing yesterday before she had finally agreed to make the formal identification. But Leslie Siebrig had no relatives in the city. Her mother was dead, and her father, who lived in Virginia, had not yet returned from a business trip abroad. Johnson had made arrangements for them to pick Hoffman up this morning, as the only way to be sure that she would come.

It was Adelia who sat next to the young woman now, smiling reassurance as the whining elevator signaled its rise from the basement. The detective stood, patting her shoulder, leading her to the window where Darius was waiting.

The gurney with its burden had arrived. The attendant, at his signal, uncovered the face. The intervening hours had not been kind to what remained of Leslie Siebrig.

Air exploded from Maggie Hoffman's chest. "That's not her." The words of denial barely delivered with the last of her breath. She had already made as if to turn, but Johnson's hand was firm on her elbow.

"Look carefully, Maggie," Adelia said.

Darius signaled the attendant to roll down the sheet to completely expose the arm. The birthmark stood out clearly in the bluish-green pallor. And, on the chest, Linsky's neat stitches, following the track of the staples.

"Oh, God." Hoffman's knees buckled as she tried to fold within herself. Her head jerked in affirmation. Face forming tears.

"Are you sure now that it's Leslie, Ms. Hoffman?" he asked.

"Yes. Yes. Please"—she was begging—"I have to get out of here."

✥

"I already answered all your questions yesterday." Tears still eased themselves from Maggie Hoffman's face, but it was clear to Darius that the prime emotion to have settled in was resentment. She might sit in Police Plaza drinking coffee, but her mind was still many blocks away in that viewing room, would be in that viewing room for a long time. *Why,* he knew she was asking herself, had she let them talk her into it.

"I know you answered them, Maggie," Adelia Johnson was saying, "but it's possible you may remember something more today, something that could help us stop this from happening to someone else." She patted Hoffman's hand and, turning on the recorder, made the preliminary statement for the record.

Darius moved in. "You told us that the last time you saw Ms. Siebrig was around midnight on Thursday at the dance club. Is that correct?"

"Yes." Hoffman seemed resigned. "I met her there after work."

"You are also a graduate student?"

"I am, but I work part-time as a waitress."

He stepped back. The ball was rolling.

"What's this club like?" Johnson's tone was conversational.

"Big. Noisy. A couple of dance floors."

"More than one level?"

The girl nodded. "There's a TV lounge and a restaurant. That's where we agreed to meet."

"In the restaurant?" Johnson asked.

"Yes. Leslie's always hungry—*was,*" she caught herself. "Leslie . . . was." The face verged on sudden collapse.

"So you had something to eat." Johnson pulled it back.

"A quick bite." Hoffman dabbed at her eyes with a tissue. "Leslie wanted to get on the dance floor."

"Tell me what that was like," Johnson said.

"The place was really packed. It seemed just like a weekend. Leslie and I were together for a while, just moving around on the floor, being seen."

"And then?"

"This guy came over and asked me to dance."

"Did you know him?"

"No. It turned out he was a tourist. He'd read about the club on the Net. Can you believe it? We danced a couple dances. He bought me a drink. Then I danced with someone else."

"And Leslie?"

"I couldn't see her, so I stayed where I was. We'd always touch base, you know. Let each other know if we'd hooked up."

"If you'd hooked up with a guy?"

"Yeah. I stayed put for a long time, but she never came back."

"And you hadn't seen her with anyone," Johnson asked, "while you were dancing?"

"I wasn't looking then. I was having a good time. I figured Leslie was too. She always did."

"Did you search for her in the club?"

"Everywhere." The voice was earnest. "I even went back to the restaurant."

"Were you worried when you couldn't find her?"

"No." The word came out low. "I was mad." A confession that started the tears again. "Why hadn't she told me she was leaving?"

"What did you do then?"

"I went home."

"And when she didn't come in?"

"I went to sleep. I didn't know she hadn't come in until morning."

"And weren't you worried then?"

"Not really. It wasn't that unusual for Leslie to spend the night out, and . . ."

"To spend the night with a man she'd met?" Darius came forward.

"Grad school is hard." The tone was defensive. "Going to the clubs was Leslie's way of letting off steam."

"There's something you're not telling us, Ms. Hoffman." He could see Johnson looking at him, wondering if he'd had some special insight. But it was only that he'd sensed the guilt of an incomplete confession.

The young woman's shoulders were shaking now. A disconnect before sobs. "I should have known something was wrong," she let out, "but I was angry and . . ."

"What happened, Maggie?" Johnson asked.

"I don't own a cell phone," Hoffman said. "But Leslie always had hers. When I couldn't find her in the club, I went to use the pay phone. I had to stand in line. It took forever before I could call her."

"And . . . ?"

"She didn't answer." Hoffman's eyes were searching Johnson's. "It was just that stupid message. And I should have known right away that something was really wrong. No matter what she was doing, Leslie always had that phone on. Even on the floor dancing, she'd have felt it vibrate. . . . I should have known."

"You couldn't have changed things," Darius said.

The woman turned to him as if he'd thrown a lifeline. "Leslie just liked to party." Her eyes still begged. "She didn't deserve this."

"No one deserves it, Ms. Hoffman."

⁂

As far as Detective Walter Talbot was concerned the trip into Pennsylvania was not unexpected, since the Fresh Kills landfill on Staten Island had been closed for some time. This morning the NYPD had joined a procession of trucks that made regular treks out of the five boroughs to disgorge unwanted accumulations of urban living.

"Nice of the locals to give us the right-of-way." Detective Johnny Rozelli bent, rechecking the protective shoe covers insulating his Gucci loafers.

Talbot smiled, refraining from comment. He gazed out at the mountains of waste, wondering what mysteries the landfill might surrender if they dug deep and long enough. If he squinted he could visualize an off-world landscape. Nothing, however, could distract him from the odor.

"This the right area?" Rozelli was pulling on latex gloves, sliding a mask down over his face.

Talbot referenced the grid he was holding. "Yes, these sections took the major hit of commercial garbage for the last six months." He snapped on gloves. "Any preference?"

His partner gave him the look he usually reserved for perps.

"Relax, Johnny, you wouldn't want to miss this prime opportunity to hone your forensic skills."

Rozelli lifted his mask. "Sakura is gonna owe us big. . . . Davis, you and Sanchez go with Mr. Smart-Ass here. Williams and Deter, come with me."

Talbot laughed, moving with his officers to Section F, thinking how like archeology was this entire drill. Garbage was just another kind of artifact. The detritus of twenty-four/seven defined a culture as much as anything else.

He lowered his mask, ready to excavate his chunk of real estate. His foot crunched on something hollow, and he glanced down in time to see a long tail slip between the seams of two garbage bags. He sensed the hurried plucking of claws against plastic. He reached down.

The day was overcast and cool, and he was grateful for small favors as his fingers cut into a tight overlay of bags, wedged like boulders. The thick dark green ones used for lawn debris never failed to resurrect the Caruso case.

Mary Ann Caruso was too young to be a mother, too frightened to tell anyone she was pregnant. Her father would have beaten the fetus out of her; her mother would have wailed and called in the parish priest. But she'd managed to keep her secret to the end. Then one night she squatted in her bedroom closet, bit into her arm to stifle her screams, and expelled her baby.

She'd stifled the infant's cries too. Two days later a homeless man, rummaging through neighborhood garbage, discovered the body deposited in a green garbage bag.

He'd been at the morgue when the coroner removed the small corpse from its plastic shroud. Its mouth open, frozen in its final effort to make its way into the world. The eyes, too, were wide, and though it was nothing more than fanciful speculation, in his mind the eyes would forever be green.

He looked up; Rozelli was waving. "Hey, Talbot, over here."

Deter had carved a deep trench through a large mound of plastic. Loose garbage spilled out. Something shiny caught the weak light overhead.

"The haulers seemed to have conveniently bypassed the recycling center." Talbot crouched down, touching a wide strip of tape binding layers of Visqueen. Inside the contents were loose, but he could feel the brittle outline of bone.

"We got soup, Walt."

"Decomp is advanced." He stood, tearing off his gloves, withdrawing his cell phone. He punched in Sakura's direct line. "We have one, Lieutenant."

The first had come too easy. But it was going to be a long haul, and somehow he knew that before day's end they would have another one.

⁂

A bright and too perfect afternoon. David St. Cyr stood near the rear perimeter of the Connecticut lot, surveying the dense copse of trees and thick underbrush. He breathed in, pleased with how well his manipulations had proceeded over the months. That precise chain of events that had brought him to this moment. Of course, there had been inconveniences, dealing with people like Patrice Attenborough. But it was a petty price to pay, since it had secured him the prize, brought him what he most wanted.

The Redmond commission. His mind drifted, placing Margot Redmond back inside the Guggenheim. Looking at the Holzer exhibition, she had appeared a rape victim herself. Her eyes wild, startled by the artistic curiosity laid bare before her. She had gawked at the silver band looping the bleached femur. A ropy blue vein throbbed in her neck as she risked reading one more line from the script: *I know who you are and it does me no good at all.*

In the rotting belly of dark, her skin polished by the LED lights, she had looked deliciously cadaverous. Her unbound rust-red hair, out of sync with the rest of her mechanized perfection, had aroused him. Though he knew Mrs. Redmond presumed he was queer. He laughed hard at her assumption. The truths and lies of first impressions.

He exhaled, assessing the land the Redmonds had chosen for their home. A man most happy when elements bent to his will, he frowned. Excessive nature required reining in. Idyllic prettiness constrained. Contemporary architecture must be dedicated to reason, possessed of a dynamic geometry that distilled and refined the human senses.

He shook off his judgments and walked into the thick of trees. He must select the right spot, must situate himself perfectly. Though a more reasonable mind challenged, a lesser self felt compelled to marry organic matter to organic matter. Reaching into his jacket, he withdrew latex gloves. Setting earphones in place, he turned up the volume and waited for the nickel-sharpened music to infiltrate his brain. Then, unzipping his pants, he withdrew his penis. He refused to allow the chill October air to interfere. Besides, he'd trained his brain to maintain a hard-on. He would masturbate to climax, spilling his live sperm onto the ground, christening the Redmond land.

A body in the landfill. He might have been sitting calmly behind his desk, but James Sakura could not control his brain. It moved with a rhythm of its own, creating its own terrible images. Made of Talbot's phone-in description, of its own uncompromising pictures. Rotting flesh folded within tight seams of plastic. A face, once distinct in life, now a greasy smudge pressing against the clear. Naked teeth, the sole architecture of a mouth, forming a bridge where lips had once been. Incongruously, the Visqueen package in his mind was a tidy layer amid mounting layers of ugly stink, a mummy bundle slid between misshapen balloons of waste.

He clutched the jade disk and breathed. Whole lungfuls of air. Pushing his mind backward to another landscape. To another time. To a spring holiday in Nara. On Mount Nyoi. Upon Bridge to Inner Temple. He stood, a boy of eight, on stone steps, moving toward the arch of the bridge. Up ahead, almost to the magic pagoda, waited Uncle Ikenobo, a paper cutout against the green in his Buddhist's robe.

All around him was the green. Woolly green shrubs and prickly bushes. Humps and lumps of green. Carved and sculpted patterns of

green. Great green arms of trees stabbing blue sky. Tangles of green forcing slick tongues up through dark earth. An archipelago of green.

He could almost taste the green. Closing his eyes, he inhaled the rich
and thick of it. Then a noise, from outside the circle of familiar warbles
and chittering his ears had memorized. His eyes widened to catch the
false note.

He ran to the middle of the bridge, his skinny boy's body leaning, the
wooden rails cutting him into halves, his eyes searching the green maze.
A flash of color. Spilled paint. A vulgar interloper against the green. And
movement. A sudden violence fusing into a steadying shimmy. Then a
single nervous quiver, alien and brief.

"Uncle," his voice sailed upward, and the once still cloud of robe
came to life, brown sandaled–feet slowly clopping down the steps.

But he was running, to where the tall stairway began, into the dense-
ness. Moving without stopping. His legs in short pants, feeling the kiss
and bite of the green, plunging as if into water.

He saw the white belly first. Then the round eyes like black marbles.
He imagined the lids blinked, but it was some trick of his mind. The
small deer was dead. He touched the muzzle, the flat of his thumb
brushing moist leather. He wiped his finger on the seat of his pants, and
saw the half-open mouth, the tip of a pink tongue. A trickle of blood ran
red onto the green.

"Akira."

He turned at the sound of his name. Until that moment he was convinced he wasn't crying. But he could feel the wet on his cheek when his
uncle touched his face.

There was a deep slash in the animal's throat. And his youthful mind
shook with questions. Who would steal the peace from Mount Nyoi?
Who had left the deer to die a secret death? *Why?* his child's heart
screamed.

"*Ahimsa.*" His uncle whispered the Sanskrit word, with questions of
his own. "Are we not taught to do no harm? To reverence all living
things? Do not some monks filter the very water they drink, wear gauze
across their faces so as not to harm the smallest of creatures? Do they
not walk the night lest they step upon some beast crawling upon its
belly?"

He felt the jade slip from his hand. He was no longer in the forest with his uncle. He was in his office. At his desk. In present time. Yet in his world someone was still stalking the innocent.

                                        ◆

Michael Darius could not deny that Gramercy Park was beautiful. A tranquil, tree-lined space at the foot of Lexington Avenue, the park was privately owned, cared for by the residents of the buildings which occupied the original sixty-six lots. He had come here straight from headquarters, and had been waiting for nearly an hour in the fast-fading light, outside the fence of the central square, watching the entrance to the handsome red-brick building.

A car pulled to the pavement, and a driver got out, opening the door for a woman and two small boys. The woman smiled, thanking the driver, who handed out a shopping bag from the car's interior. One of the boys, a compact package himself in his quilted jacket, tugged at her free hand, his round face twisting in impatience. The other fidgeted on the sidewalk. Ringlets, a good shade redder than his mother's bright auburn, escaped his blue knit cap.

Margot leaned down, still smiling, reeled the boys in with a word. Her expression changed, however, replaced by the wariness he hated, as he walked up.

"Hello, Michael. You coming in?"

"For a while." The boys were looking up at him.

"Reese is having dinner with a client." She turned, dismissing the driver. "But he'll be home before nine." She looked back at him.

"I'll be gone."

She nodded. Jason, still silent, reached up to take his hand. Margot's back stiffened, but she performed the ritual which had developed with his visits. They walked together, swinging first one twin, then the other, as each squealed with delight between them.

The townhouse, as always, was perfect. Even the toys that were scattered on the rug looked arranged. Margot was pulling off the boys' jackets and hats. They exploded away from her, running toward the abandoned toys. "They never slow down," she said. ". . . May I get you something?"

The overture so formal. "No thanks," he said. He walked to a chair near where the boys had started playing.

Jason got up, offering him a piece of the wooden train. "Wanna play?" His own blue eyes looking up at him.

"Maybe in a minute." He smiled.

Jason went back to where Damon was building up blocks for the train to knock down. Margot had put away her packages and coat. She walked past him to the kitchen that opened off the living room.

"I've got to get the boys dinner," she said.

He remained in the chair. Nearby was the armoire that held Margot's computer. She'd been working part-time at home since the twins' birth, still for the same firm that had offered them both jobs when they'd graduated from law school.

After a while she brought him the drink he'd turned down. A single-malt scotch and water. And despite the boys' protests, she sat them down to dinner at the long dining table near the window. She sat down too, but without a plate. She had poured herself a glass of the scotch.

Not long after the meal, she took the boys upstairs for a bath, and then put them to bed.

He sat in the chair till she came back. He watched her pick up the plates, carry them into the kitchen. He could hear her running water, placing things inside the dishwasher.

She came back into the living room and picked up the toys, putting them into a basket. She walked toward him and stood at the edge of the rug. "I don't know what you want, Michael," she said to him. "But I'm going to answer the questions you never ask. The ones I can hear rattling around in your head every time you decide to show up here."

He nearly spoke, but didn't. He was staring at the wooden floor, the polished planks dividing them.

"Yes," she began. "I know it was a terrible thing to do, leaving like I did, not even telling you I was pregnant. But you had me feeling I was fighting for my life. I'd been so goddamn good about you chucking the law, letting you ride out on your holy quest. But then you chucked the force too . . . and shut me out completely. Sitting around like a wounded animal, just like you're doing now. I wasn't about to put any child of mine through that."

He forced himself to look at her.

"Now the big one." She stared back. "No, Michael, I wasn't sleeping with Reese before I left you. We were good friends. We're still good friends. He's a wonderful husband . . . and father."

"Do you love him?"

His question surprised them both. He watched her suck in a breath to stop the tears that welled in her eyes. "Oh no, Michael." She was shaking her head. "You don't get to ask me that."

He stood.

"Michael . . ." Her voice, urgent, had softened. "You don't want a family. You only like to play with the idea of having us. Reese wants to adopt—"

"No!" He had cut her off. In moments he'd reached the door.

His little pussy was patient in her desires. Life had taught her unfortunate lessons. Like no pleasure without pain—a lesson fortunate for him.

She'd been waiting for hours in her hole. For the sounds of his footsteps entering the apartment. For the quiet as he removed his clothes and shoes. And now, the music starting. A tide of acid from the sound system, vibrating into walls. Reaching her in her dark little corner. A contact high, with the beat buzzing between the points where her naked shoulders touched the hardboard. And the vibe like a current running up her spine. Reverberating in her own little rhythm box. So hot for him now. The beat so promising of the fucking to come.

You'd think that he would be sick of it, after so many hours at the club. But the music was like breathing to him. The *source,* he liked to call it. His usual bullshit that she lapped up like cream.

The air wailed in the pulse of the strobe light he'd installed. Randy Lancaster smiled, admiring his erection caught in the bedroom mirror. The flash from his rings leaving metal tracks on his retina. But even his patient pussycat would be getting anxious now. He imagined beneath the music the note of a single bell.

He walked on bare feet toward the locked closet. "Here, kitty, kitty," he called.

CHAPTER

4

D r. Linsky's neat office was a relief after the long hours in the cutting room. Sakura sat waiting for the medical examiner to join him. The photo of the doctor's Russian wife smiled up at him from the desk, a contrast to the images from the autopsies that persisted in his brain— a gallery of the stages of human decomposition. He practiced proper breathing and let the pictures come. Better to endure them while the overload was numbing.

The two bodies recovered from the landfill had been badly decayed, but the eventual identification of both victims seemed probable. Dental X rays had been obtained, and skeletal muscle and dental pulp which could provide good DNA. Linsky had even managed to get fingerprints from one of them.

That particular freeze frame slotted in his brain, then ran in animation. The necrotic skin slipping away like a glove. Linsky fitting it onto his own latexed hand, plumping out the prints to get a good pattern. The attendant had been impressed by the ME's innovation. Linsky as always would go the extra mile. Sakura had instructed himself to be grateful.

The doctor came in looking drained, his fatigue more pronounced in the starched white coat. Sakura, feeling his own exhaustion, made the effort to pull himself straighter.

Linsky got to the point. "I assume you'd like a comparison with the other two victims."

"Please."

"The wrapping of the bodies appears identical," the doctor started speaking as he sat behind his desk. "The plastic was thick and carefully taped, which accounts for the level of preservation." He settled back. "If he killed them as quickly as the others, the lab should still be able to detect if they were given Rohypnol. And I saw nothing inconsistent with asphyxiation as the cause of death."

"Could you determine if the organs were reversed?"

"Decomposition was advanced. But it appears that these two bodies were cut and closed like the others. The staples are there, and the presence of the stainless wire in the cavities is certainly suggestive that the organs were also reversed."

Sakura nodded. This was as clear a declaration as he was likely to get that the killer's MO had remained consistent with respect to all four victims. His next question was more problematical. "Any idea how long these two had been out there?"

Predictably, Linsky frowned. "There are too many variables to make any kind of accurate determination. If there had been insect activity, we could have based an estimation on the stages of development in the colonies, but the plastic kept everything out. And since obviously there were no egg deposits before the victims were wrapped, it indicates they came from a clean cool environment."

"Were they out there for weeks? Months?" Sakura persisted.

"Months, for one. Weeks for the other," the doctor conceded.

"So it's reasonable to conclude that these victims fall between Helena Grady and Leslie Siebrig."

"I would say that your assumption is reasonable."

"Thank you, Doctor." He stood up. "I guess that's all for now."

"For now." Linsky's tired expression turned ironic. "Regretfully, I must assume, we will have other occasions to meet."

⁂

Victor Abbot pressed the remote control. At first the cable news program had been a diversion. Now it was his obsession. He stopped at the Fox channel. For his afternoon fix. Waiting for the host to explode across the screen. On his knees. As if before a shrine. And it didn't matter how many times he'd seen Zoe Kahn, her image always came as a shock. The insane bloom of blond hair, the excessive red lips moving, spitting words out in order to suck him in. He felt a drool of seminal fluid ease from his penis in expectation. And suddenly there she was. He reached and placed his hand over the flattened face on the screen. Flesh behind the barrier. Static electricity zapped-wiggled from his fingertips.

"So, Dr. French, if you were working in Switzerland you could carry on your research?"

Zoe's pixels spoke. He squeezed his thighs together. Camera moving . . .

"Possibly, Ms. Kahn."

Camera back on Zoe . . .

"Let me understand . . . and please call me Zoe. What you want to do is give LSD to potential serial killers to reprogram their brains. . . . But Uncle Sam is having none of it."

"A bit oversimplified. But you are correct in stating that the United States government has not actively supported LSD research in this country since the seventies."

"So we'll never know if you could have transformed a potential Ted Bundy into a choirboy."

Dancing pixels filled his brain. Cams and cogs shifting, making adjustments for his arousal.

"That's a somewhat colorful metaphor, Ms. Kahn . . . Zoe. But I do think LSD might be one of the tools we could utilize to rewire malfunctioning neural circuits in the limbic brain."

"Sounds like brainwashing. . . . What was that movie with those bad-assed British boys?"

"*A Clockwork Orange,*" the guest said.

"Is that what you want to do?"

Now he could smell it—a top note of ozone, the scent of refined petrol beneath. It filled his lungs, greased his gears.

"From the available research we know that serials are products of a constellation of events both genetic and environmental," the guest was speaking. "The evil that men do often starts early."

"How early?"

The *how* pursed Zoe's lips, so that he instantly focused on the tiny black hole forming in the center of her mouth.

"There is evidence that the progression toward serial murder may begin in childhood. With LSD we would hope to short-circuit the bad programming," the guest continued.

"To stop serial killers before they start?" Zoe asked.

The *to* and *-fore* gave him another chance at the little black holes.

"Before the primary role of fantasy sets in."

"No robots, then?"

Grind, grinder, grinding . . .

"Self-actualized human beings," the guest said.

"But you're having to do the book instead."

Grinding . . .

"I'm working on a book."

"Was the Death Angel going to be part of your research?"

He rose from his haunches.

"Yes, he was."

"Have you spoken to him since he was arrested?" Zoe asked now.

"As far as I know he is still hospitalized."

"For the viewers who might have been visiting another planet . . ."

Full face. Eyes, metallic-blue pigment rushing to white.

". . . the Death Angel was the serial killer who tallied up seven bodies last year before he was finally apprehended by the NYPD."

Zoe's pixels resettled into profile.

"Dr. French, you were assisting with the case."

"Yes."

"What was he like?"

"Intelligent. Convinced that what he was doing was not killing."

For the first time he allowed himself to consider Zoe's guest.

"A real psycho," Zoe said.

"An atypical paranoid psychotic."

The guest was so organic. Her flesh didn't want to stay inside the box. He was having trouble holding on to her pixels.

"Your official diagnosis?"

"My unofficial diagnosis."

"Are the bodies found in the Pennsylvania landfill connected to the two previous homicides?"

Zoe's pixels suddenly grew brighter, sparked . . .

"I really can't comment on that."

"Can you even tell us if you're working with Lieutenant James Sakura on this new investigation? The Visqueen Murders?"

. . . starbursts going off.

"Is that what you're calling them, Ms. Kahn? . . . And yes, I'm available if Lieutenant Sakura needs my help."

He listened . . .

"By *help* you mean profiling."

. . . with his eyes.

"Profiling is useful in painting a picture of the kind of individual who might commit a particular crime," the guest said.

"At one time you profiled for the FBI."

"I taught at Quantico for several years."

"Are you currently practicing psychiatry?"

"I'm taking on a few patients."

The tin man . . .

"Well, you heard it here. Dr. Wilhelmina French is open for business in the Big Apple."

. . . *alive.*

His thumb hit the off button on the remote. For a moment he stared at the blank screen, imagining that which had only minutes ago been Zoe Kahn and the doctor dissolve into the dark dimensions of the set. Tonight he would dream of Zoe. In full armor, sheathed in metal, jointed and mounted in bolts. Tomorrow he would think about Dr. French.

✴

Hanae had prepared a meal for the four of them, she and Jimmy, Michael and Willie, together again. She had cooked American, something she did not usually do with guests, except on holidays like Thanksgiving and Christmas. But tonight she had done the unexpected.

They had sat on the tatami floor, on cushions round the table. That much was the same. And they had eaten everything, Jimmy joking that Taiko could not have done better cleaning the plates. The meal had been good, with talk and laughter, like a fire in the night. Like the light inside her mind that tempered her blindness.

She listened to them now, her husband and her friends still laughing as they cleared the table, telling her to sit, that this was their part. *Their part.* So easily they divided things, as if they might remain separate from the thing they beheld. They had forgotten what even Western science had learned, that the act of observing was indivisible from the thing which was observed. Last year had taught them all that.

She knew they understood this, that the lie of division was an act of will, a screen that portioned their lives between work and not work. But she could not remain where they had placed her. She was one of them now. Her experience with a killer had made it so.

"Where are we going to sit?" Willie's voice near the sofa. The metallic sound of a zipper, as she opened the case of her laptop.

"Where do you want to sit?" Jimmy had rejoined them from the kitchen.

"Let's stay here." Willie had walked back toward the table. "I think my brain works better here than when I'm sitting on the sofa."

"So that's what it takes." Kenjin had come back into the room.

"I heard that, Darius."

Hanae smiled. It was good to hear the two of them. She had sensed tonight at the table how they leaned into each other, heads close, their voices seeming to emerge toward her from the same point in space. She had wanted Kenjin and Willie together. At least in this thing she had gotten her wish. Michael no longer seemed so sad as her name for him implied.

"I will fix tea." She rose as the three of them settled again on the cushions. Their discussion had already begun when she returned.

"Talbot and Rozelli have been going over the missing persons reports," Kenjin was saying, "pulling out women with a similar history."

"Have we established that Helena Grady went to clubs?" Willie's question.

"We have," Jimmy said. "She was out with friends the night she disappeared. Neither of the other women saw who she left with."

They fell silent as she placed the tray on the table and sat to pour the tea.

"That smells wonderful," Willie said.

"It is *gyokuro*. It was Jimmy's grandmother's favorite."

She filled three cups and passed them. *Had they noted the fourth?* She poured out tea for herself. She could sense their surprise. On these occasions, it was always accepted that she would withdraw. In the seconds of silence, Taiko came and settled at her side. She lifted the tea to her mouth.

"It might take a while," Willie spoke first, "matching dental records and whatever else to those bodies."

"There could be more," Kenjin said. "He could have started killing them a long time ago. There could be bodies in other landfills."

Silence again. They were looking at Jimmy, as she knew he was looking at her.

"Have you thought any more about the profile?" Her husband had turned away, his question directed at Willie.

She let out her breath. Sipped tea.

"He's finding them in bars," Willie answered. "He's drugging them, then taking them somewhere where he can kill them and hold them till he can dump the bodies." She paused. "What does that tell us?"

"That he has reliable transportation," Kenjin said, "and lives somewhere he can move them in and out of without being conspicuous."

"He's in his twenties or thirties, and he's white," Willie went on. "He's nocturnal, prowling the clubs, killing and dumping at night. He could have a day job."

"What kind of job?" Jimmy asked.

"Something dead-end where he's just marking time. Or he could be self-employed, setting his own schedule. I'm not reading this guy as a loser. He picked up Leslie Siebrig in Le Chat Noir."

"He drugged her drink," Kenjin said.

"Yes, but he had to get close enough to do it. Which means he's got confidence in social situations. He's probably attractive."

"Remember that it looks like he's killing them before they regain consciousness," Jimmy spoke again. "No bruising on the bodies to indicate that they were ever restrained. No defensive injuries. And that they died fairly quickly is also implied by the fact that the drug could still be found in their systems."

"So if he's so damn social, why does he want them unconscious when he rapes and kills them?" Willie was playing against her original argument.

"In other words what's his fantasy?" Kenjin asked.

"I don't know," she said, "but it certainly seems to center on what he's doing with the organs. Cutting them out. Then, wiring them back in reversed. . . . What did Linsky give you at the autopsies today in terms of age and height?" Willie's voice was directed toward Jimmy now.

"All the victims were in their twenties," he answered her. "And tall."

"Weight?"

"Harder to tell, but probably thin like both Grady and Siebrig."

"So that's the type," Willie said. "He doesn't seem to care about coloring. Two were blondes, two brunets."

"Tall, thin, and young," Jimmy said. "And he wants no interaction postcapture. What's that add up to?"

"A mannequin," Willie offered.

"A robot." It was Kenjin who said that. The tone of his voice chilled her.

The music annihilated space. He arced through the scene to the pulse of the strobes that flashed like razors in the carapace shield of his glasses. Midweek and the party went on. Thousands of bodies flowing and locking. The frenzy of the organic lusting for freedom.

Right-brain loathed the crowd, the sense of confinement. Left-brain didn't mind. But still he didn't dance, beyond such simple mechanics. He held the sound inside, feeling his organs dissolving, matter moving out of him in the light that streamed from his fingers. No flesh. No bone. No blood but the music, branching and jumping. Machine soul released from the grubby limits of primate brain.

In the beginning was the beat, and the beat was with God, and the beat was God.

The dancers seemed far beneath him, white bodies writhing like maggots in the dark of the cave. But for one. Tall, nearly fleshless. A perfect conductor. The music ran through her muscles as visible current in an effortless stop and flow.

For a long time he watched her dance, the wall projections splashing their colors over her body and face. Was still watching when she cut herself from the pack.

He was waiting at the bar before her in the three-deep line to order. She only seemed more perfect closer up, with the water from the misting machines beading like oil on her skin. The lasers swept by and pierced her. The music blew through, refracted. He caught her watching him back, wondering perhaps if she hadn't seen him before.

"Neat shades," she said.

He smiled at the opening, touching his glasses. "I saw you dancing," he said.

"I saw you not dancing." Her eyes were moving over him, still assessing.

"You don't know what you saw."

His answer didn't dissuade her. "The *Vibe*'s not here." Her tone dismissive. Sparks in the toss of her hair.

"Buy you a drink?" he offered.

"I like to buy my own."

"That's smart," he said. "Though I think with me you could make an exception."

"I don't think I will." She smiled. Her upper teeth were crooked. A reinsertion of the imperfect organic that brought the whole thing down.

The man ahead of him left the bar with his drink. He let her go in front of him.

"Thanks." She waited to order, then turned back. "Look," she said, favoring him again with the teeth, "the real party is this weekend." She produced a pen from her satin shorts, and wrote fate on the back of his hand.

🔱

Jimmy breathed deeply, glancing at the clock: 2:32 A.M. He turned over onto his side and listened in the darkness for his wife's regular breathing. He had spent the last two hours trying to get to sleep, blaming the new case for his insomnia. But he knew the falseness of that excuse. It was Hanae who kept him awake.

She had sat quietly, her eyes often closed, listening to the theories he, Willie, and Michael tossed around. The conversation flowed easily, though not for a minute was he unaware of her presence.

It had been a subtle calculation on her part, sitting down with them after the tea had been poured, taking into her hand the fourth cup. The cup she'd reserved for herself. And the consequences of her conduct had not been lost on him. It had been an essential gesture, one he wished he could have preempted. But then, he did not have her wisdom.

She moved onto her back, her eyes open.

He bent and kissed her, feeling her smile open against his mouth.

"Well, Wife, since neither of us are having any luck sleeping, I think it's a good time for you to tell me what you think."

"What I think, Husband?"

"About my case, Hanae Sakura."

✤

Why? The word was bile rising up into his throat. Nothing Left-brain might whisper would make the anger go away. And what excuse had been offered? *Crooked teeth.* Right-brain would have been satisfied with no teeth. It was the flesh that mattered. The sweet flesh. In layers. Ripe to the core. He pressed against the base of his penis, working the shaft with his other hand in the slow-fast rhythm he preferred.

Why the fuck had he gone out tonight if he wasn't going to bring home a little goodie. A doggie bag. Going out had only one purpose. To get the flesh to come home with him. It wasn't complicated. No convoluted destiny. Its raison d'etre was pure and simple—*get the flesh home.*

And he was beginning to run on empty. It didn't matter that Left-brain had better control. Right-brain was hungry. The eater of souls had an ever-increasing appetite, and this inarticulate slow-fast whipping of his penis could never take him where he needed to go.

CHAPTER

5

His kata practice completed, James Sakura knelt in meditation, but thought intruded, an awareness of the room, of his fellow students. It had been difficult to find a dojo in the city where training with the sword was available. Although O-Sensei, the founder of aikido, had been a master of more than one of the ancient sword traditions, after his death training with the weapon had disappeared from most aikido schools.

Sakura had been incredibly lucky to find this one, whose headmaster had trained at the fabled Kashima ryu, a school whose sword tradition stretched back for many hundreds of years. Unlike the Kashima ryu, membership in this dojo had not required a blood oath, but he considered his acceptance a privilege, and was worried about the effect of his new investigation on his continued attendance at these early morning sessions. The kata practice required some pairing, and he felt an obligation not only to the headmaster but to the other students as well.

Nor did he wish to give up the practice for himself. The rigors of the training had helped him greatly in the months that Hanae had been away, serving as an outlet for energy that could find no other. He was proud of his progress. He was already well into the second series of kata performed with the *fukuroshinai,* a training sword of cloth-covered bamboo. It would take many more levels of training, and probably many years, before he would be allowed to practice with the family sword that had been last year's gift from his father.

He had been so preoccupied at the time of Isao's visit with the pressures of the investigation. Still, he should have known that his father was not well. He had looked more tired last year than he'd ever seen him . . . vulnerable, he realized now. He had let old resentments blind him, when he should have so easily guessed the meaning in the gesture of passing on the sword.

Lupus, Elizabeth had said, when she'd finally called, defying at last Isao's wish that his elder son not be told of his illness. The trip to New York, she'd explained, had not been to attend a medical conference, as his father had implied, but rather to confer with a specialist whom he trusted on the best course of treatment for his disease. Their father had been doing well, according to his stepsister. Was now in full remission.

Remission. An interesting word, one meaning of which was absolution. Which one of them, he wondered, was in need of it most, himself or Isao?

He made a promise. When this case was successfully behind him, he and Hanae would make the trip out West. His wife would love meeting Elizabeth, who was also an artist, and he would enjoy seeing his sister again. And Paul, his brother; it might be good to see him too. Perhaps even Susan, his stepmother, might have mellowed in the intervening years. Or perhaps he had gained enough wisdom to endure the sugared barbs that dropped so easily from her tongue. In any case, he must make the trip, for himself as well as his father. There was more to healing than the physical.

The thought brought an image of Hanae last night as they both lay unsleeping in the bed. His eyes adjusted to the dimness, he could see her face as she'd rolled onto her back, her dark eyes open. How he had wanted her in that moment, a need that was too much of possession. He had simply kissed her and asked what she thought of his case.

The insight which she'd shared had been not about the killer, but him. She approved of the way he worked. He listened well, she said, drawing out the ideas of others.

But what were *her* ideas?

She had none. She too was a good listener.

He shook his head at the memory, further interrupting even the pretense of meditation. His wife had made him smile, but he knew he was not happy with this desire of hers to involve herself in what he'd always believed should be separate from their life together. He had no will to think about why, or even if, this should change. He did not want to deal with it. But he knew that he must. He sensed that his understanding and approval were, in Hanae's mind at least, the entry gates to the path that could heal their marriage.

And heal it, he must. For later in the night when he'd reached for her, he had felt her soft and pliant. But her limbs had trembled still, as if she would tear apart. He had held her, smoothing her hair, until the shaking ceased.

His wife was back in his bed. Not a dream any longer, but the flesh-and-blood woman whom he loved. His practice of aikido had been excellent for channeling the frustration of what must be endured while she was gone. But he was not a monk. Celibacy had never been a part of any spiritual life he'd envisioned. With Hanae, he must remain patient. The one who perhaps had to be hurried along was himself.

🛦

The room was a crypt, below ground and full of bones. Yet the atmosphere was anything but macabre. Dr. Wilton "Bones" Bailey had managed to create a lab that somehow defied, yet at the same time defined, its utility. A burled-wood chest laden with ancient artifacts—an Egyptian *shawabty* ogled a bare-chested Minoan snake goddess—stood opposite an old armoire, whose belly brimmed with hundreds of crusty texts. An antique torchère gave off a parchment glow, a yellow bubble inside the room's cold fluorescence. A Beethoven CD played in the background.

The center of the laboratory was Bones's work space. A wooden refectory table, likely a relic from a medieval monastery, ran half the length of the room.

"Hello, Lieutenant." The forensic anthropologist, hunched over a specimen, spoke without looking up. "Linsky said you'd be paying me a visit this afternoon."

Sakura smiled as the scientist rotated a magnifying glass over the surface of a skull. "So the two of you are communicating."

Now Bailey glanced up. His bifocals doubled the size of his blue eyes.

"Only when necessary. That man has no sense of humor." He considered the skull, an indulgent old Hamlet. "He sent over two of these."

"From the bodies found in the landfill." Sakura pulled over a stool and sat across from the doctor.

Bailey wagged his head. "Violence remains a constant, James. Assyrians, Nazis, serial killers."

And this was the very thing that kept him in the game, Sakura reminded himself. The need to make it right. "We've managed to narrow our list from Missing Persons to seven possibles," he said.

"Our killer's taste does run in a particular direction." The doctor returned the skull to the table, picked up the other.

"Tall and thin." Sakura audibilized one of the case's few certainties.

Bailey nodded. "And the bodies *are* female. Radiographs of the bony structures confirmed the sexing."

From an envelope Sakura pulled photos of the seven women who fit the criteria and who'd gone missing in the last six months. He set each photograph down, facing the anthropologist, in a line across the table. Bailey looked up, then down at the row of pictures. Six were in color, one black-and-white. A couple were candid shots, the rest formal portraits.

"Very pretty . . ." The doctor's voice seemed to waver. Then, removing his latex gloves, he selected a photograph. Tenderly, as though the paper, or the girl herself, would crack. His eyes ran over the glossy surface, then returned it to the lineup. He picked up a second, then a third, his thumb seeming to rub something off its surface. He stared at one image after another. Then he unhooked his glasses from around his ears, took a crumpled handkerchief from his pocket, and wiped the lenses.

"Young." Bailey cleared his throat on the single word. "Radiological evidence of the extent of cranial and epiphyseal fusions puts the age of the two landfill victims in their late teens or early twenties."

The doctor stood, his stool scraping against the tiled floor. "This skull"—he pointed—"has a broader, flatter, outward-sloping face. The orbital configurations are rounder. This is consistent with Asians." Now he indicated the other skull. "Whereas the orbital configurations of Caucasians are triangular, and the skull itself is generally higher, longer, and narrower."

The forensic anthropologist reexamined each of the photographs, finally choosing two from the seven. After a moment he placed the picture of a brunet with almond-shaped eyes under one skull, the photograph of a pale blonde with a wide full mouth under the other. "Of course, I'll need their dental records to be sure."

✤

Victor listened to Philip Glass whenever he masturbated to H. R. Giger. Focusing on the artist's drawings in a special coffee table edition, he would struggle to maintain the book's pristine condition. Only once did a small drool of semen hit the spread of glossy pages.

And if *Metropolis* was his favorite movie, *Species* was in second place. Sil, like Hel, another of his dream girls—not her Nordic-flesh Natasha Henstridge form, but clothed in Giger's vision. He opened his mouth, wishing to place his lips around one of those silver-capped nipples, to have those segmented articulating tentacles whip him into a frenzy.

But *Gray's Anatomy* was his bible—his road map of the pitiful physiological mask worn by human form, with its molecular swirls and twirls of flesh, its protoplasmic caverns and pockets, its greedy holes and slippery slits, its sluggish evolution in need of his hand, his refinement, till at last the steel-sleek purring core be reached.

Now he glanced up at the televison screen where his collector's edition of Tim Burton's *The Nightmare Before Christmas* was playing. Sally was working her own kind of magic with needle and thread on her severed arm. Leafing through the magazines, snipping photographs from back issues of *Elle* and *Vogue,* he found himself humming Danny Elfman's score.

As usual, his imagination worked in two dimensions. Licking his lips, he clipped the photo of the tall thin model bound and tied in Versace, in strips and strings that seemed more of aluminum than leather. Legs, white and seamless, sensible as strong shinny struts. Angling scissors, he sliced the girl off at the tops of her thighs, squinting like a painter at the disembodied pair of legs, balancing on four-inch spikes.

He placed the legs beneath the other assembled body parts. A striking fit. Opening the jar, he ran the brush loaded with rubber cement across the back of the cutout. Now all that was left was the head. And as always he had the perfect head.

He stood up from his cross-legged position on the floor and walked to the table where the latest issue of *People* magazine lay. Her image glistened from the cover, a star amidst images of other talking heads. His girl had made the big time.

He returned to his little nest on the floor, and ripped off the cover of the magazine. Then he began to excise her from her spot between Katie Couric and Paula Zahn. His scissors snipped, careful to preserve all the wisps of her hair. There. He held her head above the body he'd just constructed. He'd done well. He had a good eye. The head was in perfect scale to the body. But pixels and paper were a poor substitute for flesh. At least flesh morphed into metal.

He pasted the head onto the column of neck and smiled at his newest creation. Then he rose, carrying his "paper doll," as he sometimes called his little works of art, and entered his bedroom. He stopped at the foot of his bed, admiring his collection, staring at the same face, glued or stapled or grommeted onto the dozens of bodies he'd resurrected like Dr. Frankenstein from the glossy bits and pieces he salvaged from magazines. Her image repeated over and over. Duplicated, triplicated, quadruplicated. A hundred replicants of Zoe Kahn reclining on the smooth six-hundred-count sheets of Victor Abbot's bed.

✠

Sitting in the harshness of the overhead fluorescents, Sakura looked up at the clock to find it was late. The end of week one in this new investigation. The members of his unit had gone home, the squad room beyond the glass window of his office populated by a few stragglers, men detailed from the precincts still pecking out reports, mixed with the regular shifts from Major Case. He knew he should go home too, should take his own advice about the last weekend that any of them was likely to see for a while.

Four bodies now, and the clock was ticking. Despite today's long hours spent reading and rereading reports, he could not suppress the interior nagging voice that insisted that just one more round of sifting through the stack of DD-5s on his desk might uncover some small but significant detail they had missed—might provoke some fresh insight that could save a young woman who in this critical moment was still alive, but already stalked by the killer.

"Hello, Jimmy."

The effect of her voice was instant. His eyes jerked upward to see Assistant District Attorney Faith Baldwin standing in the doorway of his office. Her neat wool suit had nearly the same chestnut richness as her hair. The jacket's severe tailoring had the intended effect of focusing her femininity.

"It's been a while." She was smiling at whatever she read in his face. He watched her cross his office to take a seat in the chair, too conscious of the desk between them.

"Why are you here, Faith?"

"Your new case," she said. "You have to know I'm interested."

Faith had a way of attaching herself to any high-profile investigation. His serial case last year had been no exception. "It's early," he said. "We haven't developed any suspects."

"Don't tell that to the press."

"I try not to tell them anything."

"You look tired," she said now. "Why don't you let me take you out for a drink."

He shook his head. "Time to go home."

"I hear your wife's back."

"She is."

"How long has it been, Jimmy?" Her flat clear voice had changed inflection. Her green eyes were watching, daring him to pretend he didn't understand exactly what she'd meant by the question.

"Six years." He didn't deny that he did.

"I miss having you in my bed."

He shook his head. "Why are we talking about this?"

"When I want something, I ask for it."

"No," he said. He met her eyes.

She sat back in the chair, still looking at him with that directness he admired. Faith was the most self-confident person he knew. Highly intelligent, if not introspective. She had an animal grace, with no gentleness.

"I've waited all these months for your wife to get back," she said. "I wanted to play fair." She leaned forward, her breasts moving together beneath the silk of her blouse. She reached across the desk, her fingers encircling his wrist. A gesture intended to remind him of things they had done in bed.

It was pure Faith. He smiled.

She took the opening. "I don't want you for a husband. I just want to fuck you again. And you want to fuck me. Don't lie and say that's changed." She was still watching his eyes. The prosecutor now, more adept at reading the opposition than herself. He couldn't have named what he felt, but something of his jumbled thoughts had surfaced in his face. He saw her make the jump.

"Oh, hell." Her fingers released their hold. "He raped Hanae, didn't he?"

There had been nothing in the media to suggest that his wife, unlike the killer's other victims, had been sexually assaulted. That much had been kept from the press. The implication had always been that Hanae had been kidnapped by a deranged killer purely to taunt him.

Faith continued to stare. He had said nothing, but his silent affirmation seemed a worse betrayal than if he'd given in.

Faith stood. "I'm sorry . . . really." There was something near tender in her voice which didn't hold. "I still want you," she said. "No one ever guessed we were together before. No one would know now."

"We'd know."

"That is the point, isn't it?"

He stood too. "I'll keep the District Attorney's office informed of any progress."

For a moment she seemed poised to come around the desk, but she smiled instead. "Good night, Jimmy. Give us a case that will stick."

🔺

Solange Mansour glanced nervously at her watch. Nearly ten o'clock. She was glad to see she wasn't the only kid dressed like she was getting off at the subway stop. A good indication she was in the right place. The directions as usual had been pretty shitty. It was supposed to be part of the true party experience, this whole mystery of where the event would actually take place, but when you were alone this late in a not so good part of the city, the uncertainty was scary.

But she wasn't alone, she reminded herself.

She hurried to catch up with the group of kids she had spotted. They were older than her, but not much. And she was sure she looked eighteen at least, especially now with the new tattoo and piercing. There was something to be said for divorce. Play your parents off against one another, you could get pretty much what you wanted.

"Hi," she said, joining the group of two boys and three girls who had already reached the sidewalk.

They greeted her, smiles all around. One of the girls, a fat brunet in jeans, handed her a plastic bracelet, glitter hearts and stars in candy colors.

"You guys know where we're going?" she said.

"You come by yourself?" a Latino boy asked. His face showed concern.

"I'm meeting up with friends."

"You done that." He put an arm around her shoulder as they walked. He was nearly as tall as she was. "Carlos." He pointed to his chest.

"Solange."

"Cool name," said the girl with brown braided hair, half-dancing down the pavement in front of them. "We *think* we know where we're going." She smiled, looking back.

They found the warehouse twenty minutes later. Which wasn't too bad. Heidi and Paula were waiting out front for her, which seemed like a miracle now. She said good-bye to Carlos and the others, promising to look for them inside.

"I can't believe your dad bought it?" Paula's greeting.

"*I know it's your weekend, Daddy, but I really don't feel good.*" Solange croaked the words she had used on the phone, hand clutching at her fake sore throat. She broke up laughing.

"Won't he check on you?"

"Nah." Solange shrugged. "I didn't make out like I was *dying* or anything."

"But he knows your mother's not home."

"No he doesn't. She didn't want him to find out about her little three-day with Chuck. The divorce isn't final yet."

"So what if your *mom* checks?" Heidi said.

"Trust me, she won't." Solange looked bored. "So what's your alibi?"

"The usual," Heidi answered. "Our parents think we're spending the night at each other's houses. The trick is to call and check in with them. It's called a preemptive strike."

Solange gave an appreciative eye roll. Then, "God, this is cool."

"Yeah." Paula dragged the word. She dug into the pocket of her sweater, pulled something out. "E," she said, unrolling a tissue to display three small round pills.

Heidi reached out and took one.

"Well?" Paula was looking at her. "You said last time you wished we had some."

She had said that, hadn't she? She watched Paula reach with her free hand and pop a pill into her mouth. There was one left in the tissue.

Solange picked it up. What was she afraid of anyway? Everybody did it. They said it enhanced the experience.

She swallowed the pill down, her moment of fear evaporating as she smiled at both her friends. It felt so good to be here. With Heidi and Paula. With all the kids who were streaming in from every direction now. She laughed out loud. It was going to be one slammin' party.

✦

In the cold black mirror of the bedroom window, Willie's reading lamp shone in perfect double, a phantom moon that hovered over the city. She glanced at the clock. Nearly midnight, and Michael was still in his workroom, drafting a blueprint for the model he was planning to build, a replica of the cathedral at Rouen.

She wished that he would stop and come to bed. It had been a long full week of writing and seeing patients. And now with this new serial investigation, things could only get more complicated. She needed this weekend to catch up on her sleep, and she wanted to get started. But whenever Michael decided to come to bed, she knew, he was going to wake her.

Sex with Michael was always intense, but the last couple days he'd seemed driven, as if he had something to prove. And she'd woken this morning in the early darkness to find him sitting up in bed, smoking the cigarettes he'd sworn he'd given up again. He'd been to see his boys this week, and it was an easy guess that something that Margot had done or said was still eating at him. She wished he would talk to her about his ex-wife. She was reasonably certain she could remain objective, but Michael was never going to start that conversation. And she knew she couldn't.

She had been working on her book for hours. She shut the laptop down and, placing it on the bedside table, reached to switch off the lamp. The window went blank, the mirror glossiness flicking away to the dullness of reflected neon. The building, old stone, was thick as a fortress, and the city below seemed soundless, though the energy, which never ceased, was still something she could feel.

"You asleep?" Michael stood in the doorway, his body looming in the glow from the night-light in the hall.

"I just turned off the lamp." She sat up again. "I've been editing my first chapter."

"Let me read it." He started across the room.

"Not a chance." She placed a protective hand over the laptop. "I know what you think about my crackpot theories."

He sat on the bed. "I don't think your theories are crackpot."

"Liar." She switched on the light. He was smiling, his eyes that startling Welsh blue in the tanned Mediterranean face.

"We don't have to agree on everything." He kissed her.

"No, we don't. But you're still not reading the book till it's finished."

She watched him undress, tossing his clothes on the chair. She switched off the lamp again as he got into bed.

"Willie." His mood had changed. "You don't regret this, do you?"

"No." She turned toward him, but his eyes were lost in the dimness. "Do you regret asking me?"

"Hell, no." The words were a clear declaration, as was the way he reached for her, pulling her gown over her head as he slipped her beneath him. "This is good, Willie," he said.

The familiar thrill rippled through her, and the darkness came, that heaviness before the weightless oblivion that swept out everything. *This is good, Willie.* And at least for the moment, she did not believe it was only the sex that he meant.

The beat was superior, better than the clubs. Left-brain acknowledged that. There was a rawness in the setting that fed the trance. But coming here might have been a mistake.

He stayed for the sound. A Right-brain carelessness that was justified by the music's effect. A crash mix of techno and gabber. A bloodsucking oscillator having its way with his brain. He stayed for *it.* Tall. Dark-haired. Pale skin stretched over tight muscle. Machine goddess in backpack emerging from the blue of the chill-out room, strains of ambient clinging to the body like gauze. He watched from the shadows as she drifted past, stopping at the edge of the crowd.

"Lost somebody?" He was at her side.

A hesitant smile as she turned. The teeth white and perfect. She held up a hand with a strobing plastic ring. "My friend Heidi's idea," she said. "We're supposed to be able to find each other with these." She looked back toward the masses dancing in the reflection of the psychedelia projecting onto the walls, writhing in the confusion of glowsticks and glancing lasers.

"Good luck," he said.

"You a DJ or something?" She'd turned back with full attention, or however much she could muster with whatever illegal substance clouding her brain.

"Record producer," he lied. "We think it's time a major label got around to capturing this." She nodded, very serious, as if he'd said something profound.

He kept talking, some gibberish about artists and distribution. The word exchange unimportant. He blocked the sounds from her mouth, concentrating instead on the complex play of muscles that formed each new expression with the working precision of gears.

She shrugged off the backpack and produced a plastic bottle filled with juice. She uncapped it and took a swig. The action, raw and real, drew him back to the *here*. He could read her discomfort in not offering some to him.

"Hold this a minute," she said, as if ceding him this level of trust was adequate substitute for rejecting his saliva.

"Sure," he said, as she gave her attention to rearranging the pack on her back. It was almost too easy to slip the roofie into her drink.

CHAPTER

6

Early Monday. Sakura was back at his desk. He had forced himself to stay away for the weekend, checking in by phone only briefly, letting his mind rest, convincing himself he would return with fresh perspective. He had concentrated on his wife, on a pleasant two days of reestablishing routine. But it was a weekend of bad weather and false peace.

He closed his eyes and breathed deeply, moving to that dark space inside himself he called *killer mind: I am the center of the universe. My needs are superior to the needs of all others. Others do not exist as humans, only as objects. Objects for my pleasure. To move about as I please. To use in service to my fantasy. My fantasy, the only true reality. . . . And I am unafraid.*

He opened his eyes. Traveling inside a serial killer's mind was another way to understand the man who delivered death like a feature film. But the trip was not without risk. Touching evil left its mark.

He looked down to see the two pictures Dr. Bailey had culled from the group of seven photographs. One brunet. One blonde. Both young and pretty with innocent eyes full of expectation. Unknowing of the thing that would crawl from the bowels of a sewer to trap their last breaths against the membrane of a plastic bag.

Friends and relatives of the other two victims, Grady and Siebrig, were still being interviewed. Precinct officers were continuing to canvass the area where Siebrig had been found, focusing on the personnel of the restaurant whose Dumpster the killer had used to dispose of the body.

Since Grady had turned up at the recycling center, it was infeasible to pinpoint where her body had been picked up. But he had sanitation backtracking possible routes. Another detail had been sent back to the landfill in Pennsylvania to expand search zones. So far everything had added up to "no result."

Talbot was reviewing databases as far back as three years in an attempt to locate men with a history of sexual assault coupled with the use of Rohypnol. There were some prospects, but the best of the usual suspects had been incarcerated during the six-month period when the four murders had taken place.

He picked up the receiver on the first ring.

"It's Bones, Lieutenant Sakura."

He smiled, correcting his presumption that the use of the nickname was the exclusive province of first-year forensic students. "Have something for me, Doctor?"

"Thirty-two teeth present one hundred and sixty surfaces. Five surfaces on each tooth. Not to mention specific morphologic patterns. There are more than two point five billion possibilities in charting the human mouth. The bottom line, Lieutenant, is that no two mouths are the same, which makes teeth as good as fingerprints."

Bailey was famous for delivering this introductory lecture as his way of initiating the untrained to specific odontological results.

"And what did you find on these one hundred and sixty surfaces, Doctor?"

"These two ladies had good oral hygiene. Made regular trips to the dentist."

He waited; the real news was coming.

"And routine X rays were taken, and the dentists kept excellent records."

Sakura glanced down at the photos. The brunet was showing off even white teeth. He had to assume that the blonde had the same behind her closed-mouth smile.

"I should have mentioned when you were here that several teeth from one of the victims had come loose from their sockets. That's common when decomposed or skeletal remains are discovered. Linsky retrieved the missing teeth, and since the loss was not due to trauma imposed by the killer, I glued them back into the open alveoli."

He knew that the moment had arrived.

"Well, Lieutenant Sakura, there's no mistake." An indrawn breath. "I correctly matched those photographs to the two skulls. The dental identifications confirm it."

It had stormed again over the weekend, bringing in another layer of early October chill. The sky late morning had a stage-set sun. All light and no warmth, like a false note of cheeriness.

The Brooklyn Heights neighborhood was a stage set in itself, with a perfect row of nineteenth-century brownstones. The Phelps address was second from the corner, a three-story Italianate with balconies and curved iron balustrades. Darius pulled up to the curb in the narrow tree-lined street, and threw the identification plate onto the dashboard.

"Let's get it done," he spoke across the seat to Adelia Johnson.

They got out and walked to the covered porch. Johnson pressed the bell.

"You're on time," the man greeted them as he opened the door, acknowledging Johnson's badge. "I'm Arthur Phelps." He stepped aside for them to enter. "My wife, Tai Lin." He indicated the woman on the sofa.

Mrs. Phelps appeared too young to have had a college-aged daughter, but the dark almond eyes were lifeless, giving her the appearance of a discarded china doll. Her husband's animal energy was a contrast. He was above average height, and had an athletic club fitness that showed in his tailored suit. A commodities broker, he was dressed for work, having made the point when he agreed to talk to them at his home that he would need to get to his office as early as was possible. "You have some news?" he asked.

He had not offered them a seat. Nor did he sit himself. Mrs. Phelps remained silent, but the listless eyes had lifted to watch them.

"I'm sorry," Johnson spoke, "but your daughter's dental records do match one of the bodies that was found at the landfill last week."

"Do match . . ." Arthur Phelps repeated her words. He sounded as if he were assuring himself he had got it right on a stock quote, but his eyes had filled with tears.

Mrs. Phelps had not visibly reacted, was still staring at them. A sound, an animal-like whimper, seemed to issue from her pores. Certainly her mouth remained fixed, as arms locked across her stomach, her torso sank forward till her head nearly touched her knees.

Arthur Phelps had seemed to be paralyzed. Now he moved, going to the sofa, sitting beside her, his arm protectively at her back. The whimper became a keening and died. Tai Lin Phelps sat up. It was startling a moment later when her lips moved.

"The television says he's getting them at dance clubs." Her eyes were dry. Her voice, calm and flat, was entirely American.

"We believe that's true, Mrs. Phelps." It was Johnson who answered. "We understand that's where Ana was last seen."

"In June," the woman said. "She was home from college. She said I should go with her to the club, that people would think I was her sister." The memory brought the rictus of a smile.

"But you didn't go," Darius said.

The woman shook her head. "Ana was only teasing. She was going to meet her friends."

"May I see her room?"

It was Mr. Phelps who led him up the stairs and left him alone, retreating to the living room, where Johnson would be going over the reports from the time of the girl's disappearance, fishing for what might be new information. He had seen the man's grief. More than his wife, Arthur Phelps had held on to hope. Darius wondered if he'd still go in to work today.

He stood in the middle of the bedroom and glanced around. More like a child's room than a woman's, it held all the sadness of a shrine. Four-poster canopied bed. Stuffed animals on shelves.

There were framed photographs on the bedside table. Ana with friends, probably some of the girls who would have to be reinterviewed now. A portrait of Ana, her graduation picture from high school. He picked it up. He could trace every feature in the faces of her parents. Her father's mouth. Her mother's eyes and coloring. But not small like the mother. Tall and model-thin. The way that he liked them, this killer. Trolling the club scene. A happy hunting ground for him. Dark. Crowded. Packed with girls like Ana Phelps who were oblivious to the danger.

There was an image taped to the wall. He walked over to see it better. It appeared to have been printed from the computer over which it hung. Electronic icon sprung from the god on the desk. The background was New Age psychedelic, a fractal stew of purple and pink, black lines converging like magnetic tracings. Down the sides, orange-yellow letters spelled out CYBER TRIBE, the words flanking the floating newsprint image of a large infant's head. Wearing earphones. Wise beyond his months. Expression serious. Almost grave. Below in lower-case letters, black and small with no intervening punctuation: *peace love unity respect.*

"She didn't take drugs."

The voice surprised him. Mrs. Phelps had come into the room.

"It's not what they said in the papers," she insisted. "It's not the drugs. Ana went for the music. To dance." Tai Lin Phelps was animated now, not the doll on the sofa. Something after all still lived in the eyes. And the sight of it was worse.

"There were no recreational drugs found in your daughter's system," he said to her.

She seemed pleased at the affirmation. "Ana loved to go to the clubs"—she was looking at the picture on the wall—"wherever the music was. That night, when she said I should go with her, she wanted me to feel it."

She had turned to him as she spoke, but her glance was far away. He waited.

"The *Vibe*," she spoke to his silent question. "Ana said it was impossible to describe, but spiritual . . . everyone connected, like a family. She said that it made her feel comfortable. And safe." The eyes no longer looked through him. "What kind of human being feeds on a child's desire for that?"

"Not human." One cold comfort he could give.

"Stop him." She'd named the other.

The afternoon park was glorious. Hanae could feel light from every direction playing on her face, as if the sun, already past its zenith, had exploded to coat the sky. A wind blew from the lake with a bite to make her glad she had worn her favorite red coat. The chill was welcome. She liked the cold. Today was a good day to mark her return. Her first time here in nearly a year. Taiko's harness jingled as they made their way along the path near Cherry Hill. A couple passed by, trying to decide where they should go for lunch. Two small children went by in a rush, their mother behind them, scolding them not to run.

She found a familiar bench and sat down. The breeze from the lake played in her hair. She could feel the water before her as a calmness in the green of the landscape. She took off her gloves and patted the shepherd sitting on guard at her feet.

"He can no longer hurt us," she spoke to the dog, dismissing her own small and irrational fear that somehow *he* would find them here. But unthinking, her hand had gone to her belly where the child had once been growing. Two *water children* now. Despite her daily prayers, the pain of her second, and wholly unnecessary, miscarriage was with her daily.

She bent down and touched the grass, finding leaves blown from the surrounding trees. She picked one up, still green in the early days of fall. But in the edges she sensed a hint of brown curling against her fingers, the promise of orange and burning yellow to come. She had returned to autumn, to the point on the path where her steps had faltered.

Not a circle, but a spiral. A different park. A different woman. She let the leaf fall.

She could not go back; she must not try. Her life was in this moment. And it was good to be home. It was good to be home with Jimmy. Tears came. She let them fall like the leaf. Even in this moment of peace she knew she was not healed. That no matter what her mind and her heart might believe, her body would betray her.

The other night after Kenjin and Willie had left, she had wanted more than anything to make love with Jimmy. But when the time came and he took her into his arms, her body had reacted on its own, shaking so violently that Jimmy had known she was not ready. She had felt like a stranger in her skin. She feared she was a stranger to her husband.

In this moment she hated the monster who had stolen her peace. In this moment she felt rage. Taiko shifted and whined, sensing her emotion. She reached down and once more patted his coat. "I must acknowledge these things," she said aloud to him. "The Buddha does not teach us not to feel."

To be human was to suffer. She had attached herself to an image of happiness that one man had destroyed. Her body had been violated and defiled. She had lost a child. But in the truth of things she owned nothing, not even herself. Loss was an illusion that she clung to. She was an imperfect vessel. Detachment would take time. And this too must be part of her acceptance.

✦

Cold air fell as hard as a hammer as the October sun set early. The windows had frosted over with the punch of a December evening, making the borough's streets seem indistinct and softer than they were. Heat belched from radiators, and the neon ghost on the sign appeared to have slipped into the outside world through the iron grates with the steam. The spook's arms flicked back and forth in a herky-jerky rhythm, while above its ballooning head the name of the neighborhood bar burned brightly: *Hokus Pokus.*

"For chrissakes, watch the coat."

"Hey, Manny, ain't you got no respect for Johnny Rozelli's coat?" It was Lyle DeSilva who bellowed the protocol, as his partner slid into the booth beside him.

"This is cashmere, you shitheads." Rozelli reached over and rearranged his topcoat over the back of the neighboring chair.

"Cashmere . . . don't that come from a goat?" Manny Bertolli wasn't about to let it rest.

"I ain't answering that." Rozelli picked up his beer and drank straight from the bottle.

The two detectives laughed. It had become a ritual, both of them attacking his clothes. The sudden change in weather had brought out the Armani he'd purchased at Barneys at the end of the season last year. He figured they would have gone after his new tie next, if DeSilva hadn't spotted her coming in through the door and punched Bertolli. That caused him to turn, and because she had on her radar she made straight for them.

"Well, well, well, if it ain't 'Ms. Fox News' herself," DeSilva said under his breath.

"Television show or no, Zoe Kahn's still the best-lookin' broad around," Bertolli mumbled.

"I think we better give the two lovebirds some privacy."

Rozelli cringed. He had only himself to blame, letting it slip to these two apes about what had happened last year.

DeSilva stood, grabbing his glass, just as she reached their booth.

"Don't you gentlemen leave on my account." She favored the two detectives with a big smile.

"Hello, Ms. Kahn. Love your show." Bertolli was preening as he rose.

"Why, thank you, Detective." Another big smile, just for Manny.

"Later, Johnny . . . Ms. Kahn." DeSilva edged his partner toward the bar.

"Hi, Rozelli."

He looked up finally. "Slummin' tonight, Zoe?"

She gave the place a once-over. "I rather like it here. It's got character." She slid into the seat opposite him, where DeSilva and Bertolli had been. "I don't imagine you mind if I sit."

"I got a choice?"

"You always have a choice, Johnny." This time her smile was only for him. "You can ask me to get the hell out of here. You've done it before."

He could feel himself getting steamed. "I had my reasons."

"I'm sorry things had to end the way they did, Johnny."

"Don't apologize. I was nothing but a dumb cop. You were doing your job."

Why was he sitting here talking to her? There were a thousand reasons why he shouldn't. But he ignored every one of them, and forced himself to relax and go along for the ride. He could handle Zoe Kahn. Besides, she wouldn't have the balls to pump him for info now. Suddenly he laughed. Of course she had the balls.

"What's so funny?" She was slipping off her coat.

He shook his head. "Nothing."

"You going to order me a drink, or do I have to get up and get one for myself?"

He stared at her. Bertolli was right: She was still the best-looking piece of ass around. "What do you want, Zoe?"

She smiled, her lips red and wet against her teeth. "A drink, for starters."

There was the taking of the flesh *before* and *after.* Right-brain enjoyed the *before*—the skin warm, the pluck of resilient tissue between thumb and forefinger, the river of blood, still contained, a lively cadence against the inside of his thighs. And the *lub-dubbing* of the heart's chambers as he rose and fell, driving himself into the sweet package. Though he would have preferred her squirming and kicking instead of limp and inert, Left-brain warned that consciousness was an unwarranted risk. So he'd pumped her, aware of her half-lidded eyes, still sucking on life, but only moments away from *after.*

After. Postmortem. That's how Left-brain preferred it. The body cooling, the blood settling in purple pools, marbling the white flesh. The heart stilled. Life gone from the eyes. Left-brain would ride her until she'd begun to set, until rigor was free to recast her. Then, quitting, he'd stare until a fresh excitement grew, whetted by the body's unyielding. He would have to relieve himself again, working his cock with one hand, locking the other into her rigid fingers, raised above the hard right angle of her arm.

The bag from the cleaners marked the boundary between before and after. Both Right-brain and Left-brain enjoyed putting the plastic over the face, observing the fish-mouth form and re-form. Once or twice, awareness would bubble to the surface, and fear cut into the plastic like a knife.

Left-brain was meticulous about the order to be followed, cleansing the body after Right-brain removed any jewelry. This time there were a plastic bracelet, a belly bar, and a thin hoop from one eyebrow. And a childish plastic ring that had flickered till the battery went dead.

Left-brain had secured a forensic pathology text, had read that the upward range of rigor mortis was eighty-four hours. Yet never before had it lasted as long as with this one. She'd had to remain in the cooler over the weekend, until Left-brain could stand it no longer and broke the rigor.

Dead weight. He laughed now, truly appreciating the old expression, as the body was settled onto the Visqueen, the layers twisted and sealed tight with tape in preparation for the van and the dark of night that waited.

CHAPTER

7

Cigar smoke was thick in the room as Sakura entered Lincoln McCauley's office. A good indication that the chief of detectives was a less-than-happy man. The perceived success of last year's serial investigation had done nothing to lessen their mutual dislike, and the unavoidable tensions of this new case were never going to make these meetings pleasant for either of them.

"What's this I hear about another missing girl?" The chief's words were out even before Sakura sat down.

"Disappeared from a warehouse party on Friday night," Sakura said. "Her parents didn't realize she was missing till yesterday. She's only sixteen and it wasn't a dance club—she could still turn up alive."

"But I take it that except for a couple years and the location of that noise they call music, she fits the victim profile."

"Pretty much," Sakura admitted. "Missing Persons faxed over a photo and a copy of the file late yesterday. She's the same physical type."

"Tall, thin . . . pretty. They're all beautiful girls. Our killer's an aesthete," McCauley spoke with sarcasm. Then, "Have we developed anything?"

"Still no physical evidence," Sakura said. "His comfort zone appears to be citywide. And dumping them like he does gives us no connection to even a neighborhood, with the exception of the alley where Siebrig's body was found. But that was probably just a good location he stumbled upon."

"No witness to that dumping?"

"A three-block radius around that restaurant has been canvassed," Sakura said. "Best thing we could come up with is a man who sleeps above a store that backs on the alley. He's not sure, but he thinks he remembers seeing the reflection from headlights sometime that night."

McCauley grunted. His beefy face was blotched. "Nothing else?" He reached for the cigar that lay smoldering in its special crystal ashtray.

"We're working the profile," Sakura said.

"With Dr. French?"

McCauley's tone was oblique. The question was leading somewhere. "Dr. French is consulting on an unofficial basis," he answered.

"Are you aware of the interview she did last week with that Kahn woman?"

He kept his features even. McCauley had no reason yet to come at him directly, but it didn't mean the chief couldn't enjoy finding something to complain about. "Dr. French was blindsided," he said. "That interview was scheduled before the investigation began."

McCauley ignored the explanation. "I don't care how great an expert she is—you rein her in. The tabloids will crucify us, and the rest of the pack won't be far behind. No more fucking media unless we control it."

"I hope that doesn't mean a press conference."

"Not yet." McCauley blew out smoke. "But Public Relations is printing 'cover our ass' warnings to be posted in the clubs. And starting tomorrow, we're going to be running a tip number on all the local newscasts with pictures of those girls. Somebody may have seen this sick fuck with one of them."

"A good idea," Sakura conceded. "We're looking at rapists who've been released, especially any with a history of drugging their victims. Might be somebody has escalated the violence."

McCauley nodded. The cigar rolled till it caught in his teeth. "You got enough men detailed?"

"For now. I don't want things to get so big we miss something obvious."

"Fine. But we're calling it a task force."

"The task force will be working later this week with New Jersey." He worked to suppress any hint of irony. "We'll be searching the dump sites there."

"They still dumping in Jersey?"

"No," Sakura said, "but we don't know how far back these murders go. There could be more New York girls in those landfills."

McCauley's face showed what he thought of that. "Keep me informed, Sakura."

. . . and he gazes down from the magic mountain and winks at Selkie Girl. With the strobes making rainbows on her arms. The music shooting up her brain. Dance, dance, dance. The Vibe *at high tide. Sweat running down her back, between her legs. Like a silky worm. No time but now. And the Shaman winks at Selkie Girl.*

"Who is the Shaman?" Talbot looked up from the diary of Sarah Laraby, one of the two girls they'd found in the Pennsylvania landfill.

"I think he's a deejay." Candace Bennet's face was worn out from crying. "I know it's been a while, but I didn't want to believe it would turn out like this. Sarah going from being missing to dead." She glanced from one detective to the other. "You talked to Sarah's parents?"

"Yesterday." Rozelli took the journal from his partner's hand and read the last entry. "Is that his real name?"

"Whose name?" Candace was somewhere else.

"The deejay."

She shook her head. "Rave deejays are like high priests or something. They control the *Vibe.*"

" 'Vibe'?"

The roommate smiled for the first time and suddenly she was pretty. "It's the feeling ravers get. It's kind of a group thing. The music is like a drug."

"Did Sarah use drugs?"

"Some ravers use drugs. Mostly Ecstasy. But I don't think Sarah did. She said she only needed the music to get high."

"So what about this Shaman guy?" Rozelli asked.

"I don't know anything else about him. Never saw him."

"You didn't go out with Sarah?" Talbot took out his notebook.

"Once or twice. But I wasn't into the rave scene."

"And she was?" Rozelli was looking over at a photograph.

"It was her new religion. . . . That's a picture of us taken a few months back."

Talbot glanced at the photo, thinking what terrible things death did to a body. "Tell us about Sarah, Candace."

"She was a different person when she went to rave clubs." She walked over and took the picture from the chest. "Sarah was so pretty. Tall and thin. She could eat whatever she wanted and never gain a pound. And the blond hair was natural. She could have been a model." She set the photo back down. "But once she started going to raves . . ."

"What happened, Candace?" Talbot pressed the narrative forward.

"You know she used a different name when she went to those kind of clubs. Called herself Selkie Girl."

"We read that in the diary," said Talbot.

"I don't know where she got this stuff. I just found that diary. She had it hidden." She shook her head; her limp hair needed washing. "Like I told the cops before, Sarah and Selkie were two different people."

"How was she different?"

"Sarah had this incredible skin. Hardly wore any makeup. But when she went out . . ."

"What did she look like?"

"See-through blouses with black bras. Short skirts. Eyeliner to here. Red lipstick. Face powdered white. Kinda creepy, but still pretty. She even had a thing about her panties." She pulled open a drawer. "Ordinarily she wore cotton hi-cuts. But when she raved, she wore stuff like this." She pulled out a dark green thong, waved it in the air before throwing it back inside the chest.

"Who did she go out with?" Rozelli asked.

"Some people she'd gotten tight with. Met them at a club. They're the ones who introduced her to the rave scene."

"Know their names?"

"Lisa somebody. Craig. Tony."

"No last names?"

She shook her head.

"Know where we might locate them?"

"I think Lisa's number is in the diary."

Rozelli paged through the book. "Did Sarah have a boyfriend?" He looked up.

"No . . . Though she could have. A ton of guys wanted to take Sarah out."

"She didn't date?"

"Rarely."

"Did she ever talk about anyone special?" asked Talbot. "Someone from work or someone she'd met when she went out?"

"Raving isn't about sex. I mean people do hook up, but it's more about being together as a group." She shrugged. "No, she never mentioned anyone."

"You know, Candace, we might have to go through Sarah's things again." Talbot flipped a page in his notepad.

She nodded. "I'm moving out this weekend. I can't stay here now." She stopped. Fought back tears.

Talbot waited for a moment, then asked, "Do you have any idea where we might find this deejay?"

The question revived her. "You don't think . . . ?"

"We have to check everybody out, Candace," Rozelli assured her.

"You'll find him where Sarah did. At a rave club."

"And just where might we find a rave, Candace?" asked Talbot.

This time she laughed. "You gonna have to look way cooler, Detective."

✤

Jamal struggled inside his New York Jets starter jacket as he dribbled, his body leaning in, cutting off his brother. Pivot. Drive. Up. And in. *Whoosh!* Two points.

"You walked, Jamal," Cyrus screamed. "You nothin' but a cheater."

He laughed. "Come on, li'l bro, you too slow." He was blowing on his fingers. The slap of the basketball stung his hands in the chilly late afternoon. He hated the cold. It went right to his bones. Turned his blood to ice. What was worse, he couldn't move in this bulky jacket. He unzipped the starter, tossing it onto the ground.

"Mama gonna beat yo' ass, Jamal, if she sees your jacket in the dirt."

"It ain't in the dirt, Cy, it's on the concrete. And stop stalling." He angled in the ball toward his younger brother, then like lightning cut across Cyrus's lane, stealing the basketball. Dribbling for the make-shift goal, he caught a glimpse of his raggedy-assed sneakers. What he wouldn't give for a new pair of shoes. Shit, no use even thinking about it till he did something about his grades. School barely started, and he was already trying to dig himself out of a hole.

"Two!" he yelled as the ball sailed through a gray web of old net.

"Jamal . . ." It was his baby sister LaShondra, standing on the front porch, holding open the storm door, letting out Buster. In a split second, the dog burst down the steps, into the street, barking his way to freedom.

"Shit, Shondra, look what you done," he screamed in a run after the dog, Cyrus on his heels.

Buster didn't travel far, but stopped just six houses down the street, giving his full attention to the rear of an abandoned car near the end of the block.

"What that dumb dog up to anyway?" He cursed, slowing down as he got closer to Buster. "He act like he ain't never seen that pile of shit before."

"Whoa, somethin' stank, Jamal. Real bad." Cyrus had come up right behind him.

"Yeah . . ." He approached the car cautiously, noticing for the first time that the trunk was half-open. "Shut up, Buster!"

For an instant, the dog seemed distracted by his voice, but just as quickly the open trunk had his complete concentration again. His muzzle rooting like a pig's, his jaws working on something trapped inside.

He bent over, grabbing Buster's collar, pulling at the dog. "Hey, boy, what's the matter wif you?"

"He actin' all crazy, Jamal." Cyrus scrunched like a hermit crab in his brother's shadow.

"Busta . . ." Now the dog's head turned full around, just in time for Jamal to see the hand slide out of the trunk.

⚅

The car hummed along the thruway past Long Island Sound. Jimmy's fingers tapped at the steering wheel as the electric guitar wailed like a frightened cat from the radio. Hanae shook her head. She would never understand her husband's taste in music, but tonight the sound of hard rock was sweet, another small reminder that she was home.

It had been a good evening, she and Jimmy driving alone to their favorite seaside restaurant. Despite the cold that had blown from the Sound, they had rolled down the car windows so she could smell the ocean. And later, inside the restaurant, she had pressed her hand against the great sheet of glass, sensing the roll of the watery expanse that lay just beyond their cozy table.

Somehow it had seemed easier away from the apartment to fall into old ways. Jimmy had made her laugh with reports of his struggles to remaster aikido. She had begun to tell him all the funny stories about the months with her family in Japan. And it was suddenly no longer awkward to talk with her husband about the things that had happened in her time away from him. It was a moment of illumination, the months away from him receding to things past, even as she spoke of them, like a garment once binding that had slipped from her shoulders.

One short step toward healing. Another had been Jimmy's sharing the news of his father's illness and his own shame in allowing their estrangement to blind him to what should have been obvious at the time of Isao's visit. It had touched her deeply that her husband could talk with her of such things.

"Why are you smiling?" He had turned down the volume on the song.

"Perhaps I find pleasure in the music."

He laughed, and the cell phone rang. He cut the radio and answered. "Sakura," his official voice.

It was moments before he spoke again. "I've got it," he said to the person at the other end of the phone. "I'll be there as soon as I can."

"Is it . . . ?"

"Another body," he answered her. "I'll get you home."

"You must go to your crime scene."

"My unit's on the way. Michael will take care of it till I get there."

"Kenjin is many things, but he is not you, my husband. This is your case. You must be there to take charge."

She knew that he was smiling. Perhaps a little puzzled. She was a little puzzled too. She was thinking as fast as she could, not sure at all yet what it was she planned to do.

"What are you saying, Hanae?" he was asking.

"I can wait in the car. You can have someone drive me home. You are always saying there are too many people at the crime scene."

She was expecting him to argue, but he laughed again instead. She was not sure she had won till she heard him slap the flasher to the roof, and they were wailing down the thruway together.

✻

"Keep the doors locked." Jimmy was putting the keys in her hand. "I'll be back as soon as I can with an officer to drive you home." He leaned across the seat and kissed her cheek. Hanae heard the locks slide into place, the flat solid *whack* as he shut the driver door. It was the rare moment when her blindness frustrated her. She had managed to place herself at Jimmy's crime scene, but was not to leave the car. Not much that was good in that.

She rolled down the window. City sounds. Traffic from the cross street. The added buzz of police activity. An occasional shout or curse in the crude language of the ghetto—people from the neighborhood gathered like crows at the smell of death.

She rolled up the window and unlocked the door. Got out of the passenger seat and stood on the sidewalk with her long cane, her wrist twitch-tapping the hard tip at the uneven surface of the pavement. She closed the door behind her and began to move, the stick alive and searching, guiding her toward the uneasy beast—the pulse and energy of the crowd.

There was fear and agitation in the murmuring and shouts, but a warmth and connectivity. A smell. A color. She let the energy draw her, tapping into a seam, slipping like a ghost into the current of bodies. Her free hand outstretched, touching so briefly on a back or a shoulder. She could read the compass of the crowd's attention in the lift of muscles, the shuffling of restless feet. Could hear the story in snatches of conversation. *Jamal's old dog . . . boy tol' his mama . . . white girl in that trunk.*

The crowd thickened, bodies shifting away at her tapping. She could sense the faces as they turned toward her. Blind apparition. Voices rose, and died, in her wake.

Emptiness loomed. The fluttering of crime scene tape brushed her outstretched fingers. The crowd closed in, jostling at her back.

She concentrated on sound, on the knot of activity in the open space before her—the police around the car, Jimmy among them. She tried not to imagine that at any moment he would turn and see her. She breathed, focusing on what she knew was before her, the latest of the killer's victims. Yards away. The closest she might get.

It was less an impression than a wave of emotion. A blossoming of the dark and hopeless. Confusion. Dread. A boundless sadness. And outside it, as elusive as an unknown flavor, a sensation of *otherness* that she could not will to know. Then a moment when she lost herself. A rough closing like a premature healing.

A wound. A blackness sealing itself.

⁂

Just before midnight. The bedroom was dark. The mirror, like a narrow door-sized window, had collected the light. He sat in front of it nude, cross-legged on the floor, his penis sprouting obscenely from his lap. Behind him in the cabinet the television played mutely, a magic box that floated in the glass.

He wanted silence in the room. Wanted to hear his excitement, the way his breathing changed when the power approached. He studied his image and was pleased. His trophies glinted, cool and electric against his naked skin. He touched the metal to feel the energy. The rings and trinkets that would be hidden by his clothing, all on his left side.

This deliberate placement was both a joke and an appeasement. Left-brain disapproved of his souvenirs. In the mirror, left was right. All was reversed. And more. The death that flickered in the light on his face came from the ghost set in the mirror. It was his shadow self who watched the real TV across the room, who reflected its light in his phantom eyes. That same light reflected to him from the surface of the glass.

The thought of it was mesmerizing, like the sterile game of an infinite regress. But that was a left thought. What Right-brain saw was the stubborn persistence of energy.

The surgical needle lay on the plate by his knee, its cutting edge like a tease. He pretended to ignore it, stroked his penis to full erection while the video looped in the glass. Five little souls to be tasted and retasted. Five, since Left-brain had thought to record their final moments. Horning in, dividing the power.

He could hear his breath, could feel it deepening. He left his erection, picking up the needle, drawing it tight across his nipple. Drawing bright blood. Courting the pain that drew the power. A drop of seminal fluid bloomed from the head of his penis. He mixed it with the blood. Consumed it. Watching, watching the videotape in the mirror, the pale slack face that filled the frame. The kohl-lined eyes coming open in confusion beneath the plastic membrane. The smearing of red from the mouth.

Her hands rose to her face, intruding momentarily into the frame. But weakly. No real fight left. A surrender to the fish death. Mouth moving, lip-painting more smears.

He grasped the needle. Made one sure jab. No anesthetic. He wanted the pain. The agony of the current from nipple to groin. Making the holes for the power to go in, the stored power in the taped transformation. Life to death.

In the last escape of videotaped breath, he heard his scream, heard the power roaring with its dark devouring mouth from the window inside the glass. He felt the explosion from his body. Emptying, emptying, till he was nothing but a black hole to suck the universe in.

CHAPTER

8

I *wish I had a girl as white as snow, with cheeks as red as blood, and hair*
as black as ravens." Linsky whispered the words, but Sakura heard
them, glancing over at the medical examiner standing next to him.

"Snow White," the doctor said, half-smiling, turning his attention
again to where the girl's mutilated body lay inside an air-tight plastic
tent.

Sakura followed the ME's eyes. Howard Keyes had been tapped again
to do the fuming, in an effort to develop and recover possible latent fingerprints, before the body underwent the rigors of autopsy.

Linsky's reference to Snow White was unexpected, and Sakura
thought the serial's latest victim, even with her pale skin and black hair,
seemed nothing like the prettified Disney version he'd seen in the classic film. There was nothing homogenized about what lay on the gurney
table, nothing charmed about being sliced open and stapled closed, no
magic in being readied for a shroud of cyanoacrylate.

"Ever read fairy tales, Sakura?"

He retreated from his dark thoughts, turned back toward Linsky.

"It doesn't matter if you read the Japanese versions," the doctor went
on, "or the German or French for that matter. The lessons are universal."

He nodded, allowing the usually taciturn ME to ramble on, refocusing on the impending procedure. Keyes was inside the tent adjusting
one of the locations of several coffee cup warmers used for heat acceler-
ation. Small dish-shaped sculpts of aluminum foil had been placed over
each warmer, and nickel-sized dollops of superglue had been dropped

inside the foil containers. Mugs of hot water had been brought in to increase humidity. A battery-operated fan sat on a cardboard box to help with fume distribution.

"I took her out of the locker earlier to allow for condensation." Linsky was making the point to emphasize how premature moisture could destroy impressions that might otherwise be developed. Then, "Ultimately, it's about reaching sexual maturation."

"Sexual maturation?" The ME was in a rare mood indeed. The switch in topic had caught Sakura off-guard.

"The oedipal desires between father and daughter, arousing jealousy in the stepmother, forces Snow White out into the world, onto a path of self-discovery and sexual maturation."

This time he pushed himself to fix the implications of Linsky's lecture onto the body in the tent. He supposed Solange Mansour—a positive ID had been made only hours ago by the parents—could be said to resemble some modern-day Snow White, with death elevating her flesh to an almost translucent pallor. The hair was certainly black, though he suspected she had enhanced the color. And now she lay inside the plastic tent. *A glass coffin.*

The sixteen-year-old had surely been making her way in the world, and even from the most cursory examination of her lifestyle, it was clear she was on a path of self-discovery and sexual exploration. Sakura understood the significance of the story of the little girl rescued by dwarfs, even without Linsky's homily, enough to appreciate the truths the tale taught. In every undertaking lay the danger that unrestrained passion could become a young woman's undoing.

But in this reality that was too close to faulting the victim for her own death. Even those who lived on the narrowest margin were not responsible for the evil perpetrated upon them. The crime resided solely in the heart and hands of the beast.

Keyes had just finished dusting the body with black magnetic powder as he turned up the heat. "It'll take about ten minutes," the forensic tech said, exiting the tent.

Sakura observed as a fog of cyanoacrylate filled the enclosure. Ironically, the body, once so white and stainless, was now reduced to a darkened heap on the gurney.

Keyes loaded his camera. If there were latents, photographs would be taken first, before transfers were made. The tech snapped on his third pair of fresh latex gloves of the day, put on a surgical mask.

"Almost there," Keyes said, glancing at the clock.

It didn't take long once Keyes got back inside the tent. He bent over the body like a man in search of a lost contact lens. He examined the tops of the feet, the calves, the flats of the thighs. The legs were spread open from the hips, and he bent to study the surfaces of the inner thighs. He stood, checking the mound of pubis, and up toward the abdomen. He stopped. A moment in limbo. But he went on checking every square inch of skin. In the end, he left shaking his head.

Pretty damn hot, Zoe was thinking. She liked watching herself on tape. Allen, her producer, was a great guy, but she preferred putting together her own stuff. And she was taking no chances with this edit.

Are you afraid? Her recorded voice had to shout over the sound system blaring in the club, asking the question of a halter-clad girl, who'd agreed to an interview at the fringes of the crowd, though still moving with the beat of the music.

Yeah, sure. The girl was nodding, her bouncing curls backgrounded in a grid of laser light and thronging dancers. *But, I mean, what are the chances really? There's lots of us, and only one of him.*

She seemed not too bright, but she had a point. And silicone tits that shifted like softballs beneath the scanty fabric of her top. *Implants,* Zoe decided, with conscious superiority. Still, she approved of self-enhancement. And a little T&A never hurt the ratings.

She cut the player, leaning back for a moment in the padded studio chair. *Tracking the Visqueen Killer,* time-slotted for Saturday night, was going to be as good as she could make it. Thanks to her former job at the *Post,* she was used to flying by the seat of her pants, and her exclusives for the paper in last year's Death Angel case had been her key to the big time. She'd jumped from the cop beat to cable and never looked back. Her weekday show, covering hot police and court cases from all over the country, was a formula that seemed to be working, with ratings that were more than respectable for a mid-afternoon slot. This weekend prime-time special was a reward for her hard work and tougher attitude. And not too shabby for a little girl from Queens.

For no reason she thought of Rozelli, the way he'd looked at her the other night in the bar. What had she hoped for, tracking him down like that in public? Protection, in front of his buddies? Certainly, she'd known there was no way he was ever going to feed her information again. So why had she done it?

Because she wanted to see him. Simple as that. Because in all these months, there'd been no one who did it for her like Johnny. She'd said it before, and she'd say it again: Johnny Rozelli might not be the handsomest guy she'd ever been with, or even the best lover, but they just had so much fun fucking.

She missed him. And she knew he missed her too, despite the way he'd finally blown her off in the bar. Just getting up and walking out, leaving her sitting at the table with her drink. Well, she hadn't cried into it, if that's what he'd wanted. And she wasn't crying now.

Her patience had paid off. She'd gotten her exclusive by dogging an attendant at the mortuary where Leslie Siebrig's body had been sent. She had the revelation she needed in the world of cable, where every scrap of new information could be ballyhooed through a cycle, till you found another scrap. The big boys had gotten the point that Zoe Kahn could be trusted to deliver.

Take that, Johnny Rozelli!

⁂

Margot Redmond wrote in the date of the Leightons' anniversary party in her engagement book. An afternoon appointment for the twins to have their teeth checked. A change in time for Pilates class next Monday. She'd also promised the boys she would let them pick out a pumpkin. That would mean a drive out to the country before Halloween. She would also have to begin thinking about costumes.

"Hello." She picked up the ringing phone on her desk.

"David St. Cyr. I hope this isn't a bad time."

"No, I'm just getting my calendar up to speed."

"Good. Then maybe you can pencil me in. I have some preliminary drawings I want to show you."

"Great. Did you have a chance to drive up to see the property?"

"I did. It's a beautiful piece of real estate."

"I'm glad you approve. Let's see. . . . Actually, tonight would be good. Reese is coming home early. Would that be all right? Around eight?"

"Perfect. I'm really looking forward to seeing you again and meeting Reese."

"Wonderful. Tonight then. You have our address?"

"Yes, in Gramercy Park."

"Right. Cocktails at eight."

She replaced the phone. Well, that was a perfectly normal conversation. Maybe she had just been overreacting to St. Cyr; it wouldn't be the first time. Anyway, she was glad that tonight had worked out and Reese was going to be with them. Besides, David St. Cyr had been her husband's idea; she would have preferred an architect with a more traditional style. Hopefully she would like what he had worked up for them. She didn't have to love it, but it had to be something she could live with. After all, the Connecticut home was probably going to be for a lifetime.

For a lifetime. Nothing was for a lifetime. Michael Darius had taught her that lesson. She thought of his most recent visit, and hated the way she allowed him to get to her. Though she maintained her surface cool, he invariably made her feel dissatisfied, as if she were missing some vital piece of information, leaving her with a kind of hollowness in the pit of her stomach. Though she suspected the emptiness lay somewhere deeper. In her soul. Michael had always been able to keep her hungry.

An image came to her. She was standing outside his room in the hospital, in a corridor of drab green. A river of polished linoleum spread out from either side of her, rippling reflections of the overhead light. She had reached for the door, pushing it gently, only a crack, not sure at all yet if she should visit.

Michael lay in the bed. Pale as the sheets. His eyes open, staring ahead at nothing. A dark-haired woman was sitting next to his bed, her hand holding his, her eyes full of concern and something much stronger. She had not gone in. She had called the nurses' station periodically for updates on Michael's condition. But she had never called him directly. An act of pure cowardice for which she was now ashamed.

Jason's laugh caused her to look up. Fate had been doubly cruel. Not with one image of Michael, but with two, did she have to contend. Except for the bright red hair, the twins were perfect mirrors of her former husband, little faces who unknowingly judged her for some crucial lack in herself.

⁂

The day was growing late. Sakura felt suspended between the seasons. Summer, like a beast, holding the heat between its teeth. And the hard white sun seeming to steal shadows from underfoot, so that all that remained was but a still and sterile flatness. Autumn came in feisty gusts, but without much will to linger and battle the beast. So that he was left with a longing for the end of it all, and the cold pure snow of winter.

He looked up at the five photographs tacked to the chalkboard by his desk. There was at least some order now, some chronological sense. Grady. Phelps. Laraby. Siebrig. Mansour. And there existed a kind of sick order, inherent in all investigations that involved serial killers. *Target. Control. Kill.* This particular killer, like so many of his species, had embroidered upon the pattern, tailoring the action to fit the specialized demands of his fantasy. Writing upon each death his unique signature.

He drew the picture in his mind. A predator, not unattractive, was cruising the clubs and underground parties, zeroing in on young women who fit some preconceived archetype, some configuration of feature or behavior that predestined them to become objects in his lethal drama. Rohypnol was his magic potion, used to tighten the net, allowing him to hustle a seemingly inebriated date to a secure base of operations. This required transportation, and that he live alone, or at least function in a situation that precluded interruption or discovery.

And then the central act of the drama.

There was no way to know exactly what this madman did with each victim, but there were some probables. A few certainties. There was likely penile penetration, but no semen. Cause of death was asphyxiation. No signs of struggle, no defensive trauma—one strong indication that death occurred before the Rohypnol wore off, given the absence of other sedative drugs in the serology screens.

The women were found nude, wrapped in Visqueen, and dumped as so much garbage. And as centerpiece of the fantasy—the macabre drama that in serial murder took the place of motive—the opening of the chest in a mimicry of autopsy, the strange inversion of organs.

The basics of the profile were in place. But what was the meaning behind this specific mutilation? What were they missing that they could not make the leap from general to particular?

Darius came in without invitation and took a seat in front of the desk, his attention drawn to the chalkboard gallery of victim faces. Sakura watched his ex-partner's gaze shift to take in the boxes on the floor, the stacks of reports that were piling up on his desk. He knew what Michael was thinking. That in any serial case the likelihood was that the killer would be someone they had interviewed early on. That the trick was to find that single piece of data in the flood of material that narrowed the field to one.

"He's not here." Darius indicated the pile of investigative records. "He's not here," he repeated, the words coming out as a certainty.

✺

The clock above the refrigerator showed it was well after eleven as Margot walked into the kitchen with the tray of empty glasses. She had picked them up immediately, letting Reese see David St. Cyr out. She was completely startled to find the time so late.

"I don't think he's queer," Reese said to her as she came back and sat on the sofa. "It's just the Southern accent."

"Is that what it is . . . Southern?"

"Not good-ol'-boy Southern," Reese said. "Well-bred Southern. And I don't think he's even particularly weird. Not for an artist, anyway."

"No . . . I know. I told you today that he sounded fine on the phone. And the renderings for the house are beautiful."

"You like them, then? Tell the truth."

"Yes, I do," she said. "And with all the changes we talked about . . . and the separate rooms for the boys. I'm sure it will be perfect."

He leaned across the sofa to pull her closer. "You talk to Michael?" he asked her after a while.

"I tried, Reese." She pulled back to look at his face. "I got the predictable reaction. I'm sorry. . . . "

"About what? That your ex-husband can be an ass?" He smiled. "Look what you got for your second."

"I am looking." She kissed him.

"I want to adopt the boys"—he was glancing at the framed picture of Damon and Jason that stood on the coffee table—"but if Michael says no . . . well, it's just a piece of paper. As far as I'm concerned the twins are mine."

Tears burned the back of her eyes. Legalities were important to her husband. "They are yours, Reese," she said, "in every way that counts." *As I am.* She hoped it was there in her voice.

"So you're saying the house is a go." He was watching her, gently changing back the subject. "We'll keep on working to get the plans perfect. But you're satisfied with St. Cyr?"

Satisfied was not exactly the adjective she would have chosen. But Reese worked hard and deserved the house he wanted. And she hadn't lied. She liked the renderings all right. Big, but not too big. Clean-lined and functional, like living in a machine. But she'd give it her own touches. She'd make it her own.

"The house is a go." She smiled.

✤

The pygmies wanted changes. But the pygmies always did, imposing their small minds on genius. Dragging the vision down to their level rather than allowing the design to mold and uplift the dreary routine of their lives. Compromise was the price to be paid to see the vision realized. But always a crippled vision.

David St. Cyr had been walking in the chilly air, working off the energy of his anger. But he stepped off the curb now and hailed a cab, giving the driver an address on West Fourteenth. The neighborhood bar was precisely where he wanted to be at this moment. The whole area appealed to his sense of irony. A charnel house, where a committed vegetarian like Stella McCartney had opened an exclusive boutique, with reeking carcasses hanging in the street next to flower shops. A perfect metaphor for the city.

This mad juxtaposition of opposites was precisely what the Redmonds sought to escape by fleeing to Connecticut. He pictured Reese with his banker's face. And Margot. What had been on her face tonight? She still didn't know what to make of him. It was interesting that the seemingly conservative husband was the one who better appreciated his designs.

"I'll get out here." He leaned forward as the driver stopped for a light. It wasn't far and he wanted to walk again. He paid and stepped out of the cab.

Thrusting his hand into the pocket of his coat, he stroked the sharp angles of the small crystal-framed photograph he had taken from a shelf in the Redmonds' apartment. How long before Margot missed it?

✻

James Sakura sat soaking in a hot water-filled tub, the odor of his favorite soap blending with the steam. He leaned forward, elbows on knees, while Hanae, sitting on the stool behind him, worked with her fingers to soothe the knotted muscles in his shoulders and his back. The ritual familiar. Yet not the same.

It was quiet in the bathroom. Few words had been spoken since he'd come home. Indeed there had been no real conversation between them since last night when he'd told her to keep the doors locked in the car. Hanae had been sleeping when he'd returned in the wee hours, and sleeping still a few hours later when he'd left for the autopsy that had been scheduled for early morning. There had been only the brief afternoon call to let her know that he would be late, and not to worry about supper. Another familiar ritual. Too much the same.

"You are angry with me, Husband?" A question as she reached for more soap.

"No," he said, but the quickness of the denial was a demonstration of its falseness even to his own ears. "Yes," he said, reversing the unintended lie. "And I am sorry, because I do not wish to be angry. But it is so."

"Is it what I have done that angers you? Or what I have not?"

A sigh escaped him. His wife, for all her gentleness, was not without guile. She had sought to link his concern over her actions of last night with the continued lack of intimacy in their bed. If she meant to gain an advantage, she had chosen her tactic well, for surely his frustration was a part of his anger. He felt guilt in pressuring her sexually, and fear that he would push her even farther away.

Her fingers had resumed working their way down his back. He steadied his breathing, letting her hands do their soothing work. If her question had stirred his emotions, it was not done callously, to hurt. He knew her point was a true one. These things that he felt were all of a piece. And all of it had to be faced.

Her hand dipped into the water beside him. He clasped her wrist and lifted her hand to his lips. "I want my wife." The breath of his words whispered against the tips of her fingers, so she might feel their color, read their texture like braille. His mouth slipped to the cup of her palm. "I want my wife to be safe." He placed the words for keeping. "These are not two things, but one." He felt her straighten, and turned to watch her face.

"I am not a child," he went on speaking, "to demand in an instant a thing that must have time, or to demand a thing that is impossible. And no one is safe in this world. But Wife, there is foolishness and there is wisdom."

"And I have been foolish?"

"It was not safe to get out of the car."

"The question remains, was it wise?"

Subtlety. A thing could sometimes be both. He was not insensitive to what path she sought for herself. She had her gifts. She was, in her own way, as intuitive as Michael.

"You are my husband." She had spoken in his silence. "You are a detective. Is that two things, or one?"

"What do you want of me?" He had not meant the words to be harsh.

She stood to go, her tears making an end of it. "To see that there is no wall."

※

In the beginning was the *Kingdom of One*. The world made two. Water world. Air world. *Cope or die.*

Specialization, the answer. A division of tasks. Unconscious at first, then conscious. *Learn, or die.*

It was Left-brain who'd found Father's book. Right-brain devoured it. *Cannibalism in New Guinea.* A model of incorporation and survival. *Kill or die.*

The *feeding* had started with small things. A June bug, a lizard. Buzzing energy, cold blood pink-beating. Then up the chain to the small mammals. Stray cats. And the dogs that were always appearing, dropped off at the edge of nowhere, on the border of real civilization, according to Mother. Their world, the only world in the big house, with the books and the music, and the contradiction of together and apart.

It was an eternity of small red hearts before the little black girl—a stray herself, wandering over the line from the shotgun shacks in the hollow, attracted by the fire and the novelty of little white-boy naked-ness. The fires, another form of energy from death. Dead branches and twigs gathered like offerings with anything else in the woods that would burn. Stripped to the skin, sitting too close, letting the life in the flames sink with the heat inside to penetrate to the heart.

He remembered the night, the excitement at catching sight of her, little brown thing in a big brown night full of jasmine smell and mosqui-toes. Catching the reflection of flame in her huge black eyes as she sat with the dark in the ring of trees. Listening to the hot sizzle and pop, the snap and crack of twigs like breaking bones. Smoke rising with the whiff of sacrifice.

He could be patient for an eight-year-old. Physical limitation had its lessons. It was a simple strategy to let the fire draw her out. She came to sit, not far. Hunkered in her dirty rag of a dress, she was not much larger than one of the dogs.

He remembered his excitement, his absolute knowledge that every other creature had been practice. The cats and the dogs subdued with the poison meant for vermin. There was no poison now. Left-brain coun-seled caution. Right-brain moved. Had her. Heart-pump racing, feeding on its own risk. He held her down, sitting astride her tiny body, in truth no bigger than the dogs. His arms kept rigid, flat boy's hands blocking her nose and mouth, shutting in her cries and the wasted breath. Her resistance making him stronger. Skinny legs kicking muted thuds in the scrub and the grass. Arms like sticks beating at his shoulders. Then her hands like baby crabs scrabbling uselessly at his chest, scant millimeters above his feasting heart.

It was Left-brain who produced the knife and performed the cool dissection, planted the meat in earth. Not the last to lie there. No going back.

Though the opportunities were few enough—Left-brain would not allow the coincidence of another Negro child "going missing," only the occasional runaway or vagrant seeking shelter on what should have been recognized as posted land. So many lean years between, the spaces filled with far less satisfying feeds. And the knowledge of *something* growing in Mother's eyes, fueling her every vain attempt to storm the Kingdom.

It was the *something* that resulted in being sent off to the Catholic boys' school on the Coast, the theory being that the good brothers could beat out of you anything that was bad. But of course, he'd rather liked the beatings. So that blew Mother's theory to hell.

He laughed. The last laugh. He'd been having it for years.

CHAPTER

9

Friday morning, early. In the dojo. Sakura placed down his *fukuroshi-nai* and, closing his eyes, began a series of deep-breathing exercises. He understood that the basis of Kashima aikido was the concept of *shinbu*, the divine way in which one wins without fighting. To become one with your partner, embracing the negative forces aimed toward you, projecting positive forces outward toward he who attacked. The result was balance.

He opened his eyes, slowly moving into a series of bare-handed positions. Moving "with sword without sword." Using his mind, his consciousness to tap into his *ki*, extending his will beyond the flat of his palms, to the tips of his fingers.

Cutting, cutting, cutting. Invisible sword strokes into the air. Arms fluid, spiraling into the dance that forged himself with his intention. That the practice of his aikido was his way to inner peace and spiritual awareness, that it placed his feet upon a path to order and discipline, was not a lie he told himself. But it was only the half-truth. That his practice was also his way to overcome his frustration in failing with his wife was the other half.

Cutting, cutting, cutting. His arm swung to break the wall, the wall that she had said he had created. In reality he saw no barrier of his own making. And that was surely his greatest fault, his powerlessness to see himself clearly. In answer to his question of what she wanted of him, there had been only her words of "the wall." And her tears.

The tears tore at his heart, yet wore at his resolve to be patient. He hated himself for his selfishness, but there was no help for it. He wanted his wife.

He was once again the ten-year-old boy who had just discovered his own sexuality. At turns anxious and ashamed, he had also been filled with a dark wonder about his rapidly changing body, a body that felt both intimate and alien, bringing unnameable and uncontrollable pleasures.

He was at Hiro's home, poring over forbidden magazines that his friend had taken from his older brother's room. He remembered feigning excitement as he sat on the floor next to Hiro. He didn't want to seem ungrateful for this proffered bounty, and more he didn't want to seem any less than Hiro himself, whose breathing had grown more ragged with each page turned, and whose groin bristled against the confines of his khaki uniform pants.

But the bodies in the pictures seemed artificial and abstracted. Though at ten he was unable to articulate these sentiments, was unable to say exactly why he didn't find them arousing. Yet he did know the photographs were not the same as the dreams that woke him in the night, leaving him wet and sticky between his sheets. If he could have found the words, he would have said the women in the grainy black-and-white magazine photos seemed more like corpses, their contorted positions the result of some terrible crime. Instead he lied to keep face when he told Hiro, still flush with an erection, that he liked the pictures. It wasn't until he was leaving that his own erection came.

Hiro's sister, older by four years, had been coming into the house from the library as he was leaving, and he had accidentally bumped into her, his upper arm brushing against the firm bowl of one of her breasts. Their eyes had met for a moment, but as quickly his eyes fell with the rest of him to the floor to retrieve her fallen books. He willed himself not to look at her slim white ankles, the exquisite curve where ankle gave way to calf. He wanted to dig a hole through the tatami mat upon which he knelt. To hide himself from her watching eyes, to bury the shame of his blooming erection. But his wishes came to nothing; his body betrayed him as his hands scrambled for the scattered texts. Incredibly, he knew she recognized his embarrassment, but acted as if nothing had passed beyond the dropping of books. She smiled, thanking him by name, as he handed her the texts. It was a mystery she even knew his name, but "Akira" came rolling over her tongue and out her mouth, like a flower breaking through snow in early spring.

Flower. Hanae. Cherry blossom. He sliced the air a final time. With a resolve that he would do better with his wife. And with an awareness that he had an erection that soap and a shower would do little to ease.

✸

"Catch a load of those tits!" Rozelli had come up behind his partner at the computer, was peering down at the picture on the screen. "There's hope for you yet, Talbot," he said, "stealing a little computer time to sneak a peek at the babes." He grabbed a nearby chair and rolled it over to plop himself down.

"Research, Rozelli," Talbot explained. "And you're *trainspotting.*" He moved the cursor to an icon on the screen, replacing the image of the tank-topped girl with another shot, this one a blur of patterned light, a dancer with whirling glowsticks.

"I'm what?"

"Trainspotting . . . looking over my shoulder. It's what the kids say when they try to make out what record a deejay is spinning."

"So I guess you're an expert on raves now?"

"Pretty much." Talbot had swiveled toward him, was leaning back in the chair. "They call them parties," he said, "at least the underground stuff." Then, "What do you want to know?"

"Do all the babes look as good as that first chick?"

"That's strictly on a need-to-know." Talbot was grinning. "Next question."

"Okay, smart boy. Where do we find this deejay, this Shaman guy in Sarah Laraby's diary?"

"No luck on your end, huh?"

"Hell, no." Rozelli was frowning. "A couple guys at Anti-crime had heard of him. No standard gig. Spins at a lot of the local clubs. But no clue to his real name." He eyed the computer screen, where a gallery of images was unfolding—a group of scantily clad dancers, a trio of girls decked out with backpacks and strings of plastic jewelry, another girl with long blond braids sucking on a Day-Glo pacifier. He looked at Walt. "You think you could download us a list of the clubs that play this stuff, and—"

"*Download?*" Talbot mimicked amazement. "And here I thought you were still stuck on the Mario Brothers."

"Don't shit with me, Walt." Rozelli, in spite of himself, was grinning too. "We got to find this Shaman guy, and I figure now we got to go club to club."

"That what you figure?" Talbot sat up straight, letting the chair pop against his back. He swiveled to the screen, moved the cursor to the bottom, and maximized a file.

The screen bloomed black. A symbol in the middle. New Age. Southwestern. The trickster god Kokopelli with his flute. ENTER in small block letters beneath. Talbot clicked with the cursor and music played. A small box of streaming video had replaced Kokopelli. Lights flashing. A sea of writhing dancers. The camera pivoting on the shot, taking in the man on the platform above the seething mob. The angle shot over his shoulder, still on the dancing crowd. The camera panning, turning. A close-up on him now. The image of his head in the foreground, looming. The camera moving. Zooming. His face filling the box.

Blackout. The whole screen a uniform darkness. Then blazing from nothing the name. S-H-A-M-A-N in glowing letters. And the music still playing. Eerie. Electronic.

"Acid house," Talbot said.

"What?"

"Techno is divided into a whole bunch of genres," Talbot was explaining. "House. Jungle. Hardcore. Maybe twenty more. That particular track is Acid House. The Acid stuff is kind of the Shaman's specialty. Though he plays a good mix."

"Jesus H. Christ," Rozelli said. "You his press agent?"

"No, but I have been studying his website." Talbot clicked on a small icon and the page changed. A picture of Shaman. At the side of the graphic, the words: HOME—BIO—GIGS—MEDIA.

"I don't think he does any underground, what the kids would consider the real stuff," Talbot said. "But take a look at this." He clicked on

GIGS. A grid appeared listing the Shaman's club dates. Talbot's finger stabbed at one of the boxes.

"Shit," Rozelli said. "I had something going for tonight."

"Cancel, my man," said Talbot, "and get back with Anti-crime. We're going to need some way cool threads."

In *zazen* Hanae sat, eyes closed, spine straight, her legs crossed, with fingers in small circles. Empty mind. She sought empty mind. A blankness upon which to set her foot, severing time, allowing the skin of space to split around her. Not one thought did she want, beyond *this* thought of no-thought. Not one breath, beyond *this* breath she now took. And just *this* beat of blood inside her. Not the next, or the next. *Stilled* must be the very pores of her flesh, the single hairs upon her head, the impatient flutter behind the lids of her eyes. Emptiness. Nothingness. Into the All. Into the embrace of the One. Into a single wave of pure consciousness must she let herself go, riding the small vessel of self that was not self. Be and not be.

She opened her eyes. She was weeping. Tears came without will. Flowed freely from eyes devoid of sensation. No feeling of moisture or warmth upon her skin. No bitterness of salt fell into the corners of her mouth. Yet the reservoir of pain from which the tears came was real and acute. They sprang from the same source as the tears she had shed the other night.

The tears washed away her hoped-for emptiness. Brought self back to self. No Buddha-mind filled her mind. Only *his* face. Jimmy's face. And his words. Gentle and harsh. Wise yet unknowing. *I want my wife. I want my wife to be safe. These are not two things, but one.* And her words. *To see that there is no wall.*

It was this wall that now stood against her solitude, blocked the light inside. The light that had become her surest guide to both the interior and outer worlds where she had lived since birth, sightless but not without vision. When had Jimmy lost faith in that vision? Or was it possible she had fooled herself into believing he had ever accepted what he had had on her word alone?

Was this some karma she must meet in this lifetime? A dance that must be danced? Some past debt due? Greater than her blindness did this separation from her husband test her. Their lives seemingly upon a single path, only to unwind now into two.

She closed her eyes and was back in Kyoto. The day was hot and no breeze stirred inside the small enclosure of the garden. Somewhere near she could hear a steady explosion of water, gushing through a ropy rubber hose. The hard spray, spitting against the pavement, washing away the crust of the city. Inside her mouth was the wet-dry taste of dust.

She was sure that this particular day had never happened, though there had been similar days in Kyoto, in the home of her parents. *But not this precise day.* Why she did not return to an exact experience was noted, but not in any way examined. She simply let the vision flow, knowing there must be meaning inside this variance with the indelibly inked sameness of her Kyoto life.

The shuffle of her mother's geta upon stone. The smell of fresh melon. The soft *clop-clop* of wooden chopsticks against porcelain.

"Something to cool us." Mama-san's cheery voice. She set the lacquered tray upon the square wooden table, the edges of two bowls clinking.

She ran her hands across her brow, then across the nape of her neck. The hair that grew there was damp from perspiration. For only a moment did she question the shortness of her hair, its brush-bluntness against her fingers.

"Fresh from Mr. Arigato's market." Her mother was speaking again, the ripe aroma of the fruit escaping as she cut into the melon.

She reached then, and took one dimpled belly into each hand. The sweet juice ran down her forearms into the shelter of her kimono sleeves, her thumbs slipping into the centers, into the spongy nest of hair and seed. She was vaguely aware that the tough outer skin of the rind pressed a kind of cerebral pattern into her palms.

"Hanae, let me cut the melon into slices so that we might enjoy."

She knew she did not respond, but held tight the two halves. It was then she felt her mother's hand, the knife inside. The edge of sharp steel cut.

She opened her eyes to present time. Her spine was straight, her fingers rounded, her posture still in *zazen*. But the metallic flavor of blood had replaced the taste of the dampened dust of memory.

🔸

What's the bitch got this time, Sakura? McCauley's question still nagged, long after their morning meeting. Sakura gave up on his sandwich and sat back in his chair. It was not a good sign that he'd already succumbed to bad takeout.

The promos for Kahn's weekend show had started the speculation that was rife. He admitted he himself was hoping for the best, that the promise of some exclusive revelation was no more than empty hype. But the woman had certainly proven herself both clever and ruthless in the past. And security on any high-profile case was always a major concern.

So many new faces in the Operations Room this morning, new men assigned to what was now an official task force. So many officers needed for the enormous amount of legwork that an investigation like this required. But the expansion of manpower was always a double-edged sword. The wider the pool of persons possessing information, the more likely that some of it would leak. And the more likely, too, that the one really important piece of information—the detail that could break the case—could get lost in the blizzard of paperwork.

His own desk was covered in files. But despite all the canvassing and interviewing that were still ongoing, despite the hot line numbers running with the nightly news, not a single credible witness had turned up. It seemed they could not catch a break. Even without the media hype, the pressure would still be building.

It had started slow. A kind of false reprieve. Months having passed between the first body at the recycling center and the moment when it became undeniable that a serial killer was stalking young women in the city. By the time the police had caught on, by the time his unit had been given jurisdiction, four women had died. News coverage of the discoveries in the landfill had placed the public square in the loop. Solange Mansour was tipping the scales toward outrage, if not panic.

For days the dramatic footage of the recovery of her body from the abandoned car had seemed to cycle endlessly on every cable channel.

The story had gone national, with all the extra headaches that entailed. The game he hated had begun in earnest, with a press conference scheduled for Tuesday.

"Got a minute?" Adelia Johnson spoke from the door.

"You have something?"

"Cab company logs." She came in and set them on the desk. "Could be a taxi driver is our best deal for a witness. And we've got the parking tickets from around the clubs in the works, too."

He nodded. It was a long shot, but a parking ticket issued on the night of a murder had led to Son of Sam.

"But you know," Adelia was saying, "he could be using the subway. A girl doped up on Rohypnol is like a zombie. They don't pass out at first." She shifted position to fix him with a look, asked the inevitable question. "What you think that Kahn woman's got?"

"I'm hoping nothing much." Sakura sighed inwardly. "But I'm sure she's got sources in this building."

"Not Johnny." Delia was instantly protective.

Sakura smiled. The rumors about Kahn and Rozelli had seeped through Major Case last year with the inevitability of osmosis. He knew it was the judgment that he had been uncharacteristically lenient in not accepting Rozelli's offer of his badge. Speculation was still rampant as to why.

At the time, he had told himself that it simply made sense to retain a good officer who was not likely to repeat his mistake. But there had been more to it than that. Johnny Rozelli had been the beneficiary of his own guilt. His history with Faith Baldwin had given him an understanding of that particular kind of temptation.

"I wasn't thinking of Johnny," he said to Delia now. "I've no doubt we have civilian clerks who regularly pass information to Ms. Kahn. They all have their favorite reporters."

"What *is* up with Rozelli?" Delia asked. "He and Walt were makin' some big mystery of a trip to Anti-crime."

"They're getting outfitted for a little undercover clubbing tonight."

"Johnny and Walt in phatlegs and hoodies." Delia was shaking, her laugh in contralto. "Oh, mama, to be a fly on that wall."

Red explosions of light jackknifed across the afternoon's dimmer gray palette. The pair ran and scampered in the early cool, working up a doggy-smell sweat, tossing off zippered jackets to downy sweaters beneath. Hither and thither the boys raced—*monkey see, monkey do*—tumbling in crisp drying grass, skipping over scaly stones. Bright Easter eggs inside a thick lawn. Once hidden, now revealed. Ever surprising him. And like a moth to flame he had been drawn.

Inside the shelter of the park's trees, he sat on a bench. A conventional-looking man. Reading. Concentrating. Absorbing. Oblivious to the delights sparking like fireflies around him. He turned the page of the text. Adjusted the glasses on his nose. Consumed by the written word, a wayward scholar, under a jaunty cap, taking in a bit of the fading equinox. Soaking up sun and sentence and syntax.

Liar. He smiled, barely controlling his excitement as the laddies romped and rallied inside the black wrought-iron fencing, within the square's spare exclusivity. His eyes on the slant, he observed a nanny wise enough to forgo reining in twin fissions of copper penny–headed energy, two sets of legs beating a trail of maddening ever-widening circles. Little rubies. Red and brilliant and precious. Spontaneous gifts long overdue. Yesterday he'd been held prisoner, peering through the tall iron grate of the gates, captivated by the wild boys at play. Until by clever device, he'd opened passage to an infinitely greater Kingdom.

He sat cozily and happy within, licking a thumb to catch a page, his lips quivering in want of just one fox-red curl, a wet cherry rolling over tongue and throat. He set aside the book. His prop. An important piece of his invisibility. He would have to leave soon, and he removed his glasses, staring boldly for the first time today at the plump compact little bodies, somersaulting in spinwheels of color. Over and under in a patch of newly fallen rusted-out leaves.

Sleep would not easily come tonight. Instead he would stare into a volume of dark space, stilling his heart of its ancient memories, relishing the bloom of fresh imaginings of his boys. And already they were *his* boys.

Suddenly the ball rolled at Nanny's feet. In a moment they pulled up short, stood their ground before her, blue eyes stretched wide, questioning her will to become a third party to their game. He watched their chests pumping, waiting for the moment when Nanny would cross over into their boyhood. Then pairs of chubby hands reached for the ball she scooped up, held over their heads. The twins squealed, vying for possession, till one brother took ownership, the other nipping at his heels. Suddenly they were aground, all arms and legs tangled, struggling for the charmed toy. Conjoined, bound both by mutual and cross purpose. And he almost wept for joy.

⚶

Willie sat in her office, scrawling in her date book, attempting to organize her life. As if any date book could do such a thing. She laughed out loud, curling her legs up under her, twisting a strand of hair. Teeth clamped down on a pencil. She'd left Michael at Police Plaza, with a promise he'd make it home in time for dinner. She pushed back from her desk, wishing him there, puttering away in his workroom. She liked the safe solid sound of his hammer coming down, the sweet smell of the wood. Liked knowing he was never more than a few feet away.

Schedule. The word intruded. She rolled her chair forward. She had to come up with some kind of schedule. It had been days since she'd written a word. What had happened to her grand plan of writing a chapter a week? By her calculation, at the present pace, she would be lucky to finish the book in three years. Though her editor had told her to take whatever time she needed, she didn't want to push it. She already felt guilty every time she spent a penny of the advance. What if she paid herself? A fraction of the advance for every chapter she wrote. That seemed fair, and it might even be an incentive to get productive. Who was she kidding? Nothing could force her into a routine. Quantico had been her great stab at organization and discipline. And she'd been partially successful. But old habits were hard to break. She was a quantum thinker, a quantum writer, a quantum housekeeper, a quantum shopper. A quantum everything. She jumped from one activity to another. At times she half-suspected she had some form of attention deficit.

If she just didn't spread herself so thin, she could make some real headway. But there was little hope for that. Besides, she loved to mix it up. Boredom was her worst enemy. She looked down at what she had written. Time allotments for her three major undertakings: her writing, the investigation, and her patients. Speaking of patients . . . She had a new patient coming in later this afternoon. She reached over and flipped open her appointment book. Victor Abbot. 3 P.M.

🔺

The night was a large bat descending, its leathery black wings moist and heavy, promising chill hard rain. Streetlights bit sharply into the dark, but surrendered halos of saturated illumination. The air had the cold thick taste of autumn waiting in the wings.

Inside the dance club, the bat had landed, but had dropped some acid on its way down.

"Like what you see?" The man had turned over the reins to another deejay, who took his place inside the glass cage. He glanced over his shoulder, following the cops' eyes. The two girls were polar opposites. One petite, round, and blond. The other tall, angular, and dark. The height difference, however, didn't stop them from meeting breast-to-breast, tongue-to-tongue as they gyrated in what passed for dancing. Then the small one turned, flipping her long gold mane with one hand and grinding her rear into the groin of her taller partner. The flashing lights gave their movements a harder, more precise edge.

"Don't jump to conclusions. They're not lezzies. Oh, I'm not saying they're not enjoying themselves. But it's mostly a performance for the guys." He extended his hand. "Randy Lancaster. Most everybody knows me as Shaman. And you're . . ."

"Detective Walter Talbot. My partner, Detective Johnny Rozelli." Talbot watched the disc jockey examine his badge. There were silver rings on each of his fingers.

"A different world, Detective Rozelli." Lancaster was grinning now, well-defined lips curled over white even teeth.

At last Rozelli turned. "Yeah. . . . How old are those two anyway?"

Lancaster looked back at the crowded dance floor. A strobe had transformed the girls into liquid staccatoed waves. "Eighteen. Maybe younger. A lot get in on fake IDs."

"You know most of the women who come in?" Talbot asked, noticing that Lancaster's tongue was pierced. His dark curling hair, pulled back into a ponytail, made his square face squarer, his high cheekbones sharper, a corded gazelle's neck longer. Thick brows almost met above the bridge of a slightly hooked nose. Hooded eyes gave him a foxy, slightly aroused look. Though the word *satyr* came to Talbot's mind, Shaman's whole package fit his celebrity name. The deejay's look was nothing if not Native American hippie.

"I know some of the regulars. Girls come up and talk to me on my break. Ask me to play certain songs. Some offer to buy me a drink. Take me home to Mom." He laughed, the silver ball through his tongue trapping a stray bit of laser light.

"Know this one?" Talbot pulled out a picture of Sarah Laraby. "She probably would have had on heavier makeup, a different hair style. Her roommate said she went in for the club look. Even used a different name. Called herself Selkie Girl."

Lancaster reached and took the photograph, spent a few seconds examining it. "Good-looking. But can't say as I do. . . . She missing or something?"

"Or something." Rozelli took the photo. "She's dead."

"That's rough." The deejay appeared genuinely upset.

"You don't much keep up with current events, do you, Lancaster? Laraby's picture has been all over the newspapers, on TV. Along with these . . ." Rozelli forced photographs of the other victims at the disc jockey.

The deejay went through the pictures one by one, shaking his head, then handed them back. "These girls dead too?"

"Yeah. As you said, you're a pretty popular guy—know any of these women?"

"No, I don't. And I don't think I much like your attitude, Detective Rozelli."

"You don't have to like my attitude. Just answer my questions."

"I don't have to answer your questions, either. I know my rights."

"Yeah, yeah, everybody knows his rights."

"Listen, Mr. Lancaster, we're not here to hassle you." Talbot had gone into his good-cop routine. "We're sorry if we gave you that impression. We're just trying to find out what happened to these women. They were all known clubbers."

"There're a thousand clubs. And a ton of underground shit. They could have gone anywhere."

"You play any of the underground shit?" Rozelli was close to giving Lancaster the look he saved for the nastiest perps.

Lancaster shook his head. "No, I'm strictly commercial. That's where the real money is."

Talbot nodded, handing back the picture of Laraby. "I want you to take another look at this photograph, Mr. Lancaster. It's very important, because your name was in this one's diary."

Lancaster seemed surprised. Then he examined the photograph, rubbing his finger up and down the picture's edge. "I'm positive, Detective. I never saw this girl in my life."

Talbot took back the photograph, thinking that for a man who had so many girls coming on to him, he was amazingly decisive. Or lying.

CHAPTER

10

The apartment, which took up the whole of the top floor of the building, floated like an island above the dark urban sprawl. Whatever unwholesomeness the night might contain was for the moment held at bay. In deed, if not in theory. The topic was murder.

"Not budging an inch, are you." Willie stretched out opposite Michael in the bed as the TV played in the background.

"It's my Greek Orthodox background. Evil is evil."

"I'm Roman Catholic, lest you forget."

"And a psychiatrist. You people find something good in everyone. Or a reason to excuse the bad." He finished with a smile.

"That's low, Darius, really low."

"Jeffrey Dahmer."

She shook her head and laughed. "I just knew you'd start there. And that's fine. In fact, more than fine."

"Okay, make his case. Mentally ill or just plain misunderstood?"

"You're nasty, you know that, Darius."

"You're stalling."

She sat up. "Dahmer was one of the most pitiful people I ever studied. He didn't have a clue about what it meant to be human."

"So he ate his victims."

"I know it's difficult for you to understand, but that was his way of experiencing intimacy. To Dahmer, eating the flesh of his victims was an expression of love, a way of making his victims a part of him."

"*Unholy* communion?"

"Yes, but still a *kind* of communion. I'm not condoning what Dahmer did, but I can try to understand it."

"I understand it plain and simple. The son-of-a-bitch was evil."

"Not a category for people like Dahmer."

"He knew what he was doing."

"This isn't black-or-white insanity, Michael. You can't blame someone for not playing the game correctly, if he isn't given the right equipment. Dahmer's brain was different."

"Ted Bundy."

"Not so sympathetic. But a sociopath is not in the same reality tunnel as the rest of us. Somehow his programming gets skewed. His entire existence is channeled into re-creating a fantasy where humans are objects, not subjects."

"And he is the deus ex machina."

"Good." She smiled at his use of metaphor. "There was one killer who tortured his victims by tying them up and letting rats eat them alive."

"A real gentleman."

"I remember he said he watched for hours as the starving rats ran wild over a body, gnawing away at the flesh. He said he wanted to feel something, so he kept watching. Finally, when the rats had finished eating the eyes of one victim, an eleven-year-old girl, so she couldn't cry anymore because there was nothing left but empty sockets, and all she could do was scream, he said he thought something inside him stirred. Though he could never be sure, he believed what he'd experienced was the beginnings of what most humans would call pity."

"And that's supposed to make me feel better about this animal?"

"No, but it should make you see that these killers are not fully human."

"And our killer?"

She stretched back down, working her hair into a knot at the back of her head. "The same."

Michael nodded. "You were right the first time. I'm not giving an inch. They're all evil."

"At least you'll grant me they're interesting."

"I can't be that clinical." He reached for a cigarette.

"I thought you were giving it up."

He examined the glowing tip. "I'm allowed one vice."

She reached up between his legs and squeezed.

"Shit, that hurt."

"I'm your vice, remember."

"Come here, you," he said, crushing out the cigarette.

She straddled him, and let him pull her down. The half-tearing-away of clothes. Hands working. His mouth. Slowly at first, then frantically. Always moving, like there was not enough time, not enough of her to feed him. And his always coming away hungry. Begging for more.

Shadow play from the set on the wall behind them. But little chance now that they'd catch Kahn's special.

Zoe preferred doing TV live, winging it, with all her nervousness poured into the effort of the here and now. Sitting in the darkened studio and watching her special unfold on the monitor with the rest of America was way further up there on the anxiety scale.

But she knew that she'd done it, knew the special was good. She just had it, damn it. Whatever *it* was? What had that one bitch of a critic said about her weekday show? She summoned the words, still dripping with acid. *FNC's latest daytime offering is compulsive watching. An irreverent take on the U. S. justice system, the show has the same flagrant and self-admiring gaucheness that is the hallmark of its host. Zoe Kahn is an acquired taste.*

A backhanded compliment if she'd ever heard one. But it *was* a compliment. She laughed out loud, not caring who heard, and nearly missed herself introducing retired agent Gilbert Watts, formerly with the FBI's Behavioral Science Division. She would have liked a rematch with Wilhelmina French, but the psychiatrist had not returned her calls. The middle-aged Watts, though far less photogenic, had at least proved easier to manage.

The show was moving toward the end now, and Watts was the setup for her much-advertised revelation. She refocused on the screen, where Zoe on the tube was already pressing the agent for his personal take on a profile.

". . . no longer in the loop." Watts was playing it modest.

"The young women of this city are under attack." She was making herself their champion. "Any insight you can give us would be valuable."

Watts's smile said he was in on the game. "He's a white male," he began. "Twenty-five to thirty-five. Probably attractive. Can interact in social situations . . ."

"A lot of women in Manhattan might suggest that's a very limited pool"—a bit of humor, cutting through the too familiar litany—"but in reality, Agent Watts, it doesn't much narrow the field."

"Hard to be more specific with the little that's out there," he countered.

"What if there were more?"

"More?" The question, wary.

"I've learned from separate sources"—she was moving in for the kill—"that what we've actually got here is a modern-day Ripper. The victims are being slashed open, then stapled back up, as if he'd performed an autopsy."

Bombshell delivered. And it showed on Watts's face. This was substantive information that went beyond the mere speculation he'd been prepared for. He had not bargained, apparently, for treading on the toes of former colleagues.

She watched herself enjoying his reaction, her glossed lips gleaming in the studio lights. "There were weeks, months, between the deaths of the first four victims"—she was pushing her advantage, leaning into a close-up—"but only days between Siebrig and Mansour. This *New Jack* is drugging young women and abducting them, assaulting them sexually. We've all heard the rumors that he's smothering them with plastic bags. Now we know that he's ripping them open. What does that add up to, Agent Watts? Just what kind of sick . . . *guy* have we got here?"

Sick *fuck* was, of course, what she'd meant, and she'd managed to make sure her viewers knew it. A staged pause like a wink.

Watts gave in, beginning a rant on fantasy and mutilation.

It was all interesting stuff—guaranteed to hold the audience through the commercial, after which she'd do the summing up—though she wondered how accurate any of it was. Not that it mattered. Agent Watts had proved the perfect foil for her exclusive. And she trusted that the network gods were just as happy as she was.

✦

Hanae had been waiting when her husband came home, with food and scented candles, with music they both enjoyed. He had lingered in the bath while she made the final preparations for their meal. They had talked together as they ate, a most natural conversation. She spoke of her day, spent buying what she needed at the market, walking to the music store with Taiko to buy a new CD. Jimmy spoke about his case, about the inevitability of leaks, and about what had been revealed tonight on Zoe Kahn's program.

He had watched the show on the television in the Operations Room, he said. But she did not say that she too had tuned in to the program. She was glad to let him talk, to share his anger over the leak. *New Jack.* That was what Ms. Kahn was calling the killer now, a name which would surely cause greater fear. At least, Jimmy said, there had been no mention of how this serial was rearranging the organs inside the bodies. It was important to the investigation that at least some part of the killer's MO remain secret.

He had wondered how soon they might have another victim. He would have been home much earlier, he had admitted, but he had feared the call might come tonight. Might yet come. She had been happy in the comfort of his sharing, and had reached to touch his hand. A reminder that it did not matter. He had done all he could. Home or not home, murder would come when it would. His presence at Police Plaza would not change the heart of a killer.

Jimmy had insisted on cleaning up the dishes. And she sat upon the tatami mat, on her cushion at the low table, listening now to the sounds that came from the kitchen. Water running. The clatter of plates. She sat for a few moments longer, stroking Taiko's neck as he curled beside her. The candles flickered scent in their little iron lanterns. She blew them out and stood, walking into the bedroom.

He had lit candles. They had seemed to fill the room where he'd held her captive. Their warmth. Their cloying odor. She had refused to let the memory spoil them forever. This much she had accomplished in her parents' home in Japan. She had unlearned the hatred of candles.

She undressed and got into bed, pulling up the wedding quilt, waiting for Jimmy. She heard his step as he came into the room. He said nothing, perhaps believing her already asleep. Her heart jumped to her throat as he climbed into the bed, and it beat there like the wounded wing of a bird. So careful they had been not to quarrel tonight. But things could not go on as they had. Softly, as a leaf falling, a matter of gravity, she slipped beneath the covers. She felt her husband's body as a pressure next to hers, a hard smooth length beside her. Her lips were on his skin, the muscle of his thigh. Her fingers found him. Her mouth.

"Hanae . . ." So much in the simple speaking of her name. He had reached for her. His hand locking on her shoulder, he drew her up beside him. Out from beneath the marriage quilt.

He was leaning over her; she could feel his stare, hear his troubled breathing. His hand caressed her face. "I want you *here* with me," he said. "I need . . ."

"I am not ready." She was shocked by the misery in her voice. "Can you not accept what pleasure I can give?"

"There is no pleasure for me in this act. A wife may play at concubine. But you are not at play here. I will wait."

She felt her tears, a purifying rain. Would there ever be enough?

He kissed her, pulling her close. Held her. *"Aishiteru yo,"* he whispered into her hair.

"Watashi mo," she answered. *I love you too.* But the words, like the tears, did not suffice.

⚶

The night belonged to Right-brain. He loved the dark. Loved the smell of it. The black-blanket feel of it. He opened his mouth and tasted the night—air, cool and damp, full of foreign molecules, waiting to tease his olfactory nerves.

He restricted himself to Flatiron tonight, though his night journeys could take him deep into Soho, or upward toward the Theater District. He welcomed the press of flesh of theater-goers going into or coming out of a performance, offering him a heady mix of sight, smell, and sound. A night in the rain was particularly intoxicating—dampened skin, cooking in the moisture, releasing the scent of fermented perfume secreted behind an ear, or the stale stink of cigar smoke incubated in the palate hours before. And then there might be the unexpected puncture of an umbrella against a bare arm, drawing blood. Salt to the taste.

But the bodies themselves, passing him tonight as he walked Twenty-third Street toward Fifth, were not so much bodies as collections of organs, a kind of corporeal geography, suspended in time and space.

The parts greater than the whole: *Aortic isthmus, canal of Nuck, pyramids of Ferrein, rima of Glottis, Jelly of Wharton, nodes of Ranvier, Opercula of the insula, Papilla lacrimalis, Utricle of vestibule* . . .

A woman smiled as she bumped against his shoulder, though he did not smile back. Rather, he allowed his eyes to quickly calculate the capacity of her abdomen, flashing flat between the flaps of her coat, to accommodate *Douglas's pouch.* Excessively long limbs violated the prescribed space. By his estimate it would be a tight fit—*mons Veneris, labia majora, nymphae, clitoris, vestibule with meatus urinarius, Glands of Bartholin, Bulbi vestibuli, vagina, uterus—fundus and cervix, Fallopian tubes, ovaries.* He turned too late, and had to be satisfied with the *flip-flap* of her coat moving away from him. So much for that.

He laughed now, a giddy kind of laugh, though he was not particularly happy or amused. In fact, he was annoyed. He should have smiled when the woman smiled. What would have been the harm in that? He buttoned up his coat and shoved his hands into the pockets. It wasn't perfect, he thought, but it would just have to do, as his fingers slipped through the hole in the lining of the right pocket and found the zipper of his jeans, releasing his erection.

Just have to make do . . . he rubbed the underside of his shaft . . . *until something better comes along.*

✿

Jimmy slept. Hanae could hear the regular sound of his breathing. Slowly she lifted the marriage quilt and, leaving the bed, moved toward the bath. Closing the door, she waited a moment as though she might have disturbed him, and he would follow. But he slept.

She folded into herself, slowly dropping to the floor. Rocking on her knees, she let the tears come again, heavy and silent now. Swallowing the sound. Releasing the long-pent-up pain and shame. Her mind searched for the old prayer, willing her lips to form the words. Reaching behind, she loosened the gown she'd worn to bed. She was loath to touch her own body, and for one moment she wished to take up something with which to strike, to beat from her flesh the defilement that too long had festered there.

She rose naked, stepping into the tub. The prayer of *Misogi* again on her lips. Then her hand reached to free the water. The fine hot spray hit her face, a thousand burning needles running down her shoulders, pricking her breasts. The water scalded, and she prayed. Prayed that the gods wash the soil from her, make her clean. Remove from her the stain *he* had left behind, when in the same moment he had taken from her the unborn child.

For purification. For worthiness, she prayed. So that once again she could offer herself to Jimmy. Once again be wife to her husband.

CHAPTER

11

H ere, Mr. Romero, here."
The driver drove a short distance more before bearing to the right and stopping. "We can't stay long," he said. "I'm illegally parked. On the wrong side of the street. But I want to be behind you. . . . You sure you want to do this, Mrs. Sakura?" He was facing her. She could feel his eyes, the soft direct sound of his voice as he'd turned in his seat.

"It's all right, Mr. Romero. As you said, you will be right behind me. And I have Taiko with me." At the sound of his name, the dog moved, his harness making a hollow jangle in the shelter of the backseat. "Is that not true, my prince?" She bent and kissed the shepherd on his muzzle.

"This is not such a good area."

She knew he wanted to say that a black neighborhood was not a place for a blind Asian woman. Even at eleven o'clock in the morning. "It will be fine. And I won't be long." She twisted the lead in her hand and opened the door. Taiko bounded out onto the sidewalk.

The cold air was fresh against her skin, though she was glad for the coat she'd worn. A few words in Japanese to Taiko, and they moved forward. She could hear the low rumble of Mr. Romero's engine. She knew he would follow her as far as he could. An angel on her shoulder. She smiled, her feet making a wary peace with the uneven pavement. A screech of a cat. Music, loud and insistent from across the street. The *boom, boom, boom* of the bass reverberated inside her. An impatient shout. A baby's wail. A few more steps and she was there. Where the abandoned car had been left.

Issa body . . . Arm be sticking outta the trunk . . . Look like a woman hand . . . Wrapped up like garbage . . . Sho stank . . . Who done did this shit . . . Their voices a fresh litany in her head. She could almost feel them around her, though no one had actually touched her. They had parted for her as she'd moved forward inside the crowd. She had been as much an interloper as the dead inside the car . . . . *She be blind . . . See dat dog . . .*

Then, without warning, the same blackness she'd experienced that night struck. Sucked at her like a vacuum. Unzipping its mouth to take her inside itself. Emptier than empty. A nothingness beyond nothing-ness. And terrible . . . terrible in its need.

She clutched her stomach, fighting the hot ropes of saliva forming, the throbbing at her temples, matching the *boom, boom, boom* of the music. A sudden wrenching, a doubling over, and she vomited. She was conscious of the faint jingle of Taiko's harness and Mr. Romero's shout. Then his feet slamming the concrete, coming toward her, running to catch her before the blackness swallowed her and she fell.

✸

In Margot Redmond's mind, the room seemed unaccountably cold. She ran her hands up and down her arms. The gesture did not pass unnoticed. His one blue eye, one green, still unsettled her.

"Cold?" David St. Cyr asked.

"A bit. Are you? I could turn up the thermostat."

"I find it pleasant."

"I think I'll get a sweater. Excuse me. . . . Pour yourself another cup of coffee."

In her bedroom, she shivered again. What was wrong with her? Was it St. Cyr? She had to admit, the architect still made her a bit uncomfort-able. But she couldn't exactly explain why. He was nice enough. Almost too nice. And God knew he was attractive, if you liked the type. Which she did. Tall and chiseled. Reeking of breeding. Had Patrice mentioned he was gay? She could never remember. Somehow she didn't think he was. She didn't think he was anything. Maybe she was overstating it, but he seemed indifferent to any sort of physical intimacy, as though he had no appetite for it and sex simply bored him. A beautiful snake that went artfully and stealthily about its business. That was David St. Cyr. She reached into a drawer for a sweater, wishing she'd scheduled this meeting when Reese had been home.

"Back," she said, sounding overly cheerful. "Was there a problem redoing the boys' room?" She seated herself at the desk, where he'd stretched out his revised designs. "I mean, dividing the one bedroom into two separate rooms."

"No, it can be fixed."

"I'm hearing a *but*." She followed his gaze as it moved from the drawings back up to her.

"Am I that transparent?" He wore a smile that appeared practiced.

"It just seemed that there might be some problem."

"No problem." He used his pencil to indicate how easily it would be to bisect the space. "I was just thinking that since Jason and Damon are still quite young, they might enjoy sharing a room. And later when they got older, it would be a simple matter of throwing up a wall."

"Maybe . . ." She stared at the design, thinking. "No, they'll have the playroom. I want Jason and Damon to each have his own bedroom."

The wooden smile turned into a dry laugh. "I think you've been reading too much literature about twins."

"Actually I've been on-line." She didn't care a damn bit for his condescending attitude.

"Sorry, Margot, I'm cursed with 'only-child syndrome.' Individual bedrooms it shall be." This time St. Cyr's smile managed to spill over into his remarkable eyes.

⁜

The day had turned overcast, with dark clouds piling between the buildings that bordered the sculpted green. With its thrusting iron fences and autumn trees turning skeletal, Gramercy Park appeared gothic in the failing afternoon light. Michael Darius, standing near the gate, was nursing his near-wasted cigarette. For the last twenty minutes he'd been hanging around, watching the front of the brownstone, trying to decide whether to go another round with Margot.

The door opened, and a tall man came out, moving with the deliberateness of escape. Face concentrated, shoulders set, a controlled anger in the walk that carried the expensive clothes catlike.

Darius jerked at the cigarette, stubbed it in the sidewalk, and crossed.

Margot answered the door. "Oh, great!"

He ignored her comment. "Who was that?"

"What do you want, Michael?" She let him come in, but only as far as the foyer.

"I want to know who that man was."

"What man?" She was going to make this hard.

"You fucking him?"

"That's none of your goddamned business."

The rawness of the exchange shocked them both.

"Of course I'm not fucking him." She spoke first. "Why are you here?" She was again on offense.

"Where are the boys?"

"They had a play date at Peg Martin's. She has a boy of her own their age. It's almost time to pick them up. I'll have to go in a minute."

She was talking too fast, and he looked over her shoulder as she spoke. There was something on the table she didn't want him to see.

"Michael . . ."

He pushed past her and took in the plans. *Redmond House. Architect—David St. Cyr.* Some objective part of his brain appreciated the talent behind the design. "You're building . . . where?" His voice was deceptively toneless.

"I was going to tell you." Margot had followed him. She appeared deflated in the light that was coming in from the window.

"Where?" he repeated.

"In Connecticut. Not exactly the end of the earth. And nothing is definite; the plans aren't even finalized. That's why David was here. David St. Cyr. He's the architect. And he's . . . difficult." She had had to reach for the word.

"*Difficult . . .* how?"

She shook her head. "I don't know. We disagreed about some changes I want him to make in the house." She was looking at him now with something like affection. "You'd probably be on his side," she said. "Like someone had criticized your models."

Her tone was deliberately light, an attempt to diffuse the emotion that had built like thunder in the room. Layer on layer of ionized air. The charge remained.

He continued to study the plans. He could not have designed this. He was a copyist; his models of the great cathedrals were lessons. The technical aspects of this house, the materials that made its construction possible were beyond his knowledge. And something else here that was beyond him. A level of abstraction not suited for human beings. This was not a house where Margot should live. Not a house for his children.

He looked up. She was watching him as if for once she could read in his face the things he could not say.

"Michael . . ." she began, but her gaze slid past his face. "Reese just thinks that living in the country would be better for the boys."

"What do you think?"

"Do you really want to know?" she asked him.

"Yes."

"I think it's up to us . . . the three of us, to do what will make Jason and Damon happy and secure."

"And you think that keeping me out of their lives will do that?"

"I don't know. Keeping you in mine was making me crazy."

"You've said that."

"I don't know what else to say. It's confusing for Jason and Damon to have you just show up here all the time. They don't know what to make of you. Reese is their father."

"It's getting late," he said, before she could speak again. He was already walking away. "You better go pick up the boys."

✤

Victor Abbot waited in his seat for the rest of the movie audience to file out. He needed a few moments alone in the semidark to savor what he had seen. He knew he had been bad—he couldn't imagine that his obsession with the movie was something Dr. French would approve of—but it hardly seemed his fault if the revival theater on Houston had decided to schedule his favorite silent film. He couldn't resist coming here to see it played out on the big screen.

It was as if Fritz Lang could read his mind. A truly weird thought. Some film director in the twenties picking his future brain. But that was how it felt, watching his private reality unfolding up there in the dark. He could never really get enough of *Metropolis*.

The crowd had considerably thinned when finally he emerged into the pink and purple lobby. He went past the few stragglers who remained at the bar, pushed through the door to the street, and walked toward the subway station on Varick. He could feel the rods and pistons working in his legs, the metal plates inside his chest expanding and contracting. Tiny gears at the sides of his face shifted his mouth to a smile.

He had reached the stairs, and was descending now like Freder into the city's bowels. The rods moved in his thighs, their lubricated heads sliding in the grooves behind his knees. Articulated metal flexed with each step in ankle joints and toes.

It was not very late, and the subway was crowded with night-riders, city slaves in the world of the catacombs. In his private Metropolis, the hero, himself, was not the human Freder but machine. In his version, the robot Hel, and not the human Maria, was the true object of desire.

He slid his card through the slot at the top of the turnstile and went through the gate to the platform to wait behind the yellow line for his train. He stood for a moment with eyes closed, the sensors in his head filtering the machine smells from the effluvia of closely pressed bodies.

His train came. He noted his reflection distorted in the silvered pneumatic doors that parted with a *whoosh* to admit him. He found a seat across from a woman whose body fascinated. Tall and angular, muscles elongated inside the concealing skin. He longed to burn the flesh away, to reveal the gleaming structure beneath.

🐾

2:52 A.M. Margot paced her bedroom, back and forth, back and forth, from the bed to the window and back again, her thoughts looping as endlessly as her footsteps. It took a conscious will to stop, to still her feet and her brain. She made the effort, halting like an actor before the heavy curtains. Her hand parted the fabric and she peered out. But no waiting audience floated in the second-storey air. No one at all on the sidewalk beneath. Or in the park, where the trees stood dark and unmoving as cutouts. The sky itself was a murky black that trapped the city neon and occluded whatever moon still lingered.

Reese was away, which was not unusual. He had to travel a lot in his business. But his absence tonight seemed to have infected her with restlessness. She had looked forward to the quiet after putting the boys to bed, but had still found it difficult to concentrate on the brief that her law firm was expecting tomorrow. When that was finished, she'd had a harder time than usual drifting off to sleep.

And then Damon had woken with a dream, which in turn had woken his brother—something about the dark and the shadow that the night-light made on the wall. She smiled, rueful. There could be a downside to a lively imagination, something which both twins possessed. Dreams had been something that had always plagued Michael.

She had been trying not to think of him, and now she had. Which of course was the real reason for her sleeplessness. Trying to shut Michael out of her thoughts was as difficult as shutting him out of their lives. She could not forget the look on his face when he had seen the house plans today.

She let the curtain fall and returned to her bed. It was not cold in the room, but she had a sudden longing to be beneath the covers. She curled on her side and pulled the bedclothes up to her head. Sometimes it became impossible to keep up her guard. Sometimes, like tonight, she just gave herself over to thinking of her and Michael.

Never an especially pretty child, she had blossomed in high school. She had enjoyed her new attractiveness, but her parents had been watchful, and boyfriends had never been the focus of her existence. By the time she went to college she was considered a beauty, and there had always been men, but never the *one*. Not until law school.

He had walked into Torts that first day of class, and the buzz among the women around her had started. Someone had said he looked like a Cornishman's idea of the devil, with his dark complexion and corn-flower eyes. Her own description was Byronic. There had been a seriousness in his face, in his whole manner, that was more compelling to her than his looks. He seemed tragic in some overwhelming way, and her instant response was a deep and sexual attraction that made her feel ridiculous.

She had never had crushes on movie stars or rock stars growing up. But here she was waking in the mornings with that giddy "the world is wonderful" feeling just because some guy named Darius was in it—an unconscious euphoria that hit as she opened her eyes, before the censor in her brain had time to catch up. And worse, getting wet pants if he even looked her way in class, which he seemed to do more and more often. She was horrified to think he might guess her reaction.

Finally he'd approached her. She'd watched him walking toward her table in the campus coffee shop, and was surprised that she was glad, not because her girlish dreams were going to be realized, but for precisely the opposite reason. She was certain that her dreams would be smashed. The real Michael Darius was going to set her free from the imaginary man in her head.

But he hadn't. He'd begun a conversation on New York law, and the effect of Judge Cardoza's opinions. She had been completely disarmed. She possessed no natural weapons where Michael was concerned. She had had to develop defenses.

She would never be completely free of him. They could move to China, and he would still be in her head. This moment she could see him so clearly, looking at her as he had the other day when he'd asked if she loved Reese. She hadn't responded, but the answer was easy. Of course she loved Reese.

But there were other questions that he hadn't asked, and those answers were hard.

Do you still love me? Oh, yes.

Do you miss what we had? I ache for it.

CHAPTER

12

Willie sat yawning in front of Sakura's desk. "Excuse me," she said. She was watching him pull tea things from the bottom drawer, including cups for three. She had never seen Darius drink Jimmy's tea. And right now she'd rather have coffee. It had been that kind of morning, preceded by that kind of night. Michael, silent and moody at dinner, had kept her up hours after midnight. Which was fine, she guessed. Having great sex was not something she wanted to complain about. But she'd had to be up early today, joining the task force for the morning briefing. And then the real occasion, just concluded. Jimmy's first press conference on the progress of the investigation.

"I think that went reasonably well," she spoke to no one in particular.

"Considering I had nothing to say." Sakura had turned to the water boiling on the hot plate behind him.

"What bothers me"—she watched him pour hot water over the tea leaves—"is that I don't have a better handle on the profile. I can't seem to get a clear fix on what's going on with this guy."

"He's a serial killer." Darius had finally spoken from the window, where predictably he was hovering. She'd noted his habit of staring from heights whenever he felt any special pressure to communicate.

"Thanks for the insight," she shot back.

"Maybe they're supposed to be androids," Darius said. He walked over and sat in the chair next to hers. "Mechanical somehow. Stapled together. It fits with the music they play in these clubs."

"Interesting, but there has to be more than that."

Sakura pushed tea toward them. Darius picked his up. She took a sip from her cup, but the liquid was still too hot and she set it down. "Let me see the autopsy photos for Siebrig," she said to Jimmy.

He opened a drawer and handed her a file.

She picked out one of the photographs taken before the procedure. "Not an android." She pointed to the metallic tracks, like giant stitches holding the torso together. "More like Bride of Frankenstein. Cutting and reassembling. Maybe our little monster is creating the woman of his dreams."

⚶

A couple hours later Willie was shivering in the sun as a cold wind whipped up the street, a remnant of the gusts of early morning. She pulled her coat tighter, moving closer to the entrance of the restaurant. Then, glancing back, she smiled, catching sight of Hanae as she rounded the corner with Taiko in the lead. It always gave her pleasure to watch the two of them moving as a unit in the crowd.

"This place is nice," Hanae said when they had settled inside and ordered.

"It *is* nice," she said. "I eat here a lot. It's only a couple blocks from my office."

"You are enjoying your work?"

"I am. It's been a while since I've seen patients. At least normal patients." She laughed. " . . .You know what I mean."

"Patients who are not serial killers."

Not the kind of comment she'd expected. She studied Hanae's face. But the words had been simple, devoid of sadness or irony. "No serial killers," she said lightly. "But quite a few who are interesting."

"You are happy then?"

The question seemed wistful, and was not about work. "With Kenjin, you mean?"

Hanae smiled at her use of the name. "Yes," she said, "with Kenjin."

"Things between Michael and me seem to be good right now. I don't think much beyond that."

Hanae nodded, sipped at her water.

Willie had expected a little gentle gloating; it was Hanae, after all, who from the beginning had promoted the idea of Michael and her as a couple. But the silence stretched, expressive perhaps of the trouble she suspected still existed at home. The tension, so palpable in Jimmy, had not lessened since Hanae's return. His stress was, if anything, increasing.

A strain not due entirely to the pressures of a new investigation, she guessed, but more to Hanae's reaction to it. His wife's subtle maneuvering the other night to include herself in their discussion had not pleased Jimmy. Surely Hanae had earned the right, and she for one believed they would only benefit from her insight. But Jimmy had minded, despite his efforts to pretend otherwise.

The food came, looking as delicious as always, and they ate. Conversation resumed, and they laughed over things that had happened in the city, and funny stories that Hanae told about her cousins Nori and Sei. But the undercurrent of what was not spoken remained. In the end, her training took over.

"Hanae, I have to say something that you probably don't want to hear."

"What is it?" The porcelain face, emptied suddenly of expression, was doll-like.

"You went through so much last year. I just think you might benefit from seeing someone. And I'd be happy to recommend—"

"It is not necessary, Willie." The dark head had tilted downward, the white center part showing stark and childlike in the black hair.

"Then talk to *me* as a friend. . . . I know that I'm Jimmy's friend, too"—it had needed to be said—"but you can tell me anything. Ask me anything. It will stay between us."

Hanae's eyes came up to meet her own, black wells that did not at all seem sightless.

No good deed goes unpunished. The thought a sudden current in her mind.

"There is something I need to know." Hanae was smiling.

She waited, knowing she was going to regret this.

"Where exactly," Hanae asked her, "was Leslie Siebrig's body found?"

Maybe it's the blindness, Willie thought as she watched Hanae walk away from the restaurant under gathering clouds. She could only guess at what it was that made Hanae so different, although she suspected it was something fundamentally spiritual that set her friend apart. In frustration, she twisted a strand of hair. How easily she'd been trapped. Though *trapped* was perhaps too harsh a word. Rather she'd been *led* by Hanae, following her willingly down the garden path. It was still difficult to consider that any sort of guile had been used. She held Hanae above manipulation. Yet she *had* been manipulated. She had told Jimmy's wife where Leslie Siebrig's body had been discovered.

What Hanae would do with the information, Willie had a pretty good idea. She would go to the scene of the crime. And why? This too she thought she knew. It was part of Hanae's need to understand what Jimmy did, to be fully part of that other life he lived. The one he so desperately wanted to keep from her. But exclusion was apparently not something Hanae could accept any longer. Jimmy's last serial case had forced her to that boundary that divided them, and she had crossed over. There could never be a turning back.

But more, Hanae was a woman of deep and driving instincts. Living in a world honed from another kind of reality, guided by senses forged by precise and unique forces. Blindness had made of Hanae a different species. More refined, where others were awkward. More exacting, where others were grossly inept. She embodied a perfect elegance of touch and feeling. In a world of bumbling, blunted fools, Hanae Sakura was as close to being psychic as Willie would allow was possible.

It was the movie within the movie, played a hundred times. Yuppie mother driving with her spawn from the city. A bucolic excursion meant for making memories. Not for the two squirming boys, too young to later recall it. The memories are for her.

The city falls away, a discarded backdrop. The traffic is minimal after the thruway. The weather here dry and autumnal. Indian summer. The

Navigator slips through a panorama of new-rolled hay and pied cows lazing on the still green hilltops, through the woodland that separates the farms, where a leaf here, a tree there, has been set ablaze. A warning, subliminal, lurks in the Technicolor perfection. A darkness slowly piling in the ultimate blandness of blue sky and turning leaves.

They stop at a diner for the bathroom, where the gray-haired waitress dispenses pie and blessings on *the cutest little things, with all that red hair.* Then the road again, where the montage quickens. More rolling hills and farmland, then the quick-cut to the turnoff. A vehicle that passes as they stop to check the sign—*Smiley's Pumpkin Patch, 2 miles.* The Navigator follows in the fading wake of the van, pulls minutes later into the lot.

Crane shot as Mother emerges from the driver's seat. The boys freed to spill onto the withered verge, where other parents wait with their fidgeting broods for the hay wagon to depart. Mother bends to her sons, dancing roly-poly in their quilted loden jackets. A word on *behaving,* a promise of the petting zoo tossed on the air as a bribe.

Edit to the tractor as it pulls along, to the jostled group in the wagon. Edit to the field. To Mother's hyped cheeriness as they enter into the rows of orange fruit. So much time before the hay wagon will make its return. No quick-cuts in her mind. So many minutes to allocate, declaring this one too large. This too small. Too thin. Not flat enough at the bottom. Two three-year-old attention spans to harness to the search for the perfect pumpkin.

It happens as it always does in these scenes. The air full of noise and laughter so suddenly still. The bark of a dog, sharp as gunfire. Sounds becomes muffled, limited to the air inside her head, the ambience of a sinus cavity. It's Mother's POV now.

She straightens, shielding her eyes, as a flock of birds rises and vees in the air above her head. Dark shapes against the impossible blue, their arrow a signal. Instinctive little animals, the boys bolt, a tandem zigzag, like elves or hobbits dancing in the rows.

Jason . . . Damon! The names spark from her lips as she grasps the reality of their flight. She breaks and moves, speeding past parents who are oblivious, past children who look up at her with the smiles of conspirators. "Jason . . . Damon!" She is screaming the names like a primal chant, past any urban self-consciousness.

In seconds, she stops. Spins. Confused as to their direction. The green jackets and bobbing russet heads have been swallowed by the field of jack-o'-lanterns on the make, the yet-to-be-grinning pumpkins.

Fade out and cut to the twins. Jason, emerging at the far end of a row. Damon pulls up behind him, a hand going out like a tether to his brother's shoulder, not actually touching, nor needing to. The two stand, still giggling at their escape, waiting for the impulse of *what's to come next*.

Jason turns, still laughing, his gaze on the lonely tree that has wandered, it seems, into the borderland from the orchard. A movement at the bole catches his eye. An apparition has appeared in the shadows of branches. Realization spreads, a silent communiqué traced in the change of expression that passes from brother to brother. Mirror faces totter between wonder and woe. Is this something grand or ferocious, this giant with pumpkin head?

Jason. Damon. The voice of their mother sounds somewhere not far. The pull of it shows in the tightening of muscles, in eyes that too determinedly fix upon what they still seek. In the climax of tension, the giant moves first, lowering the ripe pumpkin from in front of his human face. The twins break into laughter. Pumpkin Man smiles.

"Thank God." Mother's voice sounds through the final row. Mother herself appears and fills the shot, caught between anger and relief. She settles for a time on the latter, falling to her knees, gathering in her sons, still elusive in the swollen jackets—oblivious to little fingers stabbing backward at the tree where Pumpkin Man has dissolved.

⁂

The service alley was a canyon breathing a stony dampness in the gathering chill and wet of late afternoon. Hanae stood at the mouth of the passage, conscious of Mr. Romero behind her, sitting disapproving in the car. The driver had had to circle the block so many times she'd lost count, in order to find a parking place this close to the opening of the alley. And still, he had not been comfortable with letting her get out alone. At any moment, she feared, he might defy her instructions and join her.

Not much time, then. She moved forward with Taiko, a halfhearted drizzle misting against her skin, as if the upward thrusting of the surrounding buildings increased the condensation from the air. She was aware of being enclosed, of the traffic noises muffled. And the sky too seemed close, like the lid of a box. A vibration of light like cold metal.

She had almost not come after her first experience, realizing that by coming she was involving Willie, taking shameless advantage of her friend's offer of help. Ask me *anything,* Willie had said. And she had used those good intentions.

I have become a woman of secrets. Was that not what she had said of herself last year as she walked down the path of destruction? Once again she was keeping secrets from her husband, and worse, she had drawn Willie into her deception. Brick by brick she was adding to the wall that stood between her and her husband. The madness was that she somehow believed that only in the building of it could she one day tear it down. Surely the belief was irrational.

And yet she could not stop. Because to stop meant to sit still. To do nothing. *To die.* The progression of thought was a revelation. The decision to take action in the only way that had been open to her was part of the reason she had survived last year.

And she was fighting still, seeking justification for the things she had done to remain alive for a time long enough for Jimmy to find her, but so far away from healing or any kind of acceptance. She felt guilty and defiled, though there existed at the core of her this imperative to act, to reclaim herself. Not as she was. That Hanae *had* died. To truly survive she must change.

The thought was a balm. Perhaps she was not so far from the Buddha as she feared. The concept of change was vital. She must accept what had altered inside her. Accept this path.

Unconsciously, she'd been holding her breath. She let it out now, directing Taiko forward, across the wet and cracked pavement that covered the lot. She was allowing the scent, the odor of rotting food that marked the location of the Dumpster, to draw her.

The smell became intense, threatening prematurely to bring on the nausea she'd experienced at that other scene of death. She stopped and steadied her breathing, acknowledging the wave of sickness, acknowledging her fears. She had to accept these things, then let them go. As she must also let go of her doubt. If it were foolish for her to be here, then she would be a fool. A blind woman with no expertise in these matters, except the folly of having once allowed herself to be taken in by a killer. Did that not make of her an expert? That she had touched his dark heart and been touched in return? She had been so close to that one particular evil, had known its flavor. Could a taste of this one not provide some useful insight? Perhaps. And perhaps she was nothing more than a very imprudent woman. Risking everything.

She was here now. Too late to take it back.

She stood unprotected in the rain. Reached out to touch the Dumpster, the stinking hulk that had once held the body of Leslie Siebrig. Reached for that sucking darkness that did not come. There was only the smell of rot, overwhelming. And above it, like an overripe sweetness, like a flower that blossomed in dung, was the sense-image of her remembered vision. The melon in the garden sliced in twain. The nubby rind, the pattern of seed and pulp, a strange convolution beneath her searching fingers.

The razor edge flick. Wetness in her palm. Lips sucking. In her mouth, the taste of blood.

In the waning light, Sakura watched from across the side street. The dark car was parked alongside the curb, in what could loosely be called a loading zone in front of the Water Street apartments. The driver clutched the wheel, staring off into the cold dusk. For another moment he studied Romero, observing with detective eyes, much as he might examine the scene of a crime; then he walked up to the window and tapped on the glass. Romero flinched at the sound and whirled in his seat. His face contracted in fear. Then a slow smile of recognition

"Hello, Mr. Romero. I'm sorry I startled you." He spoke as the driver rolled down his window.

"No . . . no, I was . . ." He stopped, seeming to have misplaced the words that would finish his sentence.

"Did you just drop off Hanae?"

At the mention of her name, Romero again examined the street though his windshield, then nodded. "Yes, Mrs. Sakura had some errands." His words hanging in the air with his breath.

"Is there a problem, Mr. Romero? Is Hanae—"

His hand quickly rose to fend off the question. "Everything is fine, Lieutenant. Really."

Their eyes met for a moment. Then Romero turned, seeming to slump fractionally into the upholstery. "I've been driving Mrs. Sakura almost from the day she came to New York, Lieutenant. It has been my pleasure. She is a remarkable woman."

He reached and opened the door so that Romero could exit.

In the growing twilight, the two men stood facing each other. It was several minutes before he could get the driver to break his silence, to betray what he believed to be an unspoken oath of loyalty to his wife.

There was nowhere his brain directed him. He had shifted to automatic pilot and ended up inside his office, with the blinds closed. Steam from brewing tea hovered like a cloud inside the dark, outside an arc of blue fluorescence. Sakura reached for the jade piece and rubbed his fingers across its cool surface. That Hanae could do this, that she could put herself at risk. That she could secretly defy him. All of it was beyond belief.

Mr. Romero had not been forthcoming, but in the end he had revealed her transgressions. Her pilgrimage to the scenes of the crimes. For a moment he had considered confronting her, but the very intensity of his anger held him back. Now his fear seemed to demand it.

He breathed in the sweet steam, closed his eyes, and leaned back against the padded headrest. Why was this happening? Had not their separation stood for anything? Or had the evil that had reached out and taken Hanae a year ago scarred their marriage beyond healing?

"They said you'd come back." Her voice, like the steam, settled softly inside the dark.

He opened his eyes and found Faith Baldwin standing at his door, her body backlit, so that her suit was nothing more than a nondescript blankness, the white collar of her blouse a flattened ghost around her face.

He straightened in his chair, watching her walk inside his office, set her briefcase down before she closed the door.

"Tired?" she asked, still standing.

"Yes." His admission surprised him. "What are you doing here?"

"Just nosing around a bit."

He shook his head. "Status quo . . . but you know with serials that can change in a moment."

"I wasn't necessarily referring to the investigation." She moved closer to his desk, picked up the jade piece.

His eyes followed her hand. Watched her long fingers toy with the green talisman. Her eyes lifted, caught his. "Want to talk?"

He reached and took the jade. "It's not anything that talk can help." It was an empty statement, and he knew it.

"Anything else I might do to help?"

This time he braved her gaze.

"Anything at all?" Her voice was low, as she moved around the edge of the desk. "Anything . . ." she whispered, slowly bending over him, swirling his chair around.

"Faith . . ." His voice straining.

"Long overdue, James Sakura." She separated his legs with her knee, bracing herself against the edge of the chair as her mouth came down and closed over his.

He reached to push her away. Then there was no saving himself, as his hands tightened on her arms, pressing her deeper into him, devouring the kiss she offered.

⚜

New toy. He lifted the camcorder, testing the infrared feature in the near-complete darkness of the basement. The newly purchased machine was a Left-brain embellishment, but not without its uses. The Sony, with its heightened sensitivity to electromagnetic radiation, was the favorite of ghostbusters everywhere.

He stopped recording. Set the machine onto its tripod near the table.

New toy. He felt his erection grow stronger, giddy now with the thought of what this gift offering implied. Nearly two weeks since the last kill. Twelve days of useless excuses. Almost over now.

He reveled in his nakedness. Left-brain did not allow fiber in this part of the basement. His trophies burned like ice inside his skin. His hand moved from his swelling penis to touch the latest of his mementos, the silver ring that pierced his nipple. The tape in his head was playing now. Blank eyes. Fish-mouths gasping. Five now since this new phase had started.

His left hand found his cock. Stroking. Faster and faster. The eater of souls would not much longer be denied.

New toy. Fresh meat.

CHAPTER

13

The early morning darkness had a surreal edge, as if hyping the real thing. A hush surrounded, also a bit unreal—a preternatural expectancy that gave no yield to the creeping daylight, or the traffic noises building beyond the muffle of trees. Right-brain was hungry, so Left-brain lurked. In the shadows. In the trees, in this less familiar area of the park. Wolf. Hunter. Procurer of flesh. His breathing became conscious as he stepped onto the track. His pulse beat measuring risk.

A woman, a jogger, appeared as if cued. The casting, like the stage direction, apparently perfect. She moved toward him in the wide curve ahead, fit and endomorphic, her wide thighs filling the legs of her shorts. For Right-brain, a movable feast.

He watched her with polite eyes as she neared. Runners' etiquette, letting a smile build, a short nod as she passed. Seconds counted in the beat of blood. Five before he turned, hand reaching into his pocket for the drug-soaked pad in the zip-top bag.

At the last moment, hearing his steps, she looked back. But he was already lunging, as realization scored in her eyes. He had her, and held her, locked across his chest, the pad going quickly over her mouth and nostrils.

She was strong, but he had the advantage. And her breath indrawn to mount a scream only increased the effectiveness of the drug. She slumped against him. Not out, but nearly. He let her slip to the ground. He looked around, but the hush appeared undisturbed by the sudden drama, and his own pulse had not increased beyond its slight elevation from the norm. He walked back on the path to retrieve the plastic bag and, replacing the pad, returned it to his pocket.

He went back to where the woman lay moaning, her limbs moving a little now. It was the way he needed her, if this was going to work. He crouched down, and with his arm around her, he hoisted her up. She slouched against him, nearly dead weight, her feet skipping and dragging as he walked her in the direction of the street, the bubble of silence breaking at last with a question.

Insistent. From behind. As surprising as an arrow arcing over the grass. "Sir . . . sir . . . what's the matter with her?"

🌢

The day had started slowly, then sped by in a blur of paperwork. Now it was late, and Sakura was dealing with the uneasy feeling that he had missed the real action. He pushed away files and turned off his desk lamp. With no witnesses or physical evidence, it was all the killer's game at this stage. Somehow, someway, the investigation had to become less reactive and seize some measure of control. Challenge the killer. Force him off stride. Perhaps he'd make a mistake.

"Jimmy . . ." Michael's voice penetrated his thoughts.

"What's up?"

Darius walked over and took a chair. "The taxi drivers were a bust." He frowned. "None of them remembers picking up any of the victims around the clubs." His glance drifted to the stack of files on the desk. "You find anything new on that deejay?"

"Lancaster's got a certain reputation, but no criminal record. And his background is not what you'd think. His father's a professor at UVA."

"He's hiding something."

"Hell, Michael"—he had to smile—"everybody's hiding something."

Darius nodded, tilting back in the chair, so far that the front legs lifted. It was a thing he did, this balancing act when something was on his mind.

"I noticed you came back last night," Darius finally spoke. "You were here pretty late."

"And I'll be here late a lot of nights till we solve this thing."

"Your blinds were closed."

"That didn't stop you just now."

"It didn't stop the assistant DA, either."

"You know Faith." He kept his voice even.

Michael appeared close to making some crack, but didn't. The chair legs came down, falling neatly into impressions carved in the carpet. "See you tomorrow," he said.

He watched Darius leave and reached in the drawer for his Walkman. He wanted a few minutes behind a numbing wall of sound. The first cut of *Whitesnake* started, but his thoughts didn't stop. He was remembering that Michael was Michael, and that his friend had been around six years ago. He was thinking what a fool he'd been to let himself believe that what had been going on with Faith back then could have slipped by completely unnoticed.

He had avoided his wife, having returned home very late last night, leaving before she had awakened this morning. But he could not hide forever.

He found her in the kitchen. Took her into his arms. "Is it what I think?"

Hanae nodded against his shoulder. "Lemongrass soup."

He released her, reaching behind, ladling some of the clear broth, tasting. "Like medicine. Curing whatever ails."

She shut off the burner, placing a lid on the pot. "And what ails my husband?"

He listened to his own breath, counting seconds in the hanging silence. "I have spoken to Mr. Romero."

For just a moment she seemed to freeze, a paper doll pasted in place. Then she moved, making busy, reaching for bowls and spoons. "And what did Mr. Romero have to say, Husband?"

"That my wife asked him to take her back to the neighborhood where the body was found in the trunk of the car. To take her to the bin behind the restaurant where the body of another young woman was discovered."

"I believe you refer to such places as 'scenes of the crime,' Husband."

He laughed. A dry sound. "Yes."

"I had hoped I would have been able to speak to you of this in my own time."

"Mr. Romero did not readily volunteer the information, Hanae. Do not hold him at fault."

"I do not, Husband."

"I will not ask you why you went. Rather I will ask what you discovered."

She stopped moving then and turned, her eyes finding his. "Nothing," she spoke softly. Then she dropped her head. "No, that is not correct." She looked up again. "*Less* than nothing. A darkness greater than all the dark I have ever felt. An emptiness beyond empty."

Most of the time he avoided analyzing it. But from the first body that had become the province upon which to do his duty, to every scene of death he'd witnessed since, he'd felt it. And now he was experiencing it again, its filthy lust, raping him like a whore, as bodies uncoiled from Visqueen like mummies. Laid out, spoiled and drained on morgue slabs, on the sterile cold of Linsky's cutting tables. His wife had captured the temper if not the complete truth of all serial murder. *Evil.* The absoluteness of evil.

"You are angry with me." It was not a question.

"You have felt it. You know what it is. Can you not now understand why you must not become a part of this? A part of anything I do? Have you not learned . . ." His words trailed off.

"I learned much in that cabin, Husband. Learned that I cannot shut myself away from what you do. You *are* what you do."

"No!" He shouted the word, a bitterness in the benign kitchen. "No, you cannot help!" He reached out, bringing her against him. His heart racing, his breath tangled inside his lungs. He held her face between his palms, his mouth seeking her mouth, his kiss wild and hungry, trying to wipe away all the anger and fear he felt growing inside him, all the guilt from that other kiss.

🌲

Left-brain watched the tape, observing the bubble-bubble breath of the woman beneath the veil of plastic sheeting. Transfixed as the flesh from the park pelvic-thrusted up and up and up, heels digging in to extract the final molecules of trapped oxygen. Seminal fluid oozed from his erection, and he forced himself to save his pleasure for the real thing that lay on the table.

Then a sudden flicker across the screen. A liquid dimming, followed by an intense brightening within the denser atmosphere of backlighting. Right-brain jerked, springing forward, closing in on the screen, mesmerized by the elongating globule of light, beginning to pulsate like a paramecium over the entire length of inert body.

Fuck, and double fuck. His fingers struggling to make contact with the bloated luminescence floating over the outline of flesh inside the screen. He turned, crouched like a feral beast. *Soul . . .* He dragged out the word, the hiss of a snake.

A derisive laugh in the hollow of his head. *An anomaly in the tape,* Left-brain spoke.

His tongue touched the screen. Licked the light. *Let me believe it,* he breathed. *Don't take it away from me.*

You're a smart boy. Left-brain was speaking again. *Meat is meat. That's the alpha and omega of it.*

Please . . . he cried out, half in pain, half in anger. *What of the mechanism of animation?* He grappled at his bare chest. *It's more than blood in the heart.*

Left-brain tapped the side of his head. *Electrical energy. The brain is soul.*

It's more than thought . . . Right-brain insisted, keening, drawing tight into himself, breathing in and out, a small boy who'd run a long race and almost won. Then he smiled, his face for an instant wholesome. *I like to imagine it's another kind of energy moving the meat. Something secret.*

He threw back his head and howled. *Oh yes, yes . . .* His erection rose to slap the slick of his belly as he swayed in his squat. *Hell it is—the reason for soul. The fall into the black.* Another smile, again nearly charming. *The concept of a soul going to Hell. Now that's the ticket. A real thought to chew on.*

CHAPTER

14

Harlan Kaminsky stood alone on the cobblestone street, stealing chunks of beauty—blessed minutes in the predawn before the rest of the crew came on, and the meat trucks rumbled in to gather with their loads. It was still dark. Velvety shadows ran like water in the alleys. But soon the dawn would come and the sky, backlit by the creeping sun, would glow a rich blue-purple, shading through violet to a whitened rose as it settled between the hulks of neighboring buildings. He would miss this. No matter how much more modern and finer the new plant in Hunts Point, it was still an exile from what had been. Meatpacking plants had dotted the neighborhood since the mid-1800s, over a hundred of them functioning here in the century just past, supplying the city's restaurants. Now, since the invasion of the developers, how many were left? Maybe a doomed couple dozen.

He sighed. He should be glad about the new plant. He lived in the Bronx. A shorter commute meant a few extra minutes in bed.

He closed his eyes to the dark sky, trying to catch the river smell through the closer scent of blood. He imagined that the blood scent would long remain after the last plants had gone, collected in the skin of buildings, in the creases between the cobblestones. There were organizations which had been set up to preserve the integrity of the original neighborhood, though it must be only a matter of time before many of the warehouses were torn down and the old and inconvenient cobblestones paved over. And with a punch of anger that made him smile, he knew that he hoped for the revenge of blood, its attar weeping for another hundred years through the inevitable cracks in the asphalt.

He turned and walked toward the building. He wanted to get in early and check the temperature in the locker. The compressor had been a bit touchy lately. But it had seemed smart to try and hold out, so close to the move to the new facility. Still, it would not do to let things degenerate into some major problem. Regulations were strict; he could quote them. As soon as it entered the premises, meat intended for cutting had to be placed in a refrigerated accommodation provided for its reception and storage, and there maintained at an internal temperature of not more than 7 degrees Centigrade for carcasses and 3 degrees for offal.

He reached for the keys in his jacket. Even this small motion could trigger his persistent bursitis, a malady picked up from his days on the line. The cold in the locker would not improve the pain. He was starting to think about retirement, considering it seriously for the first time.

He was standing at the metal door and had slipped the key into the large padlock before he noticed that anything was wrong. It fell with a huge dead clunk to the pavement.

He remained rooted where he was, looking down. Grasped, as if seeing it in magnification, where the metal had been cleanly cut. The seconds ticking while he mastered his shock and went into the building. Heading straight for the locker.

He saw her as soon as he entered, hanging with the other meat, in the cruel grip of the hook. Seconds more to register the glazed eyes staring. The naked body. A woman.

⚘

There was the smell of death in the air. The smell of human death below the oblique aroma of carcasses, naturally redolent in a meat processing plant. The human scent seemed blood-fresh and more elemental, wafting intermittently as the growling generator kicked on. Yet there was no scent at all. The smell existed only because he expected it. The body had been preserved at 7 degrees Centigrade.

Sakura stood in the steel locker as though in fog, though the moving refrigerated air was no more than a chill against the skin. And for a moment he was assailed with a memory of white wings stretched across tension wires. A child suspended in a church.

This, however, was no child he saw, but a woman who hung midway between sides of prime Black Angus. She had once been handsome, if not pretty, had been athletic before bad luck or bad timing had interceded. She was anchored from one of the metal hooks at the base of her skull, her head twisted at an unnatural angle, her body made heavier by death, giving in to the final forces of gravity, existential evidence of the brief and blunt brutality of life.

"He knew just where to put the hook." Linsky had come in, wearing tweed with leather patches, a jacket better suited to a college professor. He pointed up. "There's not much damage to the skull. My guess was she was hooked before being suspended."

"He knows human anatomy." He'd unconsciously made it a statement.

"I'd say so. Inserted that hook around the Arch of Atlas up into the occipital bone."

He ventured the obvious. "A doctor or med student?"

Linsky shrugged his shoulders; as always, he'd leave theorizing up to the police. "I've done all I can for now. . . . You're not ready for the gurney." It too came out as a statement.

He gazed up again, then at the ME. "No . . . not yet."

"Whenever you're ready." Linsky walked out the locker into a long exterior corridor where some techs were still dusting for prints.

Sakura returned his focus to the nude body. This was the most important time in a murder investigation. These first moments with the dead. A time to listen to the story each body told, to hear as much of its life's tale as possible, to try to understand its final chapter. And it was as close as any detective could hope to get to the killer. To peer through the window on the madness that drove him. To cross over into the house-of-horror landscape he'd fashioned. To breathe the air he breathed. To see what he saw, what he needed to see. To catch an echo of his beating heart. To take from the crime scene something of the killer himself. Something beyond fiber, or hair, or DNA. To take a piece of the killer's soul. His *tamashii*.

"He's changing." Willie walked in, Darius behind her.

"The Visqueen's gone. So is the dumping." He glanced back, nodded at Darius.

"He's exposing the body, staging something for us to look at. Or maybe something for himself. Posing."

"Remind you of anything?" Darius was gazing upward, taking in the corpse, which seemed to move fractionally as something heavy toppled over in an adjoining room.

Sakura nodded.

"But there's no reverence here." Willie reached up, stopping just short of where the staples made a steel track along the victim's chest. "He's still telling us that women are disposable. The others were garbage. This one's consumable."

"He's going through a lot of trouble. Dumping is a hell of a lot easier." Darius moved in for a closer look. "Taking greater risks, too. Breaking in through an exterior door facing Fourteenth. Came equipped with the right tools. See the size of that padlock?"

"Yes . . . a lot more is going on here." Now Willie did touch the body, at the edge of the face with the tip of a gloved finger. "This one's older, maybe in her thirties. Much heavier build."

"I don't guess we have an ID yet?" Darius examined the body, with its hard sheen, its empty glass eyes.

Sakura shook his head. "She was almost certainly murdered elsewhere. Personal artifacts kept or disposed of somewhere else. We're checking the area."

"I wonder . . ." Willie stopped. "He seemed unconcerned with decay before. But now he's taking his kill to a refrigerated locker. Beyond his need to display this victim as a carcass, preservation of the body might also hold some significance. . . . God, it's cold in here."

"I hadn't noticed."

Willie smiled. "You wouldn't, Sakura."

⁂

The eleventh-floor office, like most public spaces in the city, was temperature-controlled. And yet, glancing into space through his floor-to-ceiling window, Sakura could always get a sense of the atmosphere outside. At this moment, sitting with the husband of the killer's latest victim, he had an impression of wind that pressed against the glass. And a coldness that lurked in the late morning sunshine.

"Robin took several self-defense classes," the man seated in front of his desk was saying. "She was very aware. I can't understand how this could have happened to her."

"An attack can be very sudden, Mr. Olsen. Your wife may have had very little time to react. . . . I'm sorry."

"Sorry . . ." Lanny Olsen didn't finish whatever the word had been meant to start. He just sat there, staring ahead. The identification of his wife's body had been very difficult.

"I'll have one of my officers drive you home," Sakura said. "We can talk again soon. There are still a lot of questions. . . ."

"Ask them now." The eyes that turned on him were suddenly hard. "I want you to catch this bastard."

Sakura nodded. "You told me that your wife left very early yesterday to jog her usual route."

"That's right."

"So she had a routine?"

"Robin tried to make it to the park every morning. She was always very conscious of her weight. She said she didn't want to be one of these women who let themselves go after thirty." Olsen shook his head, blinked fresh tears, thinking perhaps that these good intentions had resulted in the ultimate futility.

"And it was your wife's habit to return home before she went to work?" Sakura prompted.

"We live pretty close to the park. She'd shower and dress. Eat something healthy for breakfast." The head shake again. "And coffee with real sugar. She couldn't give it up."

"And she didn't come home from the park yesterday?"

"We went over this."

"I want to make sure I have it right." Sakura thought he understood the man's sudden impatience. This part was difficult. It touched on what Olsen would perceive as his own culpability.

"I didn't know yesterday morning that she hadn't returned from the park," Olsen had started speaking. "I leave early sometimes myself, before Robin gets back. Yesterday just happened to be one of those days."

"When did you know that something was wrong?"

"When I came home. There were messages on the machine from her office. Her assistant had been trying to reach her all day."

"And there was no indication that she had ever returned home?"

"No. Her clothes for work were still on the bed. And the coffeepot was half-full. She liked to have a second cup before she even took her shower."

"What did you do?"

"Called everyone we knew. Then I called you."

By "you" Olsen meant the police. At approximately 7:15 last night, he had called Missing Persons.

"It's the same man, isn't it?" Olsen broke the latest silence.

"The same man?" Sakura remained noncommittal. They had taken care in the viewing room to reveal little more than Robin Olsen's face.

"You're handling the serial case," Olsen said. "It's all over television."

Not much point in hiding the truth—the media were making the same logical jump that Lanny Olsen had. "There are certain things that lead us to believe that your wife's killer is the same man who murdered these other women," he said.

"But why?" Olsen demanded. Now that his worst fear had been confirmed, he did not appear to want to believe it. "He's been killing those girls. Robin was thirty. . . . Didn't go to clubs."

"It would help if we understood exactly how your wife was targeted," Sakura said. "Maybe she was stalked because of her jogging routine, or maybe yesterday morning was simply the wrong time and place. But there could be something else about her life that caused her to cross paths with the killer. We're going to need your help re-creating the last few weeks of her life in detail, maybe even—"

"She should be here," Olsen's words cut in. From his expression, it was apparent that he was no longer listening. His focus had shifted to emotional self-preservation.

Denial. Sorrow. Guilt. In his short time with the man, Sakura had seen these stages of grief. He knew well enough that Olsen would experience them in varying degrees throughout the process of mourning and healing, if ever he did heal. At the moment, the man was beginning to feel the fourth classic emotion.

"Robin should be here," Olsen repeated. His voice was becoming more certain as the anger revealed itself. "Five women dead and this monster was still out there killing. Why was that, Lieutenant Sakura? You tell me. Five before Robin. If the police were doing everything possible . . . If you had been doing your job, my wife would still be alive."

🔱

"Are you relaxed, Victor?"

"Victor is relaxed, Dr. French."

"Does it help to keep your eyes closed?"

"Yes." A slightly giddy laugh.

"Why are you laughing, Victor?"

"My voice . . . *is* it my voice? I mean does it sound like my voice coming out of my mouth?"

"Yes, Victor, it's your voice I hear."

"It's not my voice *I* hear."

"Whose voice do you hear?"

"Not any voice in particular . . . just not my own."

"Not your own . . . ."

"Not the voice I know is my *real* voice."

"Are you inside your body, Victor?"

"Yes . . ." Another laugh. "But I don't feel like 'Victor.'"

"Who do you feel like?"

"A *what* more than a *who*. . . ."

"*What*, then, Victor?"

"A machine . . . my voice is an electronic recording."

"Does this make you feel uncomfortable?"

"Not at this moment."

She wrote in her notebook. *Persistent episodes of depersonalization. 300.6 The disorder presents exclusively. Marked and recurrent feelings of detachment. Sensory anesthesia. Displays of derealization. Some appropriate affective responses. Maintains intact reality.*

"Are you taking notes?"

"Yes."

"Writing that I'm crazy, Dr. French?"

"No, Victor, I am not."

"I *feel* crazy."

"What do you mean by *crazy*?"

"You know . . . feeling like my arms move by gears."

"But you know your arms don't move by gears, Victor, don't you?"
He nodded.

"A crazy person would *believe* his arms moved by gears."

He inhaled. Another laugh. "My lungs . . . well, not lungs really."

"But they *are* lungs, Victor. Made of cells, tissue. Filled with blood carrying oxygen."

"I know . . . but how do I say this. I'm somehow experiencing them as something else. Like metal parts. Made of plates that expand and contract when I breathe."

"Is that how you're experiencing your entire physical body now?"

"Yes. Like something mechanical."

"But you know what your body really is."

"Yes."

"And you know *where* your body is."

A noise. High-pitched. Like a child would make. "I'm not in a movie. Not this time."

"Where are you, Victor?"

"With you. In your office." He took another deep breath. Shook his head. "Smell . . . I can't smell. I know your smell, Dr. French, a nice smell. But right now I can't seem . . ." He opened his eyes finally. They were clear. Like after a cry. He stared at her. Then slowly a frown began to grow at the bridge of his nose. "Dr. French . . ."

"Yes, Victor."

"I don't feel relaxed anymore."

"Why? What's happening?"

"Happening . . . ?"

"What, Victor? Talk to me."

"*You*, Dr. French."

"What about me?"

"I can see your gears working."

⁂

The afternoon light annoyed David St Cyr, creating a frame of yellow seams across his drafting table. It was the principal problem with the apartment he'd leased. He closed the blinds and returned to the Redmond project. He had reworked the floor plan of the twins' room, dividing the space into two separate areas as Margot Redmond demanded. He hated the result. Architecturally it worked. Even aesthetically it was pleasing. But there was something wrong with the breaking up of the free-flowing space. Something inherently wrong with the division.

After another ten minutes, he dropped his pencil and moved away from the table. He drew up the blinds. The October afternoon was cooling down, and now the sharp sunlight from moments ago was beginning to drown in scudding clouds.

He looked out at the closer, denser panorama, the mid-range buildings surrounding his own, hard-carved against the spiking, less distinct skyline beyond. The city, crusted and weathered in spots, seemed tired even against the sleek alien bright of the new and nearly new. He brought a finger into his mouth, and then ran it across the wide flat of his window. How like the inside of a vagina the slick surface against his wet finger. Except that the smooth glass was cool.

He smiled at the smear of saliva. His comparison was a perfect display of his conflicted energies. Biomorphic forms could be overly sympathetic, if not infused with the cold steel of reason and utility. Yet pure functionality devoid of some canon of aesthetic seemed off-putting. How to render flesh to machine and still weep was the essential question.

Perhaps he was unsettled by Gehry's Bilbao in Spain because the architect *had* answered the question. He—St. Cyr—however, was no builder of museums, but of houses, and there seemed implied in Le Corbusier's intent that "a house be a machine for living" a conviction that *machine* was the spawn of some lesser creation, something to be endured because its time had come. He could only detest any view that seemingly "forgave" the machine for its existence, for denying its voice, made excuses for its self-revelatory beauty.

But this was mental masturbation and little to do with his displeasure over Margot Redmond's insistence that he alter the essential integrity of the house. He was to compartmentalize the twins' living space, separate, split . . . . He laughed. *Split*. Now that was an intriguing word, in more ways than one. *Split*. He'd like to split Margot Redmond, divide her pretty pink labia, plunge into the ripe red void of her sac. He was, after all, a sculptor of space. And as dear P.J. had decreed, you only do architecture when you can't help doing it.

🐦

Sakura stood looking down from his office window. With things so unresolved between Hanae and himself, he had made a promise to be home tonight at some more reasonable time. He remained unmoving, watching the shadows taking over the plaza, but it was the face of Lanny Olsen that he saw. And Lanny Olsen's voice that he heard.

If you had been doing your job, my wife would still be alive. The words had seemed to cycle endlessly at this afternoon's autopsy, impervious to any reasonable argument he could make in his defense. The abduction and murder of a young wife was not a rational event. His mind might tell him that he was doing everything possible to stop these deaths, but the rest of him remained unconvinced, on Lanny Olsen's side.

Such an emotional response was seldom useful. Empathy for the victim was a noble virtue, but justice did not require it. And emotion could be hindering baggage when it came to solving a crime.

He walked back to his desk, knowing that his promise to be home earlier would be broken, that there were many more hours here ahead of him this evening. There were no shortcuts in a serial investigation, and everything that was reasonable had to be attempted. It was nearly impossible in the mounting flow of data for one man to absorb every detail of a case. But that didn't mean he couldn't try.

He reread reports. Made pages of notes. When he got up to leave, it was late.

🐦

I move above earth, above the parquet floor down the great long hall. Gazing upon the walls, I slip into the painting as if into a pair of silk stockings. Settling myself naked upon the bed, milk-white upon my still whiter linen.

Over my shoulder, the aubergine shade of Lacassine, knowing eyes cast down, then darting as a sly smile opens her face, her teeth, fresh as hen eggs. Le Monsieur . . . Lacassine who speaks without speaking.

I touch the pale pink flower at my ear—the ear, sweet friend to his tongue. My nipples constrict with the heel-toe roll of his bare feet, the soft crush of his clothes against polished wood. For a moment I want to cover myself with the shawl at my side. No, not coyness, but something more surely honest. I hear his breathing, feel his knee come down into the soft of my bed. I close my eyes. His lips pull on the ribbon at my neck, drawing the bow undone, letting the pendant slip down between my breasts like a tear, to rest hidden in the curve of my hip.

Say it, say it, say it. "I want him . . ." Margot spoke to the dark, letting go at last the hot tears building behind her lids.

There was never a cure for it, not her life as Reese's wife, not her neatly packaged New York matron's life, not even her life as Mother, with the twins who resulted not from any sort of civilized planning but from the insanity they'd done in bed every night.

It had been her choice to leave. She laughed. There was never any choice. Stay with him or go crazy. Stay and live with being afraid all the time, and feeding off the fear like some starving mongrel. But the pregnancy had really done it, given her the courage to run away.

And run away she had. Running with her secret in her belly. Running like a thief in the night. Before she lost the will.

Talk. She turned in the big bed. Maybe that was the cure for the disease. *Talk.*

Inside the dark she was his. Lying on the remnant of carpet she was his. In the small empty closet she was his. And she was his by choice. That she wanted to be humiliated and beaten and brought to the edge, she no longer questioned. At the age of sixteen, she knew her pyramid was inverted when she preferred Ryan's slaps to his kisses. That pain, not pleasure, transported her to a space which exploded like nuclear fission inside her. That pain *was* her pleasure had been firmly established over the next two years in the small cigarette burns, in the bruises around her nipples, and now with him, in the collar that rubbed raw her thin neck. And *he* was the best pain-giver of all.

KitKat had no idea where he had learned the art of exquisite detail, or from whom he had acquired the finely articulated strokes that brought her to the threshold. But Shaman was the Master. Her Master. She crouched near the litter box that held her excrements, and waited.

She had no real sense of time. He had locked her in the closet. How many hours ago? She lifted the litter box. It felt slightly heavier, denser. That meant something. Time measured in the dark, not by a clock, but by the weight of piss and shit. The smell was a measure too. The air had thickened with ammonia. But she was content. Almost giddy, like she was high on something. A litter box, a roll of toilet paper, in the dark with her own waste. Not dripping or caked to the walls of her anus, but excreted in a small pile and a spread of wet. Safe-kept in a receptacle, so that what came out of her was still part of her.

She reached in now, her hand pawing the soiled grit. She purred. She was his precious pretty kitty. She was his pussycat. His *pussy*. She laughed at the double meaning. Somewhere she had learned what such phrases were called, but that bit of literary minutia was long forgotten, along with her knowledge of similes, and metaphors, and iambic pentameter. She had been brighter than most in that high school she had attended a thousand years ago. *A thousand years ago?* That was another figure of speech, wasn't it? *Hyperbole?* Where did she pull that from?

A key clicking in the lock. A door opening and shutting. *Purr. Purr.* Her throat rumbled in anticipation. She crouched on all fours, her fingernails plucking at the loose yarns of the carpet remnant. *Daddy Cat is home.*

When the door opened, she put one of her paws in front of her eyes, a reflex that blocked the fresh hard light coming into the closet from the strobe. "*Meow, meow,*" she mewed, arching her elegant back. The shiny chain attached to her collar jangled.

He was nude. And her tongue stroked his toes. *Sandpaper licks,* he called them. Then his hand was yanking her chain, pulling her up to her feet .

"Lick me," he hissed. And her tongue went over his face. "Good pussy." He smiled, moaning with each pink lick. Then his hand released her. The chain tumbling to the rug like a heavy snake. "You belong to me," his voice harder now. "Every part of you. Your eyes. Your teeth. Your legs and arms. Your breasts . . ." Then Randy "Daddy Cat" Lancaster reached and twisted both nipples between his silver-ringed fingers. "All parts are mine. Together. And . . . one . . . by . . . one."

CHAPTER

15

Zoe Kahn was enjoying the jog, not so much for the physical activity as for the sweet way her new shorts and T-shirt clung to her curves. Normally her workouts took place in a health club, where floor-to-ceiling mirrors could confirm that the effort to keep her natural voluptuousness within fashionable limits was worth it. Out here in the real world she simply felt fit and alive—a young and healthy female animal, not some anorexic's idea of a goddess.

She had never been in the park before sunrise, and was surprised by a looming stillness that seemed to heal with her passage, as if her presence and the activity she supported was an irritant to be isolated and diminished. She felt an irrational urge to shout, to poke a hole much larger in all this damn tranquillity.

She was coming to the curve now, and she tossed her ponytailed hair, conscious of her form, the controlled jiggle of her hips and breasts as the dark-clothed man sprang from the bushes to grab her. In an instant he was holding her with an arm across her chest. The other hand over her mouth.

She bit hard at the skin of his palm.

"Shit, Zoe!" He was jerking away from her, inspecting his wounded hand. ". . . What's so fucking funny?" He had turned on the laughing cameraman.

"Don't give up your day job, Allen," Zoe was saying. "You're a lousy serial killer. You've got to grab me like you mean it."

"I'm your producer, Zoe, not your stuntman. You drag us out here in the middle of the night—"

"The sun's practically up," she said, "and we need a perfect take. There won't be time for a full edit. I want this re-creation for today's show. Isn't that what you want too, for the show to be out in the front of the pack?"

"Yeah, yeah . . . So let's do it and get to the studio."

"Great. And this time keep your hand tight and flat over my mouth."

"Don't worry."

"And the left arm should be in a choke hold—you're supposed to be controlling me, not feeling me up."

"I've got the picture, Zoe."

She turned to the cameraman. "How's it looking in the monitor, Gabe?"

"Lookin' good, Zoe."

"Then it's back to the bushes, Allen." She flashed him her sweetest smile.

This time his heart seemed to be in it, and she admitted when it was over that he'd done a stellar job. A little too stellar, judging by the way he'd enjoyed it. Then Gabe ran the take for her right there on the monitor, and they all agreed that it looked damn scary.

A few minutes to touch up her makeup while Gabe reset the lights, then she walked over to take her mark near the tree they'd selected for the shot. She composed her face into suitable lines.

"With the murder of his sixth victim five days ago," she spoke for the camera, "this New Jack has stepped out of the shadow world of raves and dance clubs and into the world of everyday . . . and anyone.

"Robin Olsen was a young woman on the way up, an executive buyer with one of the country's largest retail chains, when she was taken by the killer in this park. What you have just witnessed was our own re-creation of what we believe happened to Robin Olsen on Thursday morning."

She paused for a breath, giving the camera a moment to register sincere concern and outrage.

"The deaths of the first five victims, young single women picked up at parties and clubs, were certainly tragic. But the police have tacitly let us

believe that the rest of us were safe from this twenty-first-century Ripper. Robin must have certainly believed it as she went about the simple
routine of her life. Her death last Thursday has spoken to the women of
this city. We are none of us safe. Information is our first line of defense.
And this reporter must ask: What else are the police not telling us?"

Hanae sat at the side of her bed. Assessing the light that filtered in
through the window, its subtle presence like vapor against her skin.
Assessing that inner light that formed itself in the space behind her
eyes. That light too had the quality of mist today, both the inner and
outer worlds in an agreement of grayness.

She stood and walked to the closet, to the place where her clothes
hung. In Japan, one must wear black to a funeral. Here one had a choice.
She took out three dresses and laid them on the bed, where even the
morning's weak light could excite their color. She ran her hand over the
cloth of each, letting the fabric ripple, feeling the difference in vibration
against her fingertips. It pleased her, this ability to discern color. Certainly it had always surprised everyone.

Still, it was not sight. Her fingers could sense color's subtle frequen-
cies; her eyes could not. Of black, white, and gray she had perhaps
the merest inkling of what the sighted called *color*. For these were the
vibrations of her inner place of light, that mental screen on which she
charted her world.

She selected a dress as gray as the day and returned the others to the
closet. The gray dress was perfect, since it was her wish to blend with
the atmosphere, to be as unnoticeable as possible on this mission she
had set for herself. She would not bring Taiko. She would rely on her
white cane. And she would call another service for a driver. She did not
care to make things any more uncomfortable for Mr. Romero. It would
not be right to place him in worse favor with her husband.

Taiko whined beside her, pushing his muzzle into her hand. "I am
sorry," she said, "but I must do this on my own. No accomplices." She
allowed herself a smile at the use of one of Jimmy's words, though its flavor was bitter.

She had no need to close her eyes to shut out the world—the world of her birth had in large measure closed itself to her. It was true that many things had changed, but so little seemed possible even now for a sightless woman in Japan. She still remembered keenly her grandmother's stories of her sister Ayano. Ayano, who had become blind when she was but a child, and so must be apprenticed to an *ogamisama* in order to be made into a *person*.

There had been no other path to independence for a blind village girl but to become an *ogamisama*, one of the sightless mediums trained to call upon the spirits of the dead. As Grandmother told it, there was much common prejudice in those days against the disabled, especially the blind, who were thought to be a particular burden. And sightlessness must be no excuse for indolence.

Mama-san had not approved of Grandmother's stories. Hanae was not Ayano, she said. There were special schools now. This was Kyoto, not some village. And Papa-san was a respected official.

She felt a smile forming, remembering the staunch protectiveness of her mother's words. And in truth she had been happy enough in her sightless world. And indulged. Hanae Miyairi might have been as indolent a maiden as she wished. But she had never wished it. She had loved school, and when her formal education had ended, she had delighted in her finches, and her sculpture, and her journeys into foreign languages. Perhaps she had sometimes, when listening to the adventures of her cousins Sei and Nori, mourned her social isolation. But meeting Jimmy that fateful day in the park in Kyoto, then returning with him to live in New York, had ended much of that.

Yet it had not changed everything. She remained who and what she was. And despite Mama-san's denials, something of Ayano's spirit certainly possessed her. How else to explain her abilities? With no training or initiation, she had yet been the one to whom her family turned for the reading of dreams and the telling intuition—what her ancestress would call *walking the lands of the dead*. This was her gift. The gift she must offer to Jimmy, whether he would have it or not.

With the thought came pain, physical and surprising . . . and familiar. So slowly had it come, this darkest and quietest of serpents, softly coiling, perceptible only in its shadow. That dimming of her inner light, and the headache gathering, merciless now, behind her eyes. She had once ignored its warning, but no more.

She sat back down on the bed, massaging the skin at her temples. Fear had uncoiled itself from her mind to touch her heart. But there was also a certain relief. For despite all her justifications, she had not truly understood the reason for her recklessness.

She understood it now, appreciating at last that there existed some special danger in this new investigation. A threat that was close. However much she might wish to, she could not doubt it. For this reason, if no other, she must remain stubbornly willing to risk the peace of her home. To risk Jimmy's love.

She sighed. She could not tell her husband of this threat, at least not until she had more fully discerned its nature, for the danger and the ugliness of his work were the very things from which he wished above all to protect her. How had they come to this, that their paths had so diverged? Certainly the seeds of this dark flower had existed from the moment of their meeting. Neither had seen. Both of them blind in this.

To live properly was to live in change. To live as husband and wife was to accept the other as he or she existed moment to moment. Present. Open. Without expectation. She must accept that her actions would cause her husband pain. She could not deny who she was. Or who she might become.

"Some kind of sports glasses," the man was saying, "with colored lenses . . . yellow, I think. And a knitted cap, pulled down. . . . And a dark jogging suit. Did I say that?"

"Yes, Mr. Grantley, you did," Sakura said to the man who sat in front of his desk. A walk-in, he seemed convincing. Not like other would-be witnesses who had not made it through screening. Mr. Marshall Grantley had been deemed worthy of the audience he had insisted on with Lieutenant Sakura. The word for the man was *tweedy,* with his British newsboy cap and Norfolk jacket. There was no pipe protruding from beneath the bushy gray mustache, but Sakura persisted in seeing one.

Just as he could not help imagining leather patches at the elbows of the
retired insurance man's sleeves.

"I should have tried to stop him, I realize that now." The man
sounded genuinely miserable. "But it happened more quickly than it
sounds. And at the time—"

"What did he say to you exactly?" Sakura cut through the self-
recrimination. They had already been over it once, how walking his
dog in the early hours of Thursday morning, Grantley had come upon
the couple.

"I asked him what was wrong with her." Grantley hadn't answered his
question. "She looked terrible, poor woman. And to think I might have
saved her." He looked directly at Sakura. "Do you think I might have
saved her, Lieutenant? He didn't seem to have a gun, or any kind of
weapon. Gordon didn't even growl."

Sakura didn't lie. "It's possible you could have helped her. But it's
equally possible that you might have become a victim yourself."

"Yes, this man is a monster. And poor Gordon is not much protection.
He's a schnauzer, you know, and nearly ten years old. Older than I, in
dog years." He tried a smile.

"You were going to tell me what the man said to you."

"Oh, yes." Grantley's hand moved to fidget with his tie, a neat bow
that was not a clip-on. "He explained to me in a rather slow, well-
spoken voice that his wife was hypoglycemic. He said that this had happened to her more than once, because she refused to follow her doctor's
instructions on proper eating."

"And he was believable?"

Grantley sighed deeply. "He was very friendly. Didn't appear nervous
at all. I think that's what convinced me that nothing really was wrong.
And then the woman . . ." He stopped.

"What about the woman?" Sakura was intent on what appeared
might be new information.

"She came around a little," Grantley said. "Her head moved, lolled
around a bit on her shoulders. I remember I was glad that she appeared
to be better."

"And the man? What did he do?"

"He shifted her on his shoulder." Grantley was literal. "It had to be uncomfortable, supporting her like that. She was a fairly large woman."

"But how did he react . . . when she started to move?"

"He spoke to her. 'It's okay, Evelyn,' he said. 'You've done it again. But I've got you, and the car's not parked far.'" Grantley shook his head. "He sounded so kind, but chiding her a bit, as one does with a wife."

"But you believe now that this woman was the latest victim?"

"I'm sure she's the woman I saw on the news. I got a very good look at her."

"And the man?"

"As I explained, he was wearing the glasses and cap. And it was still quite dark under the trees."

"But you got a good look at the woman."

Grantley smiled at this attempt to catch him out. "I was concentrating very hard on her face, Lieutenant, trying to determine how ill she was. I wasn't so concerned with the man. Of course, I know now that I should have been. But truly—stupidly, as it turns out—I never got a real sense of danger. I told you, it happened so quickly."

Sakura tried again. "I understand that his hair and eyes were covered, but you must have gotten some impression of body type."

"Above-average height. And thin, I think. Those jogging suits are bulky, but it was my impression he was thin. I remember being somewhat surprised that he was not struggling even more with her weight. As I said, she was not a small woman."

"I'd like to show you some photographs and have you ID her again. It's a bit different than seeing a picture on television."

Grantley nodded. "And the van," he said. "It wasn't a new one, but I might be able to tell the make if I could look at some pictures."

"The van?"

"Oh, yes. Didn't I mention it? The man insisted, rather strongly, that he could get his wife to their car without my help. And Gordon *would* decide at just that moment that it was time to do his business. But after I'd done the scoop, I went off after them, just to make sure that he'd gotten her in all right. I made it to the street as a van was pulling away. So it wasn't a car like he said."

"Are you sure it was him?"

"There weren't any other vehicles leaving the area, and I think I got a glimpse of him in the driver's seat. There wasn't much of anyone else around. It was still very early. The sun wasn't all the way up."

"License plate?" Sakura didn't breathe.

"Definitely New York," Grantley said. "I didn't get any numbers."

✤

Hanae paused for a moment in the wide arch of the threshold, gathering together an impression of the room that opened out in front of her. The motion of the air, the quality of sound, told her it was spacious, longer than it was wide. Most vivid was the rich smell of flowers, in which she could detect the separate note of chrysanthemums. Their earthy scent, dense and astringent, had the power to bridge both culture and religion, transporting her to other rooms where family and friends had assembled to honor and mourn the dead.

Despite this being a weekday, and early afternoon, there was a large, mixed crowd in the viewing room. She listened to the muted buzz of voices. Old. Young. Male. Female. Sad. Curious. She could sense eyes watching as she moved forward, these strangers wondering who was this blind Asian woman—speculating on what possible connection she might have to the deceased. Her connection was unfortunate but direct. Robin Olsen, a native of the city, had been the latest of the victims in her husband's serial case. She had heard on the news yesterday that these services would be held, and had spent most of the afternoon determining the location.

She moved slowly forward now, up a side aisle, her cane making quiet little thuds against the carpet. She was hoping to avoid any encounter, hoping that her presence here would in no way be challenged. There was a certain anonymity to be gained in the very size of the gathering. And sometimes the very oddity of a situation, or even a perception of weakness, engendered its own protection.

This was fortunately such a time.

She let the smell of the blossoms draw her till the scent of them became nearly overwhelming and she knew she was standing near the bier. She felt her way forward, and knelt. No difference for Buddhist or

Christian. Her head bowed, hands clasped with palms together, she whispered a sincere prayer.

Then the moment she had come for. She reached out her hand. Touched wood. The coffin was closed, shut tight on the deepest silence. She waited for *something,* be it no more than the empty sucking darkness. But the dead did not speak today.

🌿

Early evening. Cocktail time. The bar small and intimate. From somewhere in the back, a quality sound system was doing justice to a song by Nina Simone.

Faith Baldwin had removed the jacket of her crisp business suit. The silk blouse she'd revealed was deeply veed and clinging. "I'm glad you finally agreed to this," she said. "You know you look awful."

"Thanks." Sakura leaned away from her in the booth. "I needed to hear that."

"I think you did." She sat back too, stirring her martini. "I take it that the investigation is not going well."

"Oh, I don't know. Seven new confessions since the meat locker."

"Those are always fun."

"It's what you expect."

She shifted forward again, her smooth voice keying nostalgic. "Remember that crazy who came in on the Van Dyck rape. He said that the moon was telling him to impregnate women. He was so damn convincing, I think I believed him for five minutes."

He watched her waiting for his reaction.

"That was almost a smile," she said to him. "Those were good times, Jimmy. You know you miss me. Admit it."

He ignored the comment, though in truth he was enjoying this, more than he'd enjoyed anything in a while. But there was a price for pleasure, and he didn't want to pay.

"What are you thinking?" she said.

"That I must have been nuts back at Quantico to believe I'd ever want a serial case. You kill yourself with legwork and wait for a lucky break. Because if the killer's smart and he's organized, he's leaving you with nothing."

"At least this one's getting fancy. He could make a mistake." She continued to study his face. "So, how's it going with McCauley?"

"The way you think."

She smiled. "You know that's mostly bluster. And besides, you've got more leeway than the last time."

"Do I?"

"Come on, James, it hasn't been a month since they put you on this thing. And besides," she added, smiling, "you're the hero of the Death Angel case."

She had reached across the table, but didn't take his hand. Just left hers there. Soft and perfectly manicured.

He picked up his drink. "Nobody's a hero when women are dying."

She straightened, the hand retreating, pushing back the chestnut strands that had fallen into her eyes. "I heard you might be looking at some deejay."

"Where did you hear that?"

"You can't keep secrets from the DA's office. How's he look?"

"Way too soon to say." He shrugged. "He turned up in a diary of one of the victims."

"You're downplaying, Jimmy. What's your instinct telling you?"

"That it's time to go home." He swallowed his scotch. Stood up.

"One more drink?" Her fingers had curled on his wrist. Her eyes, looking up, had softened at the edges. As close as Faith ever got to pleading.

He hated how much he liked seeing it. It hardly balanced the credit that he said no.

CHAPTER

16

Sakura left the dojo, walking around the corner to his car. He had decided that the few hours he devoted to these early morning sessions was time well spent, an expenditure of energy which enhanced rather than detracted from his efficiency at work.

Normally he felt refreshed after even the most strenuous kata practice, but this morning was different. He looked up to where the sky showed cloudless between buildings, a budding blue that seemed nevertheless dusty and dispirited. The city looked worn. As worn as he felt. Not an auspicious beginning for what was going to be another long day.

The traffic moved relatively quickly, and he reached headquarters in good time, driving down the ramp to the underground garage, catching an already crowded elevator to the eleventh floor. He walked down the hall to Major Case, stopping in the Operations Room for some early morning face time with the officers who were hanging around before the daily briefing.

In his office, he brewed tea, starting the water boiling for a pot of *gyokuro*. The word translated as *pearl dew* and had to do with the special practice of shading the leaves to increase chlorophyll and reduce the tannin. His grandmother had prized the tea for the delicacy of its flavor, and always made it properly, sitting ceremoniously on the tatami floor, her best lacquer tray set with cups, teapot, and cooler.

He could not observe such niceties, but he let the boiling water cool for a while before pouring it into the pot and sitting back to savor the aroma. The scent of *gyokuro* never failed in its power to send him back to his boyhood on Hokkaido. What he remembered today was a foggy morning when he was seven, not long after his father's visit had ended with the announcement that he had taken an American wife and would be staying in the United States to practice medicine.

The boy Akira had retreated on that morning of mist, as he often did then, to the beach near his grandfather's farm. He had sat on a rocky shelf, hugging his thin knees, staring out toward the veiled swell of ocean. His grandfather had found him there, and they had sat together in silence, listening as the waves broke themselves against the faithless rocks.

"My father is a bad son," he had spoken at last, turning to look at his grandfather, the words seeming to form themselves without will from his mouth.

"Isao believes that he is following his true path, and only he can be the true judge of that." His grandfather remained staring ahead. "I have taught him always to follow the Tao. So I say that Isao is a good son."

"But Grandmother believes that this second wife has deceived him." He was stubborn. "She says that my father has been fooled into abandoning his family."

Still his grandfather did not turn to him. "Ah," he spoke, "but perhaps Isao knows better than the grief of a mother's heart that to be deceived by this woman is his path."

He had said nothing to that, pretending to himself that he did not understand.

He reached for the pot now, and poured a cup of tea. He held it in both hands, letting the thin porcelain conduct the heat to his fingers. Karma was cause and effect, but its lines of force were subtle. Did he not believe now, as Isao had then, that he walked his true path? What other life would he desire? And how else would this life have been possible without his father and his father's decisions? Yin and yang. Pleasure and pain. The resolution of opposites.

His grandfather's sorrow at Isao's departure had been as great as his own. But his wisdom had been greater. This was the way of things with youth and age. But as he must keep reminding himself, he was no longer that boy, Akira. He should pick up the phone and call his father.

"Sir . . ."

He looked up to see Walt Talbot standing in the doorway.

"I thought you'd want to see these." Talbot came forward with a stack of photographs in his hand. "The surveillance shots from the Olsen wake and funeral," he explained.

"Who'd we get?"

"Nobody." Talbot was clearly hesitating. ". . . Not anyone we believe is a suspect."

He picked up the photos from where the detective had placed them on his desk. "Anything else, Walt?"

"No, sir." Talbot seemed glad to escape.

The photo of interest was buried midway through an endless parade of strangers. Despite the fact that he'd guessed, it was still a jolt to see her. He made a conscious effort to focus away from his anger, to concentrate on how beautiful his wife looked in her gray dress and coat. How the camera had captured her confidence.

Like her tiny one-room apartment, Lisa Hennessy was a mess. Spiky hair flattened. Rings of makeup beneath her eyes. She greeted Talbot and Rozelli in pink fuzzy slippers, faded flannel pull-ons, and a sweatshirt. She'd gotten in from the airport after 3 A.M., she explained. Talbot's phone call earlier this morning had interrupted her few hours of sleep.

She locked the peeling door and rehooked two safety chains, despite the fact she'd just let in the police. Pushing rumpled blankets to the end of the sagging couch, she invited the men to sit, slouching herself in a wounded mismatched chair.

"We been trying to reach you since we found your number in Sarah Laraby's diary." Rozelli pulled out a notebook.

"I was back in Boise," Hennessy explained. "Lost my job and needed to hit the parents up for cash." A crooked smile softened the words, making her face momentarily appealing.

"But you heard Sarah's body had been found," Talbot spoke. They had gone over some of this on the phone.

Hennessy nodded, her body slightly rocking in the chair. "It was weird," she said, "seeing Selkie's . . . Sarah's picture all over the TV at home. I had to blab that I knew her back here in New York. The parents were totally freaking."

"But you had known she was missing," Talbot prompted.

"Sure." The head was still going, like one of those dashboard dolls. "I just thought she'd turn up all right."

"Why'd you think that?" Rozelli asked.

The head had stopped, as if concentration required it. "Selkie had a real life. A decent job and all." The mouth scrunched sideways. "She was just playing at being rad."

"Radical?" Talbot asked for confirmation.

"I don't mean politically," Hennessy explained. "Just, you know . . . wild."

"She take drugs?" Rozelli picked it up.

"Sure. But not the hard stuff. X . . . stuff like that sometimes."

"How else was she wild, Lisa?"

"The way she dressed and shit."

"And *shit?* You mean sex?"

"Selkie Girl was no virgin." It was meant to sound offhanded, but didn't.

Rozelli pressed. "We'll have to have a list of the guys she was sleeping with."

The open face shut down, head now moving sideways. "I'm no snitch," Hennessy complained.

"Know who Randy Lancaster is?" Talbot cut through her protest.

Rozelli shot him a look. It was clear from Hennessy's body language that the question had hit home. "Randy Lancaster?" he spoke again to prod her.

"You mean the Shaman." Her hostile expression caved, but the bedroom eyes had lost their sleepiness, the makeup rings making them look hard rather than vulnerable.

"The Shaman, yes," Rozelli repeated her words, "you know him?"

"We're not friends." The voice hard as the eyes now. "But I know who he is. A lot of kids do."

"And Sarah knew him?" Talbot said.

Hennessy turned to him, as if suddenly eager. "She was obsessed with him."

"And was Mr. Lancaster aware of that?"

"Aware? That was the way he liked it."

"What do you mean?"

"It's part of his trip. Like he's some kind of god up there. Some girls really buy into it." Hennessy's voice dripped scorn.

"We need to be clear with this, Lisa," Talbot said. "Are you saying Randy Lancaster was having sex with Sarah Laraby?"

"That's a nice way to put it," said Hennessy, hinting at knowledge that had just guaranteed her a formal statement downtown.

Evening, and her husband had come home full of anger. Hanae could feel it. Could smell it on his skin. Could hear it in the soft chomp of his stockinged feet. But in the same moment she could sense that he was seeking to conceal his anger. So that now, as Jimmy settled by her side on the tatami, she could count the breaths between his words. And his words were restrained, speaking of seeing her in a surveillance photo that had been taken at the wake of Robin Olsen. Like soft clinks of glass against glass came the sound of his words. And as he spoke, she heard in her mind the monk Saigyo's poem, reminding her of who and what she was, so that she might wisely answer him:

> loneliness without which
> living would be unpleasant

She was no monk, but a monk's life in many ways Hanae had lived. A simple monk's passage in some manner she had followed. Her solitary life, chiseled from blindness, had almost from the first been more than an accepted aloneness, more than an exceptional existence. Her sightlessness had become in time a welcomed bliss. A world filled with a blind woman's smells, a blind woman's touches. A blind woman's hearing and taste. A blind woman's instincts.

But when Jimmy had come, with the offer of his heart, leading her beyond the boundaries of her unconventional though well-ordered world, she had willingly crossed over. With her husband, in the new island city, she had stretched her separateness, not falling into an alien dark, but rather into another kind of light. Her path remaining ever constant, but greater its distance and wider its breadth.

Her husband speaking . . . "I am trying to understand what it is you want, Hanae."

She wished she did not have to speak, that he could but read her thoughts. "I want you to return what it was you gave when first we became husband and wife."

"And what is that, Wife? Please tell me. I do not want to deny you."

So difficult this was. She stood, moving to one of the cages that held her finches. "A childless wife has a most insecure position. . . . But then Mama gave birth. To a girl, small and soft, laid inside the new bed, covered with new quilts. And it was with great difficulty that Mama waited out the traditional year before her girl could come to her bed, sleep in her arms, warm and safe under the covers.

"I do not know when it was Mama discovered her baby girl was blind. I think she kept it secret from Papa for a while. But she would learn that it did not matter. Papa cared not that his girl was not perfect in the eyes of others. She was perfect in his eyes."

She turned and smiled. "Like all good Japanese mothers, Mama took her baby girl to a Shinto shrine after the first month, strapped and clinging like a kitten to her back. Then the girl learned to ride the rhythms of Mama-san's shoulders and spine. A mere bundle no longer. She was now in the world. Though it was to be a different world for her."

She walked away from the birds, sat back down beside him on the tatami rug. She found Taiko, placed his head in her lap. "He is a good dog."

"Yes, and better than mine is his understanding."

This time she laughed, tugging gently at the shepherd's ears, then again finding her husband's eyes. "The first color I ever felt was red. The bright red dresses Mama put me in. I jumped and tumbled in those red dresses, a leaf blown from a maple, feeling the impatient energy of the color against my skin. Mama laughed and told me to enjoy my red dresses, since according to custom, I would not wear red again until I was sixty. . . . Do you remember your grandmother wearing red, Jimmy?"

He shook his head.

"I was spoiled beyond my years, Husband. Because I was greatly loved. And because of the blindness. Though never did I feel shame or sorrow from my parents' hearts. Only joy."

"Hanae . . ." He moved. Touched the sleeve of her kimono. Brushed the tips of her fingers.

She pulled back. "Please, Husband, I must make you understand. You must not allow *your* heart to come between. It is not comfort I seek, but understanding."

"I am listening."

"My aunt was *ogamisama*. One who sees not with eyes, but with the constant stirrings of the heart. But the days of such women were past when I came as a blind child to my parents. And though to be blind is not what one would wish, I was never bitter. I was content in the making of my own way. My vision was both gift and burden."

She took his face into her hands. "I cannot be blind to who you are, to what you do. I cannot wish for the man you are not. That man would not be the James Sakura I love." She kissed his mouth softly. "And you must not wish for the woman I am not. Could you love such a woman, Husband?"

Her hands fell into her lap, her head bowing a little. "It is too late to deny the forces that made our two paths one. And I cannot break my bond, darken my vision, fail to seek what truth there may be." She looked up now. "I only wish to have returned what once you freely gave. Do not make of me a caged bird, my husband."

✦

Always, in his more reflective moods, he wondered if the smell had finally forced Mother, and Daddy reluctantly, to come to the decision that the boarding school run by the good brothers on the Gulf Coast was the solution. Of course, Mother had always been seeking solutions. If she had had keener instincts at seventeen, she would have arrived at the ultimate solution and undergone an abortion, flushing the festering mess out of her uterus once and for all. Even her Roman Catholicism would not have eclipsed her will if her mind had been more agile. But she was young then, and with the passing years she became more perceptive.

Of course, her instincts were less than wisdom, but something more akin to the quick lively fires he started at the age of seven between the pine and tupelo behind the big house. And she had been full of fire that year when she had Didon Petit pull up the floorboards in the bedroom and haul out his prized collections. Left-brain had warned that such things should be buried.

Still, he had enjoyed those souvenirs he could smell and hold anytime he wanted. At least until the real rot took hold. And he'd thought a great deal about skin then, skin that was created to hold everything together, as he'd sat crouched on the floor, the boards gapping between his legs like a toothless grin. Left-brain was always on alert during those times, listening for footfalls on the stairwell that would spell doom and bring down the Kingdom.

But the Kingdom did come tumbling down, and it was the smell that had finally been his undoing, that sweet odor of fresh decay that gave him even harder erections than sniffing his fingers after he'd felt up one of Bessie's nieces, who hung around the back porch like stray cats during the long hot summer.

He had thought as he rode the Sunset Limited down the tracks from New Orleans toward Biloxi, gazing through the double-wide window at the green kudzu that had overtaken everything, that in time Mother's plan would fail—flushing out the big house, like it was her seventeen-year-old womb. He had closed his eyes, letting the *chug-a-lug* of the train become his heartbeat, and fallen to sleep, his hand resting against his chest and the cloth pouch safeguarding the one dried remnant from his collection that Didon Petit had not taken away.

It had been the rape of another student that had finally wrecked Mother's plan. Though Left-brain had contemplated the idea like a calculus problem, had campaigned for a safer hole to plug, some inconsequential nobody off campus, it had been Right-brain who had pushed Amos Gainsford into the dark and ravaged his tight hairy anus.

He had been considerably more naive then, ready to pull down his trousers for the paddling from Brother Clarence he half-enjoyed. But he read another message in the disciplinarian's eyes. He was going home. And was lucky, according to Brother Alphonsus, that he wasn't going to jail.

So he went home on the same train that had delivered him, with his hand over his heart, and the voice of Left-brain screaming in his head that he should have listened. And Mother was waiting, ready to bring down the Kingdom so that its resurrection would never again be possible.

Put the bad boy away. For good. Lock the beastie in a cage. Hole him up in a sanitarium. With papers, of course. A formal commitment underwritten by Dr. Jasper Lovell, a true Southern gentleman and faithful family retainer.

But he never saw the inside of the fancy loony bin that was Mother's solution. She died before his bags could be packed. A fire burned down the big house and everything in it, the flesh steaming and simmering, an arrogant aroma, unlike the passive stink which had risen from the floorboards of his room and set the clock in motion.

CHAPTER

17

Sakura stood alone behind the one-way glass, observing the man who slouched in a chair at the scarred table in the interview room. Randy Lancaster, the deejay known as Shaman, had lied to Talbot and Rozelli when they'd talked to him at the club; for one thing, he'd given a false address. But his cell phone number had been accurate. And when contacted this morning, he had agreed to come in.

He was wearing a fringed suede jacket and jeans that were frayed at the knees, which gave the impression that he was physically at ease. But beneath it, he seemed nervous. A fact that was in his favor. It was the real criminals who were totally relaxed while waiting to be questioned. Lancaster kept glancing around, his gaze coming back to the mirrored wall, as if he guessed he was being watched. Sakura tried imagining him holding a plastic bag over a victim's face, and found it wasn't hard. "Too jumpy to be guilty" wasn't much of a rule, and the Shaman might be new to serial murder.

"Ready?" Delia was waiting for him.

Sakura nodded and picked up a folder, following her next door.

Lancaster looked up as they approached. His deep-set eyes were very dark, the irises so nearly black they seemed to absorb the pupils. The contrast with white even teeth was both sensual and sinister. And the energy he projected was palpable this close. Not fear, but an animal magnetism.

"This is Officer Adelia Johnson. I'm Lieutenant James Sakura," he said, sitting down across from the deejay.

"And I'm here . . . why?" The blunt question did not erase the smile.

"A few questions," Sakura answered.

Lancaster's eyes went to Adelia, sitting next to the mounted camera. "Maybe I need a lawyer," he said.

"It's your right to have an attorney." Sakura was matter-of-fact. "But it's only a few questions. No need to drag this out."

"What kind of questions? I already talked to the cops."

Sakura did not answer immediately. He gave Adelia the signal to start the recording and stated for the record those present in the room. "The detectives you talked to are part of my unit," he said, turning to Lancaster. "You lied to them."

"How's that?" The grin got bigger.

"You told my officers that you didn't know Sarah Laraby."

"Who says that I did?"

"A friend of Sarah's."

A shift in posture. A charge of anger. "Lisa Hennessy, right?"

Sakura waited, silent.

"Lisa doesn't know shit." Lancaster was forward in the chair again. "But all right," he said, his black gaze direct, "I admit I did know Sarah."

"So it was a lie."

Lancaster laughed, giving Sakura a glimpse of the metal ball in his tongue. There was no doubt the man liked jewelry. The multiple rings. The silver neck chain hung with a pendant of the Hopi trickster Kokopelli. "I was in the middle of a gig. I just wanted to get rid of your guys. It's not a crime."

"Lying to the police can be a crime if you intentionally obstruct an investigation."

"I don't know anything to obstruct."

"But you don't deny now that you slept with Sarah Laraby?"

"I sleep with a lot of girls." The perpetual grin was now a leer.

Sakura remained expressionless, the surest goad, it seemed, for someone as theatrical as the Shaman. "Ms. Hennessy believes that your relationship with Sarah Laraby went beyond nontraditional sex."

Lancaster's head rolled back, a breath escaping. His expression, when he straightened, made clear what he thought of such a delicate choice of words. "What the fuck is that supposed to mean?"

"That you manipulated Sarah Laraby into doing things that were in Ms. Hennessy's words 'sexually weird.' She said you do that with a lot of girls."

"Look, I rule up there. What I control is the *Vibe*." The white teeth gleamed. A challenge to the uninitiated. "Anything else is crazy."

"Was Sarah having sex with anyone else?"

"Like I know? We weren't buddies."

"Did you know any of the other girls who were murdered?"

"No."

"You answered that very quickly, Mr. Lancaster."

"I've heard about them. Who hasn't? Your guys showed me pictures."

"And you're sure you didn't know any of them?"

"Is this a trick question?" Lancaster was not hiding his belligerence. "I can't swear that I've never run into them at the clubs. But I didn't *know* any of them."

Sakura had taken a sheet of paper from the file he'd brought in. "Can you account for where you were on these particular dates?" He pushed the list forward.

"What are these dates?"

"The nights when victims disappeared from clubs."

"I can't remember where I was yesterday." The dark eyes were mocking. "But my manager keeps a schedule."

"I'd like to see it."

"Here." Lancaster had produced a pen, kept handy no doubt for autographs. He wrote a number at the bottom of the page. "My manager's name is Kyle," he said. "He'll give you what you need." He stood up.

"One more thing, Mr. Lancaster."

"And what's that?"

"Do you have access to a van?"

"A van?" He seemed momentarily thrown by the question. "Yeah," he said, "a buddy of mine lets me borrow his. To move sound equipment."

"Does this buddy of yours have a name?"

"Dustin Franks."

"Perhaps Mr. Franks would allow us to examine his van?"

Lancaster was decidedly wary. "You'd have to ask him."

"His address and phone number, Mr. Lancaster."

"I don't know the number offhand. It's a cell. And he's changed cribs since I last saw him. Don't have the new address."

"It would be in your interest to put us in touch with Mr. Franks."

"What do you want with Dustin's van?"

"Sometimes police work must proceed by a process of elimination." Sakura didn't elaborate.

"And that's supposed to make me feel good, Lieutenant? That you're working to eliminate me as a suspect in the murder of those girls?"

"I have not used the word *suspect,* Mr. Lancaster."

"Yeah, right." The deejay had started walking.

"Get us Mr. Franks's number," Sakura said, "and maybe we won't have to talk with you again."

Lancaster stopped. No longer so at ease, he still seemed cocksure. "But I might not want to talk to you, man," he said. "Like I told those other cops, I know my rights."

⁂

"He looks near the same height. Maybe a mite shorter. Quite the same build. Slight. Though I would have liked to have seen the gentleman in the same sort of jogging clothes." Marshall Grantley looked back over his shoulder, through the one-way glass, into the now empty interrogation room where Randy Lancaster had just been interviewed.

"What about the facial features?" Sakura was hoping against hope, but knew that the chance of a positive identification was virtually zero.

"That is difficult. The man in the park had on that cap and those glasses. Yellow lenses, as I mentioned before. And to be completely honest, I was looking more at the woman. Poor dear."

"And the voice?"

Grantley smiled. "Now of that I am quite sure. Not the same. Not the same at all. The man in the park spoke with a different voice quality entirely."

"Is it possible he could have altered his voice?"

"Entirely possible. Though he was in such a compromised position, holding up the woman and all, I am not sure he would have had the presence of mind to do anything of the sort. And . . ."

"What else, Mr. Grantley?"

"I would have to say the man in the park spoke in a much more culti-vated manner. No slang or any such. I take it a *crib* is a flat of some kind."

Sakura smiled. "That's correct, Mr. Grantley."

"I'm totally . . . *out of the loop.*" He laughed at his own joke.

"Is there anything—"

"Sorry, Lieutenant. Most inappropriate of me. To jest when we're about such serious business. No, there isn't anything else. Except per-haps the hair. I think the man in the park had lighter hair. Brown. But difficult to tell with that cap. And I don't think it was curly or long. Of course, it could have been pulled back just like the fellows today. But my impression was that he had short hair under that cap."

"Thank you, Mr. Grantley. If you remember anything else, please con-tact me. You have my card."

"Indeed I do, Lieutenant. I am just sorry I wasn't more observant. Maybe I could have narrowed down the model of that van. And more important, I might have noticed that that young woman was being taken against her will."

⁂

Round paper lanterns hung in the lowest branches. A chilled wind tossed them like unattached heads. Darkness waited in a flat gray sky leaching remnants of the afternoon's yellow light. Tines of the cast-iron fence threw pale shadows like long bones. Beneath the squeals and laughter of children, the crackling whisper of autumn leaves could be heard, communicating in the language of the dead.

The twins ran, their costumes barely containing the raw energy that threatened to burst through the seams and leave them naked, running like small foxes in a primeval wood. He rather liked to think of them as kits. With their heads of dense bright red hair, the alert-jerk motion of their fit little-boy bodies. Mother Fox, a vixen with a mane of blood-red hair of her own, made a faint attempt to slow her offspring, who were leading a trail of tagalong classmates round the statue of Edwin Booth in a fast getaway.

He smiled, patting where his hungry heart fed. He moved to one of the park's far corners, sheltered by a dense stand of trees where he could watch the party proceedings unobserved. A Halloween party for sweet young flesh. Ice-cream-and-cookie-fed flesh. Plump pretty meat. His ears perked as Mother Fox called. Time for a game. The band of masquerading three- and four-year-olds sprinted toward a dangling piñata, an *El Día de los Muertos* skeleton swinging low from a tree branch.

"Jason. Damon. Let your guests take their turns first," Mother Fox admonished.

"Mama . . ." whined the boys in unison, but waited, squirming for a chance to swing.

A chunky Ninja Turtle struck gold first, a hard swift swat to the rib cage, and down tumbled a rain of trinkets and candies. The flesh scrambled, stubby pink fingers scrabbling in the grass for booty.

A round of snapping for apples on strings followed, masks removed from faces as wet hungry little mouths fought for a taste of the slippery fruit. He sniffed the air, taking in the sour-milk smell of saliva, studying arching backbone and the white tissue of arcing throats, feet flat-planted in a frenzied dance to gain a threshold. The kits were best at the challenge. Each taking thick chunks out of the sides of the large red apples, exposing the white pulp like fresh wounds.

He looked over his shoulder. A wolf's moon rose, and he could sense a winding down as the children split off into smaller groups, some sitting on the grass counting treats, others in numbers of two and three playing made-up games.

He stepped from behind the tree, revealing himself. The twins were close enough for him to hear Damon draw mucus down into his throat from a runny nose. Jason saw him first, his mask off his face, perched atop his head.

"Pun'kin Man!"

Quickly he brought his index finger to his lips to make the hush sign.

"Pun'kin Man," Jason repeated, his voice child-husky.

"You came to our party." Damon reached for him, but he pulled away, retreating to the shelter of the trees.

After a moment he peeked around a trunk, smiling in the pale purple dusk. "I came just to see you. It's a secret."

"A secret?" Damon whispered, venturing closer on his frisky fox feet.

He nodded.

"We like secrets," Jason agreed. "Like our costumes? I'm Spider-Man. Damon is a vampire."

Damon smiled, placing plastic fangs over his teeth. Then, pulling them out, asked, "Know what vampires do?"

He nodded again.

"And you're Pun'kin Man," said Jason, a reconfirmation that suddenly seemed funny. And because he laughed, so did Damon.

"Shhh . . . You'll give away our secret."

The boys stopped, matching sets of deep blue eyes searching his face, waiting, it seemed, for some kind of mission he might send them on, or for some feat of magic he might perform.

"I have a treat for you." He reached inside his jacket pocket. "Close your eyes. Give me your hands." Mother Fox's choice of the piñata was delicious serendipity. ". . . Happy Halloween." The boys opened their eyes and stared down at the small sugar skulls.

"*Calacas*," he whispered, chuckling as he supposed any respectable Pumpkin Man would.

"You're very late today, Victor. We only have a short time before my next appointment."

"I'm sorry, Dr. French." His laugh, half-giddy, that she remembered from their first two sessions.

"We can't work on the things that are troubling you if you don't come."

This time he simply nodded.

"Perhaps we should explore your goals in seeking therapy."

"My goals?"

"Yes, what you want to accomplish here."

"I guess I just want to feel better."

"What do you think 'feeling better' would be like for you?"

"I would feel less . . . crazy?"

"You made that sound like a question," she said. "Are you still having episodes when you experience your body as mechanical?"

"Yes."

"Has the medication I gave you helped at all?"

He looked away. "The pills make me sleepy. And I'm not really all that anxious when it happens."

"How *do* you feel during those periods?"

"Excited, in a way."

"In what way, Victor?"

"It's kind of neat being a machine. Not . . . messy."

"And being human is messy?"

"My mother thought so."

"I think we have a good topic to explore"—she scribbled into her notebook—"which is why I'm sorry we have so little time today. We have a lot of work to do if we're going to make progress."

"Could I ask *you* a question, Dr. French?"

He had been staring at the watch on his arm, an old timepiece that showed its inner workings through a window in its face. Now as he looked up, she saw again how clear his eyes were, a transparent blue with very dark irises. They made her think of targets. But any arrows would be coming out. It was a weird thought, and she shook it away.

"What do you want to ask?"

"The man who's killing those women," he said, "do you think they're going to get him?"

She was not particularly surprised by the question. The Ripper Murders, as they were being called now, were a hot topic, and it was hardly a secret that she was helping with the investigation.

"I believe the police will catch him," she said.

"How?" He didn't drop it. "I mean, he's smart, don't you think? They say he cuts them up to see inside."

"Is that what they say?" She couldn't remember that particular formulation in the press. She didn't remember having said it herself.

"Yes," he answered. "Why else would he open them?"

The transparent eyes were impossible to read, and for a split second she felt an irrational fear.

"Are you okay?" he said to her. "You look kinda funny?"

"Yes, I'm fine." She forced a smile.

"I saw you with Zoe Kahn," he said now. "I like her show."

His flattened affect had morphed into sudden enthusiasm. She had an intuition that his decision to choose her as his therapist was the result of his seeing her on TV. "Please don't be late for your appointment next week," she said to him.

She had to admit that she was glad when he was gone. Her experience of last year was making her paranoid, and there was a definite note of falseness in the naivete that Victor Abbot projected. Everyone wore a mask, even the craziest ones. It was her job to see behind them, and despite that they were paying her for it, patients always resisted. Some more than most. Coming late for a session was an obvious strategy. A more subtle approach was to mess with the good doctor's head.

✣

The end of another week. Margot stared through the glass window at the closed blue umbrella in front of the corner bistro. Drawn in above an abandoned table, the folds of its canvas wings were whipped by the night's sun-drained wind. Another season, another place, the umbrella would have been unfurled, a cutout against a lighter blue sky, a prop against the hot Aegean sun, inflated with tipsy laughter, rising like the bubbles in the glass barely held between her fingers, her leg rubbing the white of his summer pants.

But this wasn't that time. Or that place. And the man and woman weren't the same. Over the years something essential had been altered, and lost was the false innocence of the early days, the belief that love and the passion would last forever.

So why had she called Michael? Because she was still "hungover" from the dream. Maybe it was as simple as that. Just a little reality test. Or maybe it was what she sometimes acknowledged in her weaker, more honest moments—that something unsettled lay between them. The unfinished business of lives once spent together, then torn apart.

And what was she going to say when he showed up? *I had to see you because of this dream I had. Of fucking you. And I wanted to make sure it was just bullshit.* Or would she finally do the right thing and just tell him.

Typical of him not to ask why she needed to see him. Michael didn't believe in waste. He'd find out soon enough. And why bother to ask?

With his instincts he could probably read her mind. Yet it was knowledge without understanding. Intimacy without connection. Which meant that no one could make her feel as wanting, or as complete, as Michael Darius. And maybe that was what had ultimately driven her away, made her run as far as she could, as fast as she could. Even with his babies in her belly.

Yet what she hated she loved. He'd forced her open, like a bulb in hard winter soil, rupturing the layers of her self-control, stripping away the last of her shell. How, when they made love, she would scream and moan in pleasure. And how he'd smiled in the giving of it, with his words of "Yes, Margot, yes . . ." as he looked down at her with the gaze of God in his eyes.

She ran her finger around the rim of her glass, watching the wind play tag with the folded wings of the umbrella. She glanced at her watch. He wouldn't be late. And just as she had the thought, he was standing there.

"You can sit down, you know."

He gave her something that passed for a smile, pulling out a chair. And suddenly it seemed easier to drink than talk. Lifting her glass, she watched him get the waiter's attention.

"You're looking well, Margot."

She laughed. At last able to speak and breathe. "Small talk doesn't quite suit you, Michael . . . but thanks anyway."

He had gotten his scotch, and was taking a sip.

"The last time . . ." she started.

"The last time . . . I can remember the last time." He was smiling for real now.

And she was blushing like a schoolgirl. This wasn't going according to plan. "The last time *when we talked*," she tried again, "I might have given you the wrong impression."

"I think I got everything right, Margot. Reese is the boys' real father. I confuse them. And a move to Connecticut would be best for everyone concerned. Except me, of course."

She shook her head. "Just what I thought. You heard the words, but didn't understand a damn thing."

"I'm still in love with your hair."

She knew it—she should have worn her hair up. And just what in hell was he doing? This chameleon routine was way out of character. "Don't change the subject. What is important is that you understand I don't want you gone from our sons' lives."

"Isn't that the reason you left me . . . so I would be gone from their lives?"

"One of them." She didn't sound very convincing, and she was ready for anything but his laughter. "Michael, please . . ."

He was watching her now, his eyes sad and hurt and inconsolable.

"I'm sorry . . ." The words had rusted in the intervening years. "I'm sorry," she repeated, "leaving without telling you I was pregnant."

Something small and bright seemed to catch fire in his eyes.

"I was wrong"—she was going to finish this—"and I want you in the boys' lives. No matter what. Connecticut or not. You are their father. I don't want them to ever forget that. I—"

He stopped her, his fingers touching her lips. And before she could say another word, or breathe, or think, his lips were where his fingers had been. And just as lightly.

CHAPTER

18

Back by five tomorrow . . ." Erica Talise called out, smiling wanly at the sequined Valkyrie who waved to her in acknowledgment from the door. She was tired for midweek, and half-hoped that the woman was going to be their last customer for the evening. The day had been good, even better than last Halloween, which had been the best ever since she'd taken over the shop three years ago.

She headed back to the dressing room to gather up and rehang the piles of try-ons the woman had plowed through while trying to find something "perfect." Why did the most difficult ones always wait till the last minute?

As she reached the dressing room curtains, the wolf face sprang out at her, hairy and hugely horrific, thick snarling lips curled over yellow canines.

"Damn it, Marcus." She was not the least fazed. "I could have sold that thing a dozen times in the last two hours."

"No way. I told you I was wearing it tonight. You can dock me for a rental."

"We don't rent those masks. You wear it, you're going to pay for it."

"Lighten up, Erica." Gilly was smiling, emerging like a sprite from the storeroom. "I know it's been really crazy today, but I thought you agreed that this year we were going to have some fun of our own."

Looking at her, Erica had to smile too. Her friend always had that effect. Years her junior and thinner than she'd ever been, Gilly had been working with her almost from the beginning. There was something otherworldy about Gilly, with her heart-shaped face and huge gray eyes. Her attitude might be streetwise, but her ballerina delicacy always undercut the effect.

"How do I look?" Gilly pirouetted in the fairy costume that had been part of a production of *A Midsummer Night's Dream*.

"I thought you were doing vampire." Marcus didn't hide his disappointment, but Gilly was no fool. She knew what suited her best.

"You look great, Gilly," she said, then glanced at the clock. "It's past seven. I guess we can close up."

"Do it," from Marcus.

"What are *you* going to wear, Erica?" Gilly was asking.

"Do I have to wear a costume?" *Was she the only one who was sick of the things?*

"Yes, you do." Gilly was adamant. "That's what makes Halloween so cool. You get to be something different. And, besides, the Half Moon is having half-price drinks for single women in costume."

That was Gilly all right, the fanciful dosed with the practical. She smiled again. "We'll see," she said. "I just might surprise you. You two go on. I'll close out the register and meet you there."

The Half Moon was just around the block. She stood in the doorway and watched them move down the sidewalk, the fairy and the werewolf laughing together. She felt a twinge of jealousy she couldn't help. Marcus had only been with them part-time for the last few months, hired after she'd improved her stock and had started to get some of the big-time rentals. He was a graduate student and wouldn't be staying in the city past graduation. It had begun to worry her that his interest in Gilly might be more than a workplace infatuation.

She shut the door and turned the key in the lock, switched off the front lights, and walked back to close out the register. It really was a relic, and she knew she should chuck it for something new and electronic. But she liked the ancient machine, liked the substantial sound of its jingling open, shutting solid. Just as she liked going through the small paper invoices at the end of a day. She reached for them now, impaled like square butterflies on their cast-iron spike.

She was totaling the invoices on the noisy adding machine, so it took a little time for the tapping to penetrate. A man was standing on the stoop.

She could see him fairly clearly, his face pressed against the glass insert in the door. He was staring at her while his fingers drummed the surface.

Closed. She mouthed the word, regretting that she had somehow forgotten to flip the sign in the window. "I'm *closed*," she said loudly, still exaggerating the word for him to lip-read.

He wasn't having any of it. He smiled at her cheerfully now, catching her eyes, his fingers still tap-tapping on the glass in the door to beat the goddamned band.

She sighed, and walked over to where they stood divided by the glass, determined on some principle or other to keep the bastard out. "I'm closed," she said again, this time with her own damn cheerful smile.

He had been leaning against the dusty pane to see in through the glare. Now he stood up straight. He was a well-dressed bastard.

"I'm really sorry to bother you," his voice diminished by the glass. "But I've got to have a costume, and you're it. Please," he was begging.

Damn, she was a soft touch. She frowned, but she unlocked the door.

🔻

All Hallow's Eve. Sakura stood at his office window, looking out beyond the plaza. Close to a million revelers were expected to pack the Village, and the traffic was already heavy with the overflow from the parade. He watched the headlights streaming by and tried to imagine them as *Toro Nagashi,* the floating lanterns of his boyhood, meant to guide the spirits.

But Halloween had never been his holiday, despite its obvious resonance with *O-bon.* The American version of the Feast of the Dead had lost nearly all its ancient connection to a reverence for ancestors who had crossed into the shadowland and returned for one night each year to be honored.

Only once had he accompanied Paul and Elizabeth on their Halloween rounds. He could not remember if he'd worn a costume, but his stepbrother had been a pirate, which had not suited his reserved nature at all. Elizabeth had dressed as a princess, with a conical hat dripping netting and sparkles. She had danced from house to house, equally thrilled with each new bounty of candy. He had enjoyed the night through her eyes. But by the next year, he had begun to gain the height that would distinguish him. And Susan, his stepmother, had judged him too old for such things as trick-or-treat.

"Gazing out windows, Jimmy, is not a good sign. You'll be drinking coffee next." He turned, glad to find the friend who matched the voice. Willie had come into his office.

"It's not that bad yet." He smiled. "You here to meet Michael?"

"We're supposed to be having dinner." She sat down. "You want to join us? We could call Hanae."

"Another time." He walked back to the chair behind his desk. "I want to stick around here a little longer."

"Expecting trouble?" She was leaning over, setting down the suitcase she called a purse.

"Something like that," he admitted. "It's nearly two weeks since Olsen."

She sat up. "Anything happening with the deejay and his friend?"

"Lancaster's not cooperating," he said, "and so far we've had no luck in tracking down Dustin Franks. Neither one of them seems to have a record, but Talbot and Rozelli are still on it. I want a look at that van."

"It's easy enough to imagine that Mr. Lancaster is having kinky sex with women from these clubs," she said, "but you don't really like him for our killer, do you?"

"Do you?" he turned it around. "You saw the interview tape."

"He certainly seems narcissistic enough. And this Lisa says he's into weird sex. The problem is his style's so chaotic, though the whole rebel-hipster thing could be a mask. I just have trouble believing that Mr. Lancaster is even half as smart as he thinks he is. And it's hard to picture him rerigging those organs or scrupulously cleaning bodies."

"Or taking that much care wrapping the first five," he added. "The lab found next to nothing on any of the duct tape."

"What's really freaking me out," she said, "is the radical change in the killer's MO on this last one."

"The posing . . ."

"Exactly. Posing the body may be more significant than the change in victim type. I frankly don't have a clue at this point. There's something important we're missing."

"It seems to me we've said that before."

"Last year, yes." She looked rueful. "It was true then, too. The problem is that no matter how much we study them, no matter how many similarities we manage to find in the patterns of their behavior, the truth is that serial killers are individuals. Each of them is unique, just as each of us is. I've said it a million times—profiling is more an art than a science. And right now I'm feeling like a pretty lousy artist."

"Get in line."

The children of the night. Out in full force. Shedding urban identities. Wig and wand. Lacquer and lipstick. Jack-o'-lanterns, sitting fat and full, preening on concrete steps. A pregnant moon, flash-dancing on black wings, turning feather to liquid, as autumn crows circle inside bare bones of trees. A stiff breeze, a dry rustling, and leaves tumble to ground.

He moved through the Halloween traffic, chuckling over the idea fermenting in his head. Maybe it was the pot he'd smoked earlier. Or the night. Or the thrill of the risk he was about to take. Though the attack in the park and what had happened in the meatpacking plant had been fairly audacious, they had been predetermined. So it was not unreasonable that he should be amazed by his break with protocol. Though in the selfsame moment he could hear Right-brain arguing why bother; the meat had already been trapped and vanquished.

He peered into the mirror, into the black interior of the van where the Visqueen package lay. If his plan was going to work, the goods would have to be kept nice and cold. Reaching over, he jacked up the air conditioner full throttle. He was fighting time and the natural order of things.

He headed toward the Midtown location. Toward a destiny he alone crafted. With none of Right-brain's lusty impatience or greedy quick fixes. None of the insatiable passion to move on to the next bit of business. He laughed out loud. God was in the details. And though Right-brain might see the lump in the back as so much baggage, Left-brain fancied one more turn around the dance floor.

Zach Lynch tried to put his arm around Reni's shoulders, but she pulled away. It was almost one o'clock, and she still hadn't come around. Why had they even bothered going out?

She just wouldn't let it go. It had all started when he'd told her to say her good-byes after only one drink at her office's annual Halloween party. The last thing he'd wanted was to make small talk with some computer geeks from her office. Of course, *geeks* was the wrong word to use. They were very nice people. He just didn't relate, she'd said, to any-one who wasn't a certified asshole. Then he'd nixed her idea of going to the parade in the Village. The last thing he'd wanted was to be pushed and prodded by a million drunken faggots. Of course, *faggots* was the wrong word to use.

To make matters worse, he hadn't worn the costume she'd put together for him. It wasn't as though she'd gotten him a Spider-Man out-fit, she'd said, or expected him to wear fangs and a cape and go around saying, "I want a bite of your neck." It was just a pair of blue jeans and a white T-shirt. And the leather jacket she'd found at a secondhand cloth-ing store. They would have made the perfect fifties couple, she said. Crap, if she wanted James Dean, why didn't she just go out with that jerk Mervin, who couldn't seem to get it through his thick skull that she had a boyfriend and that he should quit already with the cute messages on her machine.

"Are you ready to go home?" he asked for the umpteenth time since their big blowout hours ago.

She shook her head, her long blond ponytail flapping against her back. He had to admit she looked adorable in the poodle skirt and fuzzy sweater with the tiny collar she'd worn in spite of him.

"You hardly ate anything at the restaurant."

She wasn't taking the bait.

"Or drank any of the wine you ordered."

Nothing.

"And you might have spoken a half dozen words to me all evening."

This time she favored him with a look. A look that reduced him to something less than pond scum.

"Come on, Reni, what the fuck are we doing walking around like this?"

She seemed to pick up her pace.

He shook his head and tramped after her just like he'd been doing all night. Around midnight it seemed a reasonable penance. Now . . . he was getting pissed off. Still, he figured, in the grand scope of things he was getting just about what an ugly man with a beautiful girlfriend deserved. Though he wasn't actually ugly. It was just that Reni was god-almighty beautiful. Maybe that was the real reason he'd cut short their appearance at her office party and vetoed the parade. He was jealous.

Shit, what he wanted more than anything right now was to go back to the apartment, smoke a little dope, and make love till the wolves howled. But clearly that wasn't going to happen.

"I wasn't hungry," she said finally, turning to look at him, but still walking. "And I don't like to drink when I'm upset. You know that."

He smiled. "Finished punishing me?"

"You can call it anything you want."

"*Torture* is what I'd call it."

She stopped. "Zach, this is not the major argument of our lives. I still love you. I still want to be with you. But I'm still kind of pissed. So give me a couple more blocks to cool off, and we can do anything you want."

He watched her walk away, down a short side street toward a small collection of retail stores, her poodle skirt bouncing to the beat of her ponytail. He followed her, thinking that she was an absolute sweetheart, and that he was one lucky son-of-a-bitch.

"Reni, baby . . ." She was standing now, in a pool of yellow light, focusing on something in a shop window.

"Reni?" This time she turned at the sound of her name, her head moving in a kind of stop-animation rhythm. Her expression fixed like it too was being manipulated. Eyes too large for her face. Mouth moving as if blowing air.

"Reni?" He was next to her now, and his eyes followed her pointing finger.

Inside the window the figure was seated. A leg draped over one of the chair's arms. The hat on her head was wide-brimmed and black, with large red roses. There was an acid-green boa wrapped once around her neck in a kind of stranglehold. And she wore fishnet stockings on her fleshy legs, bright red high-heeled pumps on her feet. She fit in perfectly with the macabre cast of characters decked out in Halloween finery in the window, except this mannequin oozed real blood from a Y-track of staples running between her heavy naked breasts, down her rounded belly, and into the exposed thatch of dark pubic hair between her thighs.

⚜

It was the easiest break-in she'd ever pulled off. No prying some cheap lock with her fingernail file. No crying to the building's super that she was some Joe's, or in this case Johnny's, long-lost sister or cousin. Nope, just a simple matter of inserting a key. Johnny Rozelli had returned hers last year the night of their breakup, but she still had his. And he hadn't changed the lock.

Zoe walked into the familiar mess. The place was not exactly a dump, but Johnny wasn't here that much except to sleep, and he spent every extra penny on clothes. She could identify with that. It was only since getting her program that she'd begun the hunt for a nicer apartment herself.

She went straight to the bedroom. It was already really late, and if Johnny was going to come home at all tonight, he would be here soon. She freshened her makeup and started to strip. She enjoyed a good disguise, and had given a lot of thought to her Halloween costume. In the end she'd decided to keep it simple. Tonight's strategy was direct frontal assault. The trick was not to give him time to think.

She turned out the light and arranged herself in the bed, certain that this was going to work. Johnny had once compared her to the ice cream sundaes that his uncle had bought him on Saturday afternoons. Tonight, she would be his treat again. His Halloween treat. It was perfect.

The minutes passed slowly with no distractions in the dark, and the smell of him from the sheets was driving her crazy. But finally she heard him in the living room. And at last the bedroom light went on.

Her first impression was how tired he looked. But then he laughed. Taking in the cellophane. The wide orange satin ribbon snaking across her body from ankles to neck. The huge floppy bow tied at her throat, holding it all together.

"Unwrap your candy, baby." She smiled at him from the pillow.

"You are too fuckin' much, Zoe."

"Wrong, sweetie. There hasn't been near enough fucking lately."

"Guess we'll have to fix that." He was already pulling off his clothes, leaving a trail of Calvin and Armani.

The sex was every bit as good as she knew it would be. And good for him too—coming over and over, holding to her shoulders like a drowning man.

"What if I'd brought back some broad?" he'd said to her at one point.

"Then we'd just have kicked her ass out." They'd laughed together like kids, and screwed some more.

They were still screwing when the phone rang. She watched his face sober in the bedside light as he held the receiver close.

She kept silent as he got up and started pulling on his clothes. But her brain was racing with déjà vu, the near certainty of another murder. The whole circumstance of last year repeating itself.

"Johnny . . ." she began, not able to help herself. "It's another victim, isn't it." She raised herself on an elbow.

"Shhh." He sat next to her, pushing her back into the pillows. "Wish I could stay." He kissed her breasts.

"Mmmm . . ." She was stretching in pleasure when she heard the click and felt the cold metal closing on her wrist.

"Trick or treat . . ." Johnny was saying, springing out of her reach.

"Rozelli!" She shot straight up, but the handcuffs kept her tethered to the metal headboard. "Rozelli, get these goddamned things off me."

"Guess you got the *trick*, baby." He was so clearly enjoying himself. "But I'll tell you what I can when I get back."

⚜

No one knew who finally resurrected the canvas tarps from a small storeroom at the rear of the costume shop, but a couple of techs had the remnants from an old paint job hung in a matter of minutes across the window. Sakura stood at the edge of the sidewalk, his back to the wide cordoned-off area, watching the flashing lights from cop cars reflect off the glass onto the hanging dropcloth. He checked his watch. The witching hour had passed. They were almost three hours into the first of November.

"It's a circus." Rozelli had come to stand next to him. "Look at 'em. Pushing and shoving to get a better look."

Sakura didn't turn, but continued to stare at the shrouded window. A large crowd of civilians had gathered behind the barricades precinct had set up. Night was a good fit for death, slithering under the cover of dark, burrowing its stink in shadow. And the jackals came. The news of a fresh kill traveled fast. Press vans had been gathering for the last half hour. Already he'd been hammered with questions, shouted from behind enemy lines. Though he couldn't blame the fourth estate. It made for a great story. Murder on All Hallow's Eve.

"Halloween, Detective," he said at last.

"Shit, the way I figure, Lieutenant, every night is Halloween in this town."

"Johnson interviewing the couple?"

"As only the lady can. But the girl's pretty freaked out."

Sakura nodded. He hadn't liked what he'd seen behind the glass either.

✧

"He's posing. But this is for us." Willie stood with Darius and Sakura inside the storefront window, looking at the large woman, who was still in the chair. Rigor setting in despite the cold. "He wants the whole world to appreciate his handiwork."

Darius moved in closer. Touched the bright green boa. "He used this like a rope." The feathers ruffled, momentarily coming to life. A bizarre effect played against the dead body. "Who is she?"

"Erica Talise. The store owner." It was Sakura who spoke.

Willie crouched to get a better look at the long, puckered incision running down the victim's chest. "He's not breaking with this part of his routine. Opening them up is still important to him."

"He had to do some maneuvering. First he had to subdue her, and then he had to get her out of the store." Darius turned to Sakura. "I am assuming she was taken from here and murdered somewhere else."

"There's no evidence to the contrary."

"He must have posed as a customer." Darius looked back at the woman who'd become victim number seven. "He's got good transportation, so he takes her where he can comfortably do what he wants. Returns to the shop. Dresses her. Puts her in the window. Leaves. All of this without anybody seeing him. He must be invisible."

"He's organized and smart." Willie stood. "And he's getting off on the escalating risks he's taking."

"Halloween night in New York." Sakura walked up to the body. "Maybe no one thinks there's anything strange about a guy fooling around with a mannequin in the store window of a costume shop."

Willie nodded, staring at the face that seemed to be wearing a mask, one as horrid and fixed as the dozens that filled the store. Red circles stood out on the cheeks like abrasions. The lids were smeared with a heavy coat of green shadow, and thick black liner ringed the half-open dead eyes. Lipstick ran clumsily over the natural lines of the mouth. "He's not creating his ideal woman. Look at her."

Sakura followed Willie's eyes.

"And depersonalizing her like we'd expect," she went on. "Using her as a prop. She's just another mannequin."

"She was made to look like a whore," Darius finally speaking the words nobody wanted to say.

CHAPTER

19

It was late afternoon, and Chief of Detectives Lincoln McCauley seemed a determined illustration that stereotype was often rooted in fact. His fat Irishman's face showed especially beefy above his stiffly knotted tie, the smoke that issued from the wedged Don Diego at the side of his mouth only adding to the cartoon impression of a snorting, angry bull. Sakura, as was becoming usual, had found himself at this meeting in the role of the red cape. He watched McCauley take a another huge draw from the stout Robusto, and imagined that at least some of the smoke was venting from the chief's reddening ears.

"So what's the deal on this latest victim?" McCauley asked.

"The usual canvassing and interviews with witnesses. The autopsy's scheduled for later today."

"And that van connected to the deejay?" McCauley had zeroed in on the latest of his failures.

"Mr. Lancaster is refusing to cooperate. We're still working on tracking the friend with the van."

"But bottom line, you don't think this Shaman guy's good for the murders."

"We don't have any real evidence to suggest that he is."

"That's good." McCauley took equivocation for a yes. "Because I wouldn't want the public to ever learn that we had the killer in our hands and let him walk out for a little Halloween fun. What's bad, Lieutenant, is that you don't have anyone else who even looks like a suspect."

Seven victims and counting. Sakura offered no defense.

The chief got tired of waiting. "What about the tip line?"

"We've had thousands of tips," Sakura said. "And the daily volume's increasing. But it's all the usual thing—people calling to tell us that they're sure the killer is a husband, or a brother-in-law, or their boss. The task force is following up on every one, but nothing so far has yielded anything credible."

"Like I said, you're going nowhere. Unless you have some plan?"

"It's my judgment we should go proactive."

"Stir the bastard up?"

"Knock him off stride. He's probably feeling pretty invulnerable right now."

"He has empirical data." McCauley couldn't resist.

"We can use the media," Sakura continued. "Send him a message."

"Which is?"

"That we don't respect him; he's not that intelligent. And he's making mistakes, though they can't be revealed to the media. He'll do whatever's necessary to prove we're lying. He needs the public to believe what he believes—that he's smarter than we are."

"Why would he believe that?"

Sakura ignored the comment. He would play straight man if it meant he would be allowed to do his job. "He's already expanding beyond his pattern of simply dumping the bodies," he said, "taking greater and greater risks. Challenging him this way could force a mistake that catches him sooner rather than later."

The chief leaned forward in his swivel chair. "And we save lives even as we're provoking him to kill again?"

"He's going to kill anyway," Sakura said. "But, yes, that's the theory."

"It better fucking be more than theory, or the vultures will have the balls you're so eager to dangle out there."

Sakura wasn't sure if the private parts included the chief's, but he understood the danger to careers involved with this kind of maneuver. "Do I have your okay?" he asked.

McCauley unplugged the cigar to study its burning tip. In a single peevish motion he stubbed the glow to ashes inside the crystal ashtray. "Make damn sure this works," he said.

⁂

Leaving McCauley's office, Sakura took the metal staircase down to his own floor. Descending with measured footsteps. Parceling the moments of peace. The reverberation of his passage sounded like a haunting in the empty well.

He was relieved to have gotten McCauley's agreement to go ahead with his plan. He only wished he were as confident as he had sounded when presenting it. But there was no way to accurately gauge their chances for success. In the end it didn't matter. With the toll of victims rising, he simply was not willing to remain passive. If his game didn't work, if more victims died and baiting the killer failed to result in his capture, it would be *his* balls on the line, as McCauley had so colorfully put it. The chief himself might get some flak from the top, but that could always be handled by a showy decision to replace James Sakura with another lead investigator.

The failure would be his. And it would be fair. He would have had his chance.

Make damn sure this works. McCauley need not have wasted his breath. He had tasted a failure that others did not guess. He had no wish to revisit that dish.

In his office, he made tea and reviewed tapes of the interviews that had been conducted this morning with the employees of Erica Talise's costume shop. The young man and woman had each expressed regret for not checking on their employer when she failed to meet them as arranged. Gilly Franklin had appeared inconsolable. And Marcus Laine had admitted that, happy to be alone with Franklin, he had been all too willing to accept that Talise had decided not to join them, a decision which would not have been wholly uncharacteristic.

Neither of the two could remember any customers who seemed suspicious. Sure, they got some weirdos from time to time, but yesterday and the week leading up to it had produced no one who stuck in the mind. Each was pretty certain that Talise had locked up after them, and equally sure that she might easily have let someone in late. Their friend would not have been afraid of being alone with a customer. The Erica they had known was afraid of very little. An admirable trait that in the end had not worked to her advantage.

Franklin's interview had ended in uncontrollable sobbing over the horrible things that had been done to Talise. Apparently she had insisted, partially out of guilt, on being present with Laine for the identification of the body, feeling that she owed at least this much to her friend. Sakura did not envy her the experience, which he was soon to surpass. His unpleasant duty, as he'd mentioned to McCauley, was to attend the autopsy that had been scheduled for late this afternoon.

Margot dusted, the white cloth making frantic swirls on the dark of the dining table. The dust was imaginary. The task ridiculous. She hated housework of any kind, and Ruth, her maid, had just dusted on Tuesday. It was only that she was restless today, and in need of activity. Anything mildly physical and completely mindless would do.

Only it wasn't *doing*. And suddenly she remembered that today was All Saints' Day, and switched to regretting that she hadn't gone to Mass, though she'd been a comfortably lapsed Catholic since her first semester in college. Perhaps it was not enough that Jason and Damon be presented with a good ethical model. There was a spiritual side to things, represented by the kind of ritual she'd grown up with. It seemed suddenly terribly wrong that she had neglected this aspect of her children's lives.

Or was she simply being foolish. The twins were not yet four. There was plenty of time before she considered the complication of religion. For were things not already complicated enough? She knew that at least part of the anxiety she felt was a holdover from seeing Michael last week. She hadn't told Reese about that meeting yet, and the longer she waited, the more likely it seemed that she would appear to have been hiding it from him.

Damn Michael. She had wanted some kind of closure. To offer an apology for past sins. To proffer a promise that she and Reese had no intention of shutting him off from the boys. She had wanted to make their lives simpler. But with Michael nothing was simple. Their meeting had gone . . . too well.

The dusting had stopped, and she stared now at the white cloth stilled in her hand, as if in its soft folds answers might hide. Sunlight streamed through the gap in the curtains. And the dust, not imaginary after all, whirled in its lemon stripes, lively spiraling motes that returned to the table to die.

She had been standing. Now she sat down, as if the force of gravity was all at once too great. She had made things worse. Theoretically perhaps, Reese wanted only what was best for the boys. But how would he really react if Michael began to take a larger part in their lives? The thought had actually crossed her mind that she might call David St. Cyr and have him include a guest house in their plans, someplace Michael could always stay to visit with the boys. Would Reese interpret that idea as the practical solution she had first envisioned? Or would he think, as she did at this moment, that she was utterly mad? She didn't know the answer. And that was completely frightening. Loss of her judgment was Michael's continuing gift. Loss of control.

She dropped her head in her hands. Giving in. Remembering his kiss. She prayed she had hidden her response, leaving immediately on what she'd contrived as a friendly, civil note. When what she had wanted was more.

Jason's scream was piercing as he flew into the room, with Damon in vampire teeth chasing behind him.

"Gonna bite me. . . ." Jason ran into her arms.

"You're Spider-Man," she said. "You can take care of any old vampire." She tugged at the mask. "But I thought you weren't going to run with this on your face. You shouldn't be running at all in the house."

"Damon's gonna bite me," Jason repeated.

"No he's not."

"Am too." Damon had to remove the teeth from his mouth, happily contradicting. "He told me to."

"I know what we need to do," she said. "I want you to bring me your trick-or-treat buckets. Go get them."

She waited while they scurried off. Sometimes they could be surprisingly cooperative.

When they returned, she dumped the pumpkin-faced containers out onto the table. She should have done this last night after she'd come

back with them from trick-or-treating in the neighborhood. It was a sign
of how distracted she had let herself become, that she hadn't monitored
how much candy they were being allowed.

She looked down at what was left. The piles were nearly identical.
Jason would be the one to decide what was to be eaten, and Damon
would follow. It was a natural tendency for one twin to be dominant,
but it was something she wanted to ameliorate. It was the principal reason she wanted them to have their separate rooms.

"Pick out one more piece," she said to them. "I'm going to put the rest
away. You can have another piece after supper."

Getting them to nap was more difficult than usual, but finally they
gave out, crawling together into bed, where they curled together like
kittens. Still in partial costume, faces sticky with candy. Nanny would
have cleaned them up, but Nanny wasn't here today, and their little-boy
messiness seemed natural and endearing. She stood by the bed for a
time watching the miracle of their troubleless sleep.

In just a little while she would wake them up and bathe them. Reese
would be home early tonight, and they would all eat together for a
change. She walked to a chest to pick out fresh clothes. The twins were
beginning to take notice of what they wore, and as with the Halloween
costumes, she was encouraging them more and more to select different
things. The bottom drawer slid open on untidiness. Jason had discovered he could get into it, and she never knew what pieces of toys or
puzzles she would find within the rumpled folds of little shirts and
pants. She sat on the floor to restraighten the contents, removing bright
plastic cars and a ball, refolding clothes.

Underneath everything was a wadded black and orange napkin from
the Halloween party in the park. Her first thought was the nightmare of
stale crumpled cookies, or worse. She was faintly puzzled by the discovery of two tiny sugared skulls, a bit melted and grubby but recognizable
still.

⁂

KitKat was on her knees, facing him, tits to chest. Her arms wound
around him, massaging his back, her fingers tracing his tattoo. An
indigo line of tribal glyphs running from the nape of his neck down his

spine into the crack of his buttocks. She pinched the lids of her eyes closed, feeling his heart thud against her, the muscles of his buttocks contract and release in rhythm as he thrust himself into the dark arch of her cunt. *Slap, slap, slap*—sweaty skin against sweaty skin, meter to the gut-rumble of his grunts.

"All of my cock . . . *Can . . . you . . . take . . . it?*" He tensed in orgasm, pulling her hair hard, so that she arced back, and inside her head fine lines of ecstasy bloomed, and something close to fear. Then the moment broke and he relaxed, locking one hand around her neck in a kind of loose stranglehold. He was coming down, his breath easing off. His heart beginning to mark regular cadence. Then she saw his mouth moving down over hers.

She screamed, a sound filtered through breath and saliva and pain. And then he jerked away, arms flying up into the air, the winner of some kind of match, leaving behind pulp, her lower lip chewed and bloody. And insanely, he was laughing. Wiping the wet red stain of victory from his face with his hand.

She was lying on her back, her fingers cupping the lip. Crying; she was crying. Softly. *Weeping.* That was the word. Tears mixing with mucus out her nose.

"*You son-of-a-bitch . . .*" She gurgled the words quietly, uninflected, grabbing the sheet, stuffing it into her mouth. Anything to catch the blood, keep it from sliding back down her throat. She thought she might have raised her arm to strike him, but fingers like fat worms gripped her wrist. Something cautioned her to get up, to make it to the bathroom to throw up. But the thought was lost in the large movement of his body coming down on her, lost in the shoving of his dick back inside her. The last of her mind registering the wink of his silver rings before it turned into a solid wall of black.

✥

Lancaster watched her. Sleeping now. When she'd finally come around, she'd thrown up. All over the bed, all over herself. He'd struggled to get her off the bed and into the tub. Then there had been the stink to clean up. She'd sunk like the dead in the warm water, so he'd had to pull her out and dry her off himself. Her face had begun to swell, though he'd managed to stop the lip from bleeding. Although he didn't know how. The bite had gone clean through. He figured she needed stitches. But that wasn't going to happen. Not in his lifetime. That was the last thing he needed. Some snoopy bitch nurse asking just how she'd gotten the injury. His ass was already on the line with the cops sniffing around. Asking him questions about Sarah.

God, his head ached. Something was definitely happening. How long since half his brain had turned nasty? Gotten greedy? A little roughing up used to suit him just fine. A good spanking from Shaman satisfied. Bruise a little flesh. But something had split inside him along the way, and the game had gotten real. And he'd developed a taste for blood. And the hurting.

Shit, he had to get it together. Lay low after he patched things up with KitKat. He would have to really sweet-talk the bitch. Hopefully she wouldn't remember all the crap that had gone down. Who was he kidding? That fat lip of hers told the whole fucking story. Well, almost the whole story. Except for that little part where he'd humped her brains out while she was flat-out dead cold.

If only his goddamn head would stop hurting so he could think. He'd always been good at thinking, figuring things out. And as he saw it, the police were plenty interested in the van. Shit, where was Dustin hiding his ass? He needed to find him before the cops did. Needed to get inside that van and clean it up.

CHAPTER

20

Once, as a small boy, James Sakura had had to sing with his many cousins on the occasion of his grandmother's birthday. It was a short song of simple rhythms. And though he adored his grandmother, Akira did not enjoy performing in public. The words of the song were beautiful, and they sang inside of him. But the voice that came from his throat was as one of the small green frogs that filled garden ponds in summer.

It had been the next day that Akira had given his true gift to his grandmother. Taking her by the hand, he had brought her to a patch of earth, where he'd helped her to sit among the soft grasses. And then, as fast as his lean boy legs could carry him, he had run. Run with the sea-salted wind, lifting and coaxing his dragon kite into the air, until it soared, its long tail swishing against the sky. Grandmother had laughed at his wild spirit, clapped as his thin arm worked the winds and his dragon kite, tethered by hand and heart, danced among the clouds.

This morning, standing behind the podium, Sakura felt like that frog-throated boy of long-ago Hokkaido, wishing with all his heart to be Akira of the dancing dragon. It was not in his nature to make public pronouncements, in his will to preen power. Sakura, even at his most visible, was a private man.

"Thank you for coming this morning," he spoke quietly. "There can be no words for the families of the women who have died that will heal their grief. Yet we offer them. We are sorry for your incalculable loss.

And with our sympathy, we offer our continuing commitment to apprehend and bring to justice this killer." He paused, taking in his audience.

"We are utilizing the Department's full resources to stop this individual. There is much we have done, much we are doing, much we intend to do. We will not allow the voices of the victims to go unheeded." He looked down at the notes he had not used. "We are very fortunate to have the assistance of forensic psychiatrist Dr. Wilhelmina French. Some of you know Dr. French and her critical role in the Death Angel investigation. Before I take any questions, Dr. French has a few remarks."

Sakura moved away from the microphone bank and Willie came forward. "Good morning, ladies and gentlemen. Profiling is only a tool. Offering insights that inform good detectives, doing good detective work." She paused. "This killer is a risk-taker and an opportunist. A man without boundaries or discipline, a man of shallow intellect who acts from the basest of instincts. And he has begun to make serious mistakes."

Sakura listened as Willie played with the truth. She was tossing the bait. The serial would either answer the challenge with another murder—something in all likelihood they could expect anyway—or contact his detractors in order to mount a defense. They were counting on his ego, and the very thing they had publicly libeled—his considerable intelligence—to work in their favor. It was a chance they had to take. Continuing failure was not something Sakura could live with. And he *had* failed. The last three victims had died on his watch.

"What kind of mistakes, Dr. French?" Zoe Kahn had jumped the gun.

Sakura intercepted, as Willie stepped aside. "We cannot comment on that, Ms. Kahn."

"Sorry, Lieutenant Sakura"—Kahn was not giving up—"but it seems to me that, despite Dr. French's expert analysis, this serial killer appears to be anything but stupid, since he's managed to outsmart your good detective work, and jacked up the body count to seven."

⁂

It was one of those neighborhood bars that seemed to never close. *Day* and *night* meant nothing; the interior of Acey's was on neon time. Most customers bellied up to the bar, but Rozelli had decided on one of the three scarred tables parked in the rear. Bad choice. Too close to the johns. Urine smells competed with the odor of cigarette smoke and won.

Lammie Pie sat with a hand wrapped around a glass of diet Coke, fingers stripped of the fake nails she used to wear as much for self-defense as anything else. The nails were just one of many changes. In fact nothing about her resembled what she'd been two years ago. Back then her face had been coated in makeup, her lips greased hot pink, and her eyelids shadowed in something resembling colored glitter. She'd worn false eyelashes back then too, so thick and heavy she must have been visually impaired. But that would have been a mistake. Lammie Pie was all-seeing, all-knowing. A goddess of sorts.

Rozelli looked across the table, admiring her transformation. Face scrubbed clean, hair pulled back in a ponytail, and dressed in a pale yellow turtleneck and navy blazer, she could have passed for a Barnard coed. He thought she looked pretty and fresh and her age—two months shy of twenty. Though he had to admit he had liked the miniskirts that had barely covered the finest ass in the business, and that showed off legs incredibly long for someone who was just under five feet four. Of course, the stiletto heels might have had something to do with the illusion. Her short dark hair had been covered in those days with a curly platinum-blond wig, the source of her street name.

He had been the one to finally get her off the streets after her pimp had used her like a punching bag for turning tricks on the sly. Her new occupation brought her into contact with some of the same scum, but with fewer liabilities.

Lammie smiled all the way up to her big blue eyes. "You're the only man I ever offered freebies, Rozelli."

"That's a load of shit, Pie. Besides, I was never good enough for you."

"That's a crock, Rozelli. You're every girl's dream."

"You're making me blush, Lammie."

"I was hoping to give you a hard-on."

"You know I'm a man of steel, Pie."

She dropped the smile, and lifted her leg under the table, her foot going up between his thighs. She laughed, a smoker's laugh. "Good boy."

"Okay, Lammie, put your shoes back on. We got other business to transact here."

She let her foot slide away. "Franks is a real titty baby. Whenever things go sour, he runs home to Mommy in the Bronx. My sources say he's holed up there now. In an apartment over the garage."

"What's he know?"

"That his friend is looking for him."

Rozelli nodded. "He carrying anything?"

"I doubt it. . . . He killed those women, Rozelli?"

He shrugged, placed a couple of twenties on the table. "Don't give anything away, Lammie."

"Saving it all for you, Rozelli."

The office was quiet. Even the traffic noises seemed entirely subdued by the muffling effects of curtains and central heating. Willie sat at her desk, typing at her keyboard. Her work with the task force had been taking up a lot of her time, and she was using this interval between patients to catch up on writing her book.

She sat back and looked at her watch. Thirty-five minutes past the hour. Victor Abbot was inexcusably late, the second time in as many weeks that he'd been late for an appointment. It was not a good sign.

She saved her work and brought up his file. She wanted to review her notes from their first session together. Abbot had interested her, partly because of her research with psychoactive drugs and their effects on self-perception. Depersonalization disorder, from which Abbot seemed to suffer, could sometimes be triggered by the use of LSD, though the active ingredient in marijuana was a more likely catalyst. As was MDMA. The present epidemic of the disorder among the younger population was thought to be directly correlated with the widespread use of Ecstasy among clubbers and ravers.

Victor had denied such drug use. He claimed that his feelings of being an automaton were long-standing, and that he could remember no particular triggering event. There had been hints that his mother had been cold and demanding. And childhood abuse was one of the more traditional links to the disorder. It had been one avenue she'd wished to explore, but as yet there hadn't been time.

She suspected that Abbot, for whatever reason, was not really interested in therapy. He had seen her appearance on Zoe Kahn's show, and this had evidently inspired him to make the first appointment, but with no will for any serious follow-through. She found she was sorry. She was ashamed of the reaction she had had to him in their truncated session last week. It was foolish, letting a private patient weird her out, when in the course of her research she'd sat across from nearly every incarcerated serial killer in the country, having detailed conversations about their crimes.

That Abbot had been "messing with her head" she had no doubt. He might be lying to her on who knew how many levels. Still, she didn't think he was a fake; she believed that the symptoms he described were real. But he was someone with too much time and money who had mainly wanted to get close to a sensational investigation through some psychiatrist having her own fifteen minutes of fame.

Obviously, she had failed to engage him, doctor to patient. There were probably good reasons why she was more comfortable with research, more comfortable profiling serials who were in effect a substitute for patients. She was helping the police catch them after it was far too late for any effective intervention, when what she really wanted was to find them as children, before their destructive fantasies got the upper hand. It was the reason she was so obsessed with the reprogramming possibilities of drugs like LSD. The reason for writing this book. Maybe she was just . . . *Jesus, Willie, stop analyzing yourself.*

She glanced again at the time. It looked like Victor Abbot was not going to show at all. She picked up the phone. It might be true that she had never sensed any real honesty from him, much less received the proper commitment; but when she'd agreed to become his doctor, she had assumed a level of responsibility for his welfare. She dialed his number, and when he did not answer, she left him a message to call.

✺

It was a run-down neighborhood in the Bronx, but not half as bad as some Talbot had seen. He figured the curb appeal of the Franks domicile would improve in spring, since there was evidence that Mrs. Franks might have a considerable green thumb. Rows of clay pots lined the steps leading to the front door of the detached residence.

This was the second time he and Rozelli had circled the block. On the first circuit they had spotted a black van parked in the Franks driveway, had observed the garage apartment slumped at the rear of the property.

"Park here," Rozelli said, a block away. "We'll hoof it."

He pulled the car over, parked parallel to the curb.

It was bone-numbing cold, but he knew Rozelli was oblivious to the elements. Trapping rodents like Dustin Franks gave his partner a warm adrenaline rush. He shivered, his skinny Anglo-Saxon instincts responding to the damp 30-degree weather, and a certain level of rational fear that he hoped would keep him and his partner from getting themselves killed.

Rozelli slowed entering the front yard, opposite the driveway. He followed, crouching, moving alongside a row of shrubbery that flanked the house and marked the right boundary of the Franks property. There was an abandoned look about the house, a soundlessness that made him wary. He peered over Rozelli's shoulder.

"The van doesn't necessarily mean he's home," he spoke.

"Oh, he's home. In a dark stinking hole."

"You're loving this, Rozelli."

"I wouldn't exactly say I'm getting an erection."

Talbot laughed.

"We need to split up. I'll go around the back to make sure the weasel doesn't try to give us the slip. You take the front, head up those steps like an encyclopedia salesman."

"Are you implying I look like a nerd?"

"I'm not implying, Talbot. Although I'd bet my ass Janet Kissit's got the hots for you."

"So that means I'm not completely asexual. . . . Okay, I'll take the front."

Rozelli stayed low, moving ahead, then out of sight around to the rear of the garage.

He stood, walked back around the house, came up the driveway casually, as though he had nothing but innocent business to transact with Dustin Franks. He took the steps evenly, his hand going to the solid security of his .38 inside his jacket.

At the door, he knocked, stepping aside, his hand moving again to his gun. He waited.

No response.

Another knock.

Then he heard it, the wild scramble of someone in a hurry. A rat in a maze. Then a door opening somewhere, slamming back against itself.

"Police! Halt!"

He flew down the stairs, running around the corner of the house to the rear. He stopped short, looked up. Dustin Franks was spread-eagle, flat on his stomach, on the second landing of a rickety stairway that led from the apartment down into the backyard. Rozelli was standing over him, gun drawn, one foot firmly planted in Franks's spine. A jumble of small plastic packets, like imperfect snowflakes, spilled down the stairs and off the landing into the tall grass.

"That you, Talbot?" his partner asked, not taking his eyes off Franks.

"Here."

"Mr. Franks was making his big getaway." Rozelli grinned down at him. " With enough shit to get half the Bronx fucked."

✲

The late afternoon seemed contrived for beauty, a deep and pleasant coolness emerging from the shadows in the wake of a fading sun. Hanae, walking with Taiko in the French Garden, stopped along the stone path to listen to the play of water. She smiled, imagining for herself the Three Dancing Maidens of the central fountain circling joyfully in their surround of nodding chrysanthemums.

As to their actual form, she had only the accounts of others. And she held a momentary wish to wade through the pool and climb to the level of the three dancers frozen in their whirl of delight. To touch and take their measure.

So often had people wondered at her ability to sculpt what her eyes had never seen. They forgot that an object in space was but a set of relationships, which in her experience could be apprehended in the span of a hand or the gentle probing of a fingertip. A collection of information adding to a unity.

She had begun small, duplicating in clay the simplest of shapes. And if, after years, she had become more proficient . . . well, what was a head but a ball deformed by its characteristic hollows and dimples? She was no more nor less than any artist, comprehending and transforming the world to her vision. As a child, she had sometimes sought in earnest to penetrate the mysteries of seeing with the eyes. But all her imaginings and all the explanations that her cousins Sei and Nori had struggled to provide had failed to bridge that unbridgeable chasm. She had accepted that sight was insight, no matter what organ provided it. Her small success with her sculpture bore testament to that.

And indeed there were many sorts of vision, many ways of coming to knowledge. For the material world was so small a part of the all, and in the truest sense no more than an illusion. Her marriage to Jimmy was not an object to be weighed and measured in the world, but to be comprehended as a complex set of relationships. It could be summed, recognized, even as it changed. *Do not make of me a caged bird.* Her words. She knew that Jimmy had heard them and understood. Knew that he was struggling to accept her vision of where the pathway led. As she struggled to overcome the feelings which kept them from intimacy.

A cold breeze blew, ruffling her hair. She touched her forehead, where pain had begun to gather even in the beauty of the day. So many kinds of knowledge. So many complexities. Perhaps it was her sightlessness that stripped her of distraction, that let her apprehend things that others did not see. How to measure a sense of darkness? A warning of decay? She could not express these things. But the sum of them she knew, as she knew her own powerlessness.

She reached down to pat Taiko's neck, as if to feel the life and the strength of him in the warm thickness of his fur. But some danger she perceived drew closer. The threat of it grew.

🔱

From the beginning Left-brain had been a fly on the wall. Buzzing busily in the daylight, flitting from one dung heap to another. Gathering and assessing what was to be made of life. And Right-brain, the sewer rat, scurrying in the bowels of Earth, always inside the cavern of night.

At first the bodies had been insignificant. Rotting somewhere in the aethyr of anonymity. Stray cats to stray people. A quick satisfying squeeze around the neck, no more than copping a feel in the dark. Well within the rationalized boundaries of prepubescent curiosity and adolescent lust. At least that was the lie Right told to Left, and Left to Right.

The old city marked a kind of end. And a beginning. The heavy humidity of New Orleans had always given Right-brain an itch for fresh meat in specific ways that the dusty-wet bayou parish had not. Lichen-covered stucco, tight-corseted in black wrought iron, put new and exotic death smells in his nostrils. The ancient cemeteries sang to his soul. And sweet was the taste where the river ran, as the eye of a white urban-bound egret trapped him one purple evening inside its fragile bird-brain.

He could still feel the sharp edge of the aspidistra lining the bridle path in the park across from the university on St. Charles Avenue where he'd once sat mornings, and sometimes afternoons, dreaming his death dreams, waiting for night. He'd raised his body, a feeding beast, to the shadow world, daring to be seen in the bone-pale light of a full moon. It was an audacious act, as the green leather-leaves bit like delicious teeth against his naked calves, and he'd hunched over and sucked life out of the marrow of innocent young bones.

Left-brain had been fussy about the who, and where, and when. But never the why. The why was need. Yet the day came when the security of the old city failed, and the safe and familiar threatened like a full womb ready to spill its bloody contents. Left-brain said it was time to move. New York. New feeding fields. A thousand million places for a fly to fly. A thousand million sewers for a rat to crawl.

CHAPTER

21

Willie, like everyone working the case, felt the incalculable weight of tragic senseless death. And though what she had to say today would not catch the killer, it might at least trigger something that did. Yet she was never really comfortable lecturing cops, spouting theories from what some might perceive as her psychological ivory tower. But Erica Talise's murder Halloween night had only intensified the pressure to catch the madman before he killed again.

Most of her insights she'd already discussed with members of Sakura's unit. This morning she was speaking to the task force. She looked at her audience, aware of more than one pair of hungry eyes starving for a lead, and of the hollow ones that had too soon gone cynical. But worst were the eyes that seemed to hold out hope she'd be the one to deliver a miracle.

She glanced at Jimmy, seated at the table next to her, still calm in the midst of the storm that threatened to engulf them all. And because he hated meetings like this, Michael made himself invisible at the rear of the room. Rozelli, sitting in the front row, appeared edgier than usual. Even Talbot, who'd prepared the digital presentation for her, was subdued. Only Adelia Johnson favored her with a smile, a *you go, girl* shine in her eyes.

"He's changing," she started, "consciously to confuse us . . . or unconsciously because his fantasy is evolving."

"He's just trying to fuck with us." There was a low rumble of laughter. It was Harry Winn, one of the lead detectives who'd come up from precinct the second week after the task force had been organized.

She smiled. She could kiss Winn for breaking the ice.

She tossed it back. "How do you think he's doing, Detective?"

"Pretty goddamn good, Doc."

"Well, he may not be the fool we painted at the press conference, but maybe *we* can fuck a few things this morning."

Another round of laughter.

"Whatever's driving him, he's taking greater risks now. Olsen was abducted in near daylight in Central Park. Talise from her own retail store. He's more aggressive. Backing off social situations, where he had to 'work it.'" She moved from behind the table. "No more roofie. He used chloroform on Olsen, probably on Talise."

She tossed her notes back on the table. "He's got wheels. He couldn't do what he's doing without good transportation. One witness said it was a van."

"What color, Doc?"

"You tell me, Rozelli."

"Black."

"Good, Detective. The color choice of obsessive-compulsives. And from a practical standpoint, dark vehicles disappear. Especially at night." She sat on the edge of the table. "There are so many ways we could go with this guy, but I'd like to concentrate on three elements— *where* he's leaving the bodies, *what* he's doing to them, and *who* his victims are."

She nodded to Talbot, who brought up photographs of the first four victims on the wide-screen television set up in the room. It was important to keep it personal, make sure that no one lost sight that each of these women was once a living, breathing human being.

"The *where*—Grady, Phelps, Laraby, and Siebrig were disposed of in Dumpsters. As commercial refuse. The message—women are garbage."

"And the other three, the ones not in Dumpsters?" It was Eddie Ziober, a veteran cop, whom Sakura had brought in as soon as McCauley had started talking task force.

"I think we can consider the trunk of the car where Solange Mansour was found like a Dumpster. The body was concealed, and she was wrapped in Visqueen like the others. At this point he's not advertising what he's doing." A photograph of Mansour appeared on the screen.

"Olsen was not concealed, but displayed in a processing plant where her body would be discovered as soon as the first workers came in." Olsen in life appeared on the screen, next to a picture of her in death. "He was taking greater risks, flaunting what he's doing." She looked over the photographs on the screen. "Olsen's body was suspended from a hook in a meatpacking plant. She's so much meat. Consumable. Disposable, like garbage."

"And Talise?"

Talbot brought up a picture of Erica Talise, smiling for the camera, surrounded by her employees in the costume shop. "The disposition of Talise's body was the most arrogant, exposed in that store window for all the world to see. 'Look,' he says, 'what I have done.'"

She stood. "It's important to remember that serials don't think like you and me. So as difficult as it may be to understand, what he is doing to each victim holds some positive value for him. And that brings us to the *what*. It may look like mutilations, but those are quasimedical procedures he's performing on the bodies."

"A doctor?" It was Janet Kissit, the rookie detective, who took more than her share of ribbing about her name.

"Possibly, Detective. Or someone with knowledge of surgical techniques." She paused. Then, "I know he's been tagged New Jack by the media, but I think that's a poor comparison. The London Ripper butchered his victims. Throwing organs against the wall, which the Ripper did the last time he killed, is light-years away from the complex manner this serial handles his victims."

She was conscious that she was pacing in front of the table. "He's spending a lot of time working on his victims, which implies some level of comfort and control, maybe even concern. But I think it would be a mistake to be distracted by what we see on the surface. Because I believe that what he's doing inside the body is more important for him."

She stopped, signaled Talbot. "*Situs inversus totalis*—complete organ reversal." First an image of the torso of one of the victims, showing the stapled Y-incision, the tracks of stainless steel running down the chest, appeared. Then a split-screen image: on the right, a diagram illustrating the normal arrangement of internal organs; on the left another diagram, showing the anomaly of organs in reversed positions.

"Organ reversal occurs in nature . . . but not often. It can bring with it various medical complications. Including heart problems."

"Why is he doing this, Dr. French?" Kissit had removed her glasses. She looked fifteen.

"I wish I knew, Detective Kissit. But I believe it is the defining component of this serial's fantasy."

She smiled for the second time this morning. "I had an idea that these intricate surgical procedures had something to do with his wanting to create his ideal woman. A kind of Bride of Frankenstein. Ironically, this view of the killer's mind seemed to have more to do with love than hate. Which leads us to the final topic—the *who*."

She sat back down on the table. "His switch from young women to an older woman seemed to support my Bride of Frankenstein theory. Solange Mansour was sixteen; Robin Olsen, thirty. The first victims were really just beginning life. But Olsen was a professional woman. Successful. Confident. A woman at the height of her powers."

"Given today's youth-oriented culture, and since we're talking bodies here, Dr. French"—Kissit was challenging her—"and operating under the assumption that the killer is male, wouldn't it seem he would prefer younger, thinner women?"

"It would seem so, but organized serials usually work up to getting what they want. It's an evolutionary process. Perfecting their fantasy. So I assumed that victim number six, Olsen, was closer to the killer's ideal than victims one through five."

She nodded to Talbot. On the screen a full-body image of Solange Mansour in a swimsuit appeared next to one of Robin Olsen, illustrating the killer's changing preference in body type.

"But he hung Olsen on a hook in a meatpacking plant. So much meat. That's not any way to treat your ideal woman." Kissit was asking the right questions.

"True, but remember I theorized he was after perfection. He wasn't going to get it right the first time. Olsen might have been close, but like the other five, she was a failure."

She stood. "And then he murders Erica Talise Wednesday night." The partially nude photo of Talise, posed in her shop window, filled the screen. "Erica Talise was in the mold of Robin Olsen both physically and professionally. But what this killer did to Talise far exceeded what he did to the other victims. He chose to add another layer. An even more externalized layer, a manipulation superimposed over the stapled Y-incision. Which beg some questions: What is he doing? Where is his fantasy driving him now? Who, in the killer's mind, does Erica Talise represent?"

Sergeant Adelia Johnson had seen "the look" before. Hundreds of times. On the streets when she was too young to understand its meaning. And later, when she did. The punching bag look of a woman who thought she couldn't live without him in her life.

Nicole Hansen had "the look." She looked whipped, and maybe on the verge of being cooperative. "Dustin Franks said you and Randy Lancaster were seeing each other."

"Is that what that asshole said?" The words came out slightly garbled, since Hansen's lower face was twice its normal size and her mouth looked as if a rabid dog had chewed on it.

Adelia sat down. "Listen, Nicole, you don't look so good. We're here to help you. If Lancaster hurt you, he needs to pay."

"The Shaman never pays. He's a magic man, you know."

"You don't really believe that, Nicole, do you?"

The girl slumped over the table. "I don't know what the fuck is real anymore."

Adelia reached over, covered the girl's small hand with her own large one. "Try, Nicole."

"I can't believe he fucked me while I was unconscious. . . . That's rape, isn't it?" Hansen looked from Johnson over to Sakura.

"Nonconsensual sex is rape, Nicole." Johnson fought to keep her voice level.

"Felony sexual battery carries the prospect of long-term imprisonment if the perpetrator is convicted." Sakura was standing at the far end of the interview room.

"*Perpetrator,*" she repeated. "Pretty word for a rapist."

"Tell us what happened, Ms. Hansen," Sakura said, "from the beginning."

"Jesus, nobody's ever called me Ms. Hansen." She smiled for the first time, with effort. "KitKat is fine. Except . . ."

"Except?" Johnson had a good idea what the exception was.

"That shithead gave me that name. Way before we even started fucking. Sorry . . . about the language."

"Any way you want to tell it." Johnson gave her one of her high-voltage smiles.

"He . . . Randy said I looked like a stray cat. Scrawny. With my spiky short hair and green eyes."

"So he nicknamed you KitKat." Johnson thought the name suited.

She nodded. "But after, it was more than that. It had to do with . . ." She stopped, suddenly embarrassed. Suddenly looking pitiful and fragile and very young. "To do with the stuff we did."

"And what was that, Nicole?" Johnson asked.

"I was his pussy. His pet. Most of the time, when we were alone, at his place, I wore a leash round my neck and crawled on all fours. . . . I liked it." She stopped again. "I remember when he bought me a little silver bell. Put it on my collar. It was pretty. Made a nice sound. He liked knowing where I was all the time. And with that little bell jingling . . . I thought that was kinda sweet." She brought her head down, picked off some bright purple polish from one of her chewed nails.

"But sometimes KitKat was naughty." She looked up. "And Daddy Cat had to punish her. I mean isn't that what you do to bad pets?" She searched Johnson's face.

"Go on, Nicole."

"He would put me in the closet. With a bowl of dry cat food. Some water. And a litter box. It really wasn't as bad as you might think. In fact it was kinda . . . you know, got me excited. Especially when I could hear him calling through the door. 'Pussy? Where's my little Pussy?'"

"Did he let you out of the closet then?"

She nodded. "He'd unlock the door. Scratch me behind my ears. I'd lick his feet."

"Then . . . ?"

"We fucked."

"Was this the first time he hurt you?" Sakura had moved to the table where Hansen and Johnson were sitting.

"Before it was just part of the game. Spanking. Pinching my tits. That kind of thing. This . . . this was something different."

"What happened to change things?" Sakura asked.

"I don't know. We were screwing, nothing special. Then when he kissed me . . ." She choked on the words.

Johnson handed her a Kleenex. Squeezed her hand. "Take your time, baby. It's gonna be all right."

Hansen destroyed the first tissue, grappled for another. "Sorry." She blew her nose. "He bit me. I mean right through my bottom lip. His teeth went clean through. I guess I shouldn't have jerked away. I mean, it made it worse. I never saw so much blood. I thought I was going to bleed to death. I remember stuffing the sheet in my mouth, then I must have passed out or something. When I came to, I threw up all over the bed." She smiled. "That was the good part. Making him clean everything up. Including me. That's how I knew he banged me while I was out. I could feel his cum running out between my legs as he pulled me off the bed and dumped me in the tub."

"When did this happen, Ms. Hansen?"

"Last Thursday. I know I should have reported his ass, but I didn't."

"What *did* you do, Ms. Hansen?"

"I knew a human bite was worse than an animal bite. I waited until he fell asleep and got the hell out of there. Took a cab to an emergency room. I forget how many stitches they put in my lip. But they gave me a shot and some pills for infection. Told me to check back with them in a couple of days. But I haven't."

"Did they ask how you'd gotten bitten?" Sakura asked.

She affected another of her smiles. "I told the doc I'd fallen, jammed my own teeth clear through my lip. He knew I was lying, but there was so much shit going on in that emergency room I was the least of his worries."

"It would have been better if you would have told the doctor the truth, Ms. Hansen."

"You ever been scared?" She stared up at Sakura. "No, I guess not. But I was scared. I knew he was looking for me. I just didn't want any trouble. From him or the cops. Going to the cops usually gets complicated. I'd sorta just came outta hiding when you picked me up. So when

I saw you guys pull up in that unmarked car and all, I thought it was somebody Randy sent. And I had no idea if things were going to be friendly or ugly, so I ran." She met Sakura's eyes again. "The real truth is that I should have come in a long time ago. I mean after I saw that picture of him and one of those girls who got killed."

"Which girl?" Johnson glanced up at Sakura.

"Sarah Laraby. Boy, was she into some crazy shit."

"What shit, Nicole?"

"I saw this one picture. She was naked, lying back on the bed, playing with herself, and he had this scarf or something tied real tight around her neck. I could just see his hand."

"How did you know it was Randy?"

"Those goddamn rings of his."

✦

Zoe looked at herself in the mirror. "What do you think, Leylah?"

"Perfect."

"If this is going to work, I can't give away too much too soon. I mean everything should look business as usual." She flipped back her shoulder-length hair.

"Zoe, in five."

"I'm coming, Ray. Thanks, Leylah, you're the best."

"I know."

Leylah Vargarian followed Zoe out of the dressing room and into the studio, watched her give a thumbs-up to Allen in the control room. The makeup artist/hairstylist smiled. She knew a witch when she saw one; after all, she was descended from a long line of Romanian gypsies. And like her grandmother, whose picture she wore in a gold locket around her neck, she was a true believer. It was magic that had gotten her her present position at Fox, transforming talking heads into beautiful people.

Of course, Leylah had been blessed with natural ability, honing her skills early by practicing on all eleven of her Romanian gypsy cousins. Uncle Gregor had even trusted her to trim his mustache. Her considerable talent, hard work, discipline, and knowing some of the right people had all contributed in getting her where she was. But the heart and soul of her success was drawn from the same deep well that had helped her grandmother grow babies in barren wombs, and crops in fallow fields.

Leylah watched Zoe settle behind her desk, adjust the high mandarin collar inside her tailored suit jacket. The light on camera one came on.

"Is he playing it by a script," Zoe opened, "and is Halloween at last the perfect setting for his ghoulish acts?" She turned to camera two for a close-up. "Is he another player in the game of Murder Most Macabre? Another Dracula? Another Jason? Or Mr. Hyde? . . . Or is New Jack no respecter of the calendar, of the wheel of time, but a monster from Hell, and Halloween just another night?"

A slow pan of a lineup of victim photographs.

"Helena Grady, who wrote song lyrics on the backs of napkins, collected first editions of Nancy Drew mysteries, had two best friends—her mutt Maxi and her brother Charlie . . .

"Ana Phelps, home for the summer, whose favorite color was red, who still loved Dr. Seuss, and whose Taiwanese grandmother she was going to visit for the holidays . . .

"Sarah Laraby, *Selkie Girl,* Gaelic water sprite, who once won the butterfly in a state swim meet, who still slept with the teddy bear she'd gotten on her fifth birthday . . .

"Leslie Siebrig, whose favorite movie was *The Graduate,* who collected sea glass and kept a supply of Jolly Ranchers in her purse, who fostered stray cats whenever she could sneak them into her apartment . . .

"Solange Mansour, whose favorite thing was a silver enameled bracelet from her French *grand-mère,* who ate pita bread sandwiches and drank green tea, who loved algebra best . . .

"Robin Olsen, who read Joyce and Proust, who grew antique roses in clay pots, who leaves behind a husband who adored her, the promise of children . . .

"Erica Talise, who collected vintage clothes, loved Elsa Lanchester and Charlotte Rampling, who would rather wear a hat than show off her thick brown hair, who died doing what she loved best . . ."

Kahn was on a roll.

"Helena, Ana, Sarah, Leslie, Solange—young, at the beginning . . .

"Robin and Erica, women at the summit of their powers . . ."

Leylah realized she was holding her breath. This was it. Even Allen didn't know the punch line. She watched as camera two moved from the perfection of Zoe's face to an upper-body shot. Zoe's French-manicured fingers went to her throat, undoing the first, second, third of the tiny buttons on her blouse. It was mostly shadow, but the camera didn't miss it, the subtle suggestion of Zoe Kahn's cleavage.

And her words, underscoring the camera's intent. "It seems New Jack has switched . . . young girls no more, thin no longer in. Women in the full flower of their femininity is New Jack's pick." She'd used a euphemism, but "big tits" was there loud and clear. Her fingers caressed the opening of her blouse.

Leylah had to smile.

"So if that's what you want, New Jack, here I am. . . ."

Leylah looked around the studio. Zoe Kahn's challenge to the serial killer had struck like lightning.

⚊

The Shaman looked anything but spiritual this cold and dreary Monday, having been hauled from his apartment and dragged to Police Plaza. The self-appointed guru of rock and rave had come in reluctantly, but without the force of an arrest warrant. He definitely appeared to have fallen from grace. His dark hair was in a curling greasy knot at the back of his head. His face was drawn, and his eyes hung deep in dark sockets. Cheekbones jutted out in hard angles from pasty overnight flesh.

"We were finally able to connect with your manager, Mr. Lancaster. Your calendar seems to cover you for most of the dates the women went missing." Sakura was standing, looked up from notes. "At least for the critical time period for each of the nights in question."

For the first time since he'd walked into the room, Lancaster seemed alert. The significance of what Sakura had said registered, having the effect of resurrecting some of the deejay's customary cockiness. The sloping shoulders righted themselves in the trademark buckskin jacket, and for a fraction of a second he allowed himself to smile.

Sakura didn't smile. "You have been a very busy man since we last spoke."

"And what the hell does that mean?"

"It seems that you and Dustin Franks have transacted a little business lately."

He laughed. "You got my ass in here because I buy a little dope from that moron?"

"That moron has quite a business operating out the back of his van."

"I don't know anything about that."

"According to Mr. Franks, you borrowed his van on a couple of occasions."

"To move some sound equipment."

"He says that you might have used his van for more than moving equipment."

Shaman stood, his chair tumbling back hard against the floor. "I'm not answering any more of your questions."

"How well do you know Nicole Hansen?"

Lancaster's eyes took on their foxy look, daring Sakura to get an answer out of him. "I'm outta here." He was moving from behind the table. "You asked real polite if I would come by to answer a few more routine questions. Although I couldn't imagine what routine questions I hadn't already answered. But I agreed real polite. Now this little meeting all of a sudden doesn't seem so polite. You got something you want to know, serve me."

Rozelli had been waiting for this moment. He slid the arrest warrant across the table. "At your service."

Lancaster glanced down at the paper, picked it up like it was contaminated, and started reading.

"How about the *Reader's Digest* version?" Rozelli was smirking. "You're being arrested for felony sexual battery."

Sakura took up the dialogue. "The warrant has been issued under the jurisdiction where the alleged offense was committed. However, your relationship with Sarah Laraby is still of particular interest to the Special Homicide Unit, Mr. Lancaster."

"I never raped that bitch."

"Who, Mr. Lancaster?"

"I want a lawyer."

✸

Damn, security should know about the burned-out lights along aisle three. Holding her laptop in one hand, Zoe fumbled in her purse for the keys to the rental car. Owning a car was totally impractical, but she liked to have her own transportation when she made an extended pilgrimage home to Queens. She was thinking maybe she would go to temple with Momma when suddenly the arm went around her neck, and the hand over her mouth.

Strange what one thought when one was going to die. Would Momma bury her next to Papa? In the old Jewish cemetery with the iron fence and the large Star of David on the gate? Then a voice screamed in her head that she wasn't going to die. At least not like this. She tried to pull something from last month's program on self-defense as she began struggling against the viselike grip. *Kick him in the balls.* Wasn't that what you were supposed to do? Hit 'em where it hurt most. She tried to bring up her leg, heel him in the groin. But she couldn't get an angle the way he was holding her, stomach to back. *Eyes.* If only she could get at his eyes. *Thumb.* There had been something about the thumb. And the Adam's apple.

Breathe. Difficult to breathe with his arm in a choke hold around her neck. But he was breathing. She could feel his breath against the side of her face. And he was whispering, "This what you want, baby girl?" *What she wanted?* God, he was getting hard. She could feel his erection jammed up against her buttocks.

Suddenly she bucked. Bucked wildly against his chest, all the while fighting for air. Sweet God-delicious air. He seemed to loosen his grip, his hand slipping away from her mouth, freeing her nostrils. She sucked in a deep breath. *Fragrance.* He was wearing some kind of cologne or aftershave.

"Goddamn your rotten soul to hell, Johnny Rozelli!"

He released her. Even in the dark she could see he was wearing the infamous Rozelli smirk along with his hard-on. "And what the fuck do you think you're doing? How in hell did you get in here anyway?"

He grabbed her around the waist, slamming her against him. "Showing you any motherfucker determined enough could breach security in this goddamn parklot. You think the killer could be kept out if he wanted to get in, Zoe?" He pressed her harder against him. "You think you could have fought him off?"

"Let me go, Rozelli."

He pushed her away. "What are you doing, Zoe? I heard about your little performance this afternoon. Are you crazy? Baiting that psycho? You wanna get yourself killed?"

"My 'little performance' was a hell of a lot better than that transparent pussy effort from your Dr. French at the press conference. . . . He's going after big tits now, Rozelli. As I see it, I qualify."

He looked at her breasts. "I won't argue with that. But I think you're worth a lot more alive than dead."

"Why, Johnny, you say the sweetest things." She reached across and stroked his cheek. "I can take care of myself, Rozelli. And if I can get this son-of-a-bitch off the streets . . ."

". . . you should be good for at least a five-year extension on your contract. With bonuses."

"You're a real shit, you know that. You act like I don't care about those women who were murdered."

"I never said that, Zoe." He was staring at her, smiling.

"You might as well have, asshole."

"I love it when you talk dirty."

She reached up and put her arms around his neck. "Really, Johnny, don't worry about me. I can take care of myself." Then she reached down. ". . . and this."

He moaned, falling into her, pressing her body against the car. "Here . . . ?" he whispered on her mouth.

"Why not, bad boy, it's dark. No one can see us since security fell down on its job."

⚶

Hanae had fitted the home she shared with Jimmy with a shelf to the Shinto gods and an altar for Buddha, each receiving offerings on proper occasions. That there were inherent contradictions between the two belief systems—to a Shintoist the present life was the only worthy one, the afterlife beset with evil; to a Buddhist the opposite was truth—was inconsequential, since it was possible for a Japanese to compartmental-ize the mind and accept contrary things. Each way had its place.

Hanae had gone to both shelf and altar. But unlike a Christian, she did not pray for relief, did not ask to be granted peace. She accepted her present distress and fear as necessary consequences of living. Yet her heart sought understanding.

She knew that life held uncertainty, that impermanence was of its own necessity, that it effected its own brief beauty. Straw sandals wore out, the kimono was restitched after each washing, shoji frames were repapered twice a year. Cherry blossoms, the most cherished of flowers, lasted but three days.

She sat upon the tatami mat, her eyes closed, sitting now in posture, between Buddha and willful self. Breathing first through one nostril, then the other. Long deep lung-emptying, lung-filling breaths. The troubling dark within her spoke clearly of the certainty of uncertainty. Of the inescapable mutability of the eternal. Of that which was hidden in plain sight.

Last night's dream still haunted, wrapping its greedy hand around her heart. She had revisited that time that never was, with Mama-san, in the garden of her Kyoto home. Cutting the melon into perfect halves. The knife slipping. Her open palm bleeding. The blood falling to earth, feed-ing snails gliding in sticky ribbons, beetles burrowing deep.

It was the dark silk of dream-death woven. And the memory of the bloodletting emptied, leaving her as dry and thin as paper. With the knowledge that two were one.

CHAPTER
22

It is the scene for which he has been waiting—this new excursion. Mother Fox, with the kits in the Navigator, drives northward on the parkway.

The van hangs behind, keeping the space of three vehicles. A nondescript phantom in the depths of her rearview mirror. A new haunting amidst the sleepy hollows.

Her destination is a town along the river. She drives through tight streets where clapboard shops cluster together in pastel splendor. Antique shops and restaurants serving sandwiches and tea. Galleries hawking the latest in Hudson River art.

He is close behind her now, but nothing of notice in this sea of commercial perfection. And Mother Fox is intent on her mission. Giving up on the crowded street, she pulls into a small garage that is three storeys of drab concrete, sprouting in the narrow lot like a spore that has blown from the city. He drives in behind her, watching as she secures the SUV in the cave of the ground floor, parking at the far dark end away from the herd. No dings or dents will mar the silver finish.

She has unloaded his treasures and is moving toward him when three women with packages emerge from the sunny world outside. Their laughter is like an explosion in the low-ceilinged space. The trunk of a Lexus yawns hungrily at their approach.

Mother moves past the shoppers, who nod and grin at the redheaded bundles, their energy straining at the tethers of her hands. Mother smiles too, moving the kits in her determined wake. He restarts the engine, swinging the van in an arc toward the Navigator, sliding smoothly into the adjoining slot. He also smiles, who only sits and waits.

✤

The walls of Zoe's office were bare of mementos. She preferred it that way. Life was what happened next. And her life was good, especially with Johnny back in it, and her show as hot as it got in the afternoon ratings.

And life could stay good, as long as your determination never let up and you remembered to stay behind . . . the *glass,* was how she always thought of it. You watched it all through the glass—the crap that people did to one another, the crap that just happened for no reason at all. So close that you could see it all, the broken bodies and broken lives. So close you could pity it, could almost, but not quite, touch it. Just the thickness of the glass marking the division between you and some shit-load of disaster.

Fucking sick bitch . . . fucking vulture. She could still hear his voice, though it was years ago now. The husband, young and good-looking . . . her own age. His finger jabbing the air in front of her nose. His face twisted in an expression of hate. All his rage at the viciousness of his wife's pointless death directed at her.

It had been one of her first assignments for the *Post,* her chance to prove herself. She'd posed as a hospital grief counselor. She just couldn't think of any other way to get "the story behind the story" that her editor was demanding. And the truth was, it had been doing the husband some good to open up to her, to tell someone how it felt to have the heart ripped out of you. But the damn nurse had come demanding to know who she was. And that was that. Suddenly she was just this sick bitch with no letters behind her name.

The truth was that a grief counselor was exactly what she was. Not just to some poor schmuck whose wife had just become a victim of the latest horror, but to the public at large. The world was a very nasty place where a lot of bad things happened. Exposing it all made that somehow easier to live with. And as her editor had always pointed out when defending the *Post*'s tactics, the victims deserved acknowledgment too, deserved to be something more than anonymous statistics. Sterilizing pain, Murphy said, was not what gave it dignity.

If she made her living off tragedy, well, the same could be said for doctors. Life *was* tragedy unless you somehow managed to stay behind the glass. And it wasn't like she didn't know what it was like on the other side of that window—the little girl thrown clear in the accident that had killed her schoolmates.

She shook away the memory. What had started this bout of introspection? Satisfaction with her ratings? You were only as good as your last outing, and she had a show to do this afternoon, a show with nothing new or exclusive on the Ripper Murders.

The problem was that her regular sources didn't have anything that was new. And though she'd tried to call Johnny, she hadn't seen or talked to him since that little stunt in the parking lot. Not that she'd expected he could or would tell her much. Boundaries had been set on Halloween night. She had stuck around in his apartment even after she'd found the key to the cuffs where he'd hidden it, barely within reach on the bedside table. He'd woken her when he'd returned from the Talise crime scene, and kept his promise to share with her what he could, which wasn't really any more than was authorized for the general media. But it was a firsthand account, which at least felt like an edge. And there were other rewards for playing it straight with Johnny. She had to smile thinking about what had happened on the hood of her rented car. Hadn't that been some send-off for her visit with Momma in Queens?

"Ms. Kahn . . . Zoe?" The boy from the mailroom had interrupted her thoughts. He was standing outside her office, wearing his goofball smile. Lester was one of her admirers.

"Is that for me?" She was looking at the package in his hands.

"You said you wanted special delivery on anything that looked interesting."

"You're a sweetie for bringing it."

"No return address," he said, looking down at the brown paper wrapping. "That freaked out the screeners." He hung back in the doorway, prolonging the contact. "Not a bomb, though. Too light. . . . And they ran it through X ray."

"Could I have the package, Lester?"

"Sure." He came forward, handing it to her. "Mind if I stay and watch?"

She nodded. This might not be what she hoped. But it wouldn't be bad to have a witness. Just in case.

She was opening a drawer for the cutters when a sudden intuition hit that this might really be it, her dreamed-for contact with the killer of no fewer than seven women. For seconds while she cut carefully through the wrapping, she considered that the *glass* might be growing thin. In seconds more she didn't care.

✦

Rozelli walked to the rear of the Operations Room and switched on the television. He picked up the remote, punched in the channel. Pushing over a box of half-eaten pizza, he slumped against the desk.

"Hey, Leopold, take a look. It's Johnny. Wanna guess what he's doing?"

"No clue, Vince. Watchin' something on the Arts and Entertainment network?"

"Nah, our boy Rozelli's more interested in current events lately. A real news junkie. That right, Roz?"

Rozelli shook his head, laughing. He'd suffered through this routine before. At first he'd been stupid enough to take the bait. Lamely justifying his interest. Telling them she had better sources than they did. But he learned fast to keep his mouth shut, and take it like a man.

"Hey, Talbot, better watch out," Vince called over his shoulder. "Your partner's IQ is gonna top yours. With all this information goin' inside his brain."

"I'll take my chances." Talbot smiled, distracted for a moment from the data on the screen.

"Shh, guys, you disturbing our boy's concentration here." Vince wasn't going to let it rest.

Several other detectives had walked over, gathered around the television. Vince's ribbing usually drew a crowd.

The show's lead-in brought a round of snickers. When Zoe Kahn's image burst onto the screen, a flurry of catcalls and whistles erupted.

"I learned early, if you want something you have to go after it." Zoe's opening words. "You can't sit around and wait for life to come to you."

"Yeah, and we all know what Kahn wants." Dietz got in a punch.

"Sometimes getting what you want requires risks. And if what you want also happens to be what others want, stretches to include some common good, you have to be willing to take even greater risks."

The camera moved in for a close-up.

"This Monday, I took such a risk. For Helena Grady, Ana Phelps, Sarah Laraby, Leslie Siebrig, Solange Mansour, Robin Olsen, and Erica Talise. For all the women in New York." She paused, her features subtly realigning themselves. "My risk paid off." The camera held her face. "New Jack has sent me a message."

Rozelli was on his feet. The Operations Room fell silent, except for the scraping of Talbot's chair as he stood.

"This morning, I received a package." The camera finally left her face. Zoomed in on a box resting on a desk. The cover was off. Tissue concealed what lay beneath.

Zoe's hand came into the picture, slowly releasing the tissue. It rustled as she parted its folds. The camera's eye went deep, locking on the contents.

"I suppose I am to take this as a warning." Zoe's disembodied voice was slow and discrete.

It was just a paper doll. Like the kind children made. A leg cut out from one magazine. An arm from another. Bits and scraps glued together to make a whole form. But this doll wasn't like any design a child would craft. Rather it was created from a vision of madness. And the muse who had inspired the handiwork was easily recognizable. Zoe Kahn's head sat atop the puzzle-pieced body. A track of small silver staples followed a thin black line drawn down the doll's torso. Red ink had been added to make you remember the blood.

Then the moment was broken by movement, of Sakura parting the detectives who'd gathered round the televison, like Moses parting the waters. The lieutenant had obviously been watching a bit of television himself. His eyes found Rozelli's. And though the actual words would have been out of character, the detective read loud and clear in Sakura's steely silence, *Bring in the bitch. Now.*

✦

"Rozelli!" Zoe was shouting with all the air in her lungs, thoroughly enjoying her anger. "You're going to pay for this, Rozelli! Big time."

She gave one last scowl for the benefit of the surveillance camera and let go the bars, walking to sit on the holding cell's narrow metal bench. It was hard to hold on to outrage when what she felt like doing was laughing. Throwing her into the cooler! Was Sakura losing his mind? Didn't he have a clue as to how this was going to play?

She took a few minutes to consider tomorrow's lead-in. *This reporter harassed by NYPD goon squad.* It was too good. Her glance went back to the camera. She blew a kiss to whoever was watching. Now if only her sources could get her a copy of that tape. There was little chance of that, though it really didn't matter. Allen, bless his producer's little black heart, had commandeered a cameraman at the studio to get the footage of her arrest, or whatever the hell it was. She didn't think those words had actually been used. *Going downtown with your little package.* That's what Johnny had said. She was sure she remembered it right, because then she'd said to him that it wasn't the only little package around. And the other detective—Walt, wasn't it?—had laughed, and that had wiped the smirk off Johnny's face. As if he were going to be the only one having fun in all of this.

Speaking of fun, it was getting boring in this hole. How long was this game going to take? She hadn't even had her phone call.

She had walked up to the bars again, about to resume her shouting, when James Sakura appeared. The look on his face took the air out of her lungs. He stopped not two feet away and stood staring at her, as always so much taller than expected, his height exaggerated by his thinness. He seemed so damn grim that for once she had to work at not being intimidated, reminding herself that the hint of cruelty she had always detected in his mouth was also what she found most attractive.

"What am I doing here?" She spoke first, determined to seize the initiative.

"You're being held on a possible obstruction-of-justice charge." The tone in which he made this ridiculous statement really teed her off.

"Obstruction of justice? That's . . ."

". . . causing or inducing the alteration or concealment of any object," he cut through her protest, "thereby impairing such object's integrity or availability for use in a criminal proceeding."

"What criminal proceeding?" She shot back, unfazed now. "You don't even have a suspect."

"We could have one, Ms. Kahn, if your grandstanding hasn't destroyed any fingerprints, or other physical evidence."

"I was careful how I handled that . . . *thing*," she countered. "And I notice that you didn't say anything about *specific intent* while you were quoting me from the statute. I had no intent of keeping any evidence from you, and putting that thing on national television is the opposite of concealment."

The line of his mouth changed. It wasn't a smile. More a nonverbal touché. Perhaps she had surprised him by knowing the law. Had he actually bought into the bimbo bit? She had always given him the credit of granting her intelligence.

"Are you going to let me out of here now?" she spoke again. "You have no grounds to charge me, and I'm sure the network is sending an attorney."

"I am going to let you out, Ms. Kahn." He was all control. "But I hope I've made my point."

"Which is what, exactly? That you're a closet fascist?" Maybe he'd like that little turn of phrase.

"That you're on dangerous ground here, and I don't just mean legally."

"Why, Lieutenant Sakura, I didn't know you cared."

That kind of flippancy was a real mistake. His expression hardened. "I do care, Ms. Kahn," he said. "And this isn't the game that you seem to think it is."

And just that quickly it hit her. How much it all meant to him. How much it all hurt. He didn't see himself as the hero of the piece. He was not on her side of the glass at all.

"I'll have one of my officers let you out," he was saying now. "I assume you'll be willing to answer a few questions before you leave." He had begun walking away.

"Lieutenant . . . ," she called him back. "I really do want to help. . . . Catch this freak, I mean. Do you think it was him? That *he* sent me the package? . . . I won't quote you."

She saw him hesitating, and felt as if she'd passed some test when he turned back to answer. But he took the pleasure away.

"I don't know if it was the killer or not, Ms. Kahn. Some of us don't work from a script."

Even this late in the day, the Operations Room was a noisy hive of conversation and constantly ringing phones. Tables and desks had been warrened together as more and more officers were detailed to the burgeoning investigation, and the fiction of eight-hour shifts continued to blur with the ever-increasing load of paper and legwork.

Willie had hung around till lunchtime, leaving for her office and her afternoon block of patients. Now she'd come back to continue speaking with as many task force members as she could. Trading theories and information. Soaking up the buzz on all the excitement she had missed this afternoon, having returned only after Kahn had been released and the supposed killer's communication sent off to the lab. She had seen some Polaroids that had been taken of the object, but was reserving further judgment until she'd had a chance to get a better look from the videotape of Kahn's show that the network was sending over. But a "paper doll," even a grotesque one, was not the sort of response she'd expected from this killer. The method in this monster's madness was complex, but its expression was literally visceral. The rearrangement of organs was an ordered butchery whose essential meaning she had yet to grasp.

Preliminary tests on Franks's impounded van had found no traces of blood, but plenty of evidence that the vehicle had been used to move drugs. According to Franks, who was cooperating as part of some deal with the District Attorney's office, Lancaster had been instrumental in getting product past the safeguards at the clubs in exchange for his own personal pipeline. So the Shaman now had drug charges to deal with in addition to the assault on Nicole Hansen. He and Franks had each made bail, but she felt fairly confident that both would soon be off the streets for a while.

Until that time the task force would keep as much surveillance on the deejay as was possible, but she did not think that she had been wrong about Randy Lancaster. The self-styled "Shaman" was basically your low-rent sociopath preying on the vulnerabilities of young women. His violent impulses, exacerbated by drug use, could erupt to endanger his sexual partners, but she did not believe he was made of the stuff of a serial killer.

She glanced at her watch, feeling suddenly exhausted. She had been standing with a knot of officers, half-listening as Walt Talbot gave a rundown on the programs he'd set up for cross-checking data. Now she excused herself and, shouldering her purse, went over to where Michael was working alone at a desk. "I just realized how tired I am," she said to him. "You thinking of going home?"

"Not yet." He glanced up from the screen. "But you go ahead. Pick up something for us to eat."

"You sick of Chinese?"

"Chinese is fine. Get some ribs."

She pulled over a chair and sat watching his hands moving smoothly on the keyboard. She had no real evidence that the marked improvement in his mood had any more to do with his ex-wife than the deterioration that had preceded it. But she would have taken a bet on both. Whether it was calculated or not, Margot could still get to him. That he had seemed happier these last couple weeks was good. That his well-being could be materially dependent on the whims of his ex-wife was something that got to her.

He looked up. "I thought you were leaving."

"I decided to sit for a minute."

He shook his head, looking at her with those deep blue eyes, an expression she found unreadable. "Let's go," he said, and smiled. "I can finish this tomorrow."

"You sure?"

He nodded, started shutting down the computer.

"Sergeant Darius. . . ." A clerk was calling from a desk across the room. "There's a call for you. Line five."

Michael reached for the phone. Punched in the button. "Darius," he said.

She sat idly, watching his profile as he stared ahead. He listened, silent, for what seemed like minutes.

"Where was she was going . . . exactly?" he spoke into the phone at last. She could sense the effort to keep his voice neutral.

He picked up a pen and scribbled notes. "No," he said, "it's better if you stay put and work with the authorities here. Call me at this number if you hear anything." He was out of the chair and reaching for his jacket as he rattled off the number of his cell.

"What's wrong?" she said to him, but he was already moving away. She grabbed her purse and followed, catching up as he was signing out, the keys to a squad car in his hand.

"Who was that on the phone?"

For a moment, as his eyes turned to her, she had the horrible feeling that he had to focus to remember who she was.

"Reese Redmond." His voice was flat. He was walking even faster now, heading for the elevators. She clutched at his arm to keep up, aware that people were watching.

"Michael . . ." She heard her voice pleading. "Tell me what's wrong."

He shook away her hand in a gesture she would want to believe was unconscious. They had reached the elevators as one was going down. He pushed through the crowd, securing the final space. She was still trying to reach him as the doors closed in her face. But she'd looked into his eyes, and she'd heard his words.

The boys . . . His voice had died mid-sentence. Then terrible, wrong, and laced with truth: *My wife is missing,* he'd said.

Kiss of death.

Friday evening and the traffic was impossible. Darius used the siren. He didn't care what the rules said. He needed speed. And he wanted the noise to drown the phrase, so relentless now in his head. *Kiss of death.*

Some part of him understood what he'd just done to Willie, the stupid thing that he'd said. . . . *My wife.* But that was behind him now, the present all-devouring. Because despite the benign possibilities—that

Reese might have misunderstood the time Margot planned to return, or that Margot might have simply neglected to turn on her cell phone—there was another more ominous explanation that his gut had already laid claim to. Something really was wrong.

Because Margot was neither imprecise nor careless. And it spoke to the depth of Redmond's concern—that after his first call to the gallery in Kingswood to establish that Margot had indeed been there with the boys to pick up the small painting that had been reframed, after his increasingly urgent calls to her friends, to hospital emergency rooms, and finally to Missing Persons—that the man had been desperate enough to contact him.

He was grateful for that. Things might have changed from the days when a women seriously overdue from a shopping trip would not immediately set off official alarm bells, especially with children involved. But there would still be a lag time while authorities went back over the checklist of simple explanations, before engaging a full-scale response. Redmond would have to remain behind to deal with that frustration, fighting his every instinct to go out searching for Margot and the boys himself. Darius had no such constraint.

Kiss of death. The words continued to eat their way through his brain. But now, out of the city, he turned off the siren. Kingswood was not far, less than an hour from Manhattan.

Kiss of death.

Why had he done it? Kissed her like that the last time they'd met? Because it was what they both wanted. That much he knew. That much of the answer was easy.

They had always wanted each other in the physical sense. Part of Margot's attraction for him was the challenge of proving how much she did want him. She had looked so in control that first day he'd noticed her in class—the gray-green eyes cool and intelligent. An ice maiden despite the flaming hair.

Only she wasn't ice. And he'd known it. Known that her appraisal had been anything but cool. Known that he wanted *her*, and was going to get her. Because having Margot Connell in his life had been the first thing he *had* wanted since that day in high school when he'd come home to find his sister dead. It was in the aftermath of Elena's murder that he'd had to consider that the blackness he'd always felt reaching out from his dreams was not the exception but a permanence in his life, a poison that would sooner or later bring everything that he loved to ruin.

But he was weak, and some selfish brightness that remained had wanted to believe that things could change. Margot had seemed so practical and assured that he'd convinced himself she would be safe, that her disbelief in anything so intangible as a *curse* would give her a kind of immunity.

But it hadn't. Because Margot loved him, or at least loved what they had in bed. Her need for him was the chink in her armor, the place where the poison could get in. For, of course, he had ruined everything. He could not forget Elena's murder or his obsession with the evil that had let it happen. His legal studies were unsatisfying. The law too removed. He had not bothered to take the bar, and had been surprised at how well Margot seemed to accept his decision to enter the Police Academy instead. One lawyer was enough in the family, she'd said. She wanted him to be happy.

Life had seemed to work for a while. He had been as happy as he'd ever expected to be. Until he shot Robby Hudson. Killing an unarmed suspect, even one as worthless and violent as Hudson, had been the final blow. He'd learned he could not trust even the instincts he'd once valued. He had proved again what a danger he was to everyone around him. He had jeopardized his best friend's career, letting Jimmy put his name to a cover-up.

He'd resigned from the Department. And he'd forced Margot out of their marriage. His shame was that he let her believe that he blamed her for leaving as she had. Let her think that he didn't understand why she might want to keep him away from their children. His guilt was that he didn't have the courage to let her or their sons go completely. And now they would all pay. May have *already* paid.

What had been in his mind the other day when he'd kissed her? Or in hers when she'd kissed him back? In that moment he was sure she still loved him, but what had he thought was going to happen next? What had he really expected?

He had come to his exit. He turned off the parkway and headed downtown, following Redmond's instructions. The lighted narrow streets near the river were crowded with weekend traffic. He drove around, searching for any sign of the Navigator.

He was running out of options when he noticed the small parking garage. It wasn't that far from the gallery. According to Redmond, Margot had told the nanny she'd be back right after lunch. If she'd been in a hurry, she might not have been willing to wait for a closer spot on the street.

He drove in and found the Navigator nearly at once. Parked by itself in a far corner at ground level, eerie in the weak light. He pulled in beside it and got out, looking around and under the chassis, peering into the tinted windows. There was nothing much to see inside but the twins' car seats in the second row and a small flat package in the bay that was obviously the reframed canvas. No purse. No keys. No Margot, Jason, or Damon.

He brought out a tool from his trunk and tried the doors, preserving the surfaces for fingerprints. All doors unlocked, including the hatch. It sprung open on the lonely painting, so carefully wrapped. A frightening neatness that edged on the void.

Kiss of death. Easy to imagine the worst. Easy to believe the poison had caught up at last. That he'd foiled their escape . . . and his own. He shut down all else but raw will, took out his cell phone and called the Westchester County police. The next call he made would be harder.

⁂

If he could stand outside himself he would have said the same words. Would have screamed that what he had done was an insanity. That he was a savage beast. A cannibal. Lusting after flesh. Blood-boiling madness.

The stench of it still gagged.

The idea. How could he have so easily betrayed the idea? Surrendered the beauty of it? Razed the edifice of objectivity so carefully erected?

The process. How could he have run amok against the precise and perfect planning? Abandoned the structure? Exposed the hidden heart of it?

The product. How could he . . .

But this he understood. This was the easy part. Understanding the leaking mouth's ravaging of her flesh. Forsaking the elegance of the scalpel's articulation. Mother's mutilation had been the same. Secreted in the charred remains of the husk left behind.

He was screaming now. Spittle flying as he cursed and ranted at Right-brain. Saying that Left-brain had been but asleep, not dead. A piece. A part. A portion. Half-acted was this offense, not whole. And so that when the news of Margot Redmond's death had come alive like a pit of snakes, he had known. Had known what had been done. And who had done it.

And he, Left-brain, had freed it. This, whose hunger was never sated. Had it been merely the red hair? No, he told himself. The act of simple thievery had begotten it. Spawned from inside the purity of glass. It had been the mirror for this madness.

But the fire, like the ancient one, burned still. The smoke and soot and ash crusting inside like plaque along walls of arteries. And so many voices hiding so many secrets.

CHAPTER

23

For Darius, the night in Westchester County had been long and wasted. Waiting with the sheriff's department officers for the tow truck to come for the Navigator. Waiting at the station house for Redmond to arrive with the photos that would go out on the computers both state and nationwide. He was back in the station house now, sitting next to Redmond in a line of plastic chairs, pinned like a bug in the cold light that never changed. The minutes indistinguishable since his last ride out with the officers on patrol to find no trace of the twins, or Margot.

The cop that he was continued to function, but the control he maintained was hollow. His calm a disguise. He watched, as from a distance, a game that was over. Though motion didn't stop.

"A television station is sending a crew for an interview," Redmond spoke from the second chair down. His glance drifted somewhere near Darius's shoulder. They had been avoiding each other's eyes. The tie of shared pain. The lie of hope too easily read. "You should be on too."

"You'll do fine," he said.

"Have you found out anything new from Sergeant Schneller?" Redmond was referring to the detective in charge of the new shift, the second change of personnel since Darius's call from the parking garage more than twelve hours ago.

"Nothing yet, but a forensic team has started processing the Navigator."

"Processing?"

"Looking for evidence."

"I see." Redmond nodded. It was clear there were more questions he wanted to ask. Equally clear that he feared the answers.

Darius stood. "I'm going to have a smoke." His excuse to escape.

He walked outside into the weak morning light and lit a cigarette, allowing the thoughts he wouldn't share with Redmond. Into the second day with no ransom asked was not a good sign. And why take all three? A kidnapper would want only the children, with a frantic Margot left behind to convince her wealthy husband to accede to whatever demands had been made for her sons' safe return.

And if it were some sick predator instead? Predators singled out victims. They didn't snatch a mother and two children. This particular evil fit no pattern, and the outcome was therefore unpredictable. Even in the blackness that crowded his mind, there was that small space for hope.

He pulled out his cell, punched in numbers. "It's me," he said when Sakura answered. "I'm still—"

"Michael." Sakura's voice stopped him. "I was just going to call."

He breathed out once, and waited.

"I'm up at the morgue," Sakura was saying. A long pause to give one or both of them time. "A body was brought in here just a little over an hour ago. Female, Michael. . . . Red hair."

✥

Michael waited outside the viewing room while Reese Redmond went in with Jimmy and Adelia Johnson to identify the body. Sakura hadn't confirmed that it was Margot when he'd called, but his former partner knew what his ex-wife looked like. A female with red hair was the closest he had come to telling him that Margot had been found in the city, and that she was dead. *Red hair.* He tried to recall the statistics on redheaded people. Five times as many brunets as blondes? Three times as many blondes as redheads?

He remembered being conscious of his own body those first seconds after the telephone call. Standing outside the station house. Reminding himself to swallow, to breathe, to put one foot in front of the other. To fight the truth growing like cancer inside his brain. He'd looked down at the hand still wrapped around the phone, his fingers biting the plastic. He had wanted to run. To scream bloody hell. To curse the gods, and the world, and himself. Most of all himself. But he had willed himself to stay sane.

But it would have been easy to go crazy, to simply cave in, to curl up inside himself, hugging the empty weight of his pain as though he'd grown comfortable with it because it had always been there. And hadn't it? He thought of his sister Elena again, and his favorite photograph of her. A black-and-white taken with an old Kodak, a relic of his dad's. High summer, and she stood posed in shorts and a pretty blouse which fell off her shoulders. She was leaning against the trunk of a tree, smiling, expectant, waiting for that next moment.

It was the sucking sound that had brought him back. To what was happening on the other side of the door. An attendant, with the body on a gurney, rising in the elevator up from the basement morgue. *Charon navigating the River Styx.* A *whoosh-click* of gears stopping. Then silence. A pause, as though the scene behind the glass window must first be set. Then a signal from Sakura. *Into the land of the dead.* And there would be a slow pulling away of the sheet. And Redmond's eyes would be trying to make something identifiable out of what lay on the cold stainless. A moment of confusion, for denial, before truth.

The quiet was at last broken by Redmond, making a high keening noise. And then his long litany of *No*'s followed by a long litany of *Margot, Margot, Margot.* And after a moment, Sakura holding open the door as Redmond stumbled out, Adelia's arm wrapped round his shoulder. Accepting the kindness of a stranger. And suddenly Redmond remembered he was there, his eyes finding him. He tried to speak, moving his lips. But there was no sound, no words, just a bit of spittle at the side of his mouth. But he'd understood what Redmond had wanted to say: *Find Jason and Damon.*

Now he stood alone inside the morgue. The attendant had pulled out the drawer for him, and he stared at the white undulating mound. Looked at the terrible landscape created by a single sheet, rising and sloping above the flat steel of the shelf. If he stood long enough, concentrated hard enough, maybe he could wish away what lay beneath. So that by some miracle when he lifted the sheet, he'd find not Margot, but castaway toys, or baskets of soft old clothes gathered for some purpose or need.

When finally he removed the sheet, he saw the whole of her, naked and torn. Her always pale skin, now blue-cast in the cold hard light. He wanted to believe there was a blush of color in her cheeks, a flush in the webbing of veins at her temples, across her brow, in the soft flesh of her hands. Blood to match whatever it was that suffused every strand of her hair, alive still among so much death.

He glanced once at her ravaged breasts, remembering how he'd loved their compactness, how he'd once seen them nurse the boys. He had thought she would have asked him to leave that afternoon, his coming unexpectedly, only the third or fourth visit after almost a year of not seeing her. But she'd slipped out her breast and brought Jason, firstborn and greediest, to her nipple. He had stared in wonder and envy, understanding the power of what she was doing, knowing that whatever intimacy he might share with his sons, he could never have this.

Finally he took a step or two backward; the distance and the angle obscured the horror, and her body appeared merely white and bare. And if the mind could destroy, could it not also pity? Could it not grant him a measure of salvation even if he didn't deserve it? And if it could do that, could it not work the impossible? Could it not will his boys back alive?

⚶

If summer had lingered like a warm ghost, that season was gone now. The first week of November had ushered in a creeping chill to discourage the sun, a harbinger of the harsher winter to come.

Inside the cutting room it was always winter. The coldness of death. Sakura would have wished to be anywhere but here tonight, in the presence once again of Margot Redmond's body. But it had been vital that the autopsy be scheduled immediately, before postmortem changes made accurate impressions of the killer's bite marks impossible.

There remained so little now of what Margot had been. It surprised him that he could not more easily objectify the ruin that was left. They had never really been friends, but he had known her in life, so that the

image of what was lost was personal, and persisted. He had some understanding too of what she had meant to Michael. What she still meant. It
was one reason why he was here, as his friend's witness that these procedures would be carried out with dignity.

But there were other reasons.

Margot's abduction with the twins seemed to have taken place in
Westchester County. But her body had been recovered in Mo Martinez's
precinct, wrapped in Visqueen and dumped with the commercial trash
like the bodies of Helena Grady and Leslie Siebrig before her. Those
similarities could not be ignored, though there were differences in the
condition of her body that might mean the work of a copycat. The seven
previous victims had all been seriously violated, and yet the neat Y-track
of staples seemed weirdly civilized in contrast to Margot's ravaged flesh.

Dr. Linsky had agreed to perform the procedure, preserving continu-
ity should it be determined that Margot was the killer's eighth victim.
Despite conflicting emotions, Sakura prayed it would prove so. For if
this were the case, he knew he would be placed in charge of finding
Michael's twins. It was a responsibility he wished, if not welcomed.

He watched alongside Martinez as the preliminaries went forward.
Documentary photographs taken. Swabs for saliva and semen. Fuming
of the skin surfaces that yielded nothing. But impressions of the bite
marks on the chewed breasts offered another chance for solid physical
evidence. A proper registration of the killer's dental pattern could be
just as good an identifier as a fingerprint. Finally, after Bones Bailey had
taken the casts, and the breast tissue had been excised and preserved,
Dr. Linsky could begin the external examination.

"There is evidence of blunt force injury to the back of the skull"—the
ME had begun removing hair in the area of the cranial wound—"most
probably a blow to subdue the victim as she was leaning over, possibly
buckling one of the children into a car seat. The swelling that is so
prominent in the soft tissues around the eyes is often associated with
this kind of trauma, the so-called raccoon eyes being indicative of frac-
tures in the orbital roof with seepage of blood into the lids. . . . You
might want a look at this." He gestured them forward, indicating a long
linear wound in the freshly shaved scalp. "This was done with something like a pipe."

"Could the head injury have been the cause of death?" Martinez asked.

"It could have been the eventual cause," the ME answered. "We'll know more about that when we get inside. But I believe she was still alive when he bit off the nipples. Microscopic examination of the pre-served tissue can more definitively establish whether or not the biting occurred before death."

"Shouldn't there have been more blood on her if she was alive when he bit her?" Mo asked.

"Not if the killer cleansed the body, Lieutenant Martinez." Linsky was characteristically acerbic. He had begun rinsing away the dark residue from the fuming. Without its noxious coat, Margot's body seemed even more despoiled, her marbling flesh a livid contrast with the raw exci-sions that had been necessary to preserve the bite marks.

"You are quiet tonight, James." Linsky had turned to him. "Have you no questions at this point?"

Linsky inviting questions? Obviously there was some answer he was eager to provide. "I do have one question," Sakura said. "Is there any-thing yet to convince you that we're dealing with the same man?"

"Indeed," Linsky said. "I was present when the Visqueen was removed and packaged for the lab. The killer's method of wrapping and taping was precisely the same. As good as a signature, in my opinion."

Mo was shaking his head. "I guess that seals the deal, Jimmy."

"There's something else." Linsky was not finished. "The marks here are very faint"—he pointed out a portion of skin beneath the left shoul-der blade—"but I believe you can see the beginning of an incision."

"He was starting the Y-cut?" Mo's question.

"It certainly seems so," Linsky answered him. But he was looking at Sakura.

⚊⚊⚊

The twilit clouds seemed to boil as Willie watched them—a witches' cauldron of a sky. The clotted masses of gray and black like bubbles of curdled wool.

She turned from the window and walked to the bed to sit among the scattered piles of her clothing. There was a box of tissues on the bedside table and she reached to pull one out, dabbing angrily at her eyes. She despised tears. She had not had a real cry since Switzerland when the news of her mother's death had come, her sadness mixed with guilt for remaining with her studies through Lallie's final bout with cancer.

But she was thinking of a time before that. Sitting on her bed. In her father's house. Barely seventeen and gathering her clothes then too, clothes that were already too small in the waist. Packing in the wake of Edmond's edict that she and her mother spend the summer away. Her father had called her a whore who at least had good timing. She'd be back for senior year with no one the wiser.

But she had been wiser. And she had not cried like that again until her mother had died.

She hated that she was crying now, though she knew it was stupid to bottle emotion inside. Certainly not something she would ever recommend to a patient. She turned on the bedside lamp and stroked the gleaming wood of the headboard. It was a totally maudlin act, and she let herself give in to it. She wanted to feel it again, Michael's soul in this bed he'd made for the two of them. She feared it might be the last time.

She had no idea where Michael was now. She had seen him only briefly a few hours ago when he'd come in to change clothes. Before that she'd had only Jimmy's reports about the discovery and identification of Margot's body, the news that was no news regarding the fate of his sons. Waiting here in the apartment for Michael to come home had been the hardest hours of her life, a gaping hole in time that had forced her to confront the things she'd been refusing to acknowledge. Feelings. Hopes. All futile now.

She had tried to imagine how bad it would be when Michael finally arrived, had tried to think out every possible response to any form that his pain would take. Her imagination had failed her. All her professional experience a hindrance to simple humanity.

There was no helping Michael.

She could hardly remember his words, a mere recitation of facts. What she remembered were eyes that could not look at her. She had sat in the bedroom and listened to him shower. She had watched him dress from the chair, remaining motionless and silent as he picked up his keys. The air so still between them. The sound of the front door closing was like a gunshot.

She shook her head and made herself get up from the bed. She scooped up the clothes that were still on hangers and made the first trip down the hall to the smaller bedroom. Her friends the Jamilis were spending the winter away, and as always she would be welcome to their Greenwich Village apartment. But she could not go there, not yet. Could not leave Michael so completely to himself. Perhaps he could stand it—might even welcome it. But she could not.

The answer for now was the limbo to which she consigned herself. She would remain in the apartment, as solitary and as silent as he wished her to be. Till he or her pride threw her out.

Hanae knelt before nothing. The altar rested within her heart. A shrine to her two unborn children, her "water babies." She breathed deeply, yielding to their small spirits, allowing them to guide her, to help her focus the light behind her eyes, to fix upon a single point. A tiny dark star in the firmament of her mind. Another breath, and that which was finite grew in length and depth and breadth, expanding till it finally became . . . a nest of twigs and dried grass and browned needles of pine. And in the nest, a single egg with two yolks joined. Side by side, bound tentatively but inextricably, floating within the fragile armor of the shell. Alone in the nest, motherless because of the quick and common cunning of a cat. Abandoned in the tall tree, upon a branch that swayed in the force of wind and cold rain. The lids of her eyes quivered, and she inhaled, this time blowing her breath into the cup of her hands. She held the egg now. Close to her breast, a mother's breast. Held it in the cradle of her fingers, warmed by her gentle exhalations, sheltered from the storm that she had foreseen. Nurturing. Sustaining. Until Kenjin's sons were safely home.

She opened her eyes, permitting her arms to fall gently at her sides. And then she stood. It was difficult to live as her practice taught. To sit in calm mindfulness. To be in the moment. The world pushed and tugged and forced. And well she knew that what she *thought,* she could become. That had always been her worry for Jimmy. And for her as his wife. But she also understood that to acknowledge, to embrace a bad feeling, made of it but a single drop in a sea of a thousand drops of peace. She reminded herself that she was sorrowful, but she was not her sorrow.

Soft steps on the stairs. Frozen seconds before the door. Then the turning of the key in the lock. Metal against metal. Another twisting inside the deadbolt. A *thwack* of release. Door opening and closing. Relocking. Now shoes removed in the *genkan*. Lined against the wall. His hand reaching, making a slight, almost not there touch against the marriage kimono hanging in the entrance. The American detective safe-guarding the Japanese boy from Hokkaido.

"Hanae."

"I'm here, Husband." *Here* in this moment.

He moved toward her, kissing her, sheltering her in his arms. "This is what I need." He let out a long breath, warm against her hair.

"And much sleep, Husband."

"There is little time for sleep, Hanae."

She remained quiet, pressed against him.

"Reese Redmond has identified Margot's body."

"But you knew it was she, Husband." . . . *a thousand drops of peace.* "Did you hold hope that it was someone else?"

He let her go. She heard the dry paper-sound of the *sudare* being raised. "She didn't want Michael on the force . . . wanted him to practice law. With her. . . . She had the most remarkable red hair." He turned. "Funny thing to remember about a person. Not that she was intelligent. Or kind. Or even a good mother. . . . That she had beautiful hair."

She nodded. "Maybe it was the red hair that made one wish to know her. The door through which you would pass to see the good."

He sighed.

"And the husband . . . how is he?"

"What you would expect."

"And Kenjin?"

"I have not really spoken to him. Reese went in alone to ID the body."

"And no word of the sons?"

"No . . ." The single word faded.

"And you believe the man who killed Kenjin's wife murdered those other women?"

"Yes."

"And took the boys?"

"Yes."

"But he has not taken children before."

"No, not children."

"This I do not understand. His killing the mother and taking the sons."

"Maybe it was the press conference that caused him to strike out."

"You must not blame yourself, Husband."

"We taunted him. Belittled him."

"And this is his revenge? Killing the former wife of one of your detectives? Kidnapping his sons?" She shook her head. "No, Jimmy, this is not your fault. There is something *inside* this man, something beyond understanding that makes him do what he does."

He moved toward her, taking her into his arms again. "I feel powerless, my wife."

"Your strength has not abandoned you, James." She took his face into her hands. "And Kenjin, will he help?"

"McCauley will place him on medical leave."

"Will Kenjin accept this?"

"He has no choice."

"And will you find Michael's sons?"

"It is my case now. Part of the serial investigation."

"And will you find Michael's sons?" she spoke the words again.

"Yes, Wife, I will find them."

She nodded, leaning into his chest, cupping her hands between their hearts, remembering her trust, remembering that . . . *she was not her fear.*

✼

At first, he did not touch her. Though she had welcomed him, naked upon their bed, her kimono fallen to the floor like a shower of autumn leaves. His voice, making Ono no Komachi's poem his own.

. . . I come to you constantly
over the roads of dreams
those nights of love
are not worth one waking touch of you . . .

And then he was over her, the air between stirring. His brow touching her brow, his breath sweet with the sound of her name. *Hanae . . .* a thousand times her name. His lips upon the lids of her eyes, the lobes of her ears, resting in the hollow of her throat, catching her pulse. His hands pulling at the arch of her back, a bridge between his thighs, drawing her breasts into the soft wet of his mouth. Words in Japanese, a murmuring Akira demanding patience of himself, lest he go too fast. His long-denied need moving across her flesh. Hands anchoring her hips, setting himself, breaking the veil, finding her moist and swollen. Entering her, drawing her up by the waist, in drifting swells, plunging into the sucking dark.

Now she lay while her husband slept, her left hand caught in her unbound hair . . . *midaregami.*

Her memory, a tanka of Yosano Akiko.

My shiny black hair
fallen into disarray,
a thousand tangles
like a thousand tangled thoughts
about my love for you . . .

He had trembled afterward, in the circle of her arms. Too long had she kept him waiting, too long chaste. Her offense lay in her failure to wholly speak the truth. Her sin existed in allowing him to fault himself where no fault existed. And her greatest transgression . . . letting the loss of her unformed child seem an impediment where no impediment stood.

Wrongly, she had let him think her wish to be fully free was the boundary that stood guard round their bed. Two problems, divided, had unfairly become one. From their second beginning, always it was her shame that had kept them apart. A self-imposed defilement no water could purify, no penance satisfy. She had denied the path she had had to walk; the path she had had to leave behind. To struggle against blind fate was a fool's task. Only discernment led to truth. Only love secured the bond.

She pulled her fingers through her tangled hair and deep inside she smiled.

CHAPTER

24

The morning had no right to its beauty. Late November. A spiraling downward to the dead of winter. But dew fed the green in grasses as yet untouched by snow. And dawn light like rosy mist hung in the branches, heightening what remained of scarlet and gold.

Walking the damp fields with one of the K-9 units, Michael Darius remembered other mornings filled with the wood smoke of autumn, days when he and Elena, both too young for school, had rumbled together through piles of leaves so carefully raked by their mother. The air, cool and untroubled, had carried their laughter in that time before death had crept from the shadow of his childish nightmares.

A snatch of birdsong rang from a thicket as the searchers moved from meadow to woodland, the carpet of sodden leaves muffling the sounds of their passage. But his memories were not muffled. They fell with full weight. A roll call of loss that had begun with Elena.

Ahead of him, the dogs plunged on. With the car seats from the Navigator as scent articles, a team last night had retraced a trail from gallery to parking lot. Beyond this, they had found nothing. The conclusion being that the twins had been taken in the vehicle that had carried their mother to the city, possibly to be dumped along the way.

So the teams were out in full force today, searching in expanding circles in the wooded areas around Kingswood, with additional sweeps down both sides of the highway. If all else failed, the volunteers would be let in, kept out till last so their odors would not confuse the scent. In between would come the cadaver dogs.

He took it as a sign that he could not imagine Jason and Damon life-less. They inhabited his mind as he had seen them only days ago. Their energy defined. Their little-boy smells so easily summoned. *Snips and snails and puppy dog tails.* In his memory, Elena, who enjoyed being sugar and spice, sang out the differences between little boys and girls. In one of his more famous cases, it had been an imagined odor that helped rescue a kidnapped boy. An irony now if he failed to save his own sons.

The hound just in front of him stopped, snuffling through the brush at the base of an oak. But after only a moment the dog moved on with his handler. He pushed on in their wake, conscious of forces that warred within him. A darkness that could not be defeated and the will to hope.

He was so completely sick of being in his skin. His choices so few, but the only things he owned. Sending Willie away would be one of those choices. Being here in the futility of this moment was another. He would fight for ground. He would move till something took hold. Margot, like Elena, was among the lost. But not Margot's children. Every minute was a promise to find them.

⁂

"I want to thank you, Dr. French. Not just for this morning, but for everything you're doing."

"It's Willie, remember." She looked up into Reese Redmond's face, handsome in its way, but the eyes so damn sad. And a kindness there too. It had been easy coaching him. "You're welcome," she added. "Think you're ready?"

"I better be. I'm on in a few minutes." He gazed across the field to the satellite truck, where the local reporter was setting up with her camera-man. "I don't know why we had to do this out here," he said.

"More dramatic with the command post as a backdrop," she said. "And that's good. We want the public to see the search effort. Makes them want to take an active part."

"The reporter told me the feed's getting picked up by the network." He had turned back.

"Also good. Saturation coverage is exactly what we want. That's why you're going to do your statement again tonight on cable."

"As many times as they'll let me." He turned again as if to shield his eyes from the wind, but she guessed the gesture was more to hide a sudden surge of emotion. She had seen it overtake him more than once this morning, but an impulse to reassure him died on her lips. She wouldn't mouth false hope. Words were cheap; it was action that spoke. This morning's exercise already presumed a best-case scenario, that the boys were still alive. Her job with Reese Redmond was to craft a message that might keep them that way.

"What did you think about our meeting with the reporter?" Redmond was asking her now. "Think she'll keep to the questions we approved?"

"I wouldn't count on it. But you know what to do. Just say it's something you can't discuss and steer her back to where you want to go. You've seen the politicians do it. Answer the question you wished she'd asked."

"I imagine I can handle it." For the first time, he smiled.

"Good." She smiled back. "Because I think it's time you got over there."

"You coming?"

"In a minute."

She watched him walking away with shoulders squared. Reese was a class act. The hell he was going through showed clearly in his face, but his dignity remained. She supposed she could understand why a woman like Margot would . . . *What, Willie? Finish that totally tasteless thought. Choose Reese over Michael? What did that mean, anyway, "a woman like Margot?"* She herself would always choose Michael, and damn the consequences.

She looked up into the cloudless sky. The early damp had burned away with the passage of the sun. She shivered inside her jacket, with fatigue rather than cold. She'd been up early for the drive out to Kingswood, after a fitful night.

It was anger more than anything that had kept her up. She was just so damn mad about leaving herself so open. But that was Michael's doing. She had left New York last year with no expectations. He had been the one to come to her. And what was that room, that bed that he had made for them with his own hands?

The wind gusted up from another direction now, blowing wisps of hair to trap themselves in whatever lip gloss remained intact. She pushed them back, dragging sticky color in tracks across her cheek. She smudged it away with her hand, glad that she wasn't the one going on camera this morning.

🔺

"This is Tara Wilson of KKRX, and the gentleman at my side is Reese Redmond, stepfather of missing three-year-old identical twins Jason and Damon. We're coming to you from a wooded area near downtown Kingswood, New York, epicenter of a massive search for the two boys believed to have been abducted with their mother sometime around midday Wednesday from a local parking garage. . . ."

Willie stood listening just out of camera range. She was generally pleased with how the interview was going, pleased that the reporter kept focus on the twins. The idea was to resist the temptation to sensational-ism, especially in regard to Margot's brutal death. Too dangerous to hold up a mirror to the monster you pray is watching. Better to pretend for the moment that he is one of us, that he has concerns for the children he's taken. The notion might take his fancy. He just might play along.

Reese was giving the description. "Jason and Damon have bright red hair and were wearing green quilted jackets on Wednesday."

"You're seeing a recent photograph taken of the boys," the reporter took over. "If you have any information or think you may have seen them, or if you saw a suspicious vehicle, particularly a black van, in the downtown Kingswood area around midday on Wednesday, please call one of the numbers or log onto one of the websites that appear at the bottom of your screen."

The interview was winding down. They had come to the critical moment. "I believe you have a statement." The reporter had turned to Reese.

"Yes." He looked straight into the camera. "I have something I'd like to say to the person who has Jason and Damon."

Willie held a breath. *Calm and direct. Not judgmental.*

"You have never to anyone's knowledge harmed innocent children . . ."

Good. Put the best face on it. Don't make this sound like a challenge.

". . . and being with Jason and Damon, I'm sure you've gotten to know them a little. I bet by now you may even be able to tell them apart."

Invite him to see the boys as individuals.

"So I'd like to ask you . . ."

Cede him the power.

". . . that you go someplace that's comfortable for you, somewhere safe you can leave Jason and Damon for us to find."

Reese paused, and she held her breath, wondering if he was going to ad-lib.

"That would be . . . generous."

Be careful. Don't suggest that you're dictating the value of the act.

"And if there's anything that I can do to make Jason and Damon's return easier, you only have to let me know how I can help you do that."

They had gone back and forth on this. It might be dangerous if it sounded too much like a bribe. On the other hand, you never knew. This guy was all over the map. The son-of-a-bitch just might decide he could use the money, especially if he thought that things were getting too hot and he needed to make an escape. She had decided it was worth taking the chance. Their best chance of enticing him to communicate.

Reese and the reporter had finished. The woman was helping him remove his wire. Willie thought he had done well. The two of them had. She had given "cajoling" this monster the best shot she could, recompense for a very opposite effort. She had avoided admitting it, even to herself, but she had to wonder if the wording of that press conference had not led directly to Margot's murder and the twins' abduction. She was certain that Michael had thought of it. She did not believe it was simply her guilty imagination that put the accusation in his eyes.

Her problem was she was still such a Catholic. Toting up penance. Believing that you could weigh things in the balance and strike some bargain with God. Her work on Reese's plea had been a prayer. An effort to fix things. The question was, did it have a *prayer* of working?

She hoped so. She tried with all her might to believe it. But the real question that kept nagging was why the killer had taken those kids in the first place.

Reese was walking over. She looked at her watch. She would say a few words to him, then check in with Jimmy at the command post. She'd done what she could here, and needed to start thinking about driving back into town. She had several regular patients scheduled at her office this afternoon.

✤

The gallery was small, but bright and airy. Adelia Johnson stood looking around while she waited for the manager. She'd always thought she liked art, but she sure didn't understand half this shit, especially the little glassed-in boxes with pasted scraps of newsprint and broken spoons and stuff—the kind of trash you could find in any vacant city lot. Who would buy other people's garbage? Who would want to look at it?

Delia's favorite paintings were the ones she had seen when she and Samuel had taken that cruise to Jamaica. Canvases crammed with people and plants and animals. Color bursting out in reds and blues and greens. So bright you almost fell out. That's what she liked. To be *fucked* by art.

The thought tickled her, and she was smiling when she found a painting here that made her look twice. A canvas filled with trees. Not too realistic, and definitely alive. She could imagine sap like blood.

"Like it?" A tall blond woman in a neat skirt-and-sweater set had come to join her. *Bony ass,* in Delia's mind, but she had a kind face.

"I do like it." She matched the woman's smile.

"Lena Baker painted it. She's one of our best local artists. . . . See that?" The woman was pointing to the remnants of a tree that had toppled into the foreground. "The *rotting stump* is a theme in Hudson River art. It's what used to be known as a *memento mori,* a reminder that death lurks in the midst of life."

"I get that," Delia said.

"I imagine you do." The eyes were sympathetic. "I'm Maxie Tompkins." She extended her hand. "My assistant said you wanted to speak to me about what happened to Mrs. Redmond."

"Detective Adelia Johnson, NYPD." She shook the woman's hand. "I'd like to go over that last day Mrs. Redmond was here."

"I've spoken with the local police, but if you think that it might help find those boys . . ."

"Won't know till we try."

Another smile. "Let's go to my office."

The room was tiny but organized. A small couch was squeezed against one wall. They sat on that.

"How well did you know Mrs. Redmond?" Delia asked.

"Margot was a good customer. She'd been coming to the gallery for a couple years, buying things for the townhouse. Lately she'd told me they were planing to build in Connecticut. She said she'd eventually be needing some large canvases. It was going to be that kind of house. I don't guess it will ever be built now."

"She was here that day to pick up a painting?"

Tompkins nodded. "A small canvas that we had reframed for her. I wonder if she might not be alive had that painting been larger."

"How's that?"

"I wanted to have someone help her take the package to her car, but she tucked it under her arm and said it was fine. She had a shoulder bag, and she showed me that she still had a hand for each of the boys. She was so good with them."

The woman's gaze had turned inward, remembering. "I wish I'd insisted." She looked up. "But I did try to go after her. One of the boys had forgotten his toy."

"You saw Mrs. Redmond after she left the store?"

"No, I missed her. I went out to the sidewalk and looked in both directions. But I couldn't see her. She didn't tell me that she'd parked in the little overflow garage. If I'd known . . ."

"If you'd followed her into that garage, you might not be sitting here now." Delia said it more as a comfort than because she really believed it.

"I'm just so knocked back by this," Maxie Tompkins was saying. "You never think that things like this will happen to you or to people you know. But I guess that's what everyone says."

It sure as shit was, but Delia didn't confirm it. "Was there anyone who came into the gallery that day, or someone you'd seen hanging around, that seemed suspicious?"

"Not that I can remember," Tompkins said. "We have a lot of repeat business. And tourists. I can't think of anyone who struck me as odd."

"What about vehicles in the area?"

"I know that you're looking for a van, and I'm sure I saw plenty. There are a lot of deliveries for the stores here." She made a little frown. "I'm so sorry. I wish I could be more help. I can't stop thinking about those two little boys." She had risen and walked to her desk. She came back with a small plastic truck in her hand. "Tell me, Detective Johnson, what do I do with this?"

⁜

The sun was setting, sucking warmth and daylight, as search operations ended for the day. Sakura, walking into freezing wind, headed for his car. He found Darius leaning against it, sheltering the cigarette that had again become habit. It was the first he had seen him today. Michael had been dodging him, evading the inevitable.

"You need a ride?"

Darius straightened. "I need information." He threw the wasted butt on the ground.

"I wish I had some." He stared at Michael, not avoiding his eyes. He sought for a word to describe the change. Hollow. His friend looked hollowed out. "Maybe no news is good news," he said.

"You don't believe that."

Silence between them. When he couldn't stand it any longer, he spoke. "You're on medical leave, Michael, effective immediately. It's that or transfer to a rubber gun squad."

"Don't do this."

"McCauley called first thing this morning. You know the policy."

"I don't want to hear regulations. Margot was my *ex*-wife."

"They're your sons."

"I'll go crazy. I can't keep still on this."

"There's official and unofficial. You know I'll keep you informed."

Darius looked away, started to walk.

"Damn it, Michael," he shouted against the wind. "Don't you think I know this is my fault?"

Darius stopped moving. Turned back with dead eyes. "Your fault?"

"It was my idea to push this guy's buttons."

A sound escaped from Michael, a release of air that worked some animation in his face. The expression faded. "This isn't about you."

CHAPTER

25

Willie knew Reese Redmond had done everything in his power to keep his wife's funeral from becoming a public spectacle. He'd kept all arrangements secret, so that after the autopsy on Thursday night, Margot's body had been transported in a private hearse to an undisclosed mortuary. No obituary had been published, and only Redmond and Margot's parents had viewed the body. For the funeral, Redmond had decided in favor of Holy Trinity Chapel in the Village. Interment would take place in the cemetery of St. Ignatius Catholic Church in Chapel Point, Maryland, where Margot had grown up. Her parents would be taking her home one last time. Redmond had chosen to stay behind to do whatever he could to help find his sons.

Willie also knew that Sakura had warned Redmond of the probability of leaks and the likelihood of press intrusion, cautioning him to be prepared. And because Jimmy understood the harsher reality, he had arranged for police escorts and barricades around the chapel. What Sakura hadn't told Redmond was that he had also set up surveillance cameras.

Willie entered the small triangular church alone. Dipping her fingers inside the bowl of holy water, she made the sign of the cross. The morning's gray light filtered in sharp detail through the chapel's stained glass windows. She knelt in the last pew on the left, and for a moment returned to the church of her youth. To a day in January, when the New Orleans skies seemed more disposed to give up snow than rain.

She had waited that day, in the seventeenth year of her life, in a pew just in front of the confessional booths at the rear of the church. Those claustrophobic stalls that were the focus of so much mystery and dread. She had waited, fidgeting and anxious, preparing to tell her sins to Father, to whisper through the grille her mea culpas. Yet she had not made her confession that day, but had run from the church like evil itself, carrying her sins with her. That was the last attempt she'd ever made at Reconciliation. And though she was now only vaguely conscious of the old guilt and fear, she knew it only lay sleeping, not dead. But she'd learned over the years to live with both her real and imagined sins, often cursing her weaknesses, and the Church that had so easily made her feel shame.

Michael brought her back to the present. He sat in front, was at the funeral only because Reese Redmond had asked him to come. He appeared strangely foreign inside the dark suit he'd pulled from somewhere in his closet. She thought he'd glanced over at Margot's casket once, but that was an illusion because he stood like a man already dead inside his own flesh.

She searched until she found Jimmy and Hanae. They were sitting together near the middle of the chapel. Sakura, real and good and grounded. Hanae, luminous and pure, a light against the dark unleashed. Then her eyes strayed to the altar. To the priest fussing with his chalice. In a short time he would transform water and wine into the body and blood of Christ. The great mystery of transubstantiation. She forced herself to believe, so that she might pray for divine intervention. A prayer not for Margot, whose destiny rested beyond her petition, but for her sons, whose destinies remained so fragile and uncertain. And a prayer for Michael, that he would not abandon the best that lay inside of him. And selfishly, she prayed for herself. And for that seventeen-year-old girl she'd tried so hard to leave behind.

☩

Bleached light filtered through the office's single window, depositing a weak band across the desk, whitewashing stacks of folders and loose papers. Willie stretched out in a chair, massaging her feet, her shoes tossed aside. She glanced over and saw that Jimmy had hung up his overcoat. She had tossed hers over the back of a chair. Its hem was dragging the floor.

"You make me feel like a slob, Sakura."

He turned.

"Look at me. I've pulled my blouse out my skirt, my shoes are off, and my coat is half-hanging off the chair. You've hung up your coat. Your tie's perfect. Your suit jacket's still on. But then, you always keep your jacket on."

He smiled, pouring hot water through a strainer over tea.

"I'm sorry."

He stared at her.

"I'm chatting away like everything's right with the world." She lay her head back, closing her eyes. "Don't mind me. I don't do well at funerals. . . . I barely made it to my own mother's funeral."

He walked over and placed a cup of tea in her hand.

She looked up at him. "Doesn't it ever get to you, Jimmy?"

"You know the answer to that, Willie."

She nodded, blew at the steam coming out of the cup. "Who do you miss most, Sakura?"

"My grandmother . . . but her spirit manages to get my attention at least once a day."

"I miss my mother."

He nodded. "Pay attention."

"What?"

He smiled.

She shook her head. "Too much noise in my head lately. . . . Speaking of noise, what does McCauley have to say?"

"He's not happy. Seven dead women. Now Margot Redmond. The kidnapping is an additional complication."

"Such a sensitive bastard."

He moved back to his desk. "I have to wonder if the press conference . . ."

"Don't even go there, Sakura. This man sets his own agenda."

"And just what agenda is that, Willie?"

"God, I wish I knew."

"Those hesitation marks must mean he considered cutting Margot, opening her chest and reversing the organs."

"Instead he chews off her nipples. And takes her children."

"He did revert to his original pattern of wrapping the body in Visqueen before dumping it. Within blocks from where Siebrig was found."

"Why *take* those boys?"

He poured himself another cup of tea. "We're still searching Westchester County."

She nodded, took a long swill of tea. "I think they're alive, Jimmy." She looked up at him. "I don't know why, except that those twins are an important piece of whatever insanity is driving him."

"So his real target was the boys, not Margot?"

She shook her head. "Margot was part of what he wanted. Using his mouth to violate her breasts, instead of incising her chest with a scalpel. That was an intensely intimate and focused action, coming from a place where it had incubated a long time."

"With whom is he so angry?"

She met his gaze. "His mother."

"And Jason and Damon?"

She stood, putting on her shoes, tucking in her blouse. "If he is identifying Margot with his mother, then . . ."

". . . he's identifying himself with the twins."

"It's as good a theory as any, but I don't know where to go with it yet."

"Want another cup?" He was walking back to the hot plate.

"No, I'm done here."

He turned, the cup held in his hand like a relic. "The dead are dead."

"But the boys might be alive."

He nodded. "This shifts everything."

"So we focus on the boys, and everything else falls into place."

He set the cup down. "Wilhelmina?"

"Don't ask, Jimmy." She was tired and frustrated, and suddenly she was crying.

He walked over, handed her his handkerchief.

After a few minutes she took a staccatoed breath. Blew her nose. "Sorry . . ." she managed to get out. "I . . . I wish I were crying for her." She looked up. "Crying for Margot. But I'm not. I'm not even crying for those poor little boys." Her eyes fell, so that the crumpled handkerchief became the focus of her attention. "I'm crying for myself, James Sakura. The selfish bitch I am. I'm crying for myself." The last words brought on another fit of tears. "I hate myself. And I hate Michael." She looked up. "For what he's doing. For what he's going to do."

She fumbled with the handkerchief. "I didn't see him at all this weekend. I suppose he was out in Westchester with the searchers. Where he stayed, I have no idea. What I do know is I'm going to lose him. Because Margot dead is a lot harder to compete with than Margot alive. And even if by some miracle the boys are found safe, it still won't matter. God, two innocent children are missing, and all I can think of . . ." She was tearing up again.

He took her hand. "I'm your friend, Willie. Nothing will ever change that."

The apartment felt cold. The lamp near the sofa cut a hazy circle in grayness. Willie stood at the console and poured herself a drink, then walked to the light to sit down. Her purse and her shoes were on the floor where she'd left them minutes ago. She curled in the cushions, making a nest of abandonment.

She had sensed that Michael was in the apartment as soon as she'd come in. She'd tiptoed shoeless down the hall until she could see his back. He was sitting in the drafting chair in his workroom, staring at his unfinished model, a skeletal beginning of the cathedral of Rouen. She had waited, hardly breathing, but Michael never moved. And she let herself take comfort in believing that he had no idea she was there.

Still in her work clothes, she'd retreated to the living room, not wanting . . . no, not daring to intrude. It had been stupid to think that her relocation to the small bedroom could be even a temporary solution. Occupying the bedroom that opened onto Michael's workroom was hardly giving him space. And perhaps she had not really wanted to.

Hang in there was the latest advice she had given herself, but it was impossible to follow when the oppression and blackness in this place were like hands pushing at her back. She shuddered and finished her drink. It was not in her nature to avoid confrontation. And she wasn't going to cry again.

She went back down the hall, returning to stand in the threshold, as if she were expecting an earthquake and had secured the safest spot.

There was no physical indication that Michael as yet even guessed she was in the apartment. Certainly he hadn't moved at all. But this time she refused to believe that he was unaware of her.

"What do you want from me, Michael? I'm willing to give it, whatever it is." Her tone dared him to continue not looking at her.

He turned in the chair, the swivel pivoting as if of its own will. He didn't speak, and it was hard to describe his expression. But at least he didn't look through her, as he had in these last few days.

"You want me to go." She spoke the words which apparently he could not. Out of pity perhaps, or some crazy notion of politeness. "Say it, Michael."

She hadn't wanted to sound angry. God knew she didn't want to be a source of pain to him. What she wanted was the opposite, to be his help and his comfort. That he wouldn't let her, that he didn't want her, hurt worse than anything had in her life.

"You want me to go," she repeated. "You're going to have to say it."

His eyes shifted to blankness. But his voice was clear enough. "Go." It echoed at her back.

Kits alive. Alive in yaps ringing like bells. Alive in openmouthed, air-sucking, boy-legged sprints. *Home free.*

He smiled, savoring the image. Kits home free. No more sour-matted den. No too swift paw against folly. No leaking teat, or milk-crusted fur. No waiting for secondhand flesh kept in caches. Kits-into-dogs together on the run.

The primal wood lay within. Rabbit-stalking streaks. Bird-snapping, feather-full stomachs. Gekking and snirking in woodland romps. Leaps and nips at furry hinds. Fleet, sweet-scented paws. Berry-rouged snouts, needle-piercing teeth. Ear-pricked, nose-sniffing races. *Vulpes vulpes.* Kits alive.

One collapsed onto the back of the other, a squealing stack-of-boy.

Conjoined forever. He tasted the words, rich on his tongue.

"Mommy coming?" Jason stopped, turning to catch his eyes.

He frowned at the question, asked again.

"You are not happy in the forest?"

Jason nodded. Damon glancing at his brother, then mirror-nodding.

Like a visiting Dutch uncle, he reached with splayed fingers, tousling their hair. Feeling the precious blood-red thickness of it. *Anointing. New princes in the Kingdom.*

Then he knelt and took their hands into his, bringing a thumb from each into his mouth, and sucked. Suckled their sweet boy-honey flesh. *Holy, holy Eucharist.*

"Mommy coming?" Damon took up the refrain, like a bone now in his mouth.

And he, self-proclaimed, a new Father of Lies, lied.

"Sailing in the clouds." *Hell . . . sailing to Hell.*

For a moment they seemed confused.

Then Jason, "Mommy's in an airplane?"

Hard fooling a fox.

He made a whooshing sound, his fingers peaked to mimic a high-flying plane.

They giggled, and whooshed and swooped, with him in the lead, around the forest he had made. A merry formation zooming in the winking strings of the white Christmas lights, a spider's web pulled across the potted trees. Dipping now into the dark of a molded cave. Then out again, under the electric-globe moon. Shadow-making. An adventure in manufactured magic, in the hollow of secret concrete-constructed space. He stopped short, under the imagined sky, and gazed into their upturned faces. The primeval forest danced.

Tell them Mother Fox is dead, he whispered inside himself. *Tell them the vixen bitch is dead and be done with it. Tell them they are free. Tell them they have at last won the keys to the Kingdom.*

He dropped to his knees, then onto his back, lying on the grassy green he had laid. Arms stretched out to enfold them. And they came. Kits, alive, came to him. He embraced them against his inconstant heart.

And then Jason turned within the cradle of his arms, looking up.

"Why are you crying, Pun'kin Man? 'Cuz of your eyes?"

"Yes, Jason, yes . . ." The first time ever—a bitter joy found in tears.

CHAPTER

26

Wednesday afternoon. Sakura had gathered the three active members of his special unit for a short meeting. The small office was a little less crowded today, making everyone feel more acutely Darius's absence.

"I know we're all taking this case personally," he began. "It *is* personal. But it's more than that. Finding Michael's sons is now key to finding this killer. I'm not saying neglect other leads if they develop. Every victim in this case is important. But these children may still be alive, and that has to be our first concern.

"Adelia"—he turned to her—"you've been coordinating with the teams in Westchester. Where are we with that?"

"They're still out there"—Delia didn't sound hopeful—"searching with volunteers now. But it's a big area. He could've dumped those babies anywhere."

Sakura turned to Talbot. "What about closer to home, Walt?"

"If those boys are alive and he's brought them to the city, he's hidden them well. Three-year-old twins with red hair are pretty conspicuous. You'd hope that someone would've spotted them by now, with all the coverage this thing's been getting. And if he killed them here, where are the bodies? Search dogs and cadaver dogs have been all over the neighborhoods where he's dumped before."

"Let's expand those searches," Sakura said. ". . . Rozelli, you have something."

Rozelli sat forward, shooting French cuffs that winked gold. "Canvass-ing around Gramercy Park turned up a witness," he said. "A woman who claims she saw a dark van circling in the neighborhood the same morning Margot Redmond left for the gallery in Kingswood. No model or license plate. But she said she didn't think it was the only time she'd seen it."

"She get a look at the driver?" Adelia asked

Rozelli shook his head. "It's an old woman," he said. "Eyesight's not so good. But it's still somebody else who saw a van."

"Dr. French thinks it's possible that the killer wanted those boys," Sakura said, refocusing attention, "that it wasn't just a case of them being along with their mother. We need to keep pushing on detailing the last few weeks before their disappearance. Where they'd been. Who saw them. Anyone new who came into their lives. Get as many people as you need on it. Talk to everyone we've talked to again. And Walt . . ." He turned to Talbot. "I've been reviewing the Redmond interview list, and there are still people we haven't gotten to yet."

"I'm sorry, sir." Talbot fiddled with his tie, uncomfortable with being on the defensive. "It's the usual scheduling problems. People like the Redmonds are hard to pin down. But none of the ones who are left on the list are high-priority."

"You can't know that." Sakura let his irritation show. "Anyone can have a key bit of information, whether they're aware of it or not. Walk into a boardroom, or a bedroom, if you have to. Remind these people there are children's lives at stake."

He let it sink in, then changed subject. "Most of the forensics are now in," he said. "Nothing of significance was found on or in the Navigator. Nothing surprising in the autopsy report. The swabs were negative for DNA."

The last brought a collective groan. Despite what had been obvious—that the killer had cleaned Margot's body before wrapping and dumping it—everyone had been hoping for some residue of saliva at the site of the chewed tissue.

"As with all the other victims," he went on, "there was no semen present. And in fact, there was no evidence at all of vaginal or anal pen-etration."

"That's different," from Adelia.

"Yes," Sakura agreed. "Dr. French thinks the killer may have been expressing rage toward his mother. The chewed nipples may not be an overtly sexual act, but rather a symbolic attack against the mother who failed to nurture."

"Biting the breast that didn't feed you." Rozelli looked dubious. "Are we sure it's not some copycat?"

"We can't be a hundred percent," Sakura answered, "but Dr. Linsky feels confident that the same man wrapped and taped the Visqueen. And despite the obvious differences in the mutilation of the body, there are other constants. Margot Redmond was subdued, abducted, and murdered while still unconscious. Her serology screens were negative for drugs, but the blow to the back of her skull was more than enough to put her out, and probably severe enough to have eventually killed her. Though it's more probable that, like the other women, she died of suffocation."

"Any *good* news?" Adelia asked.

"Yes. Dr. Bailey was able to get an excellent registration of the killer's bite pattern."

"So all we need is a suspect." Talbot was ironic.

"What about that weird paper doll thing the Kahn woman got?" Adelia asked. "We ever get forensics back on that?"

"Nothing worthwhile," Sakura said. "No fingerprints. And the scraps were cut from common magazines."

"You think it was the killer who sent it?" she asked.

"I don't think it matters." Sakura was blunt. "The real message is the one he sent *us*. Those two empty car seats and Margot Redmond's body."

⚔

Sakura looked out the window onto Gramercy Park. There was an undertow of tension circling the hemmed-in square. He spotted two members of the press trying to maneuver closer to the Redmond home, and in the shroud of gray light he could sense the dry click of cameras in cold air. The empty park seemed held in a kind of time warp, in the bonds of an ill-fated enchantment.

That the park was the nexus of the kidnapping was becoming increasingly likely, since it was the place the twins were most publicly visible on a routine basis. Though how the kidnapping had suddenly intersected with the serial killings was still difficult to understand. If Willie's hypothesis was correct, the killer's fantasy had deep roots in a pathological hatred of his mother, and if the boys on some level represented him, then the kidnapping could embody a kind of rescue.

He turned and saw Reese Redmond pacing.

"Why the boys? Why couldn't he have just left them in the SUV?" He stopped, pulled his fingers through his hair. "I'm sorry. I keep going over and over the same questions."

"That's all right, Mr. Redmond. We're asking the same questions."

"And the answers, Lieutenant?"

"There is a possibility that Jason and Damon were specifically targeted."

"But I thought this was about killing women." His voice was bitter.

"Margot was not peripheral. She was an intended victim. Remember, though, a serial is not prompted by traditional motive, but operates out of fantasy."

"That includes my two boys."

"That is a legitimate conclusion, Mr. Redmond."

"Jesus . . ." He slumped into a chair.

"That's why we have to focus on your sons. Learn everything we can about their activities in the days prior to the kidnapping."

"They're only three years old."

"We understand. But sometimes the most unremarkable detail proves significant. What was a typical day for the boys?"

He shook his head. "I don't know. . . . They went to Montessori school some mornings. Other mornings were spent at storytime at the library, or a museum exhibit. Sometimes they just went along with Margot if she had errands. She was a great mother, wanted them to see and do everything." His voice broke. "I have to keep reminding myself that she's dead."

Sakura walked closer. How many times had he been tempted to say he understood how a person was feeling. But it was impossible to understand death in specific terms. Experiencing death was intensely personal. There was no way to make of it a common equation.

"I've brought Ms. Redmond's date book."

Redmond glanced up, as though trying to make sense of Sakura's statement. "The date book . . ."

"I would like you to sit with Sergeant Johnson and go over the entries again."

"I don't know what good it'll do, but I'll try." The hand through the hair once more.

"And try to develop a time line for Jason and Damon. Start the two weeks prior to the kidnapping, and be as precise as you can."

Redmond nodded. "She would have fought for the boys."

"Yes, Mr. Redmond, I believe she would have." But in truth Margot Redmond hadn't had a chance to fight for herself or her sons.

✳

Hanae wore her red coat, a soft gray beret on her head. Wool against the growing autumn cold. She stood on the steps, holding Taiko by his lead, and waved to Mr. Romero. In a moment she heard the idling engine shift gears and accelerate away from the curb. She'd told him to return in half an hour. Half an hour was all she needed.

She turned. "He will not be happy to see us," she spoke to Taiko, entering the building, listening to the clipping sound of the shepherd's nails against the floor of the lobby. She reached down and patted the dog. "I can smell him. Even here the wise old one lingers."

She moved toward the private elevator that led to his floor. "We must keep our hearts hidden, Taiko," she said as the door closed on the two of them, her fingers pressing the pattern of numbers she'd memorized. "He has been in the elevator today. This is good. He has not yet become a monk."

A small jolt and the elevator stopped. The door slid open. There was only his apartment on the top floor. She counted the steps to his door. She removed her glove, felt the smooth refinished wood. Felt him inside the wood. A centering breath before she knocked.

For a moment she believed he would not answer. Then movement inside. His feet a slow march toward the door. Indecision.

She decided for him. "It is Hanae, Kenjin."

The door opened. "Hanae."

So much in just the speaking of her name.

The apartment was cold. The air thin and brittle. Empty. How quickly his anger had driven Willie's scent from the rooms. She could feel him behind her. Then he walked up and she felt his hands on her shoulders, helping her off with her coat. She tugged on the lead and Taiko drew her into the living room, stopping near a familiar leather chair. She sat, removing her beret, stuffing it inside her purse.

She could sense he was watching her, standing still. Smelling of wool and wood and old pain. Taiko's tail tapped a muffled beat on the rug.

"Taiko is happy to see you."

"He's the only one."

"I am happy, Kenjin . . . and unhappy."

He was moving now, away from her.

"Turning your back on me, Kenjin, will not stop my tongue."

She heard his bitter laugh.

"I am truly sorry for your loss. To lose someone you love from this life is not without cost." She took in breath. "But I sense your feelings have more to do with you, Kenjin, than with your former wife."

She could feel his eyes. Hard. Curious.

"I told you once to be selfish. To do what *you* wanted." She paused. "But this time I am telling you to *not* be selfish. To do what *must* be done."

She could hear the sharp intake of his breath. "I'm on leave, and . . ."

"But Kenjin is not."

He was listening.

"It is selfish to think you have brought this sadness. That *you* have caused this dark path that has opened. Holding yourself responsible places you at the center of this misfortune." She stopped a moment. She could hear him move, come and sit on the floor in front of her. Taiko's tail stepped up its rhythm.

"Kenjin, you must become as nothing. Only then you become everything. You were not Margot's karma. You are not the karma of your sons. Margot's destiny is as it is. You must let her go in peace. Without the burden of your guilt. Without your anger. But you can affect the path that still lies before your young sons. To do nothing is to yet think of yourself."

"I can't even feel if they . . ." He couldn't finish the words.

"They live. And wait for you to come."

"I am lost, Hanae."

"No," her word harsh. "You allow yourself to feel this. You know the path. It is unclear now. But it will come. I call you *Kenjin* because I can call you nothing else. It is what you are. Do not deny your higher self."

At first, there was silence. Then the choking sound of grief. She reached and brought his face into her hands. "First tears, Kenjin. Then do."

Charlotte Ryler was failing—failing at composure, failing at hope, failing at not blaming herself.

"I should have been more alert. I mean in the times in which we live, you can't let your guard down even for a moment. I must have let my guard down. . . ." The tears came again. Big round tears down full pink cheeks. Ryler was a plain woman with a beautiful complexion. She had devoted most of her thirty-eight years to watching other people's children.

"The children weren't with you when they were taken, Ms. Ryler," Sakura reminded the nanny. "They were with their mother."

The mention of Margot Redmond caused Ryler to reach for her stomach. "I can't even think about Mrs. Redmond. It's so horrible."

"Take a minute, Ms. Ryler."

She shook her head, fumbling with a large white handkerchief. "What's happening to this world, Lieutenant?"

"I don't know, Ms. Ryler."

"I watched them every moment. I mean within reason. They were so active. Never stopping."

"Did you go to the park often?"

"Gramercy?"

"Yes."

"Most afternoons we went. They would play until they were exhausted. Or at least until I was exhausted. Of course, I could always settle them down by reading to them. They loved stories. God . . . I'm using the past tense." She stared up. "They're dead, aren't they?"

"We don't know that, Ms. Ryler."

"They can't be dead, they just can't."

"Did you notice anyone or anything out of the ordinary the last couple of weeks when you visited the park?"

She shook her head. "Except the weather. It got cooler. And I had a time getting the boys to keep their jackets on. Especially Jason. And of course, whatever Jason did, Damon followed. That's how it usually is."

"How what is, Ms. Ryler?"

"The older twin is usually dominant. Jason was older by six minutes."

"So you didn't notice anything unusual when you went to the park?"

"Nothing I would call unusual. I mean the boys were a handful. Every day was different."

"How?"

"Jason and Damon were precocious. If Mrs. Solomon was walking her poodle in the park, the boys would run over and play with it. If Mr. Hammond was feeding the pigeons, the boys would join in. Things like that."

"Would the boys talk to a stranger?"

"I'm afraid so. Both Mr. and Mrs. Redmond, as well as myself, gave them the ususal cautions. But the boys were very strong-willed. I remember . . ." She stopped.

"Go on, Ms. Ryler."

"I don't know why I didn't remember this before. I mean you just don't think that anyone who has a key to Gramercy Park would be anyone you'd mind speaking to the boys."

✳

The cold glare of late afternoon filled the single window of Sakura's office. He sat in the chair behind his desk fingering the jade disk, the long-ago present of his uncle Ikenobo. His mind was restless today, a victim of conflicting emotion. His wife was now in every sense returned to him, and the joy of it warred with so much else that he felt. Foremost of which was guilt.

He had forcefully assured McCauley that challenging the killer was the right way to proceed in an investigation that had stalled. True, when challenged, the monster might strike out, but a serial killer this developed did not stop. There would be more victims, whether the killer was publicly derided or not. If he killed a little quicker, a little angrier, well, that was the point. Stir emotion, fog the brain. The monster might get sloppy.

Or he might get even.

Despite both Hanae and Willie having sought to soften the burden of his responsibility, he had understood immediately that what had happened to Margot and the twins might possibly have been a response to what had been said at that press conference. And *possibly* was the straw at which his mind still caught. Because Darius was very low-profile, and his relationship to Margot Redmond was certainly not a piece of common knowledge. It seemed a stretch that the killer could have intentionally targeted Michael's ex-wife, and yet the likelihood that Margot had been a random selection seemed even more improbable, more so since she'd been followed up to Westchester. Certainly the media were convinced that Margot's murder and the twins' disappearance were acts of deliberate retaliation.

He stood and walked to the window, simply for the relief of movement, but the dying afternoon cast dreary shadows in the plaza. He had not spoken to Michael since Friday when they had been alone at his car. He had tried to phone, but his friend had not picked up, and he'd received no answer to the messages he'd left. He had hoped that Willie, at least, might be able to see Michael through the worst of this, but he'd hardly been surprised by her announcement this morning that she had moved out of the apartment.

He feared for Michael. But he knew that his own need to make some apology was selfish and worse than inadequate. There was nothing he could give beyond his absolute determination to find the twins and deliver Margot's killer.

The best and the worst of it was that his strategy had not failed. The killer had acted out his rage, and the pattern of his teeth in Margot's flesh would someday convict him. He had to believe that, believe that he would find the monster who matched those bite marks. The worst was that he could never forget that the price of that victory would always be Margot's life, and too likely the lives of Michael's sons.

Willie curled in a fetal ball on the sofa, the chenille throw tucked around her. The fire she'd lit was nearing the ember stage, and she knew she should toss in another log before it went out. Instead she reached for the wine bottle and poured herself another glass of Chardonnay. She let the wine slide down her throat, tight from the fresh bout of crying she'd given in to.

Besides the tears, she had been unprepared for the selfish mean streak she'd recently encountered in herself. Before, there had been selfishness, but never meanness. And where was the understanding? She was a psychiatrist, after all. Yet it was understanding, in the simplest human terms, that she seemed to have lost. An understanding of the heart. Being in love with Michael should have inspired, not limited her compassion. He had every right to feel pain and anger and despair. His withdrawal was natural. He had suffered terrible loss his entire life—Elena's murder, followed so closely by the death of his parents. What had he said? The accident had been the only act of mercy from a vengeful God. His parents had only been going through the motions of living; they had died with his sister.

And now Margot's murder . . . and the twins. She reached for another Kleenex. Her tears had a will of their own. Everything she knew about kidnapping told her the boys were already dead. And their death was a death sentence for Michael. In a quick vision, she saw him putting his gun into his mouth and pulling the trigger. Please, God . . .

God? How dare she? Calling on a God in whom she had little faith, and then only in her need. She tossed the tissue onto the floor with the others. The mound on the carpet looked crazily like a bouquet of the carnations she'd learned to make as a girl. Back then, she had dipped the ruffled edges of the handmade flowers into food coloring. The colors bleeding . . .

She looked over at the dying fire and decided to bring it back to life. She stoked the chunks of charred wood. Amber fireflies rose in flight against the poker, and she set another log in place. She knew she should eat something, but she wasn't hungry. Pretty soon she'd be drunk. When she turned to walk back to her nest on the sofa, she noticed she'd missed the table in the entryway and that her large satchel bag lay on the floor like a wounded animal.

She walked over and picked it up. Just as quickly she knew she should have left it. But she had retrieved it, and now she was unzipping it. Inside, settled into the bottom, was the small coin purse. Sometimes she would go for months without opening it. Her private little Pandora's box. A pocket of guilt toted around like Sisyphus's stone. For one stretch of time, she had gone almost three years without disturbing its contents. Good judgment told her now was the worst possible time to . . .

She reached into her handbag. Her fingers bypassing her wallet, cosmetic kit, cell phone, keys. Moving past a hundred small necessities that women carried with them. Seeking the tiny pouch of leather that held nothing and everything. She grasped the coin purse, feeling the cool metal of its crossed nubs, the smooth arch of its spine.

The black leather had cracked and softened over the years, the metal grown dull. She rubbed the dry surface, hesitating, and then with one economical twist, the coin purse was open. Her fingers went inside.

They were such simple things, innocuous, the two thin strips of plastic, one long, one short. Hospital identification bracelets, looped round each other, curling in the palm of her hand. *Patient: French, Wilhelmina. Patient: Baby Girl French.* The remains of the day.

❦

Adelia watched him over the rim of her glass. In her estimation Michael Darius didn't look so good. Oh, he was still plenty handsome. For a white boy. Those blue eyes could bring any woman to her knees. But tonight he seemed to wear the weight of the world on his shoulders. And his unshaven face looked like he'd been nursing a bottle of booze for days, though she knew better. She thought he looked marked by something. Like Cain from the Bible. Or like somebody had put the hoodoo on him. Of course, she reckoned she wouldn't look so good herself if someone took her Samuel. Now if Tyrone Johnson up and got himself killed . . . well, that was another matter entirely. Though Mama had taught her better, not to hold grudges, and her Baptist breeding preached kindness toward those less fortunate. But her ex-husband was the most unfortunate son-of-a-bitch she'd ever had the misfortune to know.

She set the mug on the table in front of her. The cold brew had gone down easy.

"Everybody sends their best. . . ." Shit, what was she doing? Small talk never made it with Darius.

He looked up, read her mind and smiled.

"Well, that was nice."

"What?"

"That smile."

He shrugged and lifted his glass. "Want another?"

"Off duty, but one's my limit. I don't want some asshole to take advantage of me on the subway home."

"Fat chance of that happening."

"You think I'm that tough, Darius."

"You know how to handle yourself."

"And you, Darius, you know how to handle yourself?"

He gave her another look. "Not so damn well."

"Probably better than you're giving yourself credit for."

"You sound like Hanae Sakura."

"She been by? I like that woman."

He nodded.

"Well, she's right. I know it's bad when you lose someone. Especially like your Margot died. But you haven't lost those boys."

"And how the crap you know that, Delia? No ransom note. No nothing. They might be lying dead in some ditch in Westchester County."

"Shut your mouth. Besides, they searched Westchester. Had all those dogs out." She stood. "Maybe I will take you up on that second beer. . . . Sit, I can find my way to the kitchen."

When she got back, she noticed he hadn't moved. His body stiff and hunched over like he was holding something inside him ready to spill out. His fingers clinched in a big knot between his legs. She hadn't noticed before, but his feet were bare. He had pretty feet for a man.

"Listen, I know you can understand this, Darius. Because that's just the way it is with you." She relocated on the sofa opposite him. "You see that movie *The Shining*?"

"Jack Nicholson."

She nodded. "Remember the old black man . . . Scatman Crothers. He told Nicholson's son he had 'the shining' on him, because he knew things before they happened. You got the shining on you, Darius. That's what makes you such a good cop. I guess all good cops have a little of the shining on them. Remember Kelly calling it a tightening in the gut?"

She saw him looking at her, but not seeing her.

"And right now I got a little of the shining on me. And it's telling me that your babies are still alive. And they want you to come and get them."

He refocused, was staring at her now.

"I know you're on leave. But nobody says you have to sit on your ass in this apartment."

🔺

Between his fingers, Michael held a small strip of wood, wood that might on another day have become a flying buttress or gothic arch for one of his models. But tonight it existed simply as wood. Holding it in his hands seemed to connect him to what he most needed. The objectiveness of the ordinary. He brought the wood to his nose, inhaling its scent. A smell that existed as did the wood itself, as something neither of good nor evil. On the side neither of gods or demons. And like the wood he simply desired to be. Without thought or feeling. Yet thought and feeling came.

He was a sophomore in high school before he ever saw a dead person, and that was his sister Elena. Dressed in a white lace dress with a ring of fresh flowers around her head as though she were a bride. Her gold hair precisely draped over her shoulders. Never had rape and murder fashioned a more beautiful sacrifice.

Out of the corner of his eye, he watched his great-aunts, seated in a short row, languid or stiff, filling the funeral parlor's Victorian sofa, grieving in the manner of the old ways because the magnitude of this occasion demanded it. In dusty black, shrouded in black veils, they appeared to his teenage eyes to be a line of crows, cawing, if not against death itself, then against the overwhelming pain of physical separation. He had suppressed a shiver as a pair of claw-bone hands reached for him. Holding his breath as she petted and kissed him, he still tasted her old woman odors that stained his cheek and the sleeves of his new black suit.

May you have abundant life. May her memory be eternal. They'd offered him condolences, squeezing his hand or embracing him. He had wanted to run away. Run from all the death and mourning. And the worst of it was he could not cry. Though his eyes and throat and chest ached for tears.

When the time had come to close the casket, his parents, one on each side of him, knelt and offered a prayer, and each in turn kissed first their daughter's face, then the gold crucifix Elena bore upon her chest, as if in testament to some duty done for God. He remembered his father nudging him to do the same, and he had looked then at his father's face, and it had seemed infinitely more dead than Elena's.

He bent over the satin-lined coffin and observed his sister's body, a soft waxen figure, where the line between her two lips had become almost indistinguishable. The curves where her nostrils met her cheeks vague. The discrete folds of skin of her eyelids lost. So that the whole of Elena was a soft beautiful blur, the rigid boundaries of death mercifully yielding.

He stood a long time looking down, then arched over into the deep of the casket and kissed her. He froze above her face. Then he was pulled away. In the dark of the car as he rode to the church, he touched his lips. Elena had felt hard. Like parched leather. But cold. Colder than anything he'd ever touched. The processors of death had tried to play a cheap trick on him with their clever cosmetic executions. Their pink plumping juices. But he'd not been fooled: His Elena was gone. That hideous masquerade in the coffin was to pacify the living.

Now he lay the wood on the worktable and rubbed his fist against his forehead. He had allowed himself to cry with Hanae. Yet grieving for Margot brought him no relief. Death did not fall somewhere between breathing and not breathing. Death was the end of breathing. But his boys . . . Were they still alive, as both Hanae and Adelia believed?

He stood and walked to the window and looked up at the flat black sky, made ragged by a tight crowd of ascending buildings. His head hurt, as the ancient memories played themselves out. His sister's service at the big Greek Orthodox church, then the interment at the cemetery, where flowers were tossed into the dark deep hole. But it was the ripe wormy smell of earth he would recall. And how later, back at his grandmother's, he'd thrown up the *kolliva,* hearing still the incessant whining of his crow-aunts.

And then the old memory stopped, and it was Margot's voice inside his head, talking to him, telling him. His fist shot out toward the window, the glass shattering into a thousand pieces, as he glimpsed the warning in what she had spoken that afternoon, when love and life were still possible.

⚜

He was good with needle and thread, and had hand-sewn each of them costumes to wear in the Kingdom. Long pants full at the ankles, waists pulled tight with drawstrings. Collarless shirts with wide cuffs. And wide capes, gathered in rippling folds around their plump shoulders.

He had enjoyed the labor, which had endowed him with a sense of completion, a finality. Pushing and pulling at the weave of the lustrous fabrics. Small delicate stitches flowing from his fingers, the glossy material slipping between his thighs. Snip, snip, the scissors. Spin, spin, the thread.

He looked out now to where the twins hopped and jumped, watched the satin-sheathed bodies, the staccatoed movement under the twinkling white lights. His kits come home. His little princes in the Kingdom. They had worn him out with their play, and so he'd settled in a chair outside the borders of the forest and sucked in air, warm-flavored with chocolate and cinnamon. He knew he was feeding them too many sweets. But concessions had to be made. And in the end none of it would matter.

Damon stopped, suddenly finding him in the shadows. Damon, the weaker one. The needier one. He smiled, but Damon's stare remained frozen. The inevitable would come. It always did. Slowly he stretched up out of the chair, and in the next moment entered the Kingdom, kneeling down, meeting Damon's eyes. He reached and pressed one of his red curls between his fingers.

"Mommy coming?"

He kissed the top of his head.

"Soon, Damon. Soon."

"I want my mommy. . . ." The words came out as little cat mews, high-pitched and anxious.

Jason stepped closer, lifting his arm round his brother's shoulders, the shining cape, a carney-colored cloud sailing after him. Jason, the superhero. "Don't cry, Damon." His cheek nestled against his twin's wet one. "Maybe tomorrow, Pun'kin Man?" he asked bravely.

"In the magic forest anything can happen, Jason. . . . Anything."

CHAPTER 27

The hours of inaction had been killing Michael Darius. Sitting all night in his SUV wasn't a whole lot better than sitting at home. But he welcomed any course at all that could pull him out of his skin, out of the hellhole of his mind where grief, and even hope, had the stink of self-pity.

It was a trinity of women's voices that had sent him here to watch for hours in front of this particular apartment building. They wound within his consciousness—a wisp or a rope. Hanae's and Adelia's urgings. Margot's struggle for a phrase to define her . . . fear?

Once he'd made his decision, the address had been easy to find within a professional list on the Internet. He had recognized the location as residential, made the simple deduction that the subject worked out of his home. A hang-up on a call made from his cell phone had confirmed that the man was in. He had only to wait here, for as long as that might take, grinding cigarette after cigarette into the ashtray.

He was opening a fresh pack when the man emerged from the building.

Coming into sunlight had no benign effect. Light glared from the pavement with a herky-jerky intensity that matched his mood. Pedestrians, moving toward him, seemed to shoot down the sidewalk like random parts of some exploded machine. The man paused, reaching into his jacket for the case with his sunglasses. Then, changing his mind about walking, he stepped from the curb to hail a cab.

In the closed taxi, the illusion continued of clockwork energy. Traffic signals and blaring horns, color and sound battering like fugitives at the windows. A manic Wednesday. The world grinding on.

He breathed in the stale and overheated air. He teetered at the edge . . . of what? It was hardly the time now to take off the blinders. Better to believe in fate, the life history set at the moment of oogenesis when the successful spermatozoon pierced the ovum, at the moment when the developing zygote . . . He shut off the thought.

Maybe it had been the morning's early phone call that had set him on edge. Not waking him—he hadn't actually slept since returning to the apartment yesterday, keeping to routine—but alerting him.

Had he been wandering the desert to fall asleep under the moon, a dark gypsy, trusting the lion who sniffed but never touched? Had he been assuaged from the first by forces not benign, though justified? Seduced by the mysteries of both will and weakness? Had he been a man sleepwalking in his arrogance? Untouchable in the safety of the unconscionable?

He had turned again in the bed, replacing the receiver. Then later, at the window, parting the curtain, a forehead's breadth . . . looking down.

He glanced up now, focusing on the SUV that persisted as an image in the cab's rearview mirror. The vehicle that he'd noticed parked on the street was two cars behind him now. The lion had quickened. Doing what a beast must do. Stalk its prey.

"Stop right here," he said to the driver. He pushed a ten into the man's hand and got out mid-block to a chorus of angry horns. He wound through cars and taxis, glancing back once at the SUV stranded in traffic. On the kaleidoscope sidewalk he slowed his pace to what passed for city normal. In another quarter block he'd descended into the underground.

⁂

Sakura sat behind his desk observing the circular movements of the squad room, listening to the drone of voices, the routine noises that seemed to drift into his office like dust. So many files and forms, reams of paper invested in an investigation gone dry. Miles walked, interviews conducted, questions asked. Lab reports and autopsy results. Conjecture and theory. A journey which had borne little beyond the sighting of a dark van and a bite pattern with no suspect for comparison.

But the heart of the investigation had switched from the serial murders to the kidnapping. And to that end, their energies had to be realigned—establishing a list of persons who had recently come into contact with the twins, creating a minute-by-minute time line of their lives, interviewing, and recording, and reinterviewing. Understanding that in dealing with the very young, the most innocent of details—a wayward ball retrieved by a stranger, a mismatched glove found at the bottom of a closet, a missing toy only now just remembered—could be significant information.

He closed his eyes, the jade piece sliding through his fingers like a coin. He was remembering the day his older cousin Washi had told of his pilgrimage to the eighty-eight temples encircling the island of Shikoku. He had listened with keen ears and a hopeful heart. But he understood that he was too young to put on the white tunic and leggings, to don the coned straw hat, to walk the one thousand miles of the pilgrimage. Though his desire was strong, his skinny boy's body would be no match for the fifty-day journey in the dark, in the cold and rain. His uncle Ikenobo, who had made the trek three times, had instructed him he would need to grow in many years and much vigor to match the strength of his good intentions, though it would be his will that would see him to the end of the journey.

Akira had understood, even in his ninth year, that to walk on foot the *henro-michi*—the pilgrim's road—would be walking in Zen. That he must not take such a journey lightly, that even seasoned pilgrims were sometimes misled by the signs along the roads—some told too much, some too little. That such a journey required each man to set his own pace—to hear one's own breathing was to walk too quickly. That the first days of the pilgrimage would be days of walking *toward* pain, the next of walking *in* pain, and the last of walking *above* pain. That such a journey was a pilgrimage more for the soul than the body, each step holding within it its own message. That the walk was a reflection of the

Buddha's life, and as such should serve as a mirror of how one's own life should be lived. And most important, that if such a pilgrimage should be attempted, one must find meaning in the process rather than the destination.

He opened his eyes. The Shikoku pilgrimage was a template to place over his investigation, but unlike the actual journey, this journey to find Michael's sons and their kidnapper, this journey to bring their mother's killer to justice, did not afford him the luxury of holding the process above the destination. The destination was everything.

᭢

Darius had been prepared for difficulty. But entrance had been easy. The flash of a badge at the downstairs desk, a simple pick to overcome the single lock, and he was in.

The apartment was ample, with high ceilings. The rooms carved from the spaciousness of a decades-old building. The colors neutral; the furniture square. The ambience as sterile as that drawing he had seen rolled out a month ago on Margot's dining table. He stood in the cold space that served as both living room and office, his vision darting. Taking it in.

Facing sofas. A huge slab of coffee table between. A drafting desk near the floor-to-ceiling windows. On the wall beside it, a honeycomb of diamond-shaped cubbyholes containing rolls of plans.

He lifted his face to the dead air. Ears pricked. A predatory inhalation. But no echo of residual energy, no molecule of scent was there to suggest that anything so alive as his children had lately breathed within these walls.

He went back to the foyer to begin a careful circuit. Beginning at the beginning. At the entrance and then through the living space. Then kitchen, bedroom, and bath. A potential crime scene to the part of his mind that was still half-rational. Something else entirely to the instinct that screamed in every nerve. The lethal impulse that would have him remain. That would beat truth out of this man.

᭢

". . . still missing." Zoe's distinctive voice filling the darkened room. Zoe's larger-than-life face hyperinflating in the pixels of the plasma wall screen in his bedroom.

"It's been more than a week now since the murder of Margot Redmond and the kidnapping of her sons, three-year-old twins Jason and Damon Darius"—a picture of the red-haired boys had replaced Zoe's image—"acts widely believed to be the work of the serial murderer who has taken the lives of seven other women in the New York City area.

"The twins' stepfather, New York financier Reese Redmond, in an appearance on Fox Network's *America's Most Wanted,* said that he has not given up hope for his children's safe return." Footage of Redmond with John Walsh.

"But time is surely running out, despite one of the most intensive law enforcement efforts of recent years." Zoe's face, now woeful, blossomed on the screen. "As was revealed last week on this show, the boys' father is Sergeant Michael Darius, who, until his recent leave from the NYPD, had been one of the prime investigators in the so-far-unsuccessful hunt for the serial killer. Some authorities now concede that recent public taunting of the killer may have backfired, providing the motive for the murder of Darius's ex-wife and the kidnapping of his sons.

"My question for our next guest, well-known psychologist Dr. Judith Singleton, is this: Was it smart tactics to bait this killer? And would the police have been so quick to provoke this monster if they had guessed he'd strike out against one of their own? Dr. Singleton . . ."

The heavy tumbler missed the screen by inches, breaking against the wall in a crash of splintery shards and amber liquid. Victor Abbot felt the heat go out of his tantrum. He didn't want to be angry at Zoe. She surrounded him as he sat in the bed, his hundred-plus little Zoes snipped, and stapled, and grommeted. Zoe was still his girl. He just felt . . . well, depressed.

It had been a whole week since she had even mentioned the special *creation* he'd sent her. It had been great that first day when she'd showed it on TV. He had it on tape—he always taped Zoe's show. And he'd played it over and over, but it wasn't the same. Not like being a real part of everything. Right now. Today.

He looked back at the screen, where Dr. Singleton hadn't shut up, claiming that the police had indeed wanted the killer to react. It was clear that she thought that what had happened had served them right. Then, quickly, she was covering, talking about the precious missing children, the odds that they might be found alive. It was stupid and boring. It made him want to scream at her that those kids were long dead.

The sharp needles of broken glass winked at him from across the room in the shifting light from the set. Messy. Very messy. He had to get hold of himself. Remember that he had a plan. *Transformation* was something that would impress Zoe, give her something new and better to talk about.

He had wanted to tell Dr. French about it first. Psychiatrists were doctors, and he'd thought she might refer him to someone who could help. But he'd been able to tell that she couldn't handle it. She'd looked at him funny that last time, and he hadn't gone back. Though he'd kept her messages. He liked to play them. Dr. French had a nice voice. Nothing like his mother's.

It was okay that he hadn't spoken to Dr. French about *transformation*. He'd been thinking about it for so long now that he knew he could do it. The first stage anyway. He'd gotten everything he needed off the Internet. All surgical stainless steel—316LSi. The best grade. It was really surprising what you could find with a little surfing.

✤

Hattie Solomon loved talking, and talking to the police about a murder-kidnapping involving people she knew was an invitation to oratory.

"The world is a terrible place, Detective. Of course, you see it all the time, I'm sure. How old are you, Detective?"

"Just turned thirty," Talbot volunteered.

"Married?"

"No, Mrs. Solomon."

"Now that's hard to believe. Good-looking, smart young man like yourself."

"I don't have much time to socialize. The job keeps me busy."

She nodded, stroking the poodle curled in her lap.

"The matchmakers will be in high gear now that Reese Redmond's on the market again. And poor Margot not cold in her grave. He's a good catch, though, and life does go on. Doesn't it, Imogen?" She kissed the dog on its muzzle.

"How well did you know the Redmonds?"

"Not well. Just enough to say hello when we saw each other. She was a lovely woman. Looked like a niece of mine. Died young too. Breast cancer. Wear my pink ribbon every day."

"What about the twins?"

She laughed. "What a pair. With all that lovely red hair. Dynamite One and Dynamite Two. Talk about bundles of energy. They always gave little Imogen a run for the money." She ran her nose against the poodle's.

"When did you see them last?"

She looked suddenly startled. "*Last?* That's an ominous way of putting it, Detective. Surely you're going to find them. I mean God couldn't be that cruel. Losing a wife like that should be enough for any one man to bear."

"We're hopeful, Mrs. Solomon. . . . You need a key to gain entrance to the park, is that correct?"

"You got it. No one without a key gets in."

"And who gets keys, Mrs. Solomon?"

She laughed again. "Now that's a stew. In order to secure a key to Gramercy Park, your residence must face onto one of the park's four sides."

"What about guests of the Gramercy Park Hotel?"

"The hotel does have a key. Guests must request to be let in by the doorman, I think. Though I don't see too many strangers in the park."

"Anyone who stands out in your mind?"

"A stranger?"

"Yes."

She shook her head. "You think those tykes were spotted in the park?"

"That's a possibility, Mrs. Solomon."

"Well, you just go out and find that son-of-a-bitch, Lieutenant. And bring those boys home."

Although he'd missed last Friday's appointment, and had been late on at least one occasion, Willie's instincts warned her that something was wrong when Victor Abbot's voice on her answering machine told her he was canceling this week's appointment, and didn't know when he would be able to reschedule. Something terribly wrong. And the feeling in her gut didn't improve on the cab ride over to his apartment, or when he didn't answer his door after she knocked, then banged and shouted. She had made enough racket to cause the lady living in the apartment across the hall to crack open her door and peep through the opening, secured by a chain, and give her the once-over. Apparently she'd passed muster, because the woman had answered her when she asked about the building super.

Her instincts manifesting now as butterflies and an acid buildup in her stomach, she stood waiting for the apartment manager, who lived off premises. She'd gotten the number from the nosy neighbor and had called him on her cell. It had taken some convincing to get him to come over. But she'd pulled out all the stops: She was Victor's psychiatrist and was afraid he had done harm to himself.

The manager's fifteen minutes had stretched to thirty. In the meantime she'd tried again to get a response by banging on the door and calling out his name. Though logic told her he could be anywhere, she felt certain he was inside his apartment and . . . She didn't want to think beyond the *and*. Although she'd told the super Victor was depressed and might have hurt himself, she tried not to believe the full import of her own words. To hell with the instincts that had driven her over here.

She was about to knock again when she heard the elevator doors open. It was the manager. She could instantly see why he hadn't wanted to come over. Any kind of movement had to be a monumental effort. The man must have weighed three hundred pounds. She watched him struggle onto the landing, and felt sorry for him.

"Dr. Wilhelmina French." She offered identification. "Sorry to make you come over like this, but I'm rather concerned."

"Monroe Kemp," he got out between bouts of breathing. He took the ID, examined it. "This looks okay. I just don't want to get into any trouble. Violate anybody's rights."

"I completely understand. And I'll assume full responsibility if there is any problem, Mr. Kemp."

"Call me Monroe." He was trudging to the door, fumbling with a large ring of keys, trying to locate the passkey that would open the door to Victor's apartment. "Too many keys. Don't even know what half of them open. Just keep collecting them. . . . Here, this is it." Reaching, he shoved the key into the lock and opened the door.

She hadn't gotten out the words "Don't touch anything" before Monroe Kemp bolted from the bedroom. Then she had fished for her cell in her purse and dialed 911. Her damn gut had been right, she thought as she moved over toward the bed, where Victor lay nude on his back, arms stretched out, legs spread-eagle. There had been significant bleeding, and she thought that exsanguination might prove the cause of death.

She bent over the body and examined the large industrial bolts driven into both of the knee joints. The hammer lay on the floor, flung aside after it had served its purpose. What was difficult to understand was how he'd been able to do it. How had he endured the pain? She shook her head. Of course she understood. What Victor Abbot wanted more than anything was to be a machine, and no price was too high to pay. She just hadn't been listening.

She would have liked to cover Victor's mutilated body, hide his pitiful madness from the world; she seemed to at least owe him that. But she would follow the rules. Though they seemed pathetically foolish when everything pointed to "death by one's own hand"—an infinitely kinder expression than "committing suicide." In Victor's mind, he had not died alone; but there was no consolation in that. For they were hideously obscene, scattered in the bed around his body, those dozens of awful paper dolls, with Zoe Kahn's face staring up at her over and over again.

⁂

Did the stars in the trees shine with less ferocity tonight, their random syncopation playing to the rhythms of his uneasy heart? If it were true, he yet had the will to blind himself to their dimming, as he had blinded himself to everything that lay outside the borders of the Kingdom. No news was good news.

Except for what he fed in, he had allowed nothing on any of the tele-
visions. He had planned ahead with a library of tapes. It turned out he
had stumbled upon his boys' favorite. Had let them watch it too many
times before he'd realized the implications of the bright and silly thing.
Finding Nemo had had to go. And that had not been pretty.

Could he admit to himself that he was tiring? That the rejuvenation
he sought remained more than ever elusive? He could control the time
and length of their sleep, but he had not wanted control. The Kingdom,
if it was anything, was freedom.

He rubbed his burning eyes, realizing it was late. But it was always
night here. He gazed up from where he sat on the artificial turf to the
blacked-out glass that kept the Kingdom safe, then over to where the
twins sat playing, a little dispiritedly, with a collection of toys. They had
begged again today to go to the park. In all his plans, he had never
factored in dissatisfaction. He did not wish even to entertain the possibility that his boys were less than perfect, his little rubies larded with
inclusions that would crack under stress. But if they were *not* fit for the
freedom he had gone to such lengths to provide, would that not explain
the continuing drain of his energy?

He did not want to believe it. Would not allow himself to believe it.
But the ticking of seconds was the beat of his heart.

"Pun'kin Man . . ."

Jason's voice surprised him. He had sunk so far within himself that he
had not sensed the boy moving toward him. "Yes?" he answered.

"Damon wants Mommy."

This was a new formulation. It was Jason, the more dominant, who
would now bear the burden of this weakness.

"Sailing in the clouds." He repeated the mantra.

"Airplane." The boy's tone stubborn now. "Coming home."

"Soon," he said simply. *He would not let Mother's anger into his voice.*
He opened his arms.

Jason did not move. "Damon wants Mommy." The boy looked back to
where his mirror sat listlessly staring.

"Time for a bath." He got up, smiling. He picked up Jason, who
squirmed, feet kicking. "Don't want a bath."

"We'll play the *game*." He focused his mind on that pleasure, ignoring his labored breathing, scooping up Damon in his other arm. The boy had been sniveling, mucus running clear and stringy from his nose. He'd caught Jason's cue, both of them kicking now as he carried them toward the bathroom.

The Kingdom was chaos. Was not rebellion a good thing?

CHAPTER

28

God, I'm glad you came last night." Willie sank into a chair in front of Sakura's desk, pulling over gratefully the cup of tea he'd offered. "I still feel terrible, and I don't mean because of lack of sleep. I feel bad about Victor Abbot."

"You said you didn't think it was suicide." Sakura picked up his own cup, leaned back in the swivel chair.

"No, I don't believe his intention was to kill himself. You saw those diagrams next to his bed. He wanted to insert those bolts into all the joints of his body. I just blame myself for not realizing how sick he was."

"I don't think there's any doubt that he sent Kahn the doll."

"Maybe I'd have figured that out too if I'd been paying better attention. How many of those things did he have? A hundred?" She set down her tea to brush back the dark hair that seemed especially wild this morning. "He talked to me once about Zoe Kahn, told me that he'd seen my appearance on her show. It was probably the reason he came to me."

"You told me last night you only saw him a couple times."

"Three if you count the third appointment, which was just a few minutes. But don't try letting me off too easy, Sakura. I'm getting good at self-pity." A wry smile, then, "Well, at least I was on target with something. I never really thought that the guy who sent Zoe that 'paper doll' was the killer."

He smiled. "Are we that sure Abbot's not our man?"

"As sure as we can be at this point. But you saw his place. No easy in and out, and all those neighbors. Awfully hard to imagine him bringing in a parade of drugged women and smuggling bodies out. . . . And no old blood or anything. The techs were very thorough; I watched them."

"He could have killed them somewhere else?"

"True. But where? And what about the van? Where'd he keep that? According to the neighbors he didn't have a vehicle. And there's nothing registered in his name with the DMV."

"And . . . ?" He was still smiling.

"And he just feels wrong," she admitted. "Michael's rubbed off on me, I guess. I'm leading with my gut. Because technically he could fit the profile."

"Well, for what it's worth, he doesn't feel right to me either. And there's nothing at all to connect him to these murders except that thing he sent Kahn. And that's really nothing. But we'll follow up just in case, check into his background and his movements over the last several weeks. Farther back if we have to." He poured more tea for himself, gestured toward her cup.

"I'm fine," she said.

"Hanae thinks they're alive," he spoke again after a moment.

She had no trouble following; she knew he meant the twins. "I hope she's right. Statistics say otherwise."

He sipped for a moment, then looked up at her. "You said the other day that the killer might have wanted the children. What's he want them for?"

"If we understood that . . . I mean he was into display with the two victims before Margot. But he dumps her, maybe because he knows the kids are the real attention-getter. So why hasn't he put them up for us to see?"

"Because he hasn't killed them yet."

"He doesn't toy with the women." She fell into their pattern of challenge and answer. "His style is to kill quickly."

"He hasn't killed children before," he came back. "It's different."

"That's good, Jimmy. That's a real possibility, especially if he identifies with them, like I said the other day. Maybe they *are* alive."

"Then how long do we have?"

"We really haven't answered your question of *why* he wants them. Identifying with them is not necessarily to the good. He may be into self-loathing. The real question is *what* he's doing with them."

"You're thinking dead might be better."

Her eyes were too bright when she answered. "Aren't you?"

⚊⚊

"Lyle Sanderson's the man," the hotel manager said.

Rozelli had expected a list, not one specific name, of guests who had stayed at the Gramercy Park Hotel over a period when the killer could have stalked the Redmonds. "You sure about that, Mr. Merck?"

"Of course I'm sure. I've already talked to the police about Mr. Sanderson."

Rozelli was not quite sure what was going on, but he was willing to play along. "Just for the record, sir, do you mind repeating what you told the other cops about Mr. Sanderson?"

The manager gave him a look reserved for third graders not grasping the concept of long division. "He never checked out. Left without settling up with the hotel. He owed for room service and parking."

"Did he leave a forwarding address?"

Merck passed him another exasperated look. "We checked, Detective, but it was a phony. So was the name."

"And the other cops checked out the name and address?"

"Yes, came up empty-handed too."

"You mentioned something about parking."

Merck laughed. "Now that should have been a big clue that something was screwy. Illinois address with New York plates. They came up stolen when you guys ran it through."

"What was he driving?"

Merck checked the file on his desk. "2003 Ford E-350 Cargo."

Rozelli wrote it down. "Did you ever have the opportunity to speak with Mr. Sanderson?"

The manager shook his head. "Hundreds of people come and go in this hotel, Detective. I wouldn't be able to recognize Sanderson if he had two heads. But Ed Jones might be able to help you."

⚊⚊

"Detective Rozelli." He flashed his badge. "Mind if I run a few questions by you?"

"Ed Jones." The doorman checked out his credentials and smiled. The scrutiny was par, but the smile was not customary for a cop with questions.

"How long you been working here, Ed?"

"My feet say too long. But for the record about twelve years." Another smile.

"You worked during October and all of November so far."

He nodded. "All October. Hope to make it through November."

Rozelli looked across Lexington Avenue to Gramercy Park, the only private park in the city. The small piece of real estate, encircled by a tall iron fence with a locked gate, had been designed to keep outsiders out.

"If I wanted to get into the park, how would I go about that, Ed?"

The doorman pushed back his cap, scratching his forehead as if he'd just been asked a complex question. "Two ways. First, if you live in one of those fancy houses facing the park, you get a key. Second, if you are a guest of the hotel."

"So hotel guests get a key to the park?"

"Oh no, Detective, it doesn't work that way. Only one key. And I got it. You want to get into Gramercy Park, I have to let you in."

"That work out okay with you?"

"Keeps things tight. And since I work days it's not a problem."

"How's that?"

"Park's only open from seven in the morning to sunset."

He took another brief look at the park through the traffic. "Remember a guest by the name of Lyle Sanderson? Stayed at the hotel part of October, part of November."

The doorman nodded his head. "Nice guy. But not much of a talker. Never looked at you when he spoke."

"He ever go to the park?"

"Lots of times. Liked to go over there and read. Always had a book with him."

"Ever see him talk to any of the children?"

"Can't say as I did. I would just let him in, then come right back. But it wouldn't surprise me, though, if he talked to the kids. Had the impression Mr. Sanderson didn't care much for adults."

"So you never got a good look at Sanderson's face?"

"Now I didn't say that." He did that forehead scratching thing again. "One afternoon there was a Halloween party going on. I remember the wind was blowing pretty hard. Shaking some paper lanterns strung up in the trees for decoration. Sanderson noticed them too. He looked up and watched them for the longest. Had a big grin on his face. That's when I got a good look at him. I've seen stranger-looking faces, but none quite like Mr. Sanderson's."

The traffic was midday thick as Talbot drove toward the financial district and his hastily scheduled meeting with Reese Redmond. The information that Johnny had picked up this morning had given him the *buzz,* that slightly jazzed feeling that something major was finally going to break. He cut it off. *Don't get ahead of yourself, Walt. Don't jinx it.*

Because what they had was only the slimmest thread. He'd been at the computer for the past couple hours rechecking it, and there was little doubt that Lyle Sanderson was indeed a false identity. A dead end. The job now, with the clock still ticking on Darius's kids, was to somehow pick up the trail.

He was pulling away from a red light when his cell phone sounded.

"Talbot."

"It's me." Rozelli in his ear. "I'm headed back in."

"You finished at the hotel?"

"Yeah. The rest of the staff was deaf, dumb, and blind."

"What about the nanny?"

"I dropped by to see her, but no help." Rozelli sounded disgusted. "Said she never saw the guy that close-up, but he could've been the one the kids talked to. . . . You on your way to see Redmond?"

"In his office. First day back. He's there for a couple hours."

A signature grunt. "Do some good."

"Has something happened, Officer Talbot?" Reese Redmond seemed to be bracing himself in the leather chair.

"We haven't found the boys." He got the words out quickly, trying to allay what he knew was the man's worst fear. These were not only Darius's kids, he reminded himself.

"What is it then?"

"We *have* turned up something, Mr. Redmond, a man who rented a hotel room on Gramercy Park for weeks leading up to . . ."

"What man?"

"The name he registered under was Lyle Sanderson. Gave an address in Illinois. You know this person?"

"No," Redmond said. "Have you picked him up?"

"We can't." He looked away. "Lyle Sanderson turned out not to be his real name. And he hasn't been seen at the hotel since the morning your family was taken."

Redmond had shifted to the edge of his seat. He rested his head in his hands now, staring down at his desk. "So this man who may have my boys has just disappeared?" There was a note of disbelief that edged on anger. "What are you doing to find him?" He looked up.

"Everything we can. Which is why I'm here. We have a description, and . . ."

". . . and I'm delaying your telling me." A hand pushed at his temple, flattening the hair. "Please go on, Detective. What does this man look like?"

"Tall and thin," Talbot said, "with brown hair. Possibly a slight Southern accent. But the real identifier is the eyes. According to the doorman, they're different colors."

Even as he said it, Talbot knew there would be a reaction. He had felt it building, but seeing the result made the *buzz* fission in his skull.

The force of it had Redmond standing. "My God, that's David St. Cyr."

🜨

Sakura knew that David St. Cyr had somehow slipped through the cracks. As the Redmond architect, he was someone new in the family's life. Someone on the periphery, and not in the red-hot center of their universe. But that was no excuse for not getting to him sooner. Good police work looked at everybody. And everybody was a suspect until cleared. Today he would interview St. Cyr and clear him. *Or not.*

St. Cyr's apartment building was an old one brought back to life. One that had accumulated layers of living under high ceilings and above hardwood floors. He imagined that a ghost or two swiveled around marble pillars or tread threadbare orientals at the witching hour. Michael owned and lived in such a building. And it was in such places that he had done most of his carpentry, bringing back, or reconstructing, some stairway or cabinet guaranteed to give the residents a sense of history and make peace with the spirits.

He checked in at the desk and took the elevator to the seventeenth floor. Apartment 1717 was at the end of the hall on the left. For a moment he stood before the door, observing the four large brass numerals, the small peephole, and the narrow nameplate. It was empty.

He knocked. He could sense movement within. A eye to the peephole. An indrawn breath. Then, just as he was ready to knock again, the door swung open. He was hoping for David St. Cyr. He got Michael Darius.

⁘

Leaving a man on surveillance at the St. Cyr apartment, Sakura rode back to Police Plaza, with Darius following in his car. The Robby Hudson killing was rattling around his head. Michael had extended the boundaries that day in the alley, just as he had done today, breaking into St. Cyr's apartment, ransacking it, then waiting all night for the architect to return. And just what would Darius have done had the man returned? He refused to speculate.

Though he could never deny Michael's instincts, those impulses that worked more often than failed, neither could he overlook some of the negative consequences of those same instincts. Michael was never good at mending fences. Bureaucratic or otherwise. But Sakura himself had learned the hard lessons over the years. Had often paid a high price. A price his former partner had always been unwilling to pay. So if cleanup was a requisite to draw upon Michael's abilities, it was a sum he readily added to his debt.

Today there was breaking and entering. *The end justified the means?* It was both a professional and a moral dilemma. He hoped there would be no overt repercussions. But, later and alone, he would have to face his own sins. He'd made sure the apartment was left as undisturbed as possible. And with that, he did as he'd done on other occasions: He turned a blind eye.

And what instinct had brought Darius to the St. Cyr apartment? He'd been prompted by some remark Margot had made about the architect. Something about St. Cyr's being difficult. Something about a kind of disagreement between them. His impression that Margot thought St. Cyr was strange. Not much to hang murder and kidnapping on. But there was more than gut feelings now.

If they had it right, David St. Cyr *was* Lyle Sanderson who had paid to stay at the Gramercy Park Hotel from 11 October to 10 November, securing the perfect vantage point for watching the comings and goings of the Redmonds. And as a guest of the hotel, he had been able to gain entrance to the private park where Jason and Damon played most afternoons. He might have even been the man the nanny said approached and talked to the twins.

But the architect had an apartment in the city. So why rent a hotel room if not to watch Margot and the boys? And maybe, most important, St. Cyr shared a physical anomaly with Lyle Sanderson—bicolored eyes, one green, one blue.

If this was one of St. Cyr's creations, Adelia Johnson wanted no part of it. The house was as cold as a refrigerator. Had as much feeling as a doctor's office. It was strange what rich white people thought was beautiful.

But the woman across from her was anything but dull. She was a cartoon drawn against a gray background. All movement. Arms, legs, mouth, eyebrows. Artsy, but not artificial. Patrice Attenborough was the real deal.

"What's he like?"

"David? Strange." She dragged out the word for emphasis.

Delia remembered something about the pot calling the kettle. "How is he strange, Mrs. Attenborough?"

"Want a drink?"

"No thank you, ma'am. You were saying that Mr. St. Cyr is strange."

"Enigmatic. Which of course makes him all the more mysterious. But you make all kinds of concessions for genius. David is really talented. Just look at this place." She did a kind of twirl like a dancer. The gold bracelets on her wrists jingled.

"How did you meet Mr. St. Cyr?"

"Sit, Detective. Relax. Your job must be stressful. Thank God for people like you. And doctors and nurses. I don't know how you do it. Sit, please."

Delia walked over to a chair that looked dangerous, and too flimsy for her wide ass. But she sat down anyway, expecting it to collapse. It was surprisingly comfortable.

"Nice, huh?"

"Excuse me?"

"The chair. Looks like something from the Spanish Inquisition. But it's cozy as hell."

Damn, it was hard keeping this woman on track. "David St. Cyr."

"Oh, of course." She perched on the mate to the Spanish Inquisition chair. Crossed her legs. "Mind if I smoke?" She didn't wait for an answer, but drew a cigarette from a pack lying on a table and lit up. She took a long drag. "Nasty habit. I'm going to quit after the first of the year."

"Where did you meet Mr. St. Cyr?"

She threw her head back. "I really can't remember now." Blew out smoke. "Maybe everything is an act with David. Except the talent. You can't fake that. And style. Can't fake that either."

"He ever mention his family?"

"Nope. Not a word."

"Where is he from?"

"Never said. It's as though he fell out of the sky. Though I suspect he's from somewhere down South. The accent. Though that could be a put-on."

"You think he fakes his accent?"

She laughed. A hard sound. "I think David St. Cyr is capable of just about anything."

Now that was an interesting observation.

"You know, David is very selective about his clients." Patrice rolled her eyes.

"But he took on the Redmond project."

"Oh, he was reluctant at first. But I told him how much the family needed to escape the big bad city. How the twins needed some fresh air. Room to grow." She jammed out the cigarette. "God, I can't believe Margot's dead." She stood, took out another cigarette, reached for the lighter, changed her mind. "You're going to find the twins, aren't you?"

"I don't know, Mrs. Attenborough."

"What a fucked-up world." Now she took the cigarette.

"Do you know where Mr. St. Cyr is at this moment?"

"David? In New York, of course." The last words were stretched out. Suddenly Patrice Attenborough was a street cat, cautious and suspicious.

"Why are you asking all these questions about David? What does David have to do with anything?"

"Routine questions, Mrs. Attenborough."

"You think David had something to do with Margot's death and the kidnapping."

"We have to investigate everyone connected with the Redmonds, Mrs. Attenborough. That's why I'm talking to you."

"Then why don't you talk to David himself?" She chewed on her lip, the cigarette burning unattended in her hand.

"There's a problem with that."

"Problem?" The ash had dropped to the floor.

"We can't seem to locate Mr. St. Cyr."

᠁

Today had started well enough. The twins waking, smiling. Damon dry, not wetting the bed. A first since he had brought the two to the Kingdom. He crushed each to his chest, breathing in their little-boy smells, incubated through the night between sheets and blankets.

Breakfast passed without incident. Cocoa Puffs was fine with both. One bowl left with a small puddle of chocolate-flavored milk, the other drained by lips pressed against the rim. And off to the bathroom. Bladders emptied. Faces washed, teeth brushed, hair combed. Then clothes tugged on. Nothing unsettling the peace of the Kingdom. Until it was time for socks and shoes, and Damon discovered the small blister on his toe.

The words came first. Almost normal, only shaky toward the end. "Mommy fix bobo." His little fingers plucking the wound. Then a brother's investigation. A comforting hug.

"Mommy fix bobo. . . ." This time the words a wail, scrambled with tears streaming down cheeks.

"Mommy fix bobo," Jason echoed, wide blue eyes meeting his own, as if his twin's plea hadn't been understood.

"Still sailing." He tried not to snap. He made the whooshing sound of the imaginary plane.

"Call her." Jason again. "On the phone."

Clever, clever kit. He allowed a smile, more genuine than any he'd gotten from Mother. "Your mommy's in the clouds. She didn't remember to take her phone."

He watched the little minds continue to work, the blue eyes like searchlights probing his face.

"Call Daddy," Jason said.

"Daddy," Damon mimicked. "Call Daddy."

"Daddy's away, on business. He can't be disturbed," he said to them both. "Your daddy wants me to take care of you."

"No!" Jason said.

The force of the word started fresh tears in Damon. He dropped to the turf in a deadweight way that was scary. "Mommy!" He screamed the syllables till they ran together in a horrible humming string. "Mommy-mommymommymommymommy . . ."

Hysteria. What followed was hysteria. From their piteous weeping to the urgent screams and churning hiccups contorting their faces and chests. To his own hysteria, running dark and deep and uncontrollable.

He stood rooted. His heart pumping in strangled beats. His limbs paralyzed with the truth of his failure. He let them scream. There was no hearing them beyond these walls. All the wounding their cries would do had already taken place.

He left them finally, going to the area that was the kitchen. He removed the pitcher from the refrigerator, brimming with the cheap punch that had turned out to be what little foxes liked best. They would wear themselves out soon enough. Their throats raw and ready.

He poured the cherry-colored stuff into the plastic cups that were printed with ponies, insipid docile beasts. The bottle had been waiting in the cabinet overhead. He got it down. Measured it into the drinks.

CHAPTER

29

Oh, God, I look awful. Who invented these kinds of lights? It had to be a man. Willie had finished brushing her teeth, was staring at herself in the rest room mirror, trying to decide if it was possible to rescue her more-than-day-old makeup. She returned the brush and toothpaste to their little plastic bag and threw them back in her purse. Then, running the water cold, she splashed some in her face, trying to avoid contact with her mascara.

Fishing for tissues and the lipstick that was the only item of makeup in the overburdened satchel, she patted her skin dry and blended two dots of color in her cheeks before applying the lipstick to her mouth. She supposed she looked better, and tried to believe that the effort had been solely to please herself, that Michael's being here had nothing at all to do with it.

She could not remember a more difficult eighteen hours. Two paths to one dead end. Michael's instinct in parallel with Jimmy's good police work. But the suspect had disappeared. Last seen by Michael as he'd descended subway stairs. Another layer of guilt. She knew Michael feared that his tail of St. Cyr had been spotted, that this had been the thing that had driven him underground, literally as well as figuratively. All night in Jimmy's office she'd watched it tear him apart. And not a thing she could do about it.

The truth of it was that their inability to locate St. Cyr was making them all crazy. Discreet surveillance had been set up around the building, but the man had not returned to his apartment. Legally speaking, they had no grounds for a warrant. Certainly, the few CDs by rave artists that Michael had found in St. Cyr's collection would not be enough to convince a judge.

Michael had been through the place thoroughly, and had found nothing else, though he had lifted a good set of prints which they presumed to be St. Cyr's. Nothing that could ever be used in a court, but Talbot had run them, was still running them through every possible database. So far with no result.

David St. Cyr was a phantom, a man who'd left no trace of his life before his university days at Tulane. They were in the process of an extensive background check, but the lack of information pointed strongly to an identity manufactured at that point.

The question they had been arguing over for hours was how soon they should become more aggressive. It was possible to put out an APB for St. Cyr as a person of interest, a move that would instantly be picked up by the media and trumpeted everywhere. The problem was they did not actually know that St. Cyr was aware of police scrutiny. Even if he had spotted him, Michael was just a man in a car. There was every possibility that St. Cyr would come back to the apartment, if they took no measures guaranteed to alert him.

The best-case scenario was that patience would result in St. Cyr's returning and leading them back to the twins, who might be alive in whatever place they were now. The worst case was that some action of theirs would push him to kill the boys and fall out of sight for good.

It might so easily happen. So many missing children were never found. Willie couldn't imagine what that kind of nonresolution would do to Michael. Or maybe she could.

She returned to Jimmy's office to find Darius standing exactly where she'd left him, at the window. Jimmy, at his desk, was brewing tea. She'd made a stop at the cold drink machine. Burnt out on black coffee, she'd kicked her diet and was chain-drinking Cokes. One shiny red can after another.

"Have I missed anything?" She sat down.

"No." Jimmy shook his head. "But I need to make a decision."

"On the APB?"

"Yes." His gaze drifted to where Michael had not moved.

"I don't know what to say that I haven't said, Jimmy," she began. "I—"

"Sir . . ." Talbot had appeared at the door with printouts in his hand. Sakura turned to him. "You have something?"

"I think I may have." Talbot came in. "And part of it's been under my nose."

"Show me," Sakura said.

Michael had come over. All of them gathered round as Talbot laid the papers down on the desk. "Look at this." He pointed to an entry in the DMV records. "A van, black, registered to a company, CyrUs, Inc. And I'd been checking the property records, looking for anything under David St. Cyr. Nothing had shown up. But CyrUs, Inc. owns a warehouse in the meatpacking district. *CyrUs*. David St. *Cyr*. I know it doesn't sound like much, but I called a buddy at the Department of Records and he checked. It's St. Cyr's name on the title."

"That's it," Michael said.

She looked to Jimmy. Saw the calculation click. That made four of them who believed.

At first, upon awakening, Hanae had lifted a window to cold and sun. But clouds had come as the morning waned. She had felt their presence in the fading warmth that fell upon her arms and face as she stood within the open frame of air. It was a fitful day, when nothing would ease the thoughts that flitted like her finches from perch to perch in her mind, thoughts of all that had happened in the weeks since her return. How she had made her noise; how her husband had listened. How despite her clumsiness, healing had come. She and her Jimmy were not, and perhaps would never be, of one mind on the question of how deeply she should share in that part of his life that was work. But their diverging roads of the year past had returned them to a path that had widened to let them walk abreast.

She had turned from the window and sought a soothing task. Warm steam filled the air with the scent of laundered cotton as she sat pressing and folding the handkerchiefs that Jimmy liked to tuck like a talisman inside his pocket. An American expression came to her. *Agree to disagree.* Her Jimmy would wish to keep her apart from everything ugly in his work. She, no stranger to darkness, wished to share the burden of all that he must face. *Agree to disagree.* And make space for the other to walk.

His phone call last night had been more than the usual short explanation that the demands of his case would prevent his coming home. Jimmy had told her all that he could. That there was a lead they were developing. That Willie was with him. And Michael. Much unsaid there, but understood. The inclusion of Kenjin was defiance of regulation. And Michael and Willie's working together in Jimmy's small office with so much pain between them could not be an easy thing.

Perhaps she should regret her part in bringing Kenjin and Willie together, but she discovered she could not. Knew that her hope was that they would come together again. They were souls that fit, as she and Jimmy were.

She found herself smiling as she considered her husband's patience these last weeks. She did not think she would test him with any more appearances at his crime scenes. It surprised her now that she had taken such measures. And it occurred to her that her restlessness today was a reflection of more than her fear for Kenjin's sons and the peril that might be involved in finding them. What she felt was frustration for the uselessness of that gift she had found it so necessary to assert. For of what value had been her visions, her sense of close and growing danger, when they had counted for nothing in preventing Margot's death or the taking of Kenjin's sons? And indeed, she could offer no special insight on where to find them now.

But her gift was a real one, and still she could hope for a time when it might make some critical difference, when the part given her to play would be more than understanding and support. And her husband, having tolerated her noise, might on that day hear her music. She prayed it would be so.

She had been folding and pressing as she thought these things. And placing a finished handkerchief on her pile, she reached into the basket for another dampened square. She smoothed it flat, hearing Taiko's gentle snore as he dozed close by at her feet. A sound of contentment that pleased her. She lifted the iron, pressed it into the starch-soaked fabric.

The vision shook her in its suddenness. Familiar now, but with a difference. The garden no longer the garden of her childhood. A mother not hers. But the voice as musical. The words in English, soft and slow. The melon offered. The halves with their coarse and dimpled rinds balanced neatly in her palms. No hairy nest of fiber at each center, but a void at the heart that filled and overflowed with blood.. Dripping wanton scarlet through her fingers.

She came to herself with the odor of scorched cotton.

⁂

Sakura cut the siren as they approached the exit from West Street, running under radar now. He glanced across to the passenger seat where Darius sat looking rigidly ahead, as if the answers he needed might be found in the air that pushed against the windshield.

No conversation on the ride. Nothing to say. What little discussion between them had come before, at the office. A rapid give-and-take, with no doubt of the outcome, about how much of nothing they actually had on this man. A possible location now with this warehouse, but still no grounds for any kind of warrant.

One green eye and one blue was not a crime. Neither was it illegal to rent a room under an assumed name. Or to rent a room in a neighborhood where two missing boys and their murdered mother had lived. When you put it in legal terms—and a gut-rumble wouldn't cut it—there was no way you could sell it to a judge.

So the plan was just he and Michael. Low-key. See what happened, and work from there. No backup called for. Which they both understood meant no one else to implicate in whatever was going to go down here.

He swung onto Washington and drove past the building. The warehouse was small by district standards, the windows of its storeys blacked out. He parked in *No Parking* and they got out of the car, Michael on the sidewalk ahead of him.

There was no bell at the entrance. Sakura knocked . . . waited . . . knocked. Interminable seconds before his fist went up again.

"Leave it, Jimmy," Michael stopped him, looking away. "You should go." He stared out at the street.

They stood together, silent on the cracked sidewalk. "They're my kids," Darius spoke again. "And you don't need to know. . . ."

"We're going in," he said. "Both of us."

"No warrant . . ."

"You want legal?" He cut through the bullshit. "It's exigent circumstances, Michael. And we're wasting time."

❦

Into the universe that was not the universe. He concentrated on the picture reflected in the mirror from the television monitor mounted on the wall. The surveillance camera was sweeping the outside world, and he feared the reality of the two men descending to the basement level. Yet he could console himself. It was after all only a reflection of a reflection of electronic impulses sent through the air. And then there was the matter of his brain interpreting the messages through the lenses of his eyes. That was the way with the looking glass. Alice knew so well. Reaching, he laid the flat of his hand against the cool surface. There was no denying the image. Of one blue eye and one green eye staring back at him. No denying the irony of reversal. How left became right, and right became left.

From the beginning it had been a dream. A dream before he had even known it as dream. A seed, sprouting in his wounded heart, sending tendrils deep, a bud bursting the surface, new life uncoiling, forcing its way out of destiny's center.

But the dream had soured. The seed stifled by unforeseen realities. Slowly spoiling in his hands, as ghosts hovered in the background, lying in wait to shrivel and dry what had once been green and promising. And in his infantile anger and despair, the ghosts all bearing the face of his mother.

❦

The basement was not dark. A yellow-green light seeped from a strip of neon over a sink; like putrid water it flooded the subterranean world of the warehouse. Michael had seen light like this before, but it had burned then, emanating from the body of a man with a gun pointing at him. And the smell of rot was familiar too. Of blood gone bad. Crawling wet in cracks and fissures, impervious to swipes of ammonia, resistant to abraded bleaching. His mouth, his throat, his lungs, his belly filled with its stench. Every membrane sucked up the flavor of dank decay.

A muffled sound forced him to turn toward where a large cooler droned. Hunched and pasty white, sunk in the dark depths of a corner. The flat of a gurney licked up the cadaverous illumination, and upon a stiff-sheeted table, the points and edges of surgical implements glittered like fins. Against a wall, a tall thick roll of Visqueen, like a cylinder of pale translucent skin.

And in the half-black space, the last breaths, the last blood-beats of the dead reverberated. A new noise. Almost not there. Darius turned. Sakura was behind him, looking up, toward a benign light, dry and warm, illuminating the stairway out of Hell.

⚜

Deathly quiet. He had never appreciated the full meaning of that phrase before. He walked bare-fleshed through the dark twinkling forest, pausing despite his haste at the spot where the kits had had their final frolic. Short of breath and he needed to hurry. Things yet to do. And he had to fill the quiet. Or he might hear Mother laughing, enjoying her revenge.

Damn Mother. He cursed the womb that had left him incomplete, one rotation short. Enough to damn *him.* Not all the energy he might suck from a thousand thousand deaths enough to transform deformity.

Things yet to do. He imagined the men he had seen on the monitor approaching his level. Unlike Mother, they were not going to win. A bitter smile. For at least, in the end, it was he who decided her victory. Granting it hours ago. The one prize she had always required.

⚜

Birnam Wood was the crazy thought in Sakura's mind—the creeping forest that hailed Macbeth's death. He inched steadily forward in the cavernous space, Darius just behind, their flashlights and drawn guns sweeping the weird landscape of artificial hillocks and potted trees that twinkled in the not-quite-silent dark.

He knew that Michael could hear what he heard, the sound growing clearer as they penetrated forward. The siren song of children's voices. But Michael stuck to discipline, keeping pace with him and what they could see and be sure of. Data on which to base the next critical judgment.

The next few inches brought the TV into their line of vision. Set on a stump. Electronic halo flickering out of rhythm with the winking lights. Like a window-cut of color in the darkness; a videotape was playing. Jason and Damon in the fake forest, alive. But how long ago?

He saw the impact of the image hit Michael. Knew his hesitation in the intake of breath. One more decision to stick to the book. For the moment after. And the next.

It was his own flashlight that picked out the wire and plaster cave. That pinned the thing within it in its beam. A white curve of exposed back. A rickrack of bone that pushed at pallid flesh. *Dead flesh.*

"Michael . . ." The name tore itself from his mouth.

Darius saw, moved, on a wave of action that crashed them both forward. Darius, gun holstered, dropped to his knees ahead of him. Scrambling into the hole, pulling . . . dragging the first body out.

"Dead," Michael said. Sakura's own thought made real.

He was on his knees now, too. The beam from his flashlight following as Darius crawled farther, illuminating the two smaller bodies within, the twin heads bright copper against the nest of moss and leaves. But the lips and nails of both boys cyanotic, unmistakably blue.

He crabbed backward, his radio out, sitting on his heels. "Sakura." He gave his call number. "I have a medical emergency." He barked out the location of the warehouse, his eyes still on Michael, watching his head go down over one small mouth. Then swiftly move to the other.

"Send the EMTs and whatever backup you've got in the area." He was still snapping requests to dispatch. "And notify Crime Scene and my unit."

A *roger* crackled back from the line.

"I need an ME van. And Linsky if he's available."

Another *roger.*

He bent quickly to the body at his feet. Flesh still warm, no obvious sign of injury, other than the piercings that decorated the man's left side. He felt routinely for a pulse at the neck, the shadow lighting from the TV screen reflecting in the metal jewelry, shifting like water over the morbid features. The dead eyes stared back at him, dimmed but yet unclouded. One iris green. One blue.

Pun'kin Man! a tiny recorded voice rang from the boxed chatter of the video.

Pun'kin Man! a second sang.

He hurried to help Michael.

CHAPTER

30

". . . and more details of Friday's successful rescue of Jason and Damon Darius are slowly dribbling out." Zoe turned into a close-up on camera three.

"This reporter has learned exclusively from sources close to the investigation that the warehouse in which the twins were found, along with their dead kidnapper, contained an artificial forest, complete with a molded landscape and potted trees strung with white Christmas lights. This evil wonderland, apparently constructed by serial killer and architect David St. Cyr himself, was all part of some complex fantasy that involved these innocent boys.

"In yesterday's live press conference, hospital officials reported that the twins, who were released to return home with their stepfather, local financier Reese Redmond, seem to have recovered completely from the drug they were given. But none of us can help wondering about the long-term emotional impact of their experience on vulnerable three-year-old boys.

"We will probably never know all that these children have suffered." She paused dramatically to let that horror take. Then, "We do know that Jason and Damon have lost their mother, and were present at the death of the man who, though he may have been a monster, was their only caretaker for the nine days he held them captive.

"When we return from the break, we'll be talking to renowned psychologist Dr. Sharon Maravich, who will offer some insight on what might be ahead for these two little boys, and on just what kind of forces may have driven the mysterious madman who killed eight women, including Margot Redmond, before his own strange death."

The camera light winked out. Zoe sat back, thinking about the things she knew but couldn't tell. Like those kids and the dead killer curled up nude together. It was past icky. And she did have her standards.

She smiled and greeted her guest as the doctor took a chair and was wired for the interview. The cameras went live again and they breezed through the segment to the end of the show, all speculation and psycho-babble bullshit, which was all that was left to do till more of the reportable facts surrounding the case were released, or could be weaseled out. The official autopsy report on St. Cyr was yet to be issued, though the police had been quick enough to leak that the cause of death was some self-injected drug.

Back in her office she got ready to make more calls, trying to come up with some new angle on what, for a few more days at least, was still the hottest story in the pack. She'd be featured tonight on one of the prime-time Fox shows, repeating her exclusive on the whole fake forest bit. But tomorrow . . . ?

The real mystery she'd like to crack was St. Cyr himself. Who was he really? What hole had he crawled out of? Despite the scramble among the media—and the hunt was intense—no one had yet succeeded in breaking through the veneer of a life created out of carefully falsified documents and transcripts.

The person who'd called himself David St. Cyr had not seemed to exist before his appearance in college. But this much was real: He had graduated from Tulane. He was a licensed architect who had done a few residential projects in and around New Orleans before heading to New York, though certainly nothing as grand as the house he'd designed for the Attenboroughs, or the home that would have been completed for the Redmonds, if it hadn't become more important to kill the wife on the way to stealing the kids.

When it came to the official line, Little Zoe smelled a rat. It wasn't that the police were hiding something they knew, but rather that they were fudging to the media on just how much they didn't know. All of them were in the same boat when it came to this psycho. She smiled for a moment, settling back in her chair, thinking there was one cop she didn't mind sharing a boat, or a bed, with.

⚜

Willie sat with Jimmy on the small balcony that was one of the special features of the Jamili apartment. The evening was clear and cold, and a sudden gust of wind sent Willie in for a shawl. She threw another log on the fire, enjoying its warm crusty smell, the pop and crackle that intermittently filtered through the sounds of nighttime traffic.

"Another glass of wine?" she called from the bar.

"I'm okay."

"Now that's a moon," she said, stepping back outside, a refill in her hand.

"*Tsukimi.*"

"Which is . . . ?" She flopped back down into a chair, stretching out her legs, hooking her ankles over the balcony railing.

"Moon-watching. In autumn, Japanese families gather to watch the harvest moon. As a boy, *aki* was my favorite season of the year."

"I like thinking of you as a boy James Sakura."

He smiled. "Akira was an awkward boy. Tall and thin."

"Akira? Your Japanese name?"

He nodded. "Akira would climb the hillside with his hundred cousins, his pockets full of chestnuts, a ripe persimmon in each fist, and race the rising moon."

"That's a nice picture, James."

"It was another time."

"You miss Japan?"

"My memories serve me well. I'm afraid I would be out of place there now."

"But you have Hanae."

"Yes. Hanae is my Japan."

"Someday I'm going to find someone who loves me like you love Hanae."

He turned and looked at her.

"No, Michael is not that man."

"I had hoped . . ."

"So did I."

He leaned deeper into the chair that was too short for his long legs. "I am glad the boys are going to be all right."

"I really don't think St. Cyr meant to kill them."

"It certainly doesn't seem that way."

"The amount of Demerol administered was calculated to put them to sleep and nothing more. He must have drugged them right before you and Michael entered the warehouse."

"Watching us on the surveillance camera helped with the timing."

"But he wanted to kill himself. That injection of Demerol he gave himself was enough to kill two people."

"Linsky said he was dying anyway."

"*Situs inversus* with *levocardia*. An anomaly within an anomaly. All the organs are reversed, except the majority of the cardiac mass is in the left chest. Levoversion is an extremely rare pathophysiology, Jimmy, and always associated with congenital heart disease."

"So how does that explain what he was doing to the women?"

"He was reversing all their organs, including the heart. *Situs inversus totalis.*"

"Which would 'normalize' his abnormality."

"Correct. Sympathetic magic. The ritual effects real change. Fix the women and he fixes himself. People with *situs inversus totalis,* or 'mirror image' pathophysiology, typically have a normal life expectancy."

"Why women?"

Willie stood, looked out over the darkening city. "I think Margot's death answers that." She turned. "At the most fundamental level, St. Cyr's fantasy involved hatred of his mother. Killing women by ritually correcting his defect punishes the woman who played the central role in the creation of that defect."

"And Margot was the culminating sacrifice."

"Yes—all the other murders were ultimately leading up to Margot. When murder after murder failed to satisfy him, when they failed to 'cure' him, there was no other choice but to kill the cause of his pain and suffering. Killing Margot was finally killing his mother."

"But why Margot specifically?"

"Why a serial chooses a particular victim is integral to the fantasy.

In Margot's case, it may have been as simple as St. Cyr's mother had red hair."

"And the twins?"

She sat back down. "That is a beautiful moon, Jimmy."

He followed her eyes.

"When you found the boys, you said St. Cyr was curled around them. That they seemed to be nesting inside the curve of his body."

"Yes, the three of them were naked inside that cave he'd built."

"The examination of the boys showed no evidence of sexual molestation."

"Correct."

She nodded. "He wouldn't abuse those boys. He loved them. In his twisted mind, the boys somehow represented him, an idealized version of David St. Cyr. Perfect in every way. So at the end, as he lay dying, he was giving birth to himself. That's why I believe he never meant to harm the twins. Damon and Jason were the reborn David."

Jimmy stood. "You're right, it's a hell of a moon, Wilhelmina French."

"Why, James Sakura, I don't think I've ever heard you curse."

"You haven't been listening."

She laughed.

"You finished packing?"

"Yes, everything's set. Dr. Rainier is taking my patients."

"Need a lift to the airport?"

"A cab is easier."

"I'm going to miss you."

"Don't go soft on me now, Sakura."

He smiled. "Call us sometimes?"

"You know I will. Besides, I'm not going away forever. Just long enough to finish my book."

"Eat some of those beignets for me."

"First thing." She reached out and wrapped her arms around him. "Why does life have to be so damn complicated, Sakura?"

"Buddha says it's because of our egos."

"Screw Buddha."

Hanae had been able to open her hands against her heart. The nest's fragile burden had been protected: The twins were free. Now was a time for healing. In meditation this afternoon, she had begun to feel peace stirring in her spirit. Her mind, contentment's journey. But tonight there was the reawakening of her body.

She straddled Jimmy's back, massaging the muscles along his shoulders.

"This is what I've waited for all day." He lay flat, with his arms curled under a pillow.

"You are not supposed to talk."

He turned over between her legs. "There are too many rules, Wife."

"Rules are necessary." She had begun to work on his chest.

"No rules at home." He took her hands into his.

She could feel his growing arousal. "I can sense you have renewed energy."

"You have worked your magic on me, Wife."

"I must be more careful or neither of us will sleep this night."

"We can sleep tomorrow. I will stay home from work and we will stay in bed the entire day."

At this she laughed.

"You doubt me."

She took her hands from his and moved them over his face. "You are a beautiful man, James Sakura."

"Your hands have failed you. I am an ugly man."

Again she laughed. "My hands never lie. But it was your heart of which I spoke."

"We are lucky, Hanae. To have each other."

"You think of Kenjin?"

"And the others. Reese. The twins. The families of all those women. So many over the years."

She nodded. "And you carry their sorrow."

"Always it is with me."

"It is your chosen path, James. You have made room for it." Then she smiled, bringing his hand to her. "Feel my heart. It sings your name."

EPILOGUE

There was a coolness in the ruins, as if heat itself had been consumed in the fire that had raged here. Of the big house, little remained but a section of the side gallery. One defiant column lifted to the sun, which seemed reluctant to penetrate beyond it.

Odin Dupre walked down crumbling steps into a cancerous garden where the weak and exotic had died to feed the wild metastasis of plainer but hardier species. The azaleas in the stranglehold of silver-lace. The prized beds of roses gone straggling, dried sticks with thorns.

Sleeping Beauty's castle came to mind. But nothing was going to wake here.

A breeze stirred, setting the mossed oaks sighing like a murmur of grieving. But beyond the destruction, the day was bright and hard, too warm for the season. He stopped to prick his finger on a thorn, enjoying the appearance of blood. Remembering how much Mother hated this kind of weather for the holidays.

He could imagine it now the way it had been. Bessie in the kitchen cranking out cookies and cakes. The air conditioner cranking out too, a false cold to match the climate in Mother's visions of what Christmas should be. Cedar boughs everywhere, gathered from the property to "deck the halls." He could smell it, the rich tarry resin that stained and raised rashes on Didon Petit's hands.

And the Christmas tree, in the place of honor in the high-ceilinged parlor. No homegrown cedar, but a giant flocked spruce trucked in all the way from New Orleans every year. Mother, like so many ladies of the

Deep South, dreamed perpetually of a white Christmas that never came. And, of course, there was always Oliver about, to spoil whatever nature left untouched. Oliver at war with the holidays. At war with Mother, and her notions of perfection.

She had given birth in the big house. A fashion of that frivolous decade, to employ a midwife. And Mother was such a romantic. No ultrasound. Everything natural. Her brain giddy with possibility. A girl to dress, a twenty-year plan for a debut and wedding. Or a boy to seal her worth. The real surprise was that there were two.

Poor Mother, giving birth to the Kingdom of One. Rival to her domain. Odin and Oliver. Mirror twins, the doctors said when the sickly things were rushed in for inspection. Replicate DNA spun on its axis. The reversal complete, from cowlicks to organs. The sole exception, one stubborn heart that failed to make its turn.

At least that was all that was noticed in the first days, when the boys lay in incubators like some mad scientist's experiment gone terribly wrong. Wrinkled and red, little old men, with distended chests and concave abdomens. Eyes like newborn kittens, anemic and pale. Milky membranes hiding what others only later were teased to discover as the other exception. This one external. Two sets of bicolored eyes. Blue, green. Green, blue.

His first memory was of the Kingdom . . . and the other differences. Differences between him and Oliver that developed as arms and legs developed. As lungs and livers. Penises and scrotums. As height and width and depth developed. His left became Oliver's right; his right, Oliver's left. It seemed they were two sides of a single brain. And he relished the dichotomy, as he loved their sameness. Polar opposites, they attracted each other. Two perfect halves of one whole. It was, after all, a single zygote that had divided in Mother's womb, a cleft in the protoplasm, producing two princes for the Kingdom where only one had been anticipated. He imagined that bloody sea, swimming face-to-face with his mirror image, anchored by umbilical ropes that twice would be severed to gain freedom's magic.

From the first they spoke their own language. Communicating in smiles and gestures. Then giggles and goos. Later in a vocabulary of words of their own making. *Gotoruma* was the signal to flee the watchful eyes of the adult world, or more important Mattie, who could see more than any fifty white folks. And they sneaked and skulked until their bedroom they had gained, for there lay the seat of the Kingdom. Where secrets brewed. And plans were laid. Where oaths were sworn and pacts made. Where the universe uncoiled from the stuff of books, and test tubes, and birds, and crickets, and frogs. Where secret touches were given beneath starched sheets, as each stared into one eye blue, and one eye green, and wished for the day that they alone ruled the Kingdom.

He was Mother's favorite from the first, as though Oliver, with his sickly heart, had poisoned the well. It was Odin this and Odin that. Odin, who respected the servants. Odin, who charmed the society ladies. Odin, who learned to hunt with a gun, and had killed his first deer at seven. And there was cause for Mother's preference. For Oliver constantly reminded the help to keep their place. Used the N-word when he didn't get his way with Bessie or Mattie. Exposed himself to one of the society lady's daughters. Hated guns, and killed with his hands.

Odin smiled, where Oliver frowned. He compromised, where Oliver pouted. He was a boy of light, Oliver a boy of the dark. Like night and day, it could be said. But it was most fundamentally a lie.

So that when Oliver first brought a kill to their room, a possum with babies still alive, crawling like ants over their mother's stiffening carcass, he had gotten an erection as long and hard as Oliver's. And when Oliver had forced one of the little dark girls, his erection had followed his brother's lead. And though he was frightened of his own passion, he had felt shivers of excitement over Oliver's first human kill, and the second and third, bodies buried deep in thick dark soil.

But he had been cautious, fearing their getting caught. And he had trembled and stood guard as Oliver trapped and tortured and killed. Planned and harnessed the victims of their ravening boyhood. But Oliver had never led him where he had not wished to go. Never once had his conscience stood in outrage as he enjoyed the spoils of the war Oliver waged against the world. Never once had morality intruded. Never once had he feared the flames of Hell, or Monsignor Bordelon's confessional. What he feared was Mother.

And he stood witness too, Odin the good twin, as Oliver was reviled and punished. And he hated himself for not letting his evil show more clearly, for not revealing that it was his brother who was the braver, the more honest. So that in the night, as they held each other and kissed openmouthed, he begged forgiveness for hiding from the consequences his brother's dark shadow cast. But Oliver would have none of it, extolling his virtues. His intelligence and cleverness. His charm and wit. And most of all his strength. For was it not he, Odin, who ventured into the world of light, who played at the good games, when it was ever and always easier to do the bad. And Oliver would curl against him, crying because of his deformed heart, crying out against his own weaknesses, against the mother who had left her mark on him like Cain.

And then there was the day Mother sent Didon Petit to find the source of the foul smell in their bedroom, and the caretaker discovered Oliver's booty under the floorboards. That finished it. Oliver was corrupting Odin. Oliver must be sent away. Father put up a feeble struggle. Saying it was not natural that the twins be separated. But Mother ranted and raved, and got her way as always. It was going to be the Christian Brothers on the Gulf Coast with their righteousness and rules who would save Oliver. But he, Odin, could not allow it. Cut off his arm. His leg. Blind one eye. He could not allow Oliver to be sent away alone. He finally settled it by convincing Mother that Oliver needed him if he were to be set upon the path of good. In truth, it was he who needed Oliver.

The good Christian Brothers, however, did nothing but feed Oliver's defiance, and when a succession of misdeeds, and ultimately the rape of another student, sent Oliver home, Odin was foolishly happy, believing the Kingdom would be at last restored. But as the days stretched into months, and Oliver's presence a bête noire upon Mother's life, she revealed other plans. Oliver was to be committed to an asylum. Sent away, no longer in the interest of rehabilitation, but incarceration. So that Mother's world could proceed without further disruptions. So that she could go on as if no fissure had taken hold in her fertilized ovum. So she could once and for all forget one had become two.

It was bonfires in the beginning, but Oliver started his first real fire when he was nine. A small experiment to see how quickly the old shed could be consumed, how fast rotted board became ash. But the true payoff had been not the destruction, but the act of destroying, as Oliver discovered, the heat fanning his face, his eyes devouring the thick licks of flames. He had almost fainted, watching the blooming blaze eating the oxygen right from the air. And then, there had been that second fire. Another outbuilding. With its secret hefted inside. And Odin watched as Oliver's eyes widened, his nostrils flaring, reaching out for molecules of charred flesh.

So the Kingdom would have to be destroyed to be resurrected. A great phoenix rising from flame. He had agreed to the plan, even helped in getting the materials. Though he wondered if the accelerant would not later be detected and nothing good would come of the deed. But discovery was never to be. Their crime buried in copious grieving over the tragic loss of the great house. Over the terrible deaths of the Dupres. And their son Oliver. Poor motherless, fatherless, brotherless Odin.

It had been easy finding another drunken vagrant, passed out alongside the railroad tracks way to the rear of the big house. They had drug him home in the deep of the night, and tucked him neatly in Oliver's bed, no one the wiser when the ruined body was discovered along with the other remains. Only Odin escaping because he had always been a light sleeper. Stumbling from the house in a daze, lungs filled with smoke, his fine hair scorched, but not a cell of his flesh burned.

And Oliver deep in the wood, smiling and safe, masturbating as he saw the rosy red glow of the flames rise over the pines, smelled the smoke bearing the scent of that misbegotten vagrant, the scent of his will-less weak father. And bearing, most deliciously, the scent of Mother. Burning, burning, burning.

The big house was lost. But money would never be a problem. The family holdings were extensive: oil and natural gas reserves; lumber interests. If nothing else, their father had been a competent businessman. At eighteen, he came into his majority. And as sole heir, took charge of liquidating the assets as soon after the fire as he could. Though he sustained losses, expediency was more important than gain, and there was enough for him and Oliver for two lifetimes.

And so began a new freedom, though remnants of the old life remained, some of necessity, some by choice. With the Kingdom half in light and half in shadow, they moved to New Orleans. He, a new young man, with a fresh identity. Oliver, a mole living underground by day, coming out at night to feed. And feed he did, his lust insatiable with the desperate conviction that the taking of life prolonged his own, would make right his damaged heart. And he, mostly a voyeur in those first years, watching and masturbating as Oliver snuffed out breaths and humped the dying flesh. But there came a time when there was one body too many, and he had done all he could in New Orleans. Graduated in architecture with honors from Tulane. Designed a few homes. Made a modest name for himself among the young and trendier set. It was time to move. To new hunting grounds.

So they packed and left, disappearing in the night. Traveling separately. Oliver overgrown in mustache and beard. Hair to his shoulders. He, cut and curried, a young talent on the move.

In New York, it was an apartment for himself, the warehouse for Oliver. And for a time, Oliver seemed content. Roaming inside the large structure like Jonah inside the belly of the whale. Until he tired of aimless discovery. Grew weary of the dark nooks and crannies of the old building. Tired of helping fix up the place so that it was livable, even pleasant. Tired finally of the lonely night walks, inhaling moonlight and neon, gas fumes and traffic noise. Tired of being a freak barred from the freak show he encountered on the seamier streets of the city. Despaired that he was growing weaker. That he could no longer wait. That he was in need. The Kingdom crumbling. And so he, Odin, the brother of light, went into the dark, a procurer, a pimp, to satisfy a lust that in truth had also become his own.

The breeze had died away. Above him in the oaks, the crows had begun to gather, as they did for their kind. The closest thing to ravens here, the birds carried memories . . . a favorite book. *The Children of Odin* had been his present from Mother for some accomplishment now forgotten. He and Oliver had devoured its pages, reading the stories over and over. Identifying with the Norse gods—he, with his namesake; Oliver, of course, with Loki the trickster. But it was Odin's ravens that defined them. Huginn and Muninn sent into the world each morning to return with everything they had seen and heard. Huginn and Muninn. *Mind and Memory . . . Possibility and Karma.* David St. Cyr had been a dream that Mind had created. And Fate destroyed.

Odin hanging three days on the World Tree, giving his eye for knowledge. Christ on the cross. *Greater love hath no man than he lay down his life for his brother.* Older by minutes, he had been there always for Oliver. Oliver, who had died for his redemption.

Odin Dupre was reborn, free this time. But that dream was Mother's. Never his. He had fled the warehouse that Friday morning because Oliver, too sick to run, demanded it. Their final joke on the world, a hat trick. But no one left to laugh, because in the math of the Kingdom one half equaled none.

He wished he had the book of Norse myths, but it was in the New York apartment, and he had never returned since the morning he'd spotted his tail, trapped two nights in the dead limbo of a hotel room. The plans he had drawn for the Redmond house were in the apartment too. He regretted that his masterpiece would never be built, a temple to the Kingdom where twins would live in the order and harmony denied to him and his brother. But Oliver had drawn his own plans, conceived in the moment he'd seen the crystal-framed photograph stolen that night from the Redmond townhouse.

That photograph of the twins, at least, was with him. Ironic that he had never seen the twins in the flesh, avoiding them when he'd come to Oliver in those final days at the warehouse. He took the picture from a duffel bag, along with the videotapes and everything else he'd taken from the warehouse. He placed them in a pile at the center of the garden. The photograph on top.

High above the crows collected, fat and black. Their cries prophetic, piercing. Sharp and dark as the beaks that issued them. Nothing left to do. He doused the pile with gasoline. The rest poured over himself.

He lit a match.